CW00919988

THE ALPHA OF BLEAKE ISLE

DRAGONKIN

BOOK I

* * *

KATHRYN MOON

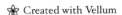 Created with Vellum

To my little dragon
(She's a cat.)

Contents

About the book   xi

Chapter 1   1
Mairwen

Chapter 2   13
Ronson

Chapter 3   29
Mairwen

Chapter 4   37
Mairwen

Chapter 5   47
Ronson

Chapter 6   61
Mairwen

Chapter 7   67
Ronson

Chapter 8   77
Mairwen

Chapter 9   89
Ronson

Chapter 10   99
Ronson

Chapter 11   111
Mairwen

Chapter 12   123
Ronson

Chapter 13   131
Ronson

Chapter 14   141
Mairwen

Chapter 15   153
Ronson

Chapter 16   163
Mairwen

Chapter 17   171
Ronson

Chapter 18   181
Mairwen

Chapter 19   193
Mairwen

Chapter 20   207
Ronson

Chapter 21   215
Mairwen

Chapter 22   225
Ronson

Chapter 23   235
Mairwen

Chapter 24   245
Ronson

Chapter 25   253
Mairwen

Chapter 26   263
Ronson

Chapter 27   273
Mairwen

Chapter 28   281
Mairwen

Chapter 29   293
Mairwen

Chapter 30   301
Ronson

Chapter 31   305
Mairwen

Chapter 32   315
Ronson

Chapter 33   325
Mairwen

Chapter 34   333
Ronson

Chapter 35   343
Mairwen

Chapter 36   353
Ronson

Chapter 37   365
Mairwen

Chapter 38   373
Ronson

Chapter 39   385
Mairwen
Chapter 40   393
Mairwen
Epilogue   405

Afterword   409
Also by Kathryn Moon   411
About the Author   413

About the book

This story was originally shared with chapter by chapter updates in rough draft form on my Patreon in starting in October of 2023. It has since been removed.

This version of omegaverse is unlike my Sweetverse series in many ways! It's my goal that the information you need to understand the world in my head is here in the book. In fact, it would be difficult for me to lay out the rules here to you, without including some lies because this world of dragons and alphas and betas and omegas is on the precipice of great change. But if it wasn't, we probably wouldn't be here.

However for those who really want clear cut terms, here are some of the "rules" of this omegaverse...some of which might be lies:

Beta and Omega are closer to alternate terms for biological sex, meaning betas are male and omegas are female.

An alpha is the strongest dragon in a geographical region, and rules over the area like a king. They can be deposed by a beta during a physical challenge.

A new alpha undergoes physical changes that lead to them going into a rut, a cycle which reoccurs every ten years.

Betas or male dragons can only be conceived during a rut. There is no mating, just partnership.

Aside from alphas, only beta dragons have wings. Some but not all of betas can transform into full dragons.

Trigger Warnings and Content Information:

Fatphobia, misogynistic culture, social ostracism, attempted sexual assault, discussions about dangerous pregnancies, bad parenting, treasonous plots, minor violence

Virginity/first-time, birth control that works, fingering, vaginal penetration, oral sex, knotting, biting, bruising, lots of breast and nipple play, but listen friends this is a different race and she doesn't have a hymen because I didn't feel like it.

You can find more content information including TWs at kathrynmoon.com

Chapter One

MAIRWEN

The melodious chatter of Lady Gertrude's afternoon fête was cleaved by a gasp of shock. I glanced up from the book in my hands, my own small squeak of surprise ringing out a moment too late.

The Alpha of Bleake Isle filled the open doorway.

Playing cards clattered to the table where Mother and her collective had gathered for whist. Crystal glasses of brandy thudded to trays and tables as Father and the other settled gentlemen sat up, their wings rustling in agitation. Even charming Adelaide, who never missed a note or ornamental trill of music on the pianoforte, struck a wrong key.

Today is suddenly so interesting, I thought, holding my breath in my chest, staring at the man who stood across from me.

No. *Stood* was too mundane a word. I'd seen the alpha, Lord Ronson Cadogan, nearly ten years ago, and another ten years before that, and the sight of him now made my heart race in terror as fast as it had when I was six and sixteen. Not that I should've expected otherwise. He hadn't changed at all. Not even by a single hair.

The man threatened his surroundings, even now, his great

height and breadth forced to slightly hunch in Lady Gertrude's otherwise accommodating entrance, glaring at us all out of those black eyes. The talons at the joint of his wings scratched against the wood frame, the sound harsh and jolting in our silence. The afternoon sun streaming through Lady Gertrude's windows did not *shine* on the alpha, but soaked into him, as if absorbed by his surly stare and dark wings.

One thought was loud, no doubt echoing through every head in the room. *What day was it? Had we somehow all lost a month of our calendars? Was it already the day of the selection?*

Because as long as I had been alive, the esteemed and feared Lord Cadogan, our isle alpha, had not courted society for any other reason. Father had said he was a stern man of business, often pushing against the interests of the beta gentlemen, but to my knowledge, he made no effort to spend time in the company of omega gentlewomen.

"M-my lord!" Lady Gertrude cried, rising in all her ruffles from the window seat where she surveyed her guests. Words failed her after the exclamation.

My own tongue was tied, but that would've surprised none of the gathered dragonkin society. No, Mairwen the Mouse would have nothing to say. At least nothing of import. The loathsome nickname had ill-suited my appearance since I'd shot up suddenly at sixteen, taller than my own father and most of the men of my acquaintance, and yet Mairwen the Mouse I remained.

Not taller than the alpha, though. I choked on my sip of tea at the thought, then froze as those black eyes found me, like a great hungry cat hearing the scratch of my creature nickname. Not a great cat at all, though. A dragon, and as unlikely to be interested in me as one of his kind might be in a mouse.

For a moment, I held that stare. It was strange enough to be seen, to be noticed, by anyone these days. I'd taken their name for me to heart, finding small corners to hide and read in. Letting these tedious afternoons pass in my own silence was easier than trying to dig my way into conversations where I wasn't wanted, where Mother's friends could pick at my appearance or the beta gentlemen went out of their way to avoid engaging me in conversation or dance. But what did *he* see, now that he was looking? Was I the mouse at first glance to the alpha too?

"Lord Cadogan, you've quite smashed our merriment in all your terrible glory."

The dark stare left me abruptly, and I realized all at once that my face was warm and my fingers were clenching the arm of the chair. I shook myself and shrank back into the cushions, into my hiding, as the alpha's attention drifted. Only Adelaide Brys could say such an atrocious thing to the man who commanded all of us, everyone on this entire island, and receive the slight hint of a smirk. It was suddenly clear to me, and perhaps even I had realized the obvious a little late, that a month from now, the alpha would choose Adelaide at the selection ceremony.

Adelaide's flirting roused Lady Gertrude back to her generally remarkable hostessing abilities, and the plumply attractive older woman hurried across the room to greet the alpha and do her duty of introductions. Dragon wings rustled in agitation, the beta gentlemen ill at ease with their superior at hand.

He's gotten sick of waiting, I realized, watching the exchange, the way the alpha's gaze picked out each young omega in the room.

"How shocking for him to just appear like this!"

I looked up to find Sophia, another omega up for the selection, paused in front of me, eyes rapt on the alpha.

"Is it?" I asked. "Surely he was invited."

Sophia blinked and glanced at me, and I realized she'd

been speaking absently, hadn't realized I was even here to answer.

"Well, he's never accepted before now," she said, as if we were all meant to go on doing exactly what we'd always done, our alpha included.

I hummed, and Sophia floated away, a pretty moth to the flame of the most powerful dragon in the room. It was said that after claiming the role, an alpha exuded the power of the ancient dragons we all descended from. I'd thought it a myth, until finding myself in a small parlor with the alpha himself. He was too potent for the delicate space, it was as if strength rolled off him in waves, buffeting against the lesser betas, catching nearby omegas like fish on hooks.

It had been half a century since Lord Cadogan had risen as alpha, and for five decades he'd neglected to select an omega to breed and bear his heir. The rumor I'd heard whispered plenty was that our alpha would not choose an omega with another dragon's scent on her. In this—as in many things, according to my father—Lord Cadogan was unlike his father before him. Our previous alpha had gleefully chosen an eligible omega girl of the gentry at nearly every selection. Lord Cadogan's own mother had only put a stop to the practice by very stubbornly refusing to die in childbirth, delivering her alpha a son at last.

The many beta gentlemen who'd all been offering beautiful Adelaide a captive audience hurried now to claim seats by their chosen young ladies, and I smirked at the sudden flurry. Only Hugh Gamesby, a hearty beta of only forty and who looked another twenty years younger still—a perfect match to Adelaide's youth and beauty—remained at the pianoforte, although his dark wings rustled and his feet stomped slightly whenever the alpha moved an inch closer to Hugh's intended.

Formerly intended.

I'd considered Hugh Gamesby quite a strong beta, experienced a faint sense of magnetism the few moments I was near him in the past. He'd seemed the sort of beta who might one day rise to alpha. Not now. Now he was a whisper, a withering note of strength that shrank against the stronger presence in the room. The one who prowled ever closer to Hugh's paramour.

Adelaide was exquisite. She was and had always been the personification of perfection. It was as if she'd been cut and stitched to be exactly to fashion. Her silky strawberry blonde hair was artfully twisted, coy curls falling to brush her collar. In her cherubic face, wide blue eyes glanced with deft and flirtatious precision. She was petite and only so gently curved as to be definitely feminine, bosom blushing prettily above her collar with the use of a good set of stays. I fidgeted in my own painfully tightened stays and tried to watch the trio slyly over the edge of my book, not that anyone would take note of my stare.

Adelaide was talented and sweet—impertinent too, but only to charm—and she had a natural omega perfume that even I found distracting. She was made for an alpha, would've been wasted on a beta like Hugh, and now it was inevitable.

Lord Cadogan would not wait for the selection ceremony, when all the young omegas had already been surreptitiously claimed by betas, marked with their scents to put him off. He would have Adelaide. I wondered if the ceremony would even take place, or if he would cart her off to his castle tonight.

It's so predictable, I thought, wishing I could rise up from my chair, turn the alpha in any other direction. Adelaide was the perfect omega, he was the precise definition of an alpha, and it was *boring*. Boring and...disappointing?

I shifted in my seat, trying to twist away from the scene, refocus on my book. I couldn't be jealous. I was lucky to even have a dragon suitor. Mr. Gryffyd Evans was over a century old, showing more than half his years, and not one of the omegas he'd chosen for a rut had survived childbirth—although several of the children had, all girls, long since grown. I'd been born in an unfortunate year, just a few months shy of having qualified for the last selection, and now by far the eldest omega available for the upcoming one. According to absolutely everyone, and most especially my parents, I ought to be delighted to be all but claimed by Mr. Evans.

I glanced in the beta's direction and found a hollow chill trickling down my spine at the sight of the old dragon, lips twisted in a sneer, proud jaw raised obstinately high.

I was lucky to have Mr. Evans's offer, and he appeared to know it. All the other omegas were now warily guarded by betas who could do no more than hover, not if our alpha really wanted to engage an omega. He would always take precedence. Only his curious distaste had prevented him from taking a rut partner in so many decades. And now he'd sorted that out for himself. But no, Mr. Gryffyd Evans was unfazed. Actually, he was frowning at me—probably not pleased with my potential—but he didn't look the least bit worried and made no move to guard my virtue or attention from Lord Cadogan.

And he needn't have been. Lady Gertrude made good work of introducing the alpha to everyone who mattered in the room. They didn't come within feet of me. No, our alpha stopped the niceties as soon as he'd reached the pianoforte, where Adelaide was playing and blushing, and ah, yes, now she was singing for him.

Good for her, I thought, not quite sure I meant it. Adelaide had given me the nickname of 'Mouse,' although she'd only been six at the time, when she found me hiding under a porch at another garden party, reading. It wasn't her fault it'd been so cheerfully adopted. And it wasn't her fault I'd let it be proven right, keeping to my corners, avoiding the stings of being corrected, rejected, dismissed by staying out of the way.

For a moment, I imagined rising from my seat, swanning across the room, *accidentally* brushing against the alpha to catch his attention...

And then what, you goose? And then my courage might fail, or I might say something rude but not coyly like Adelaide, or since a body like mine did not *swan* or *brush*, I might just end up squashing myself to the alpha and humiliating my family.

So I didn't move an inch, and I washed the bitter taste on my tongue down with a hearty gulp of tea.

To her credit, Adelaide was able to sing and play and smile, all while being glared at speculatively by those abyss black eyes. I certainly couldn't have done half that, even without Lord Cadogan towering over me like a brutal monolith of power. A handsome one, I admitted. More masculine and harsh in appearance than the beta dragons, with dark hair and a thick but short beard.

His smile was slow, predatory, and it stopped at the halfway point, as if he refused to put more effort into the act. He knew, as we all did, that he'd just found his match.

It was so obvious, actually. Inevitable.

I brought a tiny cake to my lips and lifted my book back to my nose, forcing myself to focus on the words, hoping for a better twist in the story.

"YOU MUST STOP SLOUCHING. And we'll need new irons to try for her hair. Oh, Mairwen! Would you listen?!"

My mother didn't wait for my response, wresting the book from my hands to catch my attention at last. It was getting too dark in the carriage to read anyway.

"New irons won't work. They never work," I said, frowning. "Why are we bothering with worrying about my hair?"

"She's right, Gwennie. The matter is settled," my father said, patting my mother's hand where they sat across from me. But he was frowning too.

"No, it isn't, not at all, Albert. Not now that the alpha is determined to have a girl at the selection."

I'd missed too much of their conversation and assumed the entirely wrong meaning to my mother's words, a great burst of rare laughter exploding out of me.

"He's not about to choose me, no matter what we manage with my hair," I gusted out, eyes wide.

And it struck me, as they both wore puzzled and slightly disturbed expressions in response, that they'd never believed so either.

"Hugh Gamesby won't have Adelaide, and—"

"Hugh Gamesby won't have me either," I said.

And once again, their faces said I was being obvious. Hugh wasn't as strong or huge as the alpha, but he was as handsome, fair and elegant like Adelaide rather than dark and burly like Lord Ronson Cadogan. Hugh and Adelaide would've made exquisite babies, and now I wondered what she would have instead. She and the alpha were so different in appearance, and she was slight. Her labors would be hard.

"There's going to be a great shuffling about, you mark my words," my mother continued, shooing away my comments like flies buzzing about her head. "I really do think our little Mouse could come out...well, maybe with a bit of our help, she might land George Hardaway."

I turned my head to gaze out the window of the carriage, hiding my wince. Not at George Hardaway—he would be an improvement, although still rather unlikely to choose me. No, I just hated when my parents called me "Mouse" too.

"And have me break my word with Mr. Evans? Gwennie,

it's bad form, not to mention...well, not possible," my father said. He shot me a sympathetic glance, and I suspected we were thinking the same thing.

George Hardaway wouldn't ask for me. Not even if Adelaide being pulled from the ranks did send the omegas toppling down the line like dominoes, rearranging all the fresh courtships that had started to bud with the approach of the rut selection.

"If things are rearranged, I'm more likely to lose Mr. Evans than gain one of the others," I said, trying not to sound too hopeful.

My mother let out a wounded noise, but it wasn't for my sake. She just didn't want to face the truth.

"The matter is settled. You're not losing Mr. Evans," Father said, as if it could reassure me. "And we're not breaking our word to him. The deal is done."

I held my father's gaze, and it was like looking in a mirror. I had too many of his features, and too few of my mother's. He was handsome, of course, but even her bow lips would've made my face more cherubic. No, all I had from my mother was good hips and high cheekbones. It was not enough, not for what she wanted from me.

The carriage stopped in front of the house, and I let myself down before my father or the driver could help. The night was cool, a relief on my hot cheeks.

"Perhaps we should've put her out a few months early," Mother whispered.

"No, Gwennie. Even if he had chosen her then, she'd likely be dead by now. She was too young."

Why didn't he tell her the truth? If by some miracle or poor judgment Lord Cadogan had snapped me up when I was sixteen, my father would never have been able to wager me off to Mr. Evans. A deal Father would never break, because the money made was already in the process of being spent on our keeping a carriage and a driver at all. On repairing the roof so my mother wasn't dripped on.

Father's family fortune had been dwindling for years, and his income had been lost before my birth, when the current Alpha Cadogan had put a stop to indentured servitude. I'd only heard my parents whispering about the state of our finances a few years ago, and the revelations had come with a sick kind of relief. I would rather we be poor than be dressed in finery paid for by the trade of human flesh and labor.

So we could not afford to lose Mr. Evans. Or rather, my parents couldn't. And with the burden of me gone, the load would be lighter for them. That was good too.

I marched into the house, leaving them to their discussion. They loved one another, as dragonkin couples rarely did. My father had not only chosen my mother after a rut selection decades ago, but he'd kept her at his side all this time, without ever receiving a beta heir. Most gentlemen of dragonkin would've traded their omega in for a new one by now. But not Father. He loved my mother and was sincerely loved in return. They loved me too, I was sure. I was just not quite what I ought to be. I never had been.

If I'd been a boy, it would've been an improvement in so many ways, not least of which being my features might've actually suited me. Well, the ones on my face, at least. The rest of my body was decidedly feminine. But I would've been able to seek out some employment. Perhaps find a new means of income for our family, as my father seemed resigned to watching it wither away. As I was, my worth was in who might take me on. Mr. Evans appeared to be our only option.

I hurried up to my bedroom, breathing through my nose, stamping down on the rising tide of bile and anger always at hand since Father had told me of the decision. It was not my father's fault I was unpopular or that I was not pretty enough or that when I did choose to speak, I was too blunt and never charming. He'd done what he could for me, and now I had to—

To survive. With Mr. Gryffyd Evans.

My eyes closed at the top edge of the stairs, and I wavered there for a moment, swaying, wondering what might change if I went toppling backwards.

You'll land on your ass and have a bruise, that's what. Don't be melodramatic.

I swallowed hard and carried on.

My parents would take a light supper together, probably in their rooms. And I'd eaten plenty of cakes and tarts at Lady Gertrude's.

I shut the door to my bedroom gently, pacing as I wrestled myself out of my binding clothes, stopping abruptly and scowling at myself in the mirror I'd hidden in the far corner of the room, out of my way.

I was too tall, and the baby fat around my face had never left, and I was quite too *generously* formed to look anything but lumpy in the dresses so in style. My hair was thick but determinedly pin straight, refusing to be styled, and my features were on the wrong side of plain. I couldn't begrudge Adelaide or the other omegas what would never have been a possibility for me. Even if no other dragon considered me for the selection, even if I stood on that stage naked and unscented, I would not be the alpha's choice.

My virtues as an omega were few, although my mother thought it likely I would survive childbirth and then most certainly outlive Mr. Evans. *Small mercies*, I thought, and then batted it away before I could feel dire and trapped again. But my worst deficiency of all was something not even rouge or a fierce set of laces on my stays could cure: I had almost no perfume. Sometimes, I really wasn't sure I had any at all, or if I just had a not unpleasant and nearly human sweat.

I tucked my nose to my shoulder now, found a hint of a

sweetness, and my eyes stung. I squeezed them shut and hurried away from the mirror.

Be a mouse. Hide from what frightens you.

And the best means of hiding was...

Damn. My mother still had my book. I could retrieve it from her and subject myself to the persistent and painful topic she'd latched onto for the evening, or sink into the desperate thoughts that took all my strength to keep away.

I stripped down to my stays and chemise, fingers loosening the laces automatically, my steps wandering toward the window.

The view of the alpha's castle was a black shadow against the nearly set sun, the sky over the sea smeared in vivid golds and burgundy. There was a dark shape in the sky, sailing into the wind. A dragon—the alpha, of course—flying home after unsettling us all. From this distance, he looked more like an irritating thorn in the landscape than the imposing and powerful figure he'd been in Lady Gertrude's salon.

With one eye closed, I poised my fingers with his silhouette between them and then pinched them shut, imagining squishing him between my giant's grip.

I snorted and turned away, searching for one of my other discarded books to pass the evening.

Better stories in books than in life, I reminded myself. *Happier endings too.* Although, perhaps the alpha might stir up a little more trouble in the next month. One could hope.

Chapter Two

RONSON

"What do you think of her?" I asked my half-brother, Niall, not bothering to lower my voice as we paced the edge of Hugh Gamesby's broad and meticulously manicured gardens. No one would mistake to whom I referred, and I didn't care. The rumors would've started the moment I walked into the room two weeks ago, and the rumors were right.

Niall frowned, eyes searching the party at the heart of the maze. Bringing Niall, my father's bastard, had stirred up talk, and our walk out of earshot would give the crowd time to release their flurry of shock. It wasn't as though any of the betas and omegas in attendance were unaware of Niall's existence. Perhaps some of the well-sheltered young women. No, Niall was a subject much discussed on Bleake Isle, most especially our friendship. He was half-human, his mother a maid my father had availed himself of so frequently, he'd managed to get the woman with child, when only an omega ought to have served for that particular purpose for an alpha. Niall was an aberration, and also the only man on the island I trusted completely.

"She's a little small." Niall squinted at Adelaide Brys's bright hair shimmering over the tops of the shrubs. "And I'm not sure riling Hugh Gamesby is your smartest move. But otherwise, she's perfect," he said, very blandly.

I grunted in agreement. "My mother was small. And I've hardly ridden her skirts. Hugh hasn't marked her yet."

Niall's frown only deepened. "Then he's up to something."

"Maybe he's more interested in plotting against me than he is in securing her. Maybe he already has someone else picked out," I said, but I agreed with Niall's suspicion.

"Do you like her?" Niall asked.

"She's...perfect." I repeated his own summation with a shrug. "To say she's the best of the lot would be doing her a disservice."

Adelaide was beautiful, charming, intelligent, and talented, and her mother had taken great care at our recent dinner together to inform me that Adelaide had been given control over every detail of the evening. She knew how to run a house and plan a menu. Her father said she'd been prac- ticing her nests since she was a girl. The rut with her would be not just a relief, but a pleasure—a pleasure I could imagine vividly when I was near her, her floral perfume heady and dizzying. Spending a rut in an omega's nest was a tantalizing prospect. Even with the frenzy safely weeks away from start- ing, I was eager.

Adelaide was the obvious choice. The best choice. A choice that would suit me perfectly.

And if Hugh Gamesby did manage to talk the girl into a quick fuck—he would have prettier words for it, I was sure— to secure his claim, I wouldn't feel a real loss. I frowned and turned my stare forward as the knowledge resurfaced again, in spite of my best efforts at stamping it down.

I'd been careful in my pursuit of pleasure thus far, hiring

willing humans for company, rarely and carefully. I didn't repeat my father's rare siring of a halfling like Niall, much as I was glad to have him in my life. It was hard enough for omegas to birth dragons; humans were even more ill-suited to the task.

I wanted to leave this year's selection with an omega. I was *determined* to. And for all Adelaide's extreme charms, I couldn't shake the understanding that if she weren't so obviously perfect for an alpha, I would easily choose someone else. She would be wasted on a beta, but I wouldn't miss her.

"I'm not eager to put a woman to death in childbirth," I said suddenly.

Niall's pale eyebrows rose. He had my father's coloring, shimmering copper through wheat gold, pale skin freckled from the sun. His wings were strong enough for flight, but he had no true dragon's form. Still, he looked more like the heir than I did. I had my mother's dark hair and easily suntanned skin.

"I know," Niall said. "You're worried she's too small?"

No. I worried the opposite. I worried she'd survive for many decades to come, which was every bit the cruel and brutish thought most of the isle gentry expected from me, modeled by my father. But I worried that Adelaide, for all she was the obvious right choice, might actually be the wrong choice and I would end up stuck with her.

"Who is that?" Niall asked.

Even when he nodded in the direction of his query, it took me a moment to spot the woman under the trees, well out of the shelter of Hugh's garden and tucked in the wilds of his estate proper. I frowned, staring at her, her head bent down toward a book, body stuffed in a dress just too small for her sturdy frame and one shoe kicked off, stockinged foot wiggling against the grass.

It occurred to me after a long study that I'd seen her before.

"No idea. One of the omegas' maids, perhaps," I said.

She looked up as we neared her, gaze distant and lost for a moment, as if she hadn't resurfaced from the pages she'd been studying, before latching onto us, eyes widening first in terror and then a flat kind of shock, like she was surprised to see us anywhere near her.

"Catch your eye?" I teased Niall in a hiss.

He didn't flinch or scoff. He wouldn't, because only an ass would've found me funny. "She's the most interesting person here," he said.

The woman seemed to have realized we were passing her, not approaching, and was now only giving us the occasional furtive glance, attention returning eagerly to her book.

"I think she's an omega," Niall said.

Was he attracted to the woman? Niall wasn't a prolific seducer, but I'd seen him interested in women, and they hadn't been awkward, studious, plain girls with limp brown hair.

"Why?" I asked, taking a surreptitious taste of the air. There might've been a fragrance, but it could just as easily have been the gardens.

"She arrived with the Posys; they're dragonkin. And she's not dressed like a maid."

"I defer to your knowledge of women's dress," I said, lips twitching, wanting to laugh but not quite meeting the urge.

Niall didn't rise to the bait. He never did, insufferably cool as he was. And strangely, I wanted to know what made her interesting to him but refused to ask. He would turn my teasing back on me quick as a whip. Better to be left out of the joke than let Niall make one at my expense.

We turned eventually, back into the twist of the maze. Hugh Gamesby's gardens were predictably ordered and obnoxiously forced, only one path laid out, unless we wanted to turn back and disappear into the woods like the strange young woman. Which was probably a better idea.

Adelaide beamed at me as I arrived back within the fold of the party, but there was a strain in those brilliant blue eyes, Hugh Gamesby remaining steadfastly at her side. She was a bone for the pair of us to fight over, no doubt exhausting for any young woman. But what could she or Hugh do? The moment I was within reach, her body bowed naturally in my direction. For that matter, so did the charmingly plump little brunette sitting on a blanket near my legs. My effect on omegas was biological, flattering, and somewhat irksome—part of the reason I'd avoided any courting in the past. The rut selection was in place for the alpha to choose the omega who suited him best, without the time-consuming effort of dinners and dancing and terribly polite conversation with them all beforehand. The ceremony was also a promise from the alpha to the betas to not drag all the eligible omegas into breeding nests and leave nothing for them.

Just ignore the scent marks, Niall had suggested. *The beta scents will fade by the time the rut is over.* It had never stopped my father. Nothing had ever stopped my father, and I took pride in our differences.

"You solved the maze!" Adelaide greeted.

I nodded, offered an automatic half-smile out of respect for her cheer, and glanced over her shoulder at Gamesby. "In truth, it posed very little challenge."

The omegas, even their mothers, tittered with humor. Niall twisted away from the crowd, hiding his rolling eyes.

These parties were tedious. These people weren't much better. But I was determined this year. Adelaide was perfect, my best choice in all my years of the selection, and still unmarked. Perhaps I would even conquer my aversion and take her with one, if Gamesby managed to seduce her. It would be worth it to foil him, if nothing else.

ALMOST TWO WEEKS LATER, the day before the selection ceremony, my decision was fixed.

I would bring Adelaide back to the castle at the edge of the cliffs, give her a courteous day to collect herself and build the nest, and then I would bed her. If I was left in a lackluster pairing for the rest of my life, it would be worth it for the heir she would offer. I would do everything in my power to keep her alive, which was more than she could hope for with most betas, or with an alpha like my father. Dragon births were difficult, and many betas didn't care about the loss of an omega in the process. The child's survival was always first priority. And perhaps some dragons were a little too eager to move on to a fresh choice of omega.

"You're still here."

I'd been musing, staring out the window at the sea, when Niall caught me in my office.

"Still? Did you expect me to drop dead?" I asked.

"I expected you to go claim the omega," Niall answered, helping himself to the seat across from mine at my desk.

"That's tomorrow."

"Are you *hoping* Gamesby will have her first? If you really want an omega this time, why not do what they do and place your mark the night before?"

"I'll take her with or without one," I said.

Niall tipped his head. "Will you?"

"She'll just have to bathe when she gets here," I muttered. In truth, the scent marks had never bothered me as much as the betas liked to think. I just hadn't *wanted* any of the omegas. But too much time had passed and I could no longer afford to be picky. To wait for claiming to be an intense urge, rather than a political necessity.

It would be disappointing if Adelaide did succumb to Gamesby the night before the selection. Perhaps he'd been waiting intentionally, wanting the mark fresh to better put me off. But it wouldn't stop me from flying her back here.

"I can't say I know how it feels, but you could wait another decade," Niall suggested. Niall's human genes didn't offer him much of a rut. Certainly not the agony of an alpha's.

"That's just another decade for them to stir up the idea of killing me," I said. "Achieve an heir, and I'm on safer ground." A dragon with young was considered stronger, especially an alpha. I wasn't sure if it was old folklore or a real part of our power as dragonkin, but at the very least it would make the other betas pause before pursuing my defeat.

"Letting Gamesby mark your intended the night before the selection makes you look like a fool. Taking her after the mark makes you look desperate too, now that they know how much you hate it. Go to her, Ronson. Stake your claim. If you really hate the idea, I don't know why you'd bother with her."

Which was right, of course, and Niall lounged in that chair with the superior calm of one who always managed to know better.

"You just want me out so you're king of the castle," I said, offering Niall a half-smile he mirrored. "Fine. I'll play the eager suitor."

"I'd wish you good luck, but I've seen her swoon for you," Niall said with a sneer. Which I wanted to mimic too. I resisted by opening the windows, the sudden strike of sea air shocking and sharp, drawing out an excited snarl from my lips. My wings caught me, spreading as I leapt, my claws freeing from my fingers as I flew out over the edge of the cliffs, over the crash of the sea as it met the rocks. I twisted, let the wind snap against my wings, and circled back to the isle, following the urgent gust back over land.

There were dragonkin gentlemen who elected not to use their wings, their dragon's form, considering it beastly. But flight was the only gift of our bloodline I really enjoyed. I would've gladly kept my place as a beta if I hadn't hated my father so much, seen how desperately the island needed his seat as alpha overthrown. Our omegas had been secretly fleeing on ships one by one, our human population dying under horrible working conditions. And betas took their profit and their heirs and carried on, as if all this were acceptable so long as their pockets were deep and there were young omegas for their beds.

Challenging my father to fight for the role as alpha was not solely my ambition, but my duty to the island. Most days, being alpha was more trouble than it was worth, and even the rut was an uncomfortable chore. Or it had been with only my own hand and human women to help ease the frenzy. It would be better this time, with an omega, a thought which carried me toward the modest Brys estate, set near the human village at the edge of the woods that abutted the Gamesby estate.

The Brys family had been blessed by their daughter, but were otherwise unremarkable and not quite significant. Mr. Brys made good money in trade, enough to keep his family in fashion, but their lineage was the third son of a third son or something of the like, with no titles or inheritance left to them. To have a daughter paired with the alpha would be a social boon at the least, and the expectation of titles and money was sure to sweeten the deal.

I swooped over their home, over their woods, nearly to Gamesby's house before realizing I was actively avoiding the job at hand.

I tucked my wings slightly, and flipped my body down like an arrow to land. Gamesby might try and shoot me if he saw me, pretend he thought I was wild game, but I knew how to slip through the trees and keep my steps quiet. I would use the time walking through the woods to organize my thoughts again.

Adelaide is an ideal omega, I reminded myself for the hundredth time, catching a wing talon on a tree branch and then climbing my way down slowly. *Her family has a good track record of births on both sides. An heir will settle some of the beta jostling happening behind closed doors.*

My boots touched the ground, and I gentled my steps. The only way they could take my place was by killing me, something I wasn't inclined to allow. I needed an omega, Adelaide, or at least the heir she would offer. I marched in silence toward my destination.

The thoughts were like commands in my own mind, settling a sensation that was less than nerves but more than disinterest. So strong was my determination to follow those commands that I almost missed the presence of voices. Familiar ones.

"Hugh, I'm nervous."

"Addie, pet, you've nothing to be nervous about. The plan hasn't changed in weeks. Your part will be nearly done tomorrow."

"No, it won't!"

I'd already halted my steps, taken shelter behind a vast tree, but the rough hiss of Adelaide Brys's voice left me intrigued and surprised, the sound so harsh and unlike anything I'd heard from her before.

"It all *begins* tomorrow, Hugh. If this works, if he chooses me—"

"He'd be mad not to, Addie," Hugh said, his tone so dulcet in comparison to the omega's.

"Then I have to serve him for a brutish rut. For *days*!

Doesn't the thought of an alpha rutting on top of me for hours and hours bother you?"

"It makes me furious," Hugh said, not sounding especially convincing to my mind.

There were gentle murmurs ahead, Hugh reassuring the omega of his worry and affection, but a crunch from behind sent me whirling around, surprise striking me roughly at what I found.

The strange omega woman, the one Niall and I had seen hiding from Gamesby's party, was wandering blindly through the trees, barely feet away. They called her Mouse, as I'd learned from a chuckling pack of beta dragons over whiskey after a dinner. She had her nose in another book, not even noticing a briar catching on her skirts, and definitely unaware that she was about to walk straight into an argument I was dying to hear the culmination of. If she looked up, saw me, made any noise at all, she might alert them to my presence.

I lurched forward as quietly as I could and grabbed her, clapping my hand over her lips, a suitably mouse-ish but small squeak released against my palm. With another quick, careful motion, I hauled her up off her clumsy feet and into my hiding spot with a tight grip around her arms and waist.

"Silence," I spoke roughly into her ear.

She tensed in my arms, and I noted with surprise that her stodgy-looking frame was, in fact, a very unfortunate disguise. She felt quite promising, now that I had my arms around her. Her stomach was soft, and her ass was incredibly full and plush against my hips. Interesting. Distracting, even.

"You'll enjoy the rut. You can't help it," Hugh said, gentleness disguising the lack of feeling in the words. Adelaide squawked in outrage, another new sound from her, and Hugh continued, "All you have to do is put up with him for a few days, a week or so, and then open a door when I send word."

The little mouse in my arms—Lord Posy's daughter, very unfortunately arranged for Old Gryffyd, from what I'd heard —seemed as keenly aware of the intrigue of the conversation as I was, and she stopped struggling almost as soon as the pair's voices raised. I could've let her go, told her to stay quiet, but it would've been a wasted chance to hold such a comfortably formed body. She did have a scent after all, a tiny one, but it reminded me of a perfume I'd smelled on a human woman once, designed to entice a dragon—amber and gold, warm and syrupy. It was fainter on the Posy girl, but less artificial too.

"I have half a mind to leave the door locked. If I'm so suited to a rut, I'm sure I'm suited to be an alpha's omega too," Adelaide said, sounding more herself, coy and teasing. I bit off my snarl at their casual use of me in the conversation, as if I might be the pawn in their game.

"You'll be his *broodmare*. Don't mistake his reluctance to choose thus far as him being anything less than his father's son. If you survive birth, he'll find a way to kill you off."

The woman in my arms stiffened, and I resisted the impulse to reassure her. It might've been true of my father, although I hoped not. It wouldn't be of me.

"First I'll be fine, then I'll be killed off—"

"Not in a handful of days, you won't. Don't be difficult, Addie. Worst case, you're burdened with an alpha's son, who will most likely grow up to be alpha. And if not that, then I'll be alpha next, and you'll bear me all the sons and daughters we could wish for."

A hand was clutching my arm, the omega I held shocked by the words I heard. I was a little shocked too. Not by Gamesby's ambition, but that it hadn't occurred to me they might use an omega as a trap. It was clever, and as I'd been telling myself for weeks, Adelaide was perfect. For my use and theirs.

"Admit it. You're just all in a fluff because it's been ages since we've—"

"Oh, Hugh. Why couldn't you have gotten rid of him before this? I don't want in his bed. He terrifies me."

"I know, pet, I know. And how I wish I could soothe your poor little heart with a kiss."

"More than a kiss," Adelaide urged.

The conversation took a turn, one that made the woman in my arms gasp, a surprisingly innocent sound for an omega who was almost over the edge of a desirable age.

For both our sakes, I lifted her off her toes, hiking her up at my side. Her arms wrapped easily around my shoulders, and I turned and walked us carefully away from the lovers' explicit speech.

The omega—*Mairwen!* I recalled at last—remained docile, pressed to my chest, her hands tight and almost possessive on my shoulders as I carried her. I headed roughly toward the village. The Posy estate sat on the other side of the town, in view of my castle.

"They're planning on killing you," Mairwen whispered, apparently satisfied with the distance we'd traveled.

"I gathered," I answered, lips twitching.

She huffed and started to squirm. I understood now why her clothes looked frumpy on her. The silhouettes of current fashion were too slim and straight to suit a form so inclined to volume and shape. She would look better out of her clothes than in, and I glanced down at her unjustly disguised breasts. What fool had thought to flatten them in a trap and then cover her up to her chin in fabric?

"What are you going to do?" she urged.

"Not allow them to succeed," I said easily, setting her down on her feet and offering her a rare smile.

She frowned back at me, lips twisting and pursing. She had a wide mouth, lips ample for kissing. She was still...not pretty, precisely, but I was realizing there was something there that deserved attention.

"I'm sure you can talk Adelaide out of it," she said, tone a little dubious.

She was right, of course. I absolutely could. I could order Adelaide to behave, even—demand pleasure from her too.

"It doesn't solve the issue of her having been talked into it in the first place," I said, checking over my shoulder that we were still alone.

"Katherine might suit you. She seems shy, but really she just isn't that interested in people. But she's very smart, and she thinks Gamesby is a twat." Mairwen blushed, possibly at her own language, but stared eagerly up at me. Her eyes were a comforting, warm shade, almost golden, brighter than the drowsy brown of her hair.

She was recommending me alternatives. This odd omega they called Mouse, who'd never been properly introduced to me and had never spoken a word to anyone when I'd been present, was offering her opinion on whom I might choose instead. And she hadn't started with herself, bold as her words were.

Damnit. Niall was right. She was the most interesting one of the lot. Strange and mostly plain, but also lush and a bit direct, without a proper omega's perfume.

"Where did you come from?" I asked, not entirely sure of the exact meaning I intended.

She blushed and glanced down at the book in her hand. "I was wandering. Reading."

"Not at home."

"Not at home," she agreed with a frank nod.

We stared at one another, and I understood. Tomorrow was the selection ceremony. She was promised to Gryffyd Evans. And for five selections running, the betas of the isle had thwarted my choices by scent marking the omegas shortly before.

I refused the immediate image brought to mind, of Mr. Evans trying to seduce and defile this young woman in pursuit of his own cause. She was still clean—barely even her own perfume hovered, and there was no greasy mark of his on her. But I didn't put it past Gryffyd Evans to take the chance for sex with a young omega before the selection if he thought he could get away with it. He was as notorious with the women he chose as my own father.

"I can't wander all day," she said, a dismal forced smile on her broad lips. I was about to encourage her to do just that when she turned on her heel and took the lead, continuing, "Sophia might suit you too. She's impossible to discourage. The most stubbornly cheerful creature you're ever likely to meet."

Mairwen Posy seemed to be about to wander right off now, without a curtsy or demure "my lord" or even a goodbye. I would see her tomorrow at the selection, an event whose outcome I was suddenly uncertain of. All I knew was that Adelaide wouldn't do. I didn't like her enough to try and persuade her not to kill me.

"I'd better walk you back," I said. "Clearly, I need your insight."

Mairwen hummed in agreement and then stopped, staring at me in horror. "But you can't walk me all the way to the house. If my mother saw you, she'd get all sorts of mad ideas. I know it's less than a day, but even in that amount of time she could—" She stopped herself abruptly, lips pressing flat, and shook her head, marching forward like a soldier. "Absurd," she muttered.

Mairwen's mother might see me at her daughter's side the day before the selection, might even catch a whiff of me on her after I'd manhandled her. Her mother might think I was preparing to choose Mairwen. The alpha choosing the tall, awkward, inappropriate, not clearly pretty, scentless omega.

Unlikely. Absurd, as Mairwen had said.

My lips twitched again.

"Francesca would not suit. She's very weepy and incredibly biddable. Someone like Gamesby would only have to suggest she open a door, and then the pair of you would end up playing a tug of war on her poor mind," Mairwen declared, a defense for Francesca more than a warning for my own sake.

It was a shame she was walking ahead of me. So few people ever saw me smile.

Chapter Three

MAIRWEN

I turned my head to the side, dipping my nose down to my shoulder, trying to catch another whiff of that harsh, oaky scent of the alpha. I'd bathed as soon as I got home, scrubbed myself clean and changed my dress, but I could still feel the pressure of his arm around my waist, and it seemed impossible that some evidence shouldn't still remain.

I reached for my glass, fingers pausing around the stem. Across from me at the table, Mr. Evans watched with me a faint smirk. He'd provided the wine for the evening, and it had an unpleasant aftertaste, like licorice, which was starting to turn my stomach. Or the thought of what was to come was responsible. Probably both.

I didn't see why Mr. Evans should bother to keep with the recent tradition of bedding his intended the night before the selection. He could hardly be afraid of losing me to the alpha.

Even with Adelaide Brys's recent foray into treason.

I pressed my lips firmly to the wine glass as I sipped, and some of the gassy-flavored liquid slipped in. I had a secret, and it was bursting behind my tongue, begging to be told. But what if Mr. Evans was aware of the plot, an ally to Hugh Gamesby? What if my father was?

I'd heard my father refer to our former alpha, Lord Cadogan's father, as ungentlemanly. I also knew he lacked confidence in the son, but I'd never heard him speak so ill as to suggest he might want our alpha dead.

"The wine was aged in my cellars," Mr. Evans—surely I couldn't keep calling him Mister—said, watching me take another false sip. "It is my table's signature. I rarely prefer anything else."

His smile was beatific. He'd just offered me a tidbit of knowledge of his tastes, one I would find useful—or be expected to remember—when my father handed my life over to him tomorrow afternoon.

Tomorrow. A month ago—the moment before Lord Cadogan stormed into our company—the inevitable still managed to feel quite distant, a far-off point on the horizon I might never manage to reach. Now the day was *tomorrow*, a massive wall in front of me I could find no way around or over.

My family's dining room was warm, well-heated by two small fireplaces on either end, but I felt as though I were falling backwards into a cool grave. My days were numbered now. Mr. Evans's omegas rarely lasted more than one ten-year term. If I'd been born a few months earlier, had been chosen by Mr. Evans in the last rut selection ceremony, I would already be dead by now.

As a woman walking into her grave, I decided I ought to be able to have a few last words.

"It reminds me of that candy I used to hate so much as a child," I said brightly, smiling back at Mr. Evans.

"Mairwen!" My mother's cry was sudden and wounded, as if it was her I'd insulted and not our guest.

My father let out an awkward laugh. "Aren't we lucky, then, that our tastes mature as we age?"

I went ahead and made a dubious expression, Mr. Evans glaring at me as he helped himself to his own sip of wine.

"I didn't realize you could be so outspoken, dear one," Mr. Evans said. "I do enjoy an omega who is unafraid to contradict her superiors. The opportunity to provide instruction for their betterment is quite satisfying."

It would be difficult to resist the urge to fight this man, but if he looked forward to it, I was better off denying him one.

"It must be the wine," I murmured. I looked down to my plate and frowned to find all the food already gone.

"Perhaps we'd better see that you get a little fresh air, dear one," Mr. Evans said.

"Oh yes, the gardens are lovely this time of day," my mother hurried to say.

"You mean in the dark?" I asked my mother, a little too loudly.

"They're serene," she bit out.

I huffed and sat back in my seat, glancing at my father and finding the worst kind of condemnation on his face. Worry and pleading, so much more potent than anger. I was twenty-six years old. He could hardly refuse Mr. Evans and let me wait another ten years for the next selection. And there'd been money exchanged for me already, I was sure of it.

If I insulted Gryffyd Evans too deeply, found some manner of refusal he would listen to, my father would have to pay the man back. And there would be no one ready to rescue me tomorrow.

If only I'd been just a little bit pretty, just a bit smaller and less inclined to good food and lying in the sun reading. If only my hair took the slightest curl.

I lifted the glass of wine, nose wrinkling at its smell, and stared at Mr. Evans over the rim. I could not walk into that shadowy garden alone with Mr. Evans without some kind of courage. Might as well let it be liquid. I drank the glass down in full, ignoring Mr. Evans's triumphant grin and my swirling stomach.

We rose from the table, and he remained waiting for me to circle the seat, his arm offered. I wanted to refuse the gesture, but the candlelight was spinning around me, and perhaps being docile might bore him of me quicker. I tucked my hand in his elbow, mentally comparing it to the alpha's more muscular frame. Mr. Evans was just a fraction taller than me. If I survived, he might eventually stoop with age and I would have the advantage. But even I knew that was unlikely. Betas' lives were almost triple the length of an omega's, and that was without our added risk of childbirth.

Lord Cadogan had carried me through the woods with no effort I could detect, and while I hadn't felt dainty, his hold was comfortable and I'd been less self-conscious in his company than most men's. I was not very self-conscious now with Mr. Gryffyd Evans, but that was largely to do with feeling I ought to focus on him, my body tense in preparation for his strike.

Mr. Evans led the way to the back garden like it was his home, not mine. Without an heir, with me in Mr. Evans's clutches, perhaps it would end up his. No wonder he'd been willing to put money towards it.

"You must be anxious for tomorrow," Mr. Evans said.

I was more anxious for this evening, my knees growing weaker with every step, the wine in my stomach jostling like the waves at the cliff's edge.

"Don't you find it chilly out tonight, sir?" I asked. It was lovely and temperate. "Would you rather retire to the salon? I could play music for you. I've been practicing a song on the pianoforte."

At best, I was an acceptable talent at music, and my mother said my singing voice was morbid and unsettling. Would that be enough to put the man off?

His hand covered mine on his arm, fingers biting into my wrist, latching me to him. His stride was long and quick, dragging me back through the tidy rows of poppies, peonies, and roses my mother tended with such devotion.

"I've had quite enough girlish music and simpering for one courting season. You know the tradition as well as I do, Miss Posy. I intend to have what little joy this union can offer as readily and often as I please."

My skin crawled, uncomfortably warm and clammy, and my steps stumbled as he carted me to the back of the garden. There was an old wooden bench my grandfather had built, tucked under a broad willow. It wasn't entirely out of the sight of the house, but I had no doubt that wherever my parents were tonight, they weren't going to be watching the garden.

"I don't feel well," I murmured, tripping over a root.

Mother's dinner for Mr. Evans had been designed by his own cook, and it was a heavier meal than we usually had in the evenings. And that wine, too sweet and tasting far too much like the cellar Mr. Evans had mentioned.

I was thrown down to the bench, the seat hard and the landing jolting my belly and all its contents.

"Don't be missish, you're far too old for that," Mr. Evans sneered. "Even with your shortcomings, I can hardly be the first man to take the territory."

My eyes widened at such a ridiculous statement, and Mr. Evans's bulky frame wavered in front of me. A hard grip claimed my knee, hauling my foot up to the bench, as another pushed my shoulder back and to the side, putting me at an odd angle.

No. The angle he needed, I realized, some of that wine

and thick dinner rising up my throat.

"Sir, I think I might—"

Mr. Evans's knee landed on the bench between my awkwardly spread legs, and my skirt let out a muffled cry, tearing as he pushed it up and out of his way.

He was wrong. I was twenty-six, with all my shortcomings, and no man had claimed my *territory*, as he'd called it. The hand on my shoulder grasped my neck, pinching it cruelly, and my heart sank in my chest as Mr. Evans dove down and slammed his mouth to mine. His tongue was slick across my lips and chin, and I offered myself the poor consolation prize of this being absolutely the worst first kiss in history.

"Open your mouth, chit," he snapped.

But my mouth was pressed firmly closed, stomach clenching and throat swallowing compulsively as bitter saliva and sharp bile pooled on my tongue. If I opened my mouth, I would *certainly*—

Oh. Brilliant! I thought suddenly.

I did as Mr. Evans asked of me, parting my lips as my stomach heaved once more. The wine was even worse coming back up my throat, onto my tongue, and I expelled it eagerly.

"Argh! Blech! Ughhh!"

Mr. Evans's grip on my neck was yanking me away from him now, but it was too late. I'd never been so delighted to be sick in my life, a dark stain spilling between us, over both our chins and elegant dinner clothing.

He released me, stumbling backwards, and I sat up, eagerly throwing up again, making sure it hit his pants and boots as he hurried to escape me. I wanted to crow with victory, hoot with laughter. I also wanted very much to be sick again. I felt and smelled disgusting now, but it was all worth it.

Thankfully, my voice was weak and raspy as I spoke. "Forgive me, sir. I did try to warn you. Something disagreed with me." I gagged, spat out bile to the ground, and shook my head. "I think it was the wine."

Mr. Evans shuddered and gagged softly himself. "Disgusting, absurd creature. How dare you!"

"I am so dreadfully sorry, but sir, I think there might be—"

He howled and jumped aside quickly, and I bent in half to hide my foul grin.

"Never mind. Never mind tonight. No one else would ever take you," he hissed, backing away.

I nodded to agree. And perhaps Mr. Evans would spread the word and no one would ever choose me.

"But you'll pay for this tomorrow," he snarled, turning on his heel.

My grin faltered briefly until I heard him gagging again as he all but ran toward the house, calling for his carriage. This was only a delay. A reprieve from my fate.

But I thought I might've ensured one bright reward for my future, at least.

Mr. Evans would surely never offer me more of that horrible wine. If I was lucky, I'd ruined the taste for him altogether.

I huffed a laugh and then winced. Oh, I *stank*. I rose gingerly from the bench, and the imprint of Mr. Evans's grip on me was more disturbing than the streak of vomit running down my dress.

I would have another bath. This was my last night of freedom, peace.

And tomorrow had a single bright spot to shine against the grim dark of my future misery: I would learn what Lord Cadogan had decided to do, who he would choose after Adelaide's betrayal. It was almost as exciting as something out of a story.

Chapter Four
MAIRWEN

I'd been so relieved during the last selection ceremony, aware that I'd been given a strange blessing, able to avoid the situation for another ten years. I'd ridden in the carriage with my mother and father, walked out to the large field at the center of the island where we gathered—where the harvest fair would take place at the end of the summer—and watched the girls who were just barely older than me march up onto the stage. I'd wondered then how many of them would still be with their chosen dragons by the time the next selection came.

Standing now on that very stage, the bright morning sun glaring into my eyes, I counted five of the seven of them in the audience. Not bad odds, actually.

How many of the eight of us standing now will be here in ten years?

Mr. Evans was glaring at me from the left-hand of the stage, his face red with last night's fury, a promise of retribution. I tore my stare away from his and found my parents in the seats of the audience, their expressions a little bland and nervous. They must've been aware of my failure the night before. I didn't bear Mr. Evans's mark.

It occurred to me then that today ought to have been slightly humiliating, at least to the perspective of the drag-onkin gathered. The humans wouldn't notice my smell, but the gentry dragons would. Only Adelaide and I were unmarked. If it had just been me, and I was overlooked by the alpha, even without the beta scent on me, nothing would be a stronger execution of my worth in society.

Adelaide's betrayal was my salvation. Everyone would be too shocked by his dismissal of her to think anything of him snubbing me.

Adelaide was two girls down the line, and I sent her a grateful smile she didn't see. In fact, no one saw it, because all eyes were turned to the sky as a shadow swept over our gathering.

Our alpha had arrived.

Lord Cadogan's dragon was earthy shades of black and rust, a fiery orange cast on his scaled belly. His body was long and solidly built, but not heavy and rounded like the illustrations of his father I'd seen. The dragon was as beautifully terrifying as the man, and he swooped overhead to the cheers of the human villagers standing and to the polite clapping of dragonkin.

He flew to the edges of the crowd on the right of the stage, and brought his hind legs down, body shrinking and transforming in an almost liquid shift into a man, black boots gleaming, clothes only slightly windswept, curls wild.

My stomach clenched, still woozy from the night—I'd been sick several more times before I'd finally finished expelling Mr. Evans's poisonous wine—and I rested my hand over my waist where Lord Cadogan's arm had been banded.

"Adelaide is so lucky," Sophia whispered, sighing softly.

I snorted, but she ignored me. *Adelaide would've been lucky if she'd had the sense to tell Hugh Gamesby where to stick his murder plot.*

Our alpha shook his wings, morning steam from the clouds flicking and glittering off their vast blackness, and then started forward. The islanders scattered out of his way, offering him a path to the stage stairs. I wondered how many of them—maids and gardeners to the dragonkin—already expected this to be the year the Alpha of Bleake Isle chose his omega.

I hoped he did, although I never did decide on which of the others might be best for him. I hoped he ignored the scents of the betas, dismissed Adelaide and her pure rosy fragrance, and shocked us all.

His gaze landed on me as he marched up the stairs, and I offered him a smile, feeling something like a co-conspirator of his now. He didn't answer it with one of his own, but I'd never seen him smile much in our company this past month and his eyes glittered darkly back at me.

The bubble of excitement blended with the discomfort of the night before, and I breathed slowly as black boots landed heavily on the floorboards of the stage.

Lord Cadogan spun suddenly to face the crowd, and they gasped in giddy surprise. Both times I'd watched the selection as a girl, our alpha had more or less gotten the business over with in an unenthusiastic procession down the line. Already, this year was different.

"What do you think? Is my omega amongst this year's young women?" His voice carried naturally, not a demanding boom, but as weighty as the massive wings of his dragon as they beat through the air.

The audience cheered their yeas, eyes bright with excitement, and I heard more than one "Miss Brys" amongst the shouts.

"I think so too," Lord Cadogan said lowly, turning to face us again.

But who? I thought, surely the only person in the entire field in any doubt of the outcome.

The stage trembled under his steps. So too did we omegas. Sophia on my right was breathing in short, nervous gasps. Katherine on my left was vibrating with tension. She'd been marked by William Aspley, and I'd noticed what seemed like genuine affection between them this season. He was as scholarly as she. Was she eager to see him, or anxious?

My stare was aimless as he approached from the right. I was as much a spectator of this moment as the audience, and I wished I could've been standing up against the ledge of the stage like the human shopgirls, admiring the dragon who paced in front of the omegas, waiting for him to grab one from the line.

His steps stopped, and it took me a beat too long to realize he was blocking my view, the pearl buttons of his white shirt winking at me. My eyes widened, and my chin lifted to stare up at him. But the moment I did, he moved on, the leap of my heart into my throat so absurd, so unnecessary, that I wanted to melt down into the floor.

How for a moment could I even have imagined he might...?

The crowd held its breath as he reached Adelaide, the collective so quiet, his sniff was audible. And then came the echo of his foot on the floor again, followed by a slight general gasp as he moved past her.

At my right, Sophia's eyes were huge, her mouth parted on an O and she leaned forward, gawking down the line before straightening again. He was turning around, coming back the way he came.

I appreciated his sense of the dramatic, but *who?* Who would he choose? The shocked draw of breath was louder as he passed Adelaide again without even bothering to pause. In fact, his steps were picking up, approaching.

My shoulders drooped as I realized he'd made a more sensible choice altogether—to not take any of us. No one would notice my own rejection, not in the wake of Adelaide's, but I had hoped he might do something a little more exciting. Even pliable Francesca—

I blinked as he stopped in front of me again, towering over even my height, his wings blocking me from view.

"What are you—?" I whispered, but my words turned to stone on my tongue as he bent slightly at the waist. My head fell back automatically as his face neared me, offering my throat, the combination of omega instincts and shock leaving me powerless.

His breath was heavy on my neck, like a stormy wind in my ears as he inhaled deeply, the audience so surprised, so confused, they joined him in the sudden breath.

Don't be sick. Don't be sick. Don't be sick, I chanted to my rioting stomach. Oh, to be sick on Mr. Evans was a blessing, but on the alpha? I would sooner throw myself off the cliffs.

Large hands circled my waist, bracing me, as Lord Cadogan took another deep inhale. *I have no perfume*, I wanted to say, my head so far back on my shoulders now I was watching the clouds float gently overhead. He exhaled, and his breath was as hot as dragon's fire on my throat, down into the collar of my dress, stroking my breasts and making them heavy.

He's making a joke, I thought, and my whole body ached with the bruise of the knowledge. *He will walk away, leaving Adelaide feeling as though even I might be better than her*.

He took another breath, and I wanted to strike him but I was boneless. His nose was right against my skin now. He would hear how hard my heart hammered, feel my pulse jumping.

I was going to be sick. The worst possible addition to this baffling and humiliating moment.

His nose stroked my throat, and I shuddered, his hands holding me more firmly in answer. His head lifted, and I could not bear to look him in the eye, keeping my gaze on those passing clouds, his handsome and cruel face hazy at my periphery. Was that a smile on his lips? My chest was burning up, and I wondered if an omega had ever breathed dragon's fire before.

"You'll do."

Even with his back turned to the audience, the words were clear, loud enough. He'd raised his voice for their sake.

You'll do? Do for what?

I met his stare, and the answer was obvious, and yet absurd.

Don't be sick, I thought again, but then I realized I wouldn't be sick because I wasn't even breathing. The edges of my vision were growing black. And yes, that was a smile on his lips—small, but there—and it was vanishing now, his brow creasing with worry.

Fainting was a *slight* improvement on vomiting, at least.

I HADN'T REMAINED UNDER, in the consuming darkness, for long. Just enough time for Alpha Cadogan to carry me off the back of the stage into the small retiring tent. I'd awoken cradled in his arms and promptly closed my eyes again before he or anyone else might notice I was awake.

What had he done?

No, that was obvious. The Alpha of Bleake Isle had chosen *me* as his omega. It was outrageous. Laughable. He was insane, or so spiteful he'd thought of the cruelest and least imaginable insult to Adelaide.

But he held me in his arms like I was no burden at all, his heart steady under my ear, until someone brought a cot to the tent, and then he'd settled me there, my face turned toward the soft canvas wall.

Which meant I was able to listen.

"Are you mad?" Hugh Gamesby all but shouted, bursting into the tent.

"I would've assumed you'd be relieved, Gamesby."

My lips twitched at the alpha's dry tone, and I turned my head into the prickly, hay-scented pillow on the cot.

A throat cleared, and Hugh Gamesby changed his track. "I mean, my gods, man, of course I'm *delighted* you haven't stolen the finest omega this island has seen in over a century right out from under me, but..."

But why? Hugh wanted to ask.

"I ought to claim goodwill on my part, but in truth, I picked the woman I was most interested in."

I stiffened at the words, my head blanking, heart drumming. Liar! Or did *interested in* mean *baffled by*?

Hugh had no response to that—how could he?—and a moment later, the tent was opening again, new voices arriving.

"My-my lord, you've quite—" I winced at the breathless notes from my father.

"You've foiled an arrangement, my lord," Mr. Evans bit out.

It took everything in me to keep from curling in on myself, the memory of the old dragon's harsh grip on my body still painfully fresh.

"Are you denying me the right to choose my omega, *Mr. Evans?*"

I opened my eyes and found the alpha's shadow high on the tent wall. Someone had left the curtain of the tent open. How many more acquaintances would burst inside to question the alpha on his choice of me? How many would it take before he changed his mind?

"Of course not, my lord. However, there now remains an issue for you to address as our esteemed alpha. The price exchanged between Lord Posy and myself for the honor of his daughter." Mr. Evans made no effort to quell his voice, and I wondered if I might conjure another round of vomiting now, rise from the cot and coat him in it. But now that I was lying down, my previous bout of anxious queasiness had passed, and I was loath to draw attention to myself.

"Send the receipt to me, and I'll settle it myself," Lord Cadogan said, his own voice dropping gently.

"No, my lord. I told the gentleman I could manage it myself. I fully intend to. There was no need to bring this to you."

"Don't trouble yourself, Lord Posy. I'm more than happy to take on the burden in exchange for the boon of your daughter."

I snorted and then froze, hoping the sound was muffled in the pillow. Thankfully, they carried on without me.

"You're very generous, my lord," Mr. Evans said, all silk and slime now that he'd gotten his way. "And I quite preferred the Huberts girl anyway. So isn't this a happy circumstance?"

"Our alpha has chosen an omega for the first time in almost a century," Hugh Gamesby said, low and smooth. "'*Happy*' isn't the word."

"Indeed. And now, if you gentlemen wouldn't mind, I'd like to tend to the young woman in quiet."

"Of course you would. What an auspicious beginning for you," Hugh said, finding any dig he could now that he'd wasted Adelaide in his plans.

There was a shuffle of steps and then a small and familiar clearing of a throat. "Gwenievere and I would...be grateful for a chance to say goodbye to our little mouse before you leave, my lord."

"Of course, Lord Posy. I'm sure we'll be out directly."

My father hummed, paused, and then his feet scuffed over the grass. The alpha's shadow vanished, and the light in the tent dimmed.

I must've expected the earth to tremble as the stage had, because I nearly leapt off the cot as a hand touched my back.

"You can stop pretending to sleep now," the alpha—*my* alpha said.

Chapter Five

RONSON

Mairwen jolted up from the cot I'd placed her on, eyes wide and wild and that warm shade of honey that suited her so well.

"What were you thinking?" she blurted out.

I had to check that my claws were staying sheathed after the bickering of Gamesby and Evans. The betas had grown far too bold in the past fifty years. Mairwen was also too bold, but I suspected that had more to do with her nature than a lack of respect or fear for me. And sure enough, she blanched and shrank back slightly as the words left her lips.

"Do you object?" I asked, crouching at her side.

The thoughts flitted across her face almost as clearly as if I were reading the books she'd always had on her person during the courting season. Could she object? Yes; I wouldn't drag her back to the castle with me. But would it leave her with Evans?

"I can keep the old dragon out of your way," I said, because I was more curious to see if she would choose between her own freedom and my bed, than if she would choose between Evans and me.

"I don't object, my lord," she said, and the words were measured and careful. "But I'm *very* surprised. And so will the rest of society be. I know no one should question you, but they will. You might want to think of an answer for them."

She's smart. I'd realized as much yesterday while walking her home, sharp observations about all of the isle's dragonkin just bubbling out of her. She knew more than I did, had seen more than I had, simply by hovering at the edges of events.

I rose up, and she craned her neck back, unafraid to meet my stare. "You're right. But I know I did make the right choice, Mairwen Posy."

She blinked at me, and a slight whiff of that amber-sweet scent floated up to my nose. I'd been hunting for it on the stage, wondering if I'd imagined it yesterday, and it'd been elusive, almost vanishing. But there it was, a sliver of promise, one that carved a deep hunger in my belly. This woman *was* an omega—*my* omega now, for better or worse. Perhaps the rest of dragonkin had managed to overlook her, to leave her behind for a man like Mr. Evans to pick off. I would not.

"Are you well enough to deal with their stares?" I asked, holding out my hand.

She paled again and the hint of perfume vanished, but she took a steeling breath and placed a cool hand in mine. She had a smooth palm and long fingers, comfortable in my grip —a woman's hand rather than a young girl's. I was glad that she was older than the others, even if it was only a handful of years.

The questions from Gamesby and the others were all correct. I'd surprised myself choosing her. The idea had amused me overnight, but it wasn't until I was standing on the stage that I realized I'd decided on her. It wasn't that the others were marked with beta scents. And it wasn't even that I was lucky to know Adelaide's true character.

I simply...*liked* the little I knew of Mairwen. I wanted to know more. And the thought of uncovering her softness, of taking her into my nest and pressing that secretive form against mine for the rut...

No, that certainly didn't hurt.

I wrapped my arm around her back and placed my hand on her waist, her shoulder brushing my chest and top of her head just coming to my nose. She was quieter now than yesterday, subdued by shock. I would just have to find a way to coax her character out again.

"The longer we stay, the bolder the questions will get," Mairwen warned, glancing up at me. She had thick eyelashes the same dusty shade of brown as her hair.

"I never stay for long," I said. Although in previous years, I'd left in a quiet temper. I'd thought I was being patient at my first selection ceremony, not choosing from the betas' omega lovers, not picking one of their daughters to favor over the other. I'd only just inherited my father's seat—the alpha's challenge had been an easy feat, but nerve-wracking all the same—and I wasn't overeager to ally myself with any family. But four decades later, I realized I'd given the other dragons a tool to use against me.

And now they'd given me Mairwen.

"How did you manage to avoid Evans?" I asked as we neared the tent flap. I was relieved for her, and curious too. Was she so little favored that Evans didn't even care to mark her?

"I threw up on him," Mairwen murmured.

I'd already started to step through the parted canvas as she answered, and her words struck me hard, a sudden bark of laughter rising up from my chest.

It caught the attention of the other dragons and their wives and daughters, all milling together to the left of the stage on the tidy lawn. Few of them had ever heard me laugh, and they stared now as I fought to bury my grin. I glanced down and found Mairwen's smile was nervous, but it would do. I ducked my head to whisper in her ear, aware of the picture of us, of what gossip it might stir up.

"Then I consider myself very lucky you only fainted," I said, brushing my lips against her ear.

She huffed a laugh, relaxing just a fraction into my side. "You should. I'm still a bit queasy."

Noted, I thought. We reached the others, and I spared myself a petty private moment to find Adelaide. She was at Gamesby's side, standing in profile, eyes as wide as the moment I'd walked away from her, a kind of fixed and fragile haughtiness on her face. Had I toppled the island's princess from her pedestal? So be it.

"Brace yourself," I whispered to Mairwen, leaning down and rubbing my cheek across the top of her head once in a token mark. As an alpha, my scent was stronger, my ruts were what brought on the isle wide mating frenzy—betas experiencing a mere echo of my own urges—and I had the knot to offer an omega her highest satisfaction. Now, all of that was Mairwen's.

Her cheeks flushed and her spine straightened—a warrior walking into battle armed with a tight smile and an ill-fitting dress.

A chorus of greetings awaited us, but they weren't the congratulations I expected.

"Quite a shock indeed!"

"What a surprise!"

"How unexpected, my lord!"

The omegas of dragonkin stared at Mairwen with an open and baffled kind of amusement. They understood her ascent to my side even less than she did. And the betas were somehow worse. They had no faith in my choice, and I wondered if I'd made my position less secure, or had given myself an advantage by allowing them to underestimate me. My choice of Mairwen would only lose its irony if there was an heir worthy of my father's bloodline. My bloodline.

Mairwen's arm tightened around mine, and I followed her gaze to where Lord Posy was embracing his weeping wife. Lady Posy was taller than most of the gathered women, although not as tall as her daughter, and she had a scent like a cloud of powdered sugar. She'd been at my very first selection ceremony—a perfect rosy-pink and blonde omega, like Adelaide—and she'd shaken like a leaf as I passed her on the stage.

"Oh, Mairwen! Oh, my lord!" she cried out, turning to face us. It was difficult to tell if she was overcome with delight or sorrow.

Mairwen's shoulders drooped slightly and she slid free of me, crossing to her mother, who swooned into my omega's arms with great elegance.

"Oh, my darling girl!"

"There now," Mairwen murmured, tidying her mother and handling her to stand on her own again. She reached out, wiping away the tears from her mother's cheeks. "This is nice, isn't it?"

Lady Posy's blue eyes were wide and glossy with tears, but she echoed her daughter's smile and nodded nervously, gaze flicking to me.

"Thank you, my lord," Lady Posy said, dipping into a low curtsy. "What a great honor."

It was the first sensible thing anyone had said. "The honor is mine, Lady Posy," I said, loud enough for the rest of the crowd to hear. Mairwen's expression tightened, but she only kissed her mother's cheek and returned to my side. "As soon as Mairwen and I have settled, we'll send for you to visit."

"Thank you, Lord Cadogan," Lord Posy answered, wrapping his arm around his wife.

The betas were gathering around their chosen omegas, and while I should've stayed, offered everyone an appropriate congratulations, Mairwen was shrinking under the stares and my temper was rising.

"Come, Mairwen. It's time for you to see your new home," I said.

Chuckles rose from the beta dragons, an edge of mockery in the sound that made my claws itch in my fingertips. Mairwen took my arm again, nodding up at me, and I led her toward the edge of the gathered dragonkin.

"Good luck, Mouse."

I started to turn, and it was Mairwen who tugged me forward, her own determination stony. But I glanced back at Adelaide's quiet statement, the beautiful omega's eyes narrowed on the woman at my side. Mairwen's jaw was clenched, her chin high. The words bothered her. Was it the intention behind them, or the use of that nickname?

I stopped us at the corner of the field, in full sight of the humans, celebrating around the tankards of ale and wine, and the mingling dragonkin, who were settling the pairings of omegas to betas.

"Are you too queasy to fly?" I asked Mairwen.

Her eyes widened and her steps paused as she turned to face me. "Oh! Oh, I forgot. No, I think I'll be all right."

I nodded. "Good."

For some reason, that made Mairwen wince. "Lord Cadogan, I will...do my best for you."

"I know. That's why I chose you," I said, frowning. She didn't look reassured. *It will be better when we're away from the others*, I decided.

Mairwen froze as I lifted a hand to her face, cupping her jaw gently, lifting it up. She was shocked by the touch, perhaps realizing my intention, and a little terrified too. But she stretched closer. *I won't have to hunch*, I realized with an absent kind of approval. I ducked my head, and cheers went up from the crowd of humans. Mairwen jolted briefly, my mouth hovering over hers, her eyes huge. And then her lids fell shut and she rose up to her toes.

The kiss was shy, barely a press from her, and I found myself fighting a smile. I wrapped my free arm around her waist, tugging her closer, and gently pulled her bottom lip between mine. She released a soft note of confusion but answered the gesture with a natural impulse, molding her lips to mine, arching in my arms. That sunny amber flavor was a whisper on her mouth as I licked at her, teasing her with my tongue.

Her breath hitched and her lips parted, and while I told myself I was only taking a chaste kiss for the benefit of our audience, I found myself hunting for more of that rare flavor. Mairwen was softening in my arms, her own hands sliding up to clutch the collar of my coat. She didn't know how to respond as I stroked my tongue against hers, but she shivered and her sweet breath huffed, laced with what I was sure was her perfume.

I pulled away slowly, nipping her top and bottom lip, and Mairwen's eyes fluttered open, a darker shade of honey.

Again, a gritty voice in my head urged.

I ignored it, adjusting Mairwen in my hold, lifting her off her feet and wrapping my other arm beneath her wonderfully soft ass.

"Arms around my shoulders," I said, my wings spreading wide.

Legs around my waist, the dragon in me growled, her plush body as pleasing to hold as I remembered.

Mairwen's arms were loose, her face still slack in wonder from the kiss, but her grip tightened with the first beat of my wings. She bit back a yelp of surprise as I leapt up, and we took to the air with two more rough sweeps of my wings.

"You can hide your face if you're—"

Mairwen was craning in my arms as we tipped and flew, twisting to look down at the ground. I held her tighter so she could look her fill.

"They're all getting so small," Mairwen laughed.

The isle shrank, and I gave into a rare impulse to see how high I could fly us, forgetting until Mairwen was shivering that she wasn't dressed for real flight. She laughed and gasped as I dipped down, allowing the wind to coast us along toward the castle. Mairwen had hooked her ankle around my leg, and I glanced down at her as her eyes fell shut, a blissful ease taking over her features. The wind was ruining the pinched arrangement of her hair, loosening strands from pins, and her cheeks were pink with cold and delight.

The castle staff would be waiting for us at the front entrance, but I wanted to see Mairwen's face as I showed her the view of the sea and the cliffs from this height.

"I'm too heavy for you to carry like this," Mairwen said, but she was still turned toward the view and missed my sneer.

"Don't be absurd," I said, our voices raised to carry over the rush of the wind. "We could fly like this for hours."

A wistful smile spread over her lips at that, and then she clutched my shoulders as I rotated us to the side, flying left of the castle.

"We could travel between islands, if you were dressed properly and I was in my dragon form," I added.

She bit her lip. "I've never been off the island."

"You will. Likely not long after the rut," I said. Once my frenzy had settled, there would be allies to introduce Mairwen to and we would take up our roles on the island, overseeing the relationship between dragonkin and humans, ensuring that the farms were rich and trade ran smoothly.

"Now, look down," I said as we neared the edge of the island.

I helped her turn in my hold, my arm wrapped around the firm structure of her corset. How much trouble would it be to convince her to stop wearing one? The style had been around for decades now—we were overdue for a change, and my mother had been a great influencer of fashion while she'd been alive.

But my mother had been respected.

"Oh!" Mairwen's gasp drew me back, her mouth open as we soared over the edge of the cliff.

The sea was a living creature from this height, its motion like breathing, like it was embracing the cliffs. A bit like sex too. The thrust and retreat. The wet smack against the cliffs; the familiar, reliable crash and sweeping motion. The view, and the soft form pressed chest to chest and hip to hip against me, gathered an easy heat of arousal in my groin. I imagined Mairwen's secretive perfume on the air too.

I flew in a circle for Mairwen until she was shivering from the sharp air, the pink of her cheeks turning red from the abrasion of the wind, and then pointed us toward the castle. Two familiar figures stood on the main balcony overlooking the sea, and I was tempted to carry us up to the high tower where Mairwen would build me a nest. But Niall and Beatrice were waiting, and while Niall *might* take the hint, Beatrice would hunt us down. She'd been waiting most of her life for me to take an omega, someone to share the burden of running the castle with.

Mairwen tensed in my arms as we started a slow, spiraling fall toward the balcony, her eyes already fixed to the contrasting pair. No one knew quite what to make of Niall. He had the wings of a dragon and the lifespan of one, but none of the scent marking of a beta, and no authority but what I granted him as my second. Beatrice, my half-sister, was one of the rare omegas who'd survived her beta husband. She had no heir and had returned to the castle before the age of forty, practically raising me while my mother and father oversaw the island until their deaths. Beatrice was stooped with age now, but her omega perfume still carried through the air as we neared—soothing lavender and stringent rosemary.

They were the only two people on the island whose opinion mattered to me.

Niall's face was frozen, blank, as I touched down on the balcony, his eyes bouncing between Mairwen and myself. "You made your choice," he said in lieu of a greeting.

I dipped my head. "I did."

Beatrice was already studying Mairwen with her hawkish gaze, no doubt seeing more of the woman than Niall and I had combined, but I was watching my half-brother. I'd told him of Gamesby's plot, but not about Mairwen being there with me. He had noticed her first, and I would've hated for him to point out he'd been right after all. He'd have plenty of time to do so now.

Niall stepped forward as I lowered Mairwen to her own feet, aware of the wobble of her as she caught her breath. My arm was around her shoulders, holding her to my side. The judgment of my siblings meant everything to me, and yet I almost wished I could've spared her from it. Or perhaps I was hoping to spare myself in case they thought I'd made a mistake.

"Omega Cadogan," Niall greeted, bowing to Mairwen.

Her breath caught at the title. It was what the dragonkin on the field should've greeted her with, not "Mouse." She started to curtsy, and I held her tight. Mairwen was my omega now. She curtsied to no one on this island but me.

"Mairwen, this is my brother, Niall, and my sister, Beatrice. Beatrice will help you learn the castle, the staff, everything you'll need after..." After the rut. Until that was over, she would be better occupied. I hoped.

Beatrice didn't bother lowering her gaze, and she bowed rather than trusting her old knees to a curtsy.

"It's lovely to meet you," Mairwen said to them both. Her voice was nice, low and soft when she grew shy like this, almost disappearing under the sound of the sea behind us.

"Niall is of no help to anyone. You needn't bother with him," I said, flashing a grin at my brother, who was still studying the woman pressed to my side.

Mairwen didn't laugh and Niall didn't grin, and the joke was sour on my tongue for a moment, until Niall finally looked back at me, a crooked smile on his lips, his eyes narrowed.

"Says the man who appears to have taken my wisdom to heart," Niall said.

She's the most interesting one here.

I swallowed, my jaw clenching, and at my side, Mairwen stiffened. But it was her perfume that caught me off guard. Whatever she understood of the words exchanged between my brother and I, it had elicited a soft burst of her scent. I turned my head to bow to hers, inhaling roughly, too greedy to let Niall or Beatrice have the whiff of her, fascinated by the strange phenomenon of its rare appearance. What was the key to unlocking her perfume? I wanted it in my possession. The very hint of it seemed to call the rut closer.

"Well. Hand her over to me," Beatrice snapped.

"Not now, Bea," I said, restraining my growl.

Mairwen's volleyed between us.

"Yes, now, unless you plan to lock her up to nest straight-away," Bea said, and before I could suggest that maybe that was exactly what I would do, my older sister held out one strong and elegantly gnarled hand. "Let her find her legs in this place, Ronson."

"We should discuss...matters," Niall interjected, the pair of them piling on me.

If I'd brought Adelaide home, I would've happily passed her off to Bea and went away to work with Niall, I considered.

"I would like to see the castle," Mairwen said, still too softly, but her eyes were bright. Her cheeks were still flushed from flying, hair hazily freed from pins by the wind and the sea. She looked excited now, not pale and frightened as she had when I'd declared her my choice.

You'll do. I wished now I'd thought of something better to say than that. I'd meant to tease her, but the words were a rude precursor, too aligned with the reactions of the others.

"Show her the library," I said to Bea, finally unwrapping my arm from Mairwen's shoulders. Her breath hitched, and her scent wisped into the air again, gnawing down into my stomach and lower.

Books were part of the equation then. *Noted.*

Mairwen skittered away from me, eager enough almost to offend. Beatrice grunted in agreement and caught Mairwen's hand, tugging her inside. I glanced at Niall and wondered if I could escape with them, follow Beatrice and see the castle through Mairwen's eyes.

"Do you approve?" I asked Niall as the women disappeared.

Niall's lips flattened, and something sank inside of me. "I'm not sure that I do."

My temper flared. It didn't matter what Niall thought. Except even I wasn't certain of my choice. *Mairwen* wasn't certain.

"I'm not sure that I don't, either," Niall said, relaxing and shrugging. "We'll see. For now, we need to consider what their next move will be, how they will try and use this one."

This one. Mairwen.

"She's too smart for them," I said, and I wished she'd been at my side to hear it.

"Perhaps," Niall said, turning to go inside, leaving me to follow.

My hands clenched at my sides. Mairwen was in safe hands for now, and Niall was right. Gamesby and his ilk wouldn't give up so easily. I had better things to do with the day then chase little whispers of my omega's perfume. I would have plenty of time for that come evening.

Chapter Six

MAIRWEN

The castle spun around me. Partly because it had been almost a day since I'd had a meal I'd managed to keep down, and partly because of the incredible pace Lady Beatrice Cadogan set. She was half my size, and yet her mincing steps carried her through the twisting halls, up and down the endless staircases, as though she had a pair of wings to rival her brothers'. I couldn't catch my breath to ask her the questions that raced through me with every soaring and empty hall we passed through, every vast staircase we swept down and climbed up, all the ancient castle wings we crossed into, the dozens of faces we passed who stared eagerly.

I was sweating as we entered the colossal kitchens, down in the belly and feet of the castle. I was sure I looked more like the harried men and women who labored in the steam and blaze of the kitchen stoves, their faces flushed and brows dewed. This kitchen was the liveliest place I'd seen yet in the castle, full of more activity than all the other wings and halls combined, and I helped myself to a rare pause in Lady Beatrice's speech to gasp for air and take the space in. The room smelled understandably wonderful, warm loaves of bread being pulled out of ovens, herbs hanging from the rafters, meat sizzling on spits.

And in the middle of it all stood a tall, broad woman, barking orders and sampling salt. She glanced up at us, her eyes narrowing. She looked to be about middle-aged, the same as my mother, but somehow more *vital*, powerful. *Almost as powerful as our alpha*, I thought.

"This is she?" the woman snapped.

I looked over my shoulder before I remembered, of course I would be the *she* in question, the newest and most notable arrival to the castle. Which was all wrong, if I gave it too much thought.

Lady Beatrice nodded, gesturing between the slow approaching woman and myself.

"Omega Cadogan, Cook Guinney."

"Mairwen," I declared, determined to hold onto my name.

Cook Guinney paid no attention, but I thought I caught a smile from Lady Beatrice. "If you've changes for tonight's menu, you'd better have them out now. Tomorrow's too, for that matter," Cook Guinney groused up at me.

She grabbed a bound notebook from a worktable and brought it to the doorway where Lady Beatrice and I were safely out of the way of the workers.

"No changes tonight," I said quickly, because I wasn't stupid, but I helped myself to a glance at the open page of the notebook I was passed.

Meat, meat, meat, potatoes, bread. I snorted without thinking, and Cook Guinney cleared her throat. "The alpha needs good, hearty food for a rut."

I nodded, because it made sense, and there was something decidedly masculine about the simplicity of the fare. "Roast the potatoes with sprouts and carrots. And..." I stalled, searching around me, patting at my pockets and finding a pencil I kept for notations as I read. I scribbled in the margins. "A sauce for the fish. Tart juice and bitter greens."

I was not an ideal omega, and if I stopped to think of the days ahead, the months and years, there were more expectations I was terrified of failing than those I had any hope of meeting. But I did quite like planning menus.

I mumbled a few more notes, scribbling a recipe onto the page, and then tapped the pencil against my pursed lips. "This will do for tomorrow." I reached to turn the page and check the next day, but Cook Guinney had had enough of me and snatched the book out of my hands.

"You can look your fill at the rest of the week tomorrow morning. I've work to attend to now," Cook said, frowning down at my notes. But her frown faded into speculation, and I squared my shoulders, confident in my choice.

"It's time to take you up to the nest," Lady Beatrice said to me, turning from the kitchens. She was definitely smiling now, although it might've been at Cook's expense. Or even mine. "I see you have your hands busy, Guinney, but send a luncheon up for Omega Cadogan."

"I can carry a few——" My words died on my tongue at the arch look Beatrice gave me. Offering to carry my own meal up to the nest was not the act of the alpha's omega. I tucked my hands behind my back and followed in silence, back up through the winding stairs and halls of the castle, sweat dripping down my spine, my toes pinched in my shoes.

I missed Lord Cadogan's wings. Going up to the towering height of the castle was so much worse than descending from it, and I was embarrassed by my own huffing and puffing when Beatrice's steps finally slowed outside of the large single door at the top of the turret.

"After the rut has concluded, we will likely find you your own permanent room," Beatrice said, pulling a key from the chatelaine that clinked against her hip. "Until that time, you will sleep here with the alpha."

I nodded, but my head ceased its dizzy bobbing as the door opened. The room was huge! It was round with beamed, peaked ceilings and an intimidatingly huge bed sitting on a platform of stairs at the heart. To my left, an enormous balcony faced the island, small specks of homes folding into the green hills. To my right, a large arched window faced the sea, with a cushioned bench that tempted me closer.

The few nests I'd built had been for myself, in my bedroom. They were small and personal, smaller than the bed I was now gaping at. The alpha's bed had four short, decorative posters, and the beams of the ceiling had a number of hooks, but I had no notion where to start on building a cozy nest for Lord Cadogan and myself in such an enormous space.

"Your things will be brought here by the end of the day or tomorrow," Beatrice said, moving slowly into the room. I noticed, with a little resentment, that she wasn't busy catching her breath. She was used to these endless stair-cases, and probably the enormous rooms too. "The maids will bring you a selection of linens for the nest, but you'll have to give them instruction on what more you'll need. You won't see Ronson before dinner, not now that Niall has him. Ask the staff to find me if you have any more questions."

She turned in the room, eyeing it critically. I had thousands of questions. Did the alpha sleep here normally? There were a few bits of evidence, like the open wardrobe of clothing and a pair of dusty boots by the door, but the room didn't look very personal. Was there a particular way I was meant to build a nest to share with a dragon in rut? Except I should've known that already.

"The nest will keep you busy," she said, pursing her lips and studying me with a hawkish look.

"Of course, yes," I said, wondering how obvious my complete lack of preparedness was to her keen gaze.

She nodded her head in one firm jerk and then marched toward the door I was blocking. I ducked out of the way before she plowed right through me.

The room felt even larger once I was left alone. With Beatrice's fresh omega scent gone, the deeper woodsy and smoky alpha notes teased at my nose and my tongue. Yes, he slept here. The room was clean and sparse, but it smelled like him. I wet my lips and glanced over my shoulder, making sure I was alone again as I pulled and yanked on my dress and the tight stays beneath it that were now uncomfortably soaked with sweat.

Maids would be arriving with food and materials to build a nest I had no notion of how to construct. I wanted to strip myself free of my confining garments and roll into those clean and crisp looking sheets, see if I could reach the corners of the bed as I stretched—I suspected not. But I didn't want to be caught sweating like a pig and lazing about, not when I was so sure the entire castle—and probably the island—was waiting to see what absurd mistakes I would make.

Still, a bit of fresh air would be nice. It was cooler by the sea. I crossed to the balcony, grunting as I opened the doors made of wrought iron and poured glass. They creaked, and I gasped as a chilly burst of air rushed around me, making the world a little clearer and cooling the sweat under my layers of clothing.

I had never seen the island from such a high vantage point, and it took my breath away. Bleake Isle seemed enormous. It was all I'd ever known of the world, but from here in this high tower, looking down on the grid map of the village in the distance, almost able to make out the distant edge of the island where docks waited, it revealed itself as a small kingdom.

Still too large to be ruled by you, I thought, lips twisting wryly.

But the alpha had chosen me. Perhaps to spite Adelaide and Hugh Gamesby. Perhaps because my inability to keep my mouth shut had made him see me as an ally.

I know I did make the right choice, Mairwen Posy.

I flushed and closed my eyes as the wind rushed over me, sharp with sea air but familiar too, with the woods and the hay from the farms and the meadows of wildflowers.

Lord Ronson Cadogan had chosen me as his omega after half a century of refusing others. He claimed he'd made the right choice, even as every other omega and beta likely thought he'd made a terrible mistake.

I *wanted* to believe him. Him and not them. But it wouldn't be so simple. I wouldn't blossom into the perfect omega just because he had stopped in front of me and declared me his choice. If I wanted his choice to be right, I had to help prove it so.

The door opened, and a flurry of maids called to me, their arms laden with fabric and pillows and cords and hooks. I smoothed my hands down my wrinkled skirts and straightened my shoulders, turning on my heel and determined to start now.

Build a nest for the alpha, Mairwen. I swallowed hard and fought my blush. *For you both.*

Chapter Seven

RONSON

"**D**o you think Grave Hills is ready for a new alpha?" Niall asked, one leg crossed over the other as we sat on opposite sides of my desk.

I grunted and shrugged. "You know how these things go. The old guard resists, but there's nothing any of them can do. If Torion can best Lachlan, then he has the strength to rule the betas."

Niall hummed and nodded, but I snorted, wondering if I could read my half-brother's mind.

"And then starts their scheming," I said, thinking of my own less than stable control over the island.

"Torion is even more stubborn than you. Either he'll take an omega straight away, or he'll go twice as long refusing them all," Niall said, crooked smile flashing.

At the mention of omegas, my eyes slid past Niall's shoulder to the doorway, as if Mairwen might have appeared there. She had no reason to come to my office, and Beatrice was unlikely to bring her here. I kept catching the faintest traces of her perfume on my clothes, lingering and clinging after our flight, and it was driving me a little bit mad.

"If Torion does move soon, you'll have an ally against the betas here," Niall noted, catching my attention once more.

"I have an omega now too, which works in my favor," I said. Niall made a soft sound, and my eyes narrowed. "You were the one to point out her superiority. I didn't expect you to have such doubts about Mairwen."

Niall's eyebrows rose. "I considered her *interesting*. But she's obviously not respected by local dragonkin. You took an omega to prove to the betas that you could, that you'd have an heir. But it seems you took the one they valued least."

"That's their mistake, not mine," I snapped, pushing back from my desk and rising to standing.

Niall stared at me for a moment, blinking, and his lips parted. "Ronson. You like her."

I huffed. "I know that."

"Oh. I didn't."

I scowled at him for a moment, reaching up and scrubbing my hand over the eager bristles of my beard. Should I shave before dinner, or would it be better to let it grow out? I wouldn't shave during the rut, and it might chafe Mairwen's skin to start.

"From what you've told me, you can trust her, which is good. And if you like her, then...then that's good too," Niall said, his lips twitching.

I resisted the urge to snarl, but my face was growing warm. "I'm not— It isn't— She was the best of the lot, and she wasn't marked," I spat out.

Niall wasn't chastened, and I regretted speaking the words, the way they belittled the odd omega whose company I'd been craving all day.

"Fair enough," Niall said too lightly. "It's late. I'm sure Cook's chomping at the bit to serve dinner."

I spun, looking out the windows and sighing. The sun was setting. It was time for dinner. This baffling day was almost over, and I would end it with Mairwen, alone at last. Maybe I could take her flying again.

Or maybe I'll just drag her into the nest and keep her there until I've finally discovered what's under all those boned and bound layers of hers.

My shoulders were tight, wings squeezed close to my back, as we left my office and started the trek to the dining room. My own steps thundered in my ears. Mairwen had been pale this morning, and she'd been sick the night before, thanks to damned Gryffyd. Maybe I could have our own dinner sent up to the nest. I wasn't sure I wanted to share her with Niall, who'd been picking at my choice all day, and Beatrice, who wouldn't say a word out loud but would absolutely deliver all of them with a look. Except if we were alone in the nest, I probably wouldn't be thinking of food, and she'd been *sick* the night before because of *Gryffyd*, and—

"Ronson, if you're going to rip my wings off, I wish you'd get it over with," Niall muttered, edging away from me.

I cleared the snarl from my throat and shook my head, shoving aside the horrifying imaginings of Gryffyd Evans cornering Mairwen.

We'd reached the dining room, Beatrice waiting outside with a straight back and her hands folded over her skirt, and a pair of footmen pushed open the doors. I searched the hall.

"Where's—"

"Coming!" a bright voice called from the far end.

I swallowed my own tongue as a flushed and disheveled blur rushed closer. Mairwen's cheeks were splotched with color, her dress rumpled, and the high-collared, opaque fichu she wore under her dress had been abandoned, revealing a spectacular array of soft flesh from her neck down to her heaving and flattened breasts. Their form spilled slightly over the straight neckline of the dress, eager to escape, and my mouth watered. How full would they be once she was out of that corset? I *needed* to know, far more than I needed anything as silly and useless as a meal.

"I'm starving," Mairwen admitted in a soft blurt, flashing me a quick smile. Her skin was patched pink and red from exertion, but would be creamy-pale when calm.

"So is Ronson," Niall said, patting me hard on the shoulder. "Just look at him. Practically salivating."

I growled at my half-brother, and Mairwen's shoulders hitched up toward her ears. I was going to make a terrible mess of the evening, I just knew it.

MY CLAWS DUG into my palms as I watched Mairwen chew on her lip. We ascended the stairs up to the nest together, one of her arms linked through mine, the other fussing and fisting around her wrinkled skirt. Her nerves had become increasingly obvious throughout the evening, as she'd grown silent and avoided my gaze across the dinner table.

I, on the other hand, had become increasingly aware of a simple fact—I was attracted to Mairwen. To the young woman I'd considered irrefutably plain just a week ago. I wanted to sink my teeth into her flesh as it bloomed with color, fill my hands with those hidden curves beneath her dress, and I wanted those *damned* amber-gold eyes staring at me.

"Lord Cadogan—"

"Ronson," I said, but it came out as a snarl, and I covered Mairwen's hand on my arm before she could pull away. "You no longer need to be formal with me, Mairwen." *Especially when you consider where I'm leading you and what I plan to do when we get there.*

Her cheeks blushed and her steps faltered, and that wickedly tempting and evasive scent whispered to me. "Ronson, I was late to dinner because, well... It's just that I...I don't think the nest is very good. I just wanted to warn you."

Without an omega to guard and hoard for my own pleasure, I hadn't needed a nest in the past, although I'd built myself utilitarian versions of the structures for privacy. I still didn't understand the supposed perfection of an omega nest built for an alpha. It was another piece of our dragonkin mystery that I had yet to experience, but at the moment, it was the least of my concerns.

Mairwen was fidgeting and blushing, and she was going to bruise her poor bottom lip unless I found a way to soothe her. We'd reached the door to my bedroom and I stopped, grasping Mairwen's shoulders and turning her to face me. She stiffened in my grip, but she released her lip from the abuse of her nibbling.

"The rut won't start tonight, Mouse," I said, ducking my head down. The nickname slipped from my lips—I'd heard it too many times today, and she had that skittish nature at the moment—but I paused as her expression fell, the warmth receding from her startled gaze. Damn. She hated that nickname. I ought to have banished it from my thoughts, and I regretted it ever landing on my tongue. I slid one hand up from her shoulder, greedily learning the texture of her skin, beautifully smooth and delicate. I sheathed my claws and ran the backs of my fingers up her throat, nudging my knuckles under her chin. Her lips were parted, but I'd lost her scent with that stray comment. *Never again*, I vowed to myself.

"Mairwen," I purred, and her pupils widened. It was a start. "Are you nervous?"

Her brow furrowed. "Of course I am."

My lips curved up at her honesty. She might be nervous, but she was braver than most to admit as much.

"A kiss." I'd meant to ask a question like a gentleman, but instead, the words were a softly growled order.

Mairwen eased slightly, and my impatience won out. I tipped my head to the side and slanted my mouth over hers, catching the salt from dinner on her lips. My left hand stroked down her spine, drawing her into me, as my right cupped her jaw and held her in place.

What was the solution to the puzzle of this omega? I wanted to know all of her secrets, not just her perfume or the shape of her or why everyone—even her parents—called her by a nickname that made her shrink away. What would it take to know this woman I had chosen on a whim after decades of waiting to find someone?

She hummed as I licked the seam of her lips, then sighed and opened to me. She wasn't timid in the kiss, but she was certainly still learning the pattern. I pulled away slightly, searching her face and smiling as I found her eyes shut and her cheeks flushed.

"Have you kissed before today, Mairwen?" I asked, rasping.

She blinked, and I shooed away my pride at her dazed expression. Her nose wrinkled as she answered, "Only last night with Mr. Ev—"

I growled, and my hand on the base of her back tugged her closer. "He doesn't count."

Her lips pursed, and she stared openly up at me. "I'm not doing well, am I?"

I huffed out a laugh and pressed a quick peck to the round tip of her nose. "On the contrary."

And there it was—amber syrup and warm gold, richer than before, clinging to her lips as her breath hitched. I snarled and caught her mouth roughly with my own, impatient for that flavor.

Compliments, I noted for later, too busy drawing Mairwen closer, discovering the soft swell of her ass under layers of fabric and shamelessly digging my fingers into her. She whimpered as my tongue stroked hers, and her arms swung around my shoulders, grasping at the back of my jacket.

Kisses too, I added as Mairwen's perfume bloomed a little more. My knees bent, my body searching for the fit of her against me, muscles tensing when I was denied by the restrictive dress. The open hall at my back became oppressive, a dangerous pressure on my spine, warning me that I had *my* omega out in the open. And yet it was all I could do not to tear her dress open and feast.

Mairwen gasped as I reared back, and I nearly lost any good sense I clung to as I stared down at her. Her breasts were so ripe, straining at the collar of her dress, and the red stain of her flush had the odd effect of making my mouth water and my teeth ache.

"Open the door," I said, clearing my throat to shake out the urgent snap in my tone.

"What?" Mairwen asked, still panting for air.

"Open the door, Mairwen," I said. I couldn't do it, because my hands refused to release her. My thumb stroked the hollow of her cheek in resolute protest.

She hummed, unable to turn and look at the door when I was holding her jaw in my firm grip, and her hand fumbled until she found the knob, twisting it and throwing the door open. She squeaked as I bent and lifted her up, one arm banded under her bottom. It put her chest at eye level, and I groaned and stumbled, burying my face between her breasts. Her fingers slid into my hair as she whimpered, her touch combing through curls and pulling gently on strands. I considered the advantage of the floor beneath us and how it might serve as well as a nest for my purposes of *being inside Mairwen as soon as possible*.

The nest.

She was worried about the nest. Compliments made her perfume. I would—

I lifted my face from her now brilliantly pink breasts—there was a rough mark that must have been from my mouth, and I licked my lips, delighted by the taste of salt and honey—and turned toward the bed.

"Ah."

No, Ronson, you idiot, I cursed as Mairwen's perfume withered and she sagged in my arms.

"I warned you," she breathed.

She had, unfortunately, been right. It was not a very good nest. Mairwen had draped several sheets over the posters of my bed and tied them in a knot at the center, slightly tented by a rope hanging over one of the hooks from the beamed ceilings. It was thin, small, and probably not very secure.

In her defense, she had never had to build a nest that would stand up to a dragon, let alone one in the middle of the rut's sexual frenzy.

She's nervous and she's inexperienced, I reminded myself.

She was also squirming. My arms tightened around her briefly and then relented, setting Mairwen down on her toes.

"I can—I can do a bit more now," she said, turning toward the nest.

I caught her by her shoulders and yanked her back to my chest. "No," I said, softening the harsh word with a kiss to the crown of her head. "This will do very well for tonight."

"You don't have to—"

I spun her, muffling her words with another kiss, pleased as she sank into me, opened her lips and sighed as I swept my tongue briefly against hers. My interest hadn't cooled, but my good sense had clawed its way up from the haze of lust.

"I have an idea," I murmured, grazing my mouth back and forth over Mairwen's.

"Hmm?"

She was delicious, and for a moment I wavered. Even inexperienced, she was so sweet, so responsive. I could easily ensure her enjoyment and my own tonight. I could have her stripped and under me in the shabby nest. I could have my hands and mouth everywhere I wanted them.

Because I was the alpha.

I swallowed hard and stood straight, combing the loose strands that had escaped Mairwen's tight twist of hair back behind her ear.

"The rut will come soon and I will need you, badly," I said, and Mairwen's eyes fluttered open, glowing brightly. She nodded, and I wanted to groan and give into all my base wishes at that dazed surrender. "But until that time, I think we ought to...explore one another."

"Explore?" Mairwen echoed.

I nodded. "You should have a slower introduction to sex than...than what I might like to do at the moment," I said with a rueful smile.

Mairwen's lips twisted, and her eyes cleared. "Like practice, so I know what I'm doing during the rut?"

I frowned. The words were right, but I also somehow felt as though I misstepped.

"Yes, and so I know what to do for you, Mairwen," I said. "So you know what to expect and aren't frightened, or uncomfortable."

She wet her lips with a pink tongue that I was already craving another taste of, and her gaze slid away from me. She scowled at the nest she'd built, and I found myself staring at the mark I'd made on her chest. Had I...*bitten* her? And why couldn't I recall?

"Could we take turns?"

My mouth went dry at the question.

Chapter Eight

MAIRWEN

I slid out of the alpha's—*Ronson's*, I corrected myself— grip and felt as though I could catch my breath for the first time since we'd left dinner alone. I hadn't given a great deal of consideration to his mouth before he'd pressed it to mine, but it was *marvelous*. And shocking, and very, very skilled, because I couldn't feel anything but the swollen tenderness of my lips and a deep ache in my core.

"It's true that I...I'm not really prepared for your rut," I said, braving a glance at Ronson, choking on air slightly at the sight of his dark and probing gaze. He'd been sending deadly looks to my dress all night, but it wasn't censure to *me*, and my uncomfortable corset had never been more of a strain to wear than it was now. The scratch and drag of his stubble against my breasts was still vivid in my head, and my hand fluttered up to cover the spot he'd nipped at and swirled his tongue over.

"I've never seen a man naked," I blurted out, stumbling backwards.

Ronson's eyes narrowed, and his smile was the curved edge of a blade. "Would you like to?"

"If it was you," I admitted, my face on fire.

Ronson stiffened and his eyes fell shut, a low, rumbling purr rising from his chest. His shoulders rolled, and then he was pulling at the snaps and ties that fastened his jacket in place.

"Wait!" I cried out, and he stopped immediately, coat sleeve still clinging to one thickly muscled arm. I swallowed hard and unclenched my hands. "You said...you said we should explore each other."

Ronson nodded, and I wondered if he realized how absolutely terrifying his expression was. I was reasonably sure he wasn't mad at me. He was rough and growling and glaring, but his mouth had been much gentler than Gryffyd's as he kissed me, thorough but tender.

I tiptoed tentatively back to his side, and he released the fabric of his coat, giving me his arm instead so I could complete the task.

"You undress me, I undress you, we take turns?" Ronson asked.

I winced at the idea of him unbinding my laces and corset and seeing me in all of my...me-ness. "Well. I was thinking tonight would be my turn to explore you, and then...maybe... tomorrow—"

"You're not getting into my nest until I get you out of that awful contraption," Ronson grumbled, a shameless finger hooking between my breasts and down into the collar of my dress to tug against my corset, the warm digit wedged against sensitive skin and making me break out in gooseflesh. "Even if it is your turn."

It *was* an awful contraption, and I let out a snort at the masculine snarling pout on his lips.

"I get to keep my chemise on," I bargained. It was quite thin, but in the shadow of the nest it might offer a little disguise.

Ronson was silent, and I glanced up to find him staring speculatively down at my chest again. Surprisingly, he blushed when he realized I was watching him.

"Fine," he said.

I sighed and tugged his coat sleeve away at last, stepping back to study his white linen shirt. There were carefully disguised buttons under a folded placket that ran across the line of his shoulder and then down his back to his wings. I reached up and started on his right side, relieved as he tipped his head back and away, eyes lifted up to the ceiling and giving me a break from their oppressive focus.

"I won't know what I'm doing," I murmured, unpicking the buttons one at a time and taking the opportunity to admire the strong lines of his throat, the shadow of a beard that hadn't been on his face this morning.

"Hm?"

"When I'm...exploring. Touching you."

"That's the point of doing it," he said, shrugging.

"Well, yes, but...you'll have to give me *some* indication when it goes right."

His eyes closed, and his chest shook. I considered attacking the line of buttons down his chest but moved to his left shoulder instead, repeating the process.

"I will endeavor not to hide my pleasure from you, Mair-wen. But I don't predict that being a problem."

I paused, both of his shoulders unbuttoned, the first dark curls of hair on his chest exposed. "Really?"

He lifted his head and stared down at me. "Have I seemed indifferent thus far?"

My mouth opened and shut. He had at dinner, sitting at the opposite side of the table. But in the hall...his hands gripped and squeezed me, dragging me closer, dark sounds of hunger echoing from his mouth into mine.

"I suppose not," I said, taking a solid breath and plucking

one silver button after another down the line of his chest. He had a glimmer of rust and gold scales under the dark hair covering his chest, and I fought the urge to touch him for a moment before realizing that was precisely the bargain we'd made together.

Ronson groaned and his head fell back as my fingertips slid into the curls, stroked down, and tapped against the smooth and tensing planes of his stomach. He was the largest man I'd ever met, which was only right considering he was the alpha, but I'd always felt too tall, too heavy. He dwarfed me. And he lifted me off my feet with one arm, flying me around the island and carrying me through the castle as if it required no effort on his part.

He could've tossed Adelaide around like a feather, I supposed, frowning slightly.

And then Ronson's hands covered mine over his stomach, and I forgot about the other omega, the one who by pure and strange luck—and terrible judgment—had lost her chance at being chosen by this alpha. Ronson guided my hands down to his hips, where a twin line of buttons would open his trousers.

"We can stop," he offered in a low, rough tone.

My hands were shaking slightly, and it was more obvious as his steady grip held mine. I was stubbornly avoiding thinking about one moment to the next, about the fact that I'd agreed to undress down to my thin slip, about how small I'd made the nest around the bed and how close Ronson and I would be, alone and surrounded by the thin swathes of cotton.

But I was curious.

"No," I said, continuing as his hands had guided, working on either line of the buttons at the same time.

Ronson's breath made his chest fill and sigh quickly, and he jerked his arms back, pulling his shirt off as I opened his trousers. He had another single line of buttons down a short placket over his groin, keeping his drawers fixed around his hips, and I undid those as well, until the layers of black wool and cream linen sagged. The dark hair of his chest narrowed to a thick line leading down between two beautiful arcs of muscle, and then widened again to a familiar, thick coat of curls, not entirely unlike the one at the V of my own hips.

"I forgot about my damned boots," Ronson muttered. "Come to the nest."

I blinked as he spun us around, ignoring the loose hang of his pants as he strode toward the bed. I gaped, remaining in place for a moment, watching his golden back shifting between the frame of massive black wings. I certainly hadn't taken *those* into account when I'd built the nest.

He had dimples at the base of his back, and he had to shuffle as his pants continued to droop, revealing a round swell of a firm ass.

He chose me? I thought. And I'd just declared that I would explore him for the night. Have my turn first. Perhaps that had been a mistake. I'd been recalling the rough force and uncomfortable jerks of my body Mr. Evans had delivered the night before and thinking it would be better if I could hold onto some control to start. But Ronson's touches and kisses had left me weak and melting and biting down on my tongue to keep from begging for more.

"Actually, I'd better deal with the boots myself," Ronson said, grunting as he yanked on the heel of a boot.

My lips quirked at the sight of him. He was seated on the bed, the curtains of the nest I'd built draped open and hanging over his wings. I twisted my arms behind my back, pulling the laces of my dress loose, checking to make sure he was distracted as I lifted it up over my head. One boot thunked against the floor, and I turned at the waist, attending to the ties of the petticoat around my middle.

My maid had dressed me in one of the longer corsets,

attempting to flatten and slim my shape according to my mother's instructions, but it meant the laces were all in the back and harder to reach. I wrestled and strained for a few moments, glaring at the glittering sea out of the large windows, until a warm and large pair of hands caught mine.

"Let me."

My breath froze in my chest and my hands hovered behind my back as Ronson's warmth billowed around me, the bindings of my laces tugging and loosening as he pulled them through their loops. My arms drooped, hands hanging numbly at my side, and I shivered and swallowed a whimper when his knuckles grazed through my thin chemise along my spine.

"Why do you wear these so tight?"

I had to swallow twice before I could answer. "It's fashionable to be...willowy and small. I am neither." Not that he would've needed me to point as much out.

His breath puffed over my shoulder, down into the increasingly loose collar of my chemise. "I've been looking forward to taking this off you all day, Mairwen," Ronson rumbled.

I had no idea what to say to that, and then the laces were gone and I could breathe, breathe and groan as my back bowed and my breasts pounded, aching and unbound. Ronson shoved the stern panels of the corset to the floor, and his arms wrapped around my soft stomach, tugging me back into his chest. I could feel the soft brush of his chest hair through the thin fabric of the chemise, and the gentle prod of his— Oh!

I tried to twist, but he was surrounding me, rubbing his evening beard against my hair. His lips grazed the shell of my ear and his voice purred, warm and low, "If tonight was my turn, I would take your breasts in my hands and squeeze and stroke them. I'd pull your collar open until I could kiss the marks of the corset away, make you all pink and tender with my mouth. Are your nipples sensitive, Mairwen?"

I let out a strangled noise, and then Ronson lifted one index finger up, grazing over my left nipple, and it budded to a tight peak. I whined, and the alpha holding me rumbled.

"Oh, very sensitive," he rasped, and then his head ducked, burrowing his face against my throat, his breath cascading hotly over my flesh. "Tomorrow, I'm going to suck and bite and lick your perfect, full breasts until you gush, omega."

My eyes widened, and if it weren't for Ronson's arms around my waist, I would've collapsed. I ought to have been entirely ignorant to what he meant, but mostly I was just shocked at the idea that such a thing were possible. Just from...my breasts? Usually it took—

"Oh!" I gasped, clutching my arms around Ronson's shoulders as he caught my legs with one arm and carried me toward the nest. "It's—I could f-fix the nest a little more if—"

"Leave it," Ronson ground out, catching the edge of one sheet with a hook of his wing, pushing it aside and ducking down. He nearly took the whole thing down with us, and the bedsheet was cool against my back as he slid us both into the small hollow of space I'd created at the heart of the vast bed.

"B-but," I stammered, eyeing the way his wings grazed and hooks snagged on the shelter I'd created.

"Mairwen, if you want us to simply sleep, or...um...talk," Ronson started, brow furrowing at the offer he was making, "we can do that instead. But you're not fussing with the nest tonight. And I need just a moment of...mmmm."

My breath hitched as the many many inches of Lord Ronson Cadogan's huge frame pressed onto me from above. He was heavy and wonderful and so warm, and his hips were thick between my thighs, chest hair prickling through my chemise to tickle at my stomach and breasts. He sighed, lying on top of me, his rough cheek scrubbing into my hair.

"Your corset is a crime. I'd like to burn it."

I laughed as much as I was able under his weight, and my hands grew curious, sliding from his shoulders to the base of his wings. I remembered going swimming in the stream of the woods with my father once when I was a little girl, clinging around his neck between his wings, their leathery surface hot from the dappling summer sunlight. It was the one and only time I'd ever had an opportunity to touch wings until now, and I remembered less of that part of the afternoon than the joy of having my father's undivided attention.

My father's wings had seemed enormous at the time, but he was a small man compared to Ronson, and the leather of his dragon was a softer taupe shade than Ronson's gleaming violet-black.

A silent gasp ruffled the hair against my ear as I tiptoed my finger over the tough join of his back to his wing, up the protected bone to the strong and hollow spines, and the curiously rough texture of the skin between them.

"No one's touched my wings in a long time," Ronson mumbled in my ear. They flexed gently, spreading as much as they were able in the small space I'd afforded them, shadowing us from the candlelight of the room outside.

I was curious about so many things. I wanted to know the texture of his hair around his brow, and how it differed from that on his chest and the scratch of his beard. I was curious about the gentle poke of his own nipples against my chest, almost close enough to touch one of mine. I was *very* curious about the long pressure against my right thigh, and the way every few seconds his hips would nuzzle between mine, rubbing that length to me.

But...

"Lie down on your belly," I said, pulling my hands from his back. Ronson grunted, not in outright refusal but probably disinterest, considering he didn't move a hair. "I'm exploring, and I'm starting with your wings."

He huffed at that, rising just enough to glare down at me. "My wings?"

I nodded. "Go on. Move."

Ronson's lips quirked and then he groaned, pushing against the mattress to lift himself above me, shuffling around my body. I caught a brief glimpse of a long, thick protuberance and nearly changed my mind about where to start, but Ronson dropped down at my side with a wince and a shuffle of his hips.

It took me a moment to scramble out from under Ronson's wing, tugging my chemise from where he'd trapped it with his thigh, and the whole nest rustled as I sat up, but the view was worth the struggle.

He had the most absurdly round, and *perfect* ass. It didn't matter that I hadn't known what a perfect ass *might* look like before now. I was wholeheartedly confident this one was. My mouth watered at the sight of the globes, of the curve and hollow of muscle along the sides. I forgot my goal of exploring his wings at the sight of the quick dip against his thighs, also decorated with dark curling hair, and my hand reached out of its own accord, helping itself to a squeeze of his flesh. Ronson chuckled into the bed, and his hips flexed, tightening and changing the shape of the thick muscle under my hand.

"That's not my wing—"

"Shh. You'll have your turn tomorrow," I mumbled, ignoring the mess the tented sheet was making of my hair as I swung one leg over both of Ronson's and stared down at the exquisite, bronzed form below me.

He laughed, a quick bark of sound. "And I will be planning my attack every minute until then," he warned. But he squirmed, spreading his thighs until the hair on them brushed the inside of my own legs.

I watched as his motion revealed a softly furred mound of flesh between his thighs, and I reached down, grazing my fingers, marveling at the strangeness. Ronson bit off a garbled yell into the mattress, his hips kicking and wings beating once.

My eyes widened. "What's this?"

He let out a long, muffled groan, wings tucking back in, candlelight wavering through the rustling sheets of the nest. "My sac. Balls. Very sensitive," he ground out.

I snatched my hand away. "I'm sorry, I didn't meant to hurt—"

"It didn't hurt, Mairwen," he rumbled.

Oh.

I hesitated, torn between more curious exploring or moving onto safer territory.

"Touch me again." The words were a velvety rasp, and I glanced up, past the slight curtain of Ronson's wings, to see his knuckles pale where they fisted a pillow. "Please."

I hummed and scooted back, and Ronson's thighs spread eagerly, offering a clearer and more explicit view. I blinked for a moment, staring at the secretive shadows, the curve of his ass tucking down into the soft hair of his sac. He must've been lying on his length.

If Mother knew what I was looking at—

I cut the thought out of my head and focused on the moment. I was exploring the Alpha of Bleake Isle, who had chosen me as his omega, we were alone, and tonight the rest of the island did *not* exist. I reached out, cupping one cheek of his ass in my hand and pushing it aside. Ronson shuddered, and I did my best to not think about him returning this study in kind tomorrow evening. With my other hand, I gathered up the tender mound between his legs, rolling it against my palm. Ronson hissed and groaned and rocked against the bed, and I bit my lips hard to avoid giggling.

It was lumpy and pulsing in my hand, and he was clearly... tortured by the touch.

He cursed and moaned my name, and I enjoyed a strange, thrilling victory. This was better by far than being chosen on a stage as hundreds of dubious eyes watched on. I had our alpha in my hands, whimpering and shivering, and all because I held a small, warm, and vulnerable part of him against my palm. His ass was clenching and his hands were scrambling in the sheets and his feet were shifting restlessly. He gasped as I squeezed him, groaned as I tugged on the handful, and let out a soft, broken cry as I molded the soft form in my grip.

"Mairwen! Stop, I'll-I'll—"

I did stop, although I was a little disappointed to have my power called away.

Ronson sagged and let out a soft laugh, muttering to himself, "Not against the sheets like a boy." He twisted, glancing at me over the ridge of his wing. "Can I roll over now?"

I hummed and shook my head. "I haven't done what I came for."

His eyes narrowed. "Fine. But...no more of that just yet. I'll embarrass myself."

I wasn't entirely sure why, but that claim made me feel quite warm and delighted.

Chapter Nine

RONSON

This is what comes of letting a curious, fearless virgin have free rein to explore, I thought, burying my panting breaths into the bed as Mairwen feathered light touches over the surprisingly sensitive stretch of my wings. And in spite of the sticky pool of arousal pressed between my belly and the mattress, and the painfully sharp ache of my erect cock, and the fact that Mairwen had been over my wings twice now and studied every inch of what was available to her from my position face down while leaving me simmering and ready to burst, I was grinning.

Mairwen was perfuming.

I was gasping at the air, searching for every lick of the heady, dizzying scent of her, trying not to rut into the bed and set myself off into the sheets. Although perhaps that would be better. Maybe Mairwen would elect to leave me face down for the rest of the night. Or maybe she would let me roll over and approach my dripping, throbbing cock with the same studious determination she'd met my sac with, and I'd shoot off at the first chance and terrify her with my roar.

But I didn't care what happened next. She was *perfuming*.

I groaned as her hands pulled away from my wings, brushing briefly around my hips, and my grin turned into a frown as she shuffled off the back of my legs. I liked her heat against me.

"Roll over."

My brain stalled at the gentle command.

"Can you lie on your wings, or will it hurt?"

Roll over, damnit, I snapped at myself. I pulled my wings in close, ignoring the odd, reluctant pang, as if they already missed the young woman's touch, and pushed myself up from the mattress, grimacing at the wet stain I'd left on the sheet. I would have to either lie on top of that, or let Mairwen see what she'd done to me. And then probably have to answer carefully posed and torturously innocent questions about *why* my cock was weeping.

I sighed as I turned and then collapsed roughly at the picture of Mairwen kneeling at my side. I landed in the wet spot, and my cock bounced and slapped against my belly.

She was...*lovely*.

Her hair was mussed, and strands rose and clung to the sheet around her head like a chaotic halo. The candlelight that bled through the sheets into our nest made a valiant effort at cutting into her chemise too, revealing a cruel glimpse of the lushest curves I'd ever even imagined. Her cheeks were flushed, eyes bright and fixed to my stomach— no, my cock, I realized—and her lips pursed in consideration, growing full and tempting.

"Mairwen," I called.

"Hmm?" She trailed her fingers through the hair on my thighs, grazing around the taut line of a tensing muscle, but her eyes remained focused on my twitching length. It was eager for an introduction to those exploring fingers.

"Come here," I said.

She blinked and glanced up, brow furrowing.

"Come explore my mouth for a moment," I continued. *I want to kiss you.*

She smiled, and I bit off a moan as her hand made an absent path up my thigh, over my hip and chest, skirting my needy length as she stretched out at my side. It was meant to be her night, but I was impatient, and I grabbed for her, dragging her to lie on top of me, claiming the back of her neck in one hand to draw her mouth down to mine.

I told myself to be gentle, tentative, but Mairwen sighed and her breath was sweet and her perfume was stronger up close like this, and I'd lost the grasp on my control a quarter of an hour ago when she'd nuzzled her soft cheek against the back of my thigh. I groaned and licked into her open mouth, devouring her whimper with a swirl of my tongue, searching her mouth for her flavor and then mourning the loss as I stole it away.

My hands were equally greedy and unmanageable, helping themselves to full handfuls of her flesh through the soft chemise. I stroked her thighs, then couldn't help but wrap my arms around her waist to yank her closer. The barrier of the cotton between our bodies caused boiling frustration to race through me, and I rooted for the hem before settling on gathering it up with fistfuls of her perfect, plush ass.

"Ronson!"

I growled against her lips, then scraped my teeth over them and found them slick and swollen from kisses. Was she slick and swollen between her thighs too? Could I move the chemise and plant her pussy on my cock, rock against her until we both found relief?

Delicate fingers wrapped around my wrists, and I arched up, grinding myself into cotton and soft flesh. The fingers tightened, cuffing my hands.

"Ronson," Mairwen called, tone sharp and cutting through the haze.

My head cleared enough to release her, and she drew my cuffed hands away from her body, pushing them back into the pillows under my head. My eyelids drooped, and my hips bucked in a plea. I did not mind being at Mairwen's mercy in the least, not with the collar of her chemise coming loose, offering me exquisite shadows to guess at.

"It's *my* turn still," she said, smiling.

"You're doing too good a job," I answered, groaning as her perfume richened in the air. *Compliments.* "And you feel perfect on top of me, don't you think? Bring your mouth back, Mairwen."

The pink stains on her cheeks were running down her throat, and she tore her gaze from mine. "This was easier when you weren't looking at me."

I laughed, and she straightened, still holding my hands down, not that I was fighting her. I hadn't offered to let women lead in bed very often, but Mairwen made a compelling case for the dynamic, as shy and unpracticed as she was. She released my hands slowly and one at a time, eyes narrowed like she was expecting me to grab at her again. I left them in the pillows, the picture of surrender.

She rose up on her knees, brushing her hair back, frowning at the partially pinned tangles she found. They clung to the low roof of the nest and gathered static, tickling at her cheeks. When she scooted back, the skirt of her chemise caught on my cock. I hissed, arching and twisting, trying to rise into the brief pressure, but she was quick, snatching the fabric away to reveal my swollen and darkened flesh.

There was a shiny dribbling trail leading from my belly to my cock, and Mairwen hummed, stroking her thumb through the mess. I held my breath, my eyes growing so wide, I thought they might fall out of my face, as she raised her thumb to her nose, sniffing briefly and then parting her lips.

Her eyes caught mine, tongue poised against her bottom lip, and she froze.

"Don't stop," I gasped out.

Mairwen blinked, expression wavering as she struggled over a decision, probably between obeying my request or asking me a dozen questions. *Why was I leaking? Why did she like the scent? Why did I like the idea of her tasting me?* Instead, she glanced away and pressed her thumb to her tongue. Her eyelashes fluttered and her lips curved in a smile. An alpha would taste almost as good to an omega as an omega would to an alpha. Which only made me torn between encouraging her to taste me or begging her to come and hover her sex over my mouth.

"There's so much of you," she murmured. I broke out into a rakish grin at the announcement, but she didn't look at my face, just continued. "So much that's unfamiliar, but also..."

I was only briefly disappointed that her gaze left my cock, because she moved her hands up to my chest next, planting them over the thick muscles and coarse curls and squeezing, not unlike the way I wanted to be squeezing her breasts. She blushed and shied her stare away.

"Close your eyes," she said.

"Don't ask that."

"Please?"

I chewed over my refusal. She'd been brave enough to fondle my balls when I'd been on my belly, and she hadn't so much as accidentally nudged my cock now that I was looking at her. With a heavy sigh, I closed my eyes.

Waiting like this was torture. I stiffened as Mairwen's breath rustled over my chest, and the soft, light weight of her chemise grazed my cock.

"Would I really gush just from you...you know, like you said earlier?" she asked.

I peeked one eye open, and a strangled moan rose from

93

my chest as Mairwen traced a fingertip around my small, dark nipple. "I th-think so," I rasped out. "It's possible, and I'd like to try."

"Hmm," she mused, and I forced my eye shut once more, clenched them tight, and braced as Mairwen's head lowered to my chest.

Her mouth was warm and gentle, tracing over my chest in small kisses, tongue occasionally peeking out.

"Let me touch you," I begged as she covered me in those tiny wet marks.

"Only a little," she answered. "Hold my hair back?"

My hands shook, but she was too busy to notice, and her hair was silky and smooth as I gathered every stray strand back, combing pins out of limp curls, struggling not to force her mouth where I wanted it. There were too many directions to choose from anyway. Aside from the obvious need to shove her down to my aching cock, was an almost equal imperative to drag her up back up to my mouth, to direct her toward all the small places she'd missed earlier and had yet to greet. One of her hands was circling fingertips around my right nipple until it was so sweetly sore I thought I might burst, and the other was gently scratching her nails over my hip, close but not close enough to my length.

"Mairwen, please," I whispered.

I didn't know what I was begging for, but it wasn't my decision anyway. Mairwen was *exploring*, and when her open mouth covered my neglected nipple, tongue circling at the same patient pace as her fingertips, we were both in uncharted territory. My breathing was ragged and full of whimpers, my hips lifting from the bed until I found her belly, grinding shamelessly against her.

"This is what you want to do to me?" she asked, voice so light and calm in comparison to the devastation she was raining down on me.

"Yes, and—" It took me several tries to swallow.

"And?" she prompted.

"And suck."

She let out a small sound of curiosity, and then she was sucking on me. My eyes opened wide at the first beautiful tugging sensation, a lightning-sharp zing of pressure down to the base of my balls. My wings burst out from under me, snagging and tearing on the sheet walls of the nest, tugging one free from the knot she'd formed and dropping it down on top of us.

Mairwen pulled away, and I choked on an agonized roar, pulling my fingers free from her hair to tear the sheet back off, throwing it over the edge of the bed with a curse.

"Oh dear," she said, in the smallest voice.

"It doesn't matter," I snarled, fighting the urge to gather her to my chest, to tear the rest of the nest down, and roll her into the mattress, to bury myself inside of her and never leave until I'd explained in detail and action every other depraved thing I would've liked to explore with her.

Except I saw her face, fallen and disappointed, wincing at the brighter light of the candles, her shoulders hunching high.

Compliments, damnit. And...

"Please, Mairwen. Please don't stop."

She blinked, her shoulders dropping, and her eyes found mine.

"Fang's fire, omega, don't stop touching me. I'll... Mairwen, *please.*" Only a tiny percent of my pained pleas were calculated to distract her from the disaster of the nest.

A tiny smile curved her lips, and she knelt between my spread legs, staring down at me. Her chemise was stuck to my slick cock, and she peeled it away, finally giving my eager length the attention I'd craved from the start. The hand that had been holding my hip skirted closer, and I held my breath for a moment, until I realized she was watching me again.

"*Please*."

Her fingers circled me gently, and I collapsed with a groan, wings limp and eyes rolling back. Her touch skirted away and then returned, the smooth back of her hand stroking up my length, fingers petting down. She bent her head and kissed down my chest, nose nuzzling against the dark trail of hair, her own loose locks grazing against my clenching stomach.

I was shamefully close to the edge, but at least Mairwen wouldn't realize how easily she'd unmade me, turned me into a weak and desperate puddle of an alpha. Then again...

"You're very good at exploring, omega," I growled, victory blending with hunger as her perfume curled shyly in the air. "*Too* good. You're going to make me spill."

Mairwen's hand grasped me tightly, and it was nearly done. I scrambled in the sheets, shuttled weakly in her fist.

"Am I?" she asked brightly.

I laughed at her excitement and then grunted as she released me once more.

"You will. Just...just hold me. Yes, fuck, Mairwen, like that." More perfume to drown in. I peeked my eyes open and watched her smiling and blushing down at my cock as if I'd just kissed the back of her hand. Except what I'd done was dribbled my arousal over her fingers. "Like that. Stroke me, up and—" I bit a howl off behind clenched teeth, rocking in her gentle grip. "Down, yes. Fuck. This is...this will be your cunt holding my cock like this, Mairwen. Do you know that?" Did she know enough about sex to understand that much? *Please say yes.*

"Mmhm, although I've never tried to...you seem awfully thick, Ronson," she mused.

I fought my grin. I was thick. And long. I was the alpha, after all.

"Is this your knot?" she murmured, and then her other

hand joined in, pressing her thumb to where I was starting to thicken and swell. I released a garbled yelp as she circled that spot too, unable to close her grip around me.

"Yesss," I hissed, nodding roughly back into the pillows.

"It looks like it hurts."

"It does and it doesn't—Oh, Mairwen, tighter—" I moaned, twisting an arm back to prop my head up. Oh, she was sweet, a little furrow between her brow as she focused on squeezing and stroking me. "I'm close. Do you know-know what—" I couldn't finish my sentence because she'd started to twist her hand around my length back and forth, right at the head of my cock where I was most sensitive. Instead, I gaped like a fish and whined, bucking into her soft palm, my sac growing tight and pounding.

"You're dripping a great deal. Do you know, you taste like something familiar... I can't place it."

I was fucking her hand, bucking too roughly, and her grip tightened around my knot to hold me in place at the same moment that she ducked her head down, lips parted and tongue peeking out. The sight, the promise of what she meant to do, and the warm squeeze of her hand on my knot was too much. I came with a bellowing shout, a shocking crack of pleasure racing through me, painful and perfect, snapping hard and making my body bow upwards. Mairwen squeaked as I burst, a hot lash of release splashing out, my arms and legs thrashing as I howled in relief.

She was laughing.

My eyes were shut, my body turning limp and weak. Her grip on my cock was too tight now that I'd finished, and Mairwen was giggling. I growled, and she muffled the sound of her humor. I hissed as she stroked my length and released me gently, petting me once more.

An alluring, wet sound finally forced my eyes open, and the sight was enough to make my cock throb and spill another quick gush of release against my thigh. Mairwen was scooping a dribble of opal white from the soft swell of her breast, and she lifted the finger to her tongue, lapping it clean. I groaned, and my wearied cock bobbed up, valiant and eager to offer her more.

"Mairwen," I called roughly.

Her gaze was warm, smile soft. "I didn't know that would happen, no."

It was my turn to blush. "I'm sorry, I—"

"I liked watching you," she said, head tipping to the side. She glanced down and then tugged at her collar, revealing another slow drip sinking between her breasts. I was outrageously jealous of my own release.

"Come here."

She licked her lips, cleaning another finger, and I wondered if I hadn't reached rut after all, because I was absolutely certain that if she did that one more time, I would be pinning her down in the bed and having my way with her. She knew a little more of what to expect, at least.

"I'm not done exploring," Mairwen said primly, and then she scooted out of reach, an inviting waft of her perfume billowing closer in response, making my eyes fall shut in satisfaction.

Chapter Ten

RONSON

I was perfectly and deliciously aware of the situation as I woke the next morning. My cock was stuffed comfortably against Mairwen's ass, barely deterred by her tangled chemise. My hands were full of the wonderful weight and squish and heft of her breasts, although one of my arms was numb, trapped between her waist and the mattress. My mouth was full of Mairwen's hair.

The sun was shining, just high enough to beam over the edge of the final remaining sheet wall of the nest Mairwen had built. The one I'd nearly torn to bits as she'd had her adorably, curiously, innocently wicked way with me. I'd come once more, this time against the belly of her chemise as she wiggled on top of me, pinching my nipples and kissing me until my lips were numb. I tried to return the favor, but Mairwen pushed my hands away every time until finally falling asleep on top of me, her lips pressed over my heart and her hand around my cock. I'd succumbed within minutes, my own hand possessively claiming her full ass.

Mairwen's perfume was softer now, as thin as her nearly transparent chemise, but it covered the bed and traced over my skin. My mouth watered and my gut clenched, greedy for more. I couldn't pull my arm out from under Mairwen without jostling us both, and even with the numb, heavy sensation, I was far too comfortable to think of moving.

Except for perhaps...

I flexed my working hand, shifting my fingers and palm carefully to study their surroundings. I found the soft bud of Mairwen's nipple—relaxed and warm under cotton—with a stroke of my pinkie, then turned my hand. I recalled the slow circle her own fingertips had practiced on me last night and mimicked it now.

I'd known from our first conversation that Mairwen was observant, clever, and a quick thinker. I hadn't considered how she might apply those traits in bed with me, her keen stare watching my every action, noting every hitch of my breath and low groan. It would be a challenge to remain equally alert with her when I had so many goals and desires already clamoring in my head.

And yet when Mairwen's breath sharpened and her breast butted into my teasing fingertips, my attention was entirely hers. I curled my legs against hers, nudging her hair away from my face to rest my rough jaw against her shoulder, delighted by the view I'd afforded myself, all the wonderful round inches of creamy skin now on display right below my nose.

"Good morning, omega," I growled, grinning as Mairwen shivered.

The tie of her chemise had loosened in sleep and the collar was now stretched down, nearly exposing her. I reached one fingertip up to the ruched edge and then lost the train of thought as Mairwen rolled her ass back against my hard length, stretching in my hold, thrusting her breast back in my palm. We moaned together as I squeezed her flesh.

"It's not—What are you—?" Mairwen squeaked as I

pinched her nipple and tugged, burrowing my face into her throat to lick away the taste of her, drawing that perfume onto my parched tongue.

"Tomorrow is today. It's my turn."

"Um...today is not tonight," she answered breathlessly.

I laughed, rising up and pulling my arm out from under Mairwen, swallowing the grunt as my blood rushed through my veins with a sharp stab of pins and needles. One hand was really not enough when it came to touching Mairwen. Considering the only one that was working at the moment was already overflowing with her beautifully pliable and soft flesh, I suspected even two wouldn't feel adequate.

Mairwen was staring up at me, lips parted and one cheek marked from the creases of her pillow, her brown eyes wide and dazed, glancing between my eyes and the enormous smile I wore.

"One kiss," I bargained.

She blinked, and her head jerked in a little nod.

She was only waking up. I ought to have leaned down and pressed my lips gently to hers, treated her as a young gentlewoman who would've been raised to believe a dragon treated his omega with care and respect, even if we all knew that was mostly a lie in the end.

Instead, I hooked my finger into the loose collar of her chemise, tugging gently. Mairwen's brow furrowed, but she huffed out a laugh and rolled her eyes.

"I know I am inexperienced, but I don't think that's what that's called," she said as I scooted down and lowered my starving lips to the slow expanse of pink and pale skin I revealed.

"Of course it is. Weren't you kissing me in any number of places last night?" I said.

I paused in my progress, admiring the flush that flooded her chest at the reminder of the night before. I wanted to tease her more, but I had a granted kiss to take and I wasn't going to waste the opportunity.

Mairwen stiffened as I pulled her collar down to expose one breast, full and round, peaked with a dusky rose—a perfect color, in my opinion—pucker of flesh, the tip firming and rising up toward my lips as if in offering.

One kiss, I reminded myself. *Make it count...and then ask for more.*

I took her breast in an open-mouthed kiss, tracing my tongue around her nipple, pursing my lips as she shivered and gasped, growling in victory as her chest arched closer. I suckled and laved, and Mairwen moaned, her hands sliding into my hair. The sting and throb of my arm still waking up cut through the pleasure of her voluptuous, tender flesh on my tongue and her luxurious flavor. My working arm slid under her back, hand sliding up to brace around her neck and hold in her place.

"Ronson!"

My body seemed to swell at the call of my name on her lips. She was holding me to her breast, one leg rising to curl around my back. I shifted, not releasing the treasure between my lips, just in case she might consider the kiss finished, and settled between her parting legs, groaning as her damp core kissed my belly. She was wet.

Why hadn't I considered kissing her cunt? Except that was probably a step too far, or it had been before she'd grown slick, rocking herself into the hair on my stomach in a way that assured me she would absolutely enjoy the moment I worked my way down—

Knock, knock.

Mairwen let out a charming squeak, jerking in my grasp as if she had anywhere to go now that she'd tangled herself around me.

"Ronson," Niall called from the other side of the door.

I debated my choices. I could release my divine mouthful —I licked around Mairwen's nipple once more in objection to this idea, and she sighed—in order to tell Niall to fuck off. Or I could carry on as I was and hope he took the hint.

Considering my left arm was now capable of moving and was making its way up Mairwen's side, cupping under her neglected breast and claiming the spot, I chose the latter. I suckled Mairwen once more, giving her more of my weight to grind against, and she bucked back responsively.

"Ronson, I'm sorry—"

Hinges creaked, and Mairwen wrenched herself free. I rose with a snarl, turning toward the door.

The last stalwart sheet was blocking Niall's view, thank goodness, or my half-brother might've lost his eyes for daring to enter the room.

"—there's a dispute amongst the dragons," Niall continued.

"Out!" I snapped, not really satisfied with the thin barrier of the sheet guarding my omega from view. I glanced back and let out a heavy sigh. Mairwen had tugged the drawstring of her chemise so tight, it looked like the ruffled collar might be choking her. Her knees were tucked under the skirt, body bundled together and arms wrapped around herself. Her cheeks were as red as ripe apples—equally tempting to take a bite—and her eyes were huge.

"Is it the rut?" Niall asked, still standing in the room, out of view.

I didn't like having him in here with us. I wanted to rush off the bed and grab him by the collar and throw him down the stairs. Or perhaps out the window? No, the window would bring him into view of the bed.

Hmm, was this the rut? No. If it had been, Niall would've been testing the strength of his wings out my window already. But that didn't mean I didn't want to make use of the hours until the rut in bed with Mairwen, teaching her all about what we'd enjoy together.

"No," I admitted in a grumble. "I'll join you outside."

There was no other answer but the squeak of the door as it shut behind him. I groaned as I fell back in bed, and Mairwen leaned over, upside-down in my view and wearing a shy half-smile.

"Tonight," I warned her, low and dark.

Her cheeks pinked and she placed her hands on either side of my head, ducking down and grazing her lips sweetly over mine. "Tonight," she murmured.

I grasped her face, licking into her mouth as she gasped, humming as her tongue brushed against mine. Fuck Niall. Fuck the other dragons.

Fuck Mairwen, my brain corrected.

She pulled away, still blushing, smiling wider, turning her face away but glancing down the length of my body from the corner of her eye. I wanted to stretch for her gaze, let her admire in daylight all the places she'd studied so sincerely by muffled candlelight.

But the sooner I was done with whatever tussle the other dragons needed mediated, the sooner I could return to the castle and declare it evening. *My turn.*

"Frannie, you promised."

"Oh, I did, and I did *mean* it, Jeffery, you must understand."

"Quit manipulating the girl, Bexam. We've established that Francesca gave out a great *many* promises."

"The fact remains, gentlemen, a contract was drafted between myself and her family," Gryffyd Evans declared, putting a clawed hand on the delicate omega's shoulder.

The girl withered, and her eyes dropped to her skirts.

This was *absurd*. Somehow, Francesca Huberts had promised herself to a half-dozen of the gentry dragons of the island. *She's very weepy and incredibly biddable*, Mairwen had said. And now here I was, faced with the truth of that observation. Francesca was indeed weeping, and with every reminder of her devotion, she renewed the sentiment to the gentleman in question, in spite of just having declared it a moment ago to another. Even her parents could not agree on whom Francesca preferred.

I cleared my throat, and the many eyes in the room all turned in my direction. I focused first on the easiest suit to clear, narrowing my gaze onto one dragon in particular.

"You seem to draft a great many contracts, Beta Evans," I said, glaring at Gryffyd.

His chest puffed, but his face was spotty with color. "I put very little stock into girlish vows and prefer concrete, legal—"

"There is nothing more legal on this island than my decision, yes?" I prompted, and Gryffyd paled and bowed his head obediently. "When was the contract drafted?"

"Yesterday, my lord, after the selection," Mr. Huberts, a generally jovial man, answered. His hands were twisting nervously in front of his rounded stomach, and he had yet to meet my eyes.

"Presumably after Francesca's other agreements?" I asked.

A chorus of *yes* rose up from the other five dragons.

"Then it does not stand," I said, waving a hand.

"With all due respect, Alpha Cadogan," Gryffyd said, starting a bow. "Mine is the only written contract in question."

"I don't care, Beta Evans. You were too late."

"But—!"

"You are dismissed."

Gryffyd blustered. "Am I to have no omega—?"

"Not this time," Niall answered, shrugging. "Best of luck in a decade."

I hid my quirked lips behind my hand and studied the other five dragons as Gryffyd Evans was ushered from the room. I was only going to secure the favor of one dragon today, and I needed to consider this lot carefully.

Gideon Millward was a fair dragon, still quite young and without influence, but it might serve me to cultivate a good relationship early. And yet he was now glancing at Francesca Huberts—who was admittedly a very pretty omega, even as fat teardrops rolled out of her glassy green eyes—as if he was wondering whether she were really worth the trouble.

Redmond Palmer was an ass. He was friends with Hugh Gamesby, had *traded out* his last omega when she offered no issue over a decade—a very ungentlemanly although still technically excusable act—and generally pissed me off every time he sniffed his nose and opened his pompous mouth to speak. Even if I did grant him the right to the Huberts girl, he probably wouldn't shift his opinion of me.

Jeffery Bexam was the fourth son of a fourth son, with barely a cottage to his name and no influence to speak of, but of the lot of them, he seemed the most distraught by Francesca's betrayal. I wasn't sure if that was due to a highly delicate ego or genuine affection.

Tybalt Dunne and Julian Dunne were twin brothers, and I was hazarding a guess that Francesca's favors were a bone they'd chosen to fight over. One might speak in my favor with the right incentive, but the other would become an enemy.

I resisted the urge to groan. I didn't want to be responsible for this decision. One, it was a stupid waste of my time, which I was feeling especially bitter about, considering what the summons had dragged me away from. Two, it didn't sit right with me. Surely the girl had some stronger opinion she was too nervous to voice?

"I would like to speak with Miss Huberts for a moment," I said.

The girl gasped and froze. She was scarcely eighteen years old, and I considered whether we were really putting young omegas into courting at quite the right age. She seemed *very* young. Mairwen was practically on the shelf by dragon standards, but there was no chance of me mistaking her for anything but a woman. An extremely—and yet also surprisingly—tempting woman.

Mrs. Huberts nudged her daughter forward, and the girl stumbled out of the grasp of the dragons who surrounded her. None of the betas moved."Alone, please."

Mr. Huberts gave his wife a hopeful glance, and I understood the look with a sick twist of my stomach. They were hoping I would take her for myself. As if they hadn't witnessed my choice yesterday. My hands clenched to fists, and Francesca released a small sound of terror, stepping back toward the wall. Jeffery Bexam had the decency to glare at me, but he filed out of the comfortable sitting room with the rest of the gathered dragonkin.

Francesca remained across the room, quivering against a sideboard laden with delicate porcelain trinkets that rattled in sympathy with her terror.

"Sit."

I tried to keep my tone gentle, but Francesca jerked and stumbled toward an armchair as if I'd put the full roar of an alpha's command into the word. Her russet curls bounced as she dropped into the cushions, a wave of cloying omega perfume wafting toward me. It wasn't an entirely unpleasant scent, something like honeysuckle and caramel, and my mouth did water, but it wasn't *right*, either, too sticky. I resented its presence washing over the lingering taste of Mairwen.

I glanced over my shoulder to Niall and nodded my head

toward the door the others had left from. "Keep an eye on them. Keep things civil." He grimaced, but nodded and joined the others, leaving Francesca quaking and crying, teardrops splatting against her hands.

"You don't need to be frightened," I said, my jaw grinding.

"Of course not, Lord Cadogan," she answered with a wobble and a sniff.

"I only asked to speak to you alone so you might feel you could express your preference freely."

I caught the furrow of her brow before her face lifted, eyes wide and baffled. "My preference?"

I stared back at her, and her gaze dropped once more. "Your preference of the gentlemen."

Lace around her collar ruffled as she swallowed. "I will of course prefer whomever you deem best."

"What? No, that's not—Which of the dragons do *you* choose, Miss Huberts?"

This time, I could've sworn she scowled, but her expression smoothed too quickly. "They are all very fine. Very good gentlemen. I would never presume to know better than you, Alpha."

I opened my mouth to ask about Jeffery Bexam, but then shut it just as quickly. If I so much at hinted a name, she would probably immediately agree. This was beyond *biddable* and had crossed into the territory of stubbornly submissive. Certainly there were men who might assume any woman was this much of a...blank drawing board for them to sketch out their own desires on. But I'd grown up with Beatrice for a sister and seen my father's heavy hand on women and the way it crumbled the person inside of the body he coveted. I did *not* want to be another man in a woman's life telling her what she would prefer.

My nose wrinkled, and I backed away from the girl. "Stay here," I muttered to her.

I needed someone with sense. Someone who knew more about this omega and these dragons, had *seen* more of them, than I had. I hurried to the door, yanking it open and ignoring the many expectant faces until I found Niall.

"Get me Mairwen. *Now*."

Chapter Eleven

MAIRWEN

✿

"**S**eems an awful lot of pomp and flourish for a duck," Cook muttered, but she edited her recipe and added ingredients to the list, just as she had for my other suggestions.

"Lord Cadogan may not need more than a slab of beef and a few roasted potatoes, but I assure you, these additions and adjustments will be appreciated," I said, adding privately, *if not by him, then by me.*

It felt almost scandalous to be planning such a decadent menu. At home, economy required simplification and using scraps and leftovers in creative ways. To be allowed to ask for *anything*, and in any quantity, was almost daunting.

"Now, as to the meals that will be delivered during the rut," I said, trying not to let my words tremble.

"If you think his lordship wants purees and confits during his—"

I laughed and shook my head. "No, no, it's not that. Only that I think I would be grateful for some fruit, along with all the cheese and bread and cured meats, if you can manage it."

'If you can manage it' was the secret password to getting

my way with Cook, a challenge to her determinedly capable authority over the kitchen.

She made another note. "Easily enough. His lordship doesn't drink enough water during the rut."

I blinked, and for a moment, I struggled imagining how the stout elderly woman might know such a fact. She turned and glared up at me.

"Doesn't go through the jugs we send up. Not fast enough, by my reckoning."

My hands twisted behind my back, and I nodded. "I see. I'll do my best to...to—"

"See that you do. Need wine?"

I tried not to recall the dark sparks in Ronson's gaze, the glitter of sweat on his chest and brow. Cook and I were meeting in a lovely sitting room that overlooked the sea, and I'd thrown open the windows to enjoy the cool breeze, which meant there was no logical reason for me to be so flushed.

"Omega Cadogan?" Cook snapped.

"Sorry, yes, a little wine would be lovely."

Sharp bristles scraping against my breast, his hot tongue—

A soft knock on the door sounded, but once again, the halfling dragon, Niall, didn't wait before entering. I was sure my face was in flames now.

"Apologies for the interruption, Omega Cadogan, but Ronson sent me to fetch you."

Tonight.

I whipped my head toward the window, as if I would see the sun setting, as if time might've passed at the alpha's will. But no, it was still midday. Not that he'd seemed incredibly patient this morning.

"He requires your assistance in regards to a dispute amongst the dragons."

"What?" I gasped, turning back to Niall. That was even more absurd than the alpha willing the sun to set.

Niall's expression gave away nothing. "The carriage is ready. If you would forgo any additional preparation before leaving, that would be best. He is waiting."

Which only reminded me that I was dressed in yesterday's clothing, corset tied as tightly as the dress required, my hair uncurled and hanging down in a long, plain braid. Cook rose and nodded to me, passing Niall at the doorway.

"What kind of dispute?" I asked, smoothing my skirt and crossing the room.

"A Miss Huberts—"

"Oh, dear. Frannie? Never mind, we'd better hurry."

Niall huffed, and his lips twitched. He eyed me briefly before stepping out of the way and gesturing for me to walk ahead of him. It was strange to lead the way, especially as I barely knew my own way around the castle, and Niall had certainly lived here all his life. I'd never had precedence in my life. My father wasn't important; I wasn't popular, and I wasn't even bossy.

And now I must sit at the left hand of the alpha and walk in front of all others. That was my status as long as I was the alpha's omega—ahead of all but Lord Cadogan.

It might've been fun, if only I knew my way around.

———

I REALIZED what had happened as soon as we stepped from the hall into the sitting room. The dubious glances of a number of dragon gentlemen landed on me, glanced away, and then returned in force as if they had simultaneously all recalled who I was.

They stood, and delivered low bows while barely able to tear their eyes from me in narrowed speculation.

Oh Francesca, what have you gotten yourself into? And why on earth are the Dunne twins part of it?

My knees wobbled with the impulse to curtsy, but I was startled by the sudden bang of the door opposite me thrown open. In spite of the thunderous expression on his face and the heavy waves of harsh smoky scent that wafted from him, I found myself relieved to see Ronson standing in the doorway.

"Finally. Come."

The betas parted to offer me a path through the room, and Ronson puffed up, eyes darting a glare from one group to the other. His hand extended, and I caught it, stifling my gasp as he yanked me to his side. His wings spread, one curling around my back to shield us from view as his head lowered, brushing his jaw against my cheek. A heavy sigh rushed over the top of my head.

"What's happened? Did Francesca not make up—Never mind, of course she didn't," I whispered.

"I can't get an honest answer out of her," Ronson muttered.

"No gently bred dragon lady would dare give the alpha an opinion unless she was sure it was his too," I said, my lips twitching at Ronson's sneer. Perhaps I was becoming immune to his expressions.

"You always do," Ronson said, arching an eyebrow.

I flushed and ducked my head, but he caught my chin between thumb and forefinger, refusing to let me shy away.

"Please don't stop. That's why you're here, Mairwen."

I wasn't sure if he meant here in the Huberts' home or here at his side, and if my blurted opinions the day in the forest were why he had chosen me, but it wasn't the time to ask. Francesca was rising from a window seat in the small, sweet sitting room, crossing closer.

"Oh, Mouse! It's so good to see you. But you look as if you've rushed here," Francesca cried.

I twisted the end of my plain braid in my fingers and tried

to catch my breath against the pressure in my chest. I had rushed here, and I wasn't properly dressed or with perfect ringlets like Francesca, but that was only because of whatever mess she'd accidentally cooked up.

"We did drive very quickly," I admitted, pretending I was here for a social call and helping myself to a seat she hadn't offered in one of the overstuffed armchairs. I turned to look back at Ronson, who towered over us both, even as Francesca remained standing. "We'll be all right," I said.

He shot Francesca one last glare, which sent her all but wilting into the chair across from me, and then swept from the room.

"Good gracious, he's terrifying. You poor thing. And you look exhausted. What an absolute surprise yesterday was. Do you think you'll be all right? I was quite shocked, and imagine how Adelaide must feel!"

"Adelaide was always partial to Hugh Gamesby," I reminded Francesca, then plowed ahead before she could start another unflattering ramble. "But look at you, Frannie! You've played it quite close to the chest. Five suitors! I thought you and Bexam..." I raised my eyebrows in polite suggestion. Francesca had arrived at the selection a bit muddled with scents, but I was sure it was Jeffery Bexam's violet and pine fragrance I'd caught the strongest whiff of.

"Oh, Jeffery is very sweet." Francesca nodded and smiled benignly, but her gaze flitted away in a manner that was more avoidant than dreamy.

"Of course. Mr. Millward is very handsome too," I said, sliding in a new direction.

"Mmm," she hummed, nodding once more.

I stared at her for a moment. Ten years ago, Francesca had been a wild monster of a girl, screaming through weeds as high as her wild halo of red curls, brandishing sticks as swords and collecting snakes to leave in the party picnic baskets. She was a child, of course, curious and rebellious, but she'd outshined the beta boys she'd run with for pure and unbridled mayhem. My mother said Lady Huberts would regret not keeping the girl under control when it was time for her to join society. In the end, the Huberts had hired a stern and commanding governess for their wayward daughter, and Francesca had grown and matured as all young ladies must. I'd considered it a shame she'd become so meek, but my opinions were usually contrary to society's. Still, the Huberts and their governess were successful. Francesca's youthful havoc had been thoroughly stomped out.

Unless...

"I remember when you were ten."

Francesca blinked and glanced at me.

"That governess of yours—Oh, what was her name?"

"Odalie Jones," Francesca answered.

I nodded, grinning. "'Odalie the odious,' you called her. She'd just arrived, only a month or so of staying with your family, and all of a sudden no one could find you. We had to search the whole island. You'd made it to the docks, and you were trying to sweet-talk a captain into giving you passage to Skybern."

Francesca's eyes lit up, even as her placid smile melted away. "I would've tried to stowaway if he hadn't agreed."

"I don't doubt it," I said, nodding. "I thought you'd manage it the next time—running away, that is. Or at least that you might end up finding your way out into the world sometime later."

Francesca's chin wobbled, her eyes filling, and my heart ached for her, for the clear longing that broke through the polite mask she'd learned to wear.

"I did it on purpose," she whispered, one tear spilling down over a peach-blush cheek, rich curls quivering with her tense trembles. "I had to make sure the alpha wouldn't choose me, of course. Then I'd *really* be trapped, or worse, *dead*. But I thought, if I could just make enough of a tangle, they'd spend more time arguing with each other. And I could just..." A sob broke free. "Oh, Mairwen! I don't know! Just put it off a little longer."

I rose and hurried to Francesca's side, wrapping my arms around her and drawing her into a hug. Francesca's breaths were rough and ragged. This was more than her usually fragile show of delicate, beautiful tears. This was *true* sorrow. Real fear.

"I don't want to get pregnant! What if I die?! Or what if I don't and I'm just stuck here, on this damned island, with one of *them*. *Bleake* Isle indeed. Oh, I don't know what to do!"

Francesca let out an inelegant wail against my breast, and the door cracked open, Ronson's head darting in to assess the scene.

"Why is it always *who* will *they* choose, and not *what* will *we* choose?" Francesca sobbed.

She was right, of course. I'd been preoccupied with my sealed fate with Mr. Evans, and it hadn't occurred to me that someone like Francesca, sure to receive decent offers from tolerable dragons, might still have a complaint with her own. Her fate was better than mine might've been at the hands of Mr. Evans, but that was an awfully low bar. Why weren't we omegas allowed to wish to leap higher? But Francesca had wished for more, and had even tried to scheme her way there, or as close as she could.

"You don't want any of them," I said, holding Ronson's gaze as he winced.

Francesca sniffled and sat up straighter, not noticing our audience as she stared up at me, frowning. "Don't you want to leave here? I want to see the world!"

I tried to ignore Ronson's stare and give her question real

thought. "Personally? Yes, I'd like to see some of it. But I do like the isle."

She huffed and rolled her eyes. "Well, you're certainly stuck with it, now you've been chosen."

"I don't mind. I like him, actually," I said, fighting my own smile as Ronson carefully snuck back out and shut the door behind him. "And I think you should tell them the truth."

Francesca made a number of unladylike sounds that made me wish we might've taken the opportunity to get to know one another before now.

"Oh, Mouse, are you mad?!"

Or maybe not. Come to think of it, upon surrender to her family and society, Francesca had always tried to model herself a little too closely to Adelaide.

I pulled away, and Francesca pouted as I stood. "I'm not mad, and I'm Omega Cadogan now," I said. I was starting to think of my title as armor I might don while dealing with the dragons of the island. "You're not going to accomplish anything but wasting the alpha's time with this plan."

Francesca's perfectly blushed cheeks turned tomato red, and she reared back as if struck. I fisted my hands in the folds of my skirt and swung toward the door.

"Alpha!"

Ronson was clearly waiting, and he stepped inside immediately, a hum of male conversation simmering outside of the room. "A decision?" he asked.

"Not exactly," I answered, and then turned to stare down my nose at sweet, delicate Francesca Huberts. "Go on," I said.

Francesca gaped at me, eyes wide, stare bouncing between us. "I...I...I want to leave the island," she blurted out, and the words rushed forth once they began. "I want to go to the sea, and I want to visit Skybern and see the Dire Peakes, and perhaps go even farther."

Ronson's brow furrowed. "I think Gideon Millward might have some dealings in exports?"

"I don't want to be a dragon's rut partner! I don't want to be a mother who raises a daughter and then crushes her into a mold," Francesca spat. "I want to travel. That's all. Without being a beta's omega. I just want to be *me*, damnit."

Francesca was panting for her breath as Ronson's eyebrows rose steadily higher on his brow.

"So you'll have to...to order me to take one of them, and I don't care which. No, that's not true. Not the twins. They're both terrible kissers," Francesca admitted in a rush, cheeks darkening further.

There was a pause of quiet, and Ronson's gaze traveled slowly to me with a flicker of hope as if I might've suddenly declared this was a jest. Then he sighed and scratched his nails over the beard that was already growing back in, neat and thick on his jaw. How would it feel against my skin when it was more than just bristles? I shook the thought away and tried to focus on the problem at hand once more.

"I see," Ronson said, moving to a chair and sitting down heavily at the edge of the cushion, wings spread at his back to avoid being crushed. "Well, I don't have a boat to offer you, so we'd better think of a more sensible plan than just 'off you go into the world.' Your parents won't agree to that, I'm sure."

I wasn't sure how Francesca took this answer, because I was too busy reeling myself. I'd guessed this man, this alpha, might listen. I'd even thought he'd likely make sure Francesca could avoid accepting a beta's suit for the rut too, although it was practically unheard of. But the part about the ship had seemed...like a fantasy.

"Mairwen? Come here, you look about to faint again. Have you eaten?"

I wandered to Ronson's side and sank obediently to his

knee where his hands on my hips guided me. My own hand braced against his shoulder and he ducked his head, stroking his jaw on my arm, marking me absently.

"What do you think? It's a difficult request," he said, tipping his chin up to wait for my answer.

It was absurd—the idea that an omega could go off on her own, on a ship, to see the world, without a male dragon at her side.

It was outrageous, and he was trying to make a plan. A plan to do as Francesca wanted, *really wanted*, with her life. She hadn't begged or batted her long, bright lashes, or even wept. She'd spat the words at him, and he'd listened.

I grasped Ronson's face in both hands and lurched forward, planting a clumsy but determined kiss to his lips. He grumbled an objection as I pulled away, and Francesca's jaw hung low in shock, but I ignored them both, my head running riot with new ideas.

"Perhaps we can say...she's too sophisticated for the island. She'll need a chaperone when she goes, but Lady Nightingale might do. She's quite fashionable."

"She's scandalous!" Francesca cried.

I shrugged. "You'll be scandalous too, you know. You'd better reconcile yourself to that quickly, or this won't work."

Francesca blinked and her face brightened. "Oh, I see. Yes, you're right. And she is stylish. And very witty. Mother says the most awful things about her, but she can't stand not to be invited to her soirées."

"You'll need to convince Francesca's parents that she'll find a much better match with a grand tour, and some sophistication," I said to Ronson, holding a hand up to halt interruptions. "I know that isn't the real goal, but we can hardly present the idea of her independence straight away. We're buying Francesca time."

"It probably won't take much. They're very proud of me,

and they were sure if it weren't for Adelaide I would've— Well, never mind," Francesca said, blushing and glancing between us once more.

"As for the betas..." I chewed on my lip, and Ronson reached up, pulling it free and soothing his thumb over the damp spot.

"I'll manage the betas," he said.

"They'll be angry," I murmured.

"Only one of them was going to be pleased," Ronson answered back, lowering his voice.

I thought that being offended over not being chosen was one thing, but having it declared that no beta on the island would be good enough was going to be quite a different problem. Especially since there was already a *treasonous murder* plot hatched. But I couldn't talk about that now, not with Francesca right there, watching us like we were a gossip column in live action.

Ronson rose from the chair, lifting me easily and setting me back on my toes. He turned us, and his wings provided privacy for the brief kiss brushed over my lips.

"I will manage from here, Mairwen. Tell Niall to take you to speak to Lady Nightingale? Do you mind that part?"

"Not at all," I said. I liked Lady Nightingale, who never once called me by anything but my name and would lend me scandalous books from her personal library.

"If she agrees to our scheme, have Niall take you back to the castle and then send him to me," Ronson said.

"I could also—"

He ducked down, and my breath caught in my chest, lips parting and preparing for a kiss, but his lips moved to my ear, almost grazing. "I want you back at the castle. To build the nest. For *tonight*," he rumbled.

I skittered toward the door, ignoring the dark chuckle at my back.

Chapter Twelve

RONSON

My wings burned and my ears rang as I approached the castle, the many cries and complaints I'd heard on repeat still circling in my head. What kind of precedence was I setting? What objection did I have to my own citizens, aside from a conspiracy to murder me that I wasn't ready to address yet? What was I *thinking*?

The truth was, I wasn't sure. Niall had left with the betas to go and fetch Lady Nightingale, agreeing to keep a subtle eye on the men for the rest of the day, and I'd remained stuck with the Huberts, negotiating their daughter's freedom. Freedom from a tradition that dated back a millenium. Freedom from the men who were seeking to challenge my role as alpha. Freedom from the island I ruled over.

Why? a dozen beta voices chorused in my head.

I slowed my flight, a leisurely fall to the balcony where Niall waited. Either he'd been standing there for hours, or he really did have a sixth sense of when I was arriving. The lamps were lit high in my office, prepared for a sleepless night of scheming and plotting, planning new strategies to build fresh alliances to make up for the disaster I'd just created.

And *why?*

"Palmer took the Dunne twins to Gamesby's estate, of course," Niall announced as I touched down on the balcony. "Bexam went home to deliver a speech against women to his sympathetic mother."

"And Millward?" I asked, pacing back and forth in front of my brother.

"He went to see Lionel Buchanan," Niall said, something hidden in his voice.

"Buchanan? What would they have to do with one another?" I asked.

Niall wet his lips and raised his eyebrows. "Rather a lot, by the look of it. I think they'll...see each other through the rut."

Oh. It was a commonplace secret that betas might seek each other's company for physical relief when an omega wasn't at hand. It had been outlawed long ago, one of the absurd laws I'd been looking forward to undoing when the opportunity presented itself.

"Fair enough," I said, shrugging.

Niall nodded. "That's what I thought. Your omega didn't come to dinner."

"What?" I asked, straightening and glancing up the length of the castle to my tower.

"Maids said they left her working on the nest. It was a good dinner, by the way, better than Cook usually bothers with," Niall mentioned. I glared at him. "Are you going up?" Niall's voice was carefully neutral.

I ought to have said no. To pump Niall for information about Millward—how we might advance him, curry his favor.

"Anything that can't wait?" I asked instead.

"Nothing I can't start on by myself," Niall answered, a half-smile on his lips.

I nodded. "Then I'm going up." I paused and stared at

Niall, who studied me with his usual calm. "You're the only one who hasn't asked why I did it."

"I know why you did it," Niall said, lips curving higher at the corners.

I grimaced and rolled my eyes, turning away. He would make me ask, force me to admit that even I didn't know. Having a brother who knew me so well was irksome.

My wings stroked through the air, and Niall laughed.

"You did it because she would've been miserable. And you're not your father," Niall called to me as I flew.

I dropped briefly, startled by the mention of our father, confused too, but there was a soft glow coming from the tower and a much more pleasant goal ahead of me. I swept my wings into action again, bracing against the evening chill, eager to return to the warmth of the nest. And to discover what Mairwen was up to, if she'd skipped dinner.

I twisted around the castle and climbed over the parapet of the balcony to my nest, pausing and staring through the glass for a moment. Mairwen's nest had improved, taller than before, with thicker layers of sheets, although still a bit small for when my dragon took over. Most of the candles were put out, and I wondered if she'd done that herself, if she was trying to hide my view of her when I went "exploring." Luckily, dragons had very good night vision. Then again, it wouldn't hurt to light a few more and offer myself the best possible view.

The door creaked as I opened it, no other hint of sound in the room, no rustling sheets or fussing omega. Was she not here in the nest, either? I frowned, hunting for her perfume in the air, and only finding the remains from the night before. But Mairwen's perfume was shy, and there was a little flicker of light from inside the nest worth investigating. I rounded the draped walls, unbuckling and shedding my clothes, pausing on the opposite side of the large construction at the picture I found.

Mairwen was asleep. She'd pushed the curtained walls of the nest she'd built aside and propped them open by pinning them under large books. She lay splayed across the sheets, still dressed, surrounded by open tomes, lips slightly parted as her chest rose and fell with slow breaths.

The ache in my back faded as my shoulders settled, hands unclenching from the waistband of my trousers, the corners of my mouth quirking at the sight of my exhausted omega. She'd made me a nest of books.

As quietly as I could, I kicked off my shoes and then left my trousers behind on the floor, tiptoeing closer to the bed, tilting my head and squinting into the shadows. Her cheek was resting on a page, littered with the most miniscule script, and a few sketched illustrations of...

I stopped, casting a shadow over Mairwen and the sheets and her collection of books on architecture. I glanced at one, open and slightly crushed under her knee, a familiar text I'd been force-fed as a young man: *A History of Dragonkin*. I stepped closer, bumping my toes into more pages, and leaned down, lifting up another text regarding the nesting habits of omegas that had slipped from the bed. I smoothed my fingers over the slightly creased pages and then silently shut the book, resting it on a stack Mairwen had built on the floor, more titles to prove the sweet and strangely vulnerable fact that this young woman had spent the evening researching how to be...mine.

I swallowed hard and, one by one, lifted and closed and stacked the books Mairwen had left abandoned on the bed after falling to sleep, until the last of them was the one she remained resting on. Mairwen stirred as I pulled the book out from under her cheek, and my gaze fixed to her face as she blinked and startled, stiffening as she found me towering over her.

"You're back," she said, voice thick and cracking with sleep.

"I am. Stand for a moment. Don't sleep in your dress," I said. *I like to feel your shape when I hold you.*

Mairwen blushed as she sat up, her stare snagging on the stack of books I'd arranged for her. "I've been thinking..."

About building me nests? About dragonkin and being an omega? I wondered.

"I shouldn't have encouraged Francesca to leave the island, or for you to help her," Mairwen said instead.

"Why not?" I asked, taking her by the shoulders and turning her to face the bed. She ought to have a maid to do this job for her, but I liked to be alone with this woman. And I didn't really want anyone else undressing her, no matter how absurd that was.

"The betas are angry, aren't they?" she asked, but didn't wait for me to respond before continuing, "And we know there's already animosity against you. More than that, actual conspiracy! And I suppose giving...giving omegas the right to refuse gentlemen in this way will upset them, won't it?"

"It will."

Mairwen lifted her arms with just a slight tug of her dress on my part. "Which will probably give Gamesby new fuel for plotting against you."

"Perhaps."

Mairwen sighed, and I wondered if it was because I was unlacing her stays, freeing her breasts from their trap, or the conversation. Probably the latter. *I* was the one fixated on her breasts, not her.

"I'm sorry, Ronson."

I blinked, ran through the words we'd spoken—mostly her—and shook my head. *Pay attention.*

"Do you think omegas shouldn't have the right to refuse?"
I asked instead.

Mairwen stiffened, breath stilling, and didn't so much as
twitch when my fingers brushed against her chest as I nudged
her stays down her arms and to the floor.

"I...I think it would be better," she whispered, turning to
meet my eyes. "Do *you*?"

Did I? I'd certainly considered the women of the island
better off without my father. I'd hated the idea of Mairwen
trapped with a man like Gryffyd Evans. Had I followed the
reasoning this far before now, or had I remained stuck in the
loop of my own concerns, of the social structure I was
raised in?

"I'm glad you were there today to convince that young
woman to speak the truth for herself," I said.

Mairwen gasped as I bent and hauled her up into my
arms, climbing onto the mattress with her cradled against my
chest.

"You're glad?"

I choked around the groan that wanted to rise in my
throat when Mairwen's perfume bloomed. We fell clumsily
into the mattress, and I wasted no time burying my face into
her throat, soaking up that scent after too many hours of
withdrawal.

"Do you wish you'd had the right of refusal?" I asked. I
should've given her space to think through the questions, but
my hands were hunting for their favorite pieces of her to grip
and hold.

"I suppose, but it wouldn't have made a difference,"
Mairwen said.

My gut turned to sludge, and I granted myself one last
deep breath of her before rolling onto my wings. "Because
you can't refuse the alpha?"

"Hm? Oh, not you. I was thinking that even if I was able

to refuse Gryffyd, my father needed the money he was given for me too much," Mairwen said with a careless wave of her hand that dropped a crushing weight onto my chest. "I ought to thank Adelaide for how it turned out. And you, of course," she added in a rush, blushing.

I don't mind. I like him, actually. The words had caused a sensation in my chest that reminded me of flying, and behind the safety of the door, I'd used my wings to hide the warmth that flooded my cheeks.

"You wouldn't take the first boat off the island if you could?" I asked, unable to keep from pressing the point, aware I might regret discovering Mairwen's limit to welcoming me.

Mairwen was quiet for a long time until I could resist the urge no longer and turned back onto my side, laying my wings out behind me, to watch her face shift.

"It's not very noble of me, I suppose, but Ronson, I think I prefer adventure in stories," Mairwen said, wearing a sheepish smile. "I did like flying, though! But sometimes I get queasy with a long carriage ride, and everything I've read in books says boats are *much* worse."

I laughed and Mairwen joined me, cheeks rounding and turning pink, her smile sweet as ripe fruit and equally tempting to consume.

"I meant what I said. I like the isle. I only want..." She trailed off, eyes shying and shuttering.

"Tell me." *Tell me, so I can grant it.*

"I want... Well, never mind. I'm working on it myself," she murmured, frowning up at the ceiling of the nest.

I thought of the stack of books beside the bed, of the way the other dragons spoke of Mairwen, spoke *to* her. I stretched my arm out in her direction. "Come here."

She startled and turned toward me, a flick of her pink tongue wetting her lips. I was jealous of the privilege. She scooted close enough for me to catch her and draw her against my chest.

"I forgot. Tonight."

She was tense and her perfume had faded. I stroked my hands over her sides, wrapped my arms around her back, and tucked her head under my chin. I'd left my drawers on, and she was still in her chemise. She'd looked a little tired today at the Huberts', and she'd fallen asleep while researching *architecture*, of all things.

"What do you say to...tomorrow morning?" I asked, rubbing my hand over her spine, smiling to myself as she softened against me.

"In the morning? I...I *am* tired."

"I am too," I said, shifting my hips away just enough for her to not be prodded with the physical interest that argued otherwise.

I didn't want Mairwen simply comfortable with me. I wanted her *begging* for me. But the former probably needed to come before the latter, in that case, and a good night's sleep together would be safer than helping myself to her body after a day of her worrying.

Mairwen's nose burrowed into my throat, and I held my breath as she brushed a shy kiss over my pulse.

Patience. It would be my mantra for as long as I could hold the rut at bay.

Chapter Thirteen

RONSON

❧❧❧

"**D**eRoche is walking over," Niall muttered in my ear.

I grunted and stiffened, the indigo shadows of Alpha Seamus DeRoche's great wings blocking out the glare of sunlight from the corner of my eye and the lush, rolling green landscape of Grave Hills. He paused for a moment as if posing, and a damp breeze greeted him, blowing his long, dark hair in an irritatingly heroic manner.

"Cadogan! I wondered if we'd see you today," the roguish dragon called, reaching me and clapping his hand heartily against my shoulder. "If I didn't know better, I'd say you weren't happy with the outcome for Torion."

"Not at all." I ran my tongue over my teeth, flexing my jaw to ease the tense clench. It was only being stolen from bed before the sun was up, stolen from Mairwen's soft curves and the promise we'd whispered the night before, that was putting me in a rotten mood.

But Torion had been my friend for decades, and I'd seen my own determined rise to alpha in his struggles against his father. I was glad for his sake. Even if I might've—absolutely —preferred to be in bed with my omega.

"It's your rut," Seamus DeRoche said with a nod. "Don't suppose you've finally taken your island in hand and stolen an omega out from under those betas running circles around you."

Another year, and I would've made a weak excuse to leave Seamus's irritating company. Today, I found myself smiling grimly.

He laughed, a boisterous sound, as if the man was in constant competition with the sound of thunder and waves. "About damn time. I'm surprised you bothered attending, in that case."

I shot Niall a glare from the side, and he rolled his eyes.

"I seriously considered abstaining," I admitted, and the memory of Mairwen's giving frame was far too easy to conjure and almost impossible to banish. I restrained my own groan.

"I look forward to meeting the chit," Seamus said. I snarled before I could contain the reaction, but thankfully, the man was determinedly amused and his laugh covered the inappropriate reaction.

"Are you waiting to get a word in with Torion?" I asked, turning back to the small milling crowd of dragons. I'd brought Niall with me, but the few other alphas of our region had brought entire parties of betas with them. Seamus's own crew of piratical-looking not-quite-gentlemen was drifting through the gathering, meeting women from Grave Hills, likely looking for bedpartners for the night. Not many omegas chose to take to the sea, and as far as I or my spies knew, DeRoche hadn't a single woman on his own boat.

I wonder if I ought to point Seamus in Francesca's direction, I thought, smirking. It would serve him right to deal with the contrary girl.

Seamus shrugged. "I only need to speak to him briefly,

just to secure the usual trade agreements. But I like Torion. I want to congratulate him properly."

Seamus DeRoche held a unique position amongst dragonkin. While every alpha here maintained their own territory of land, Seamus's rule surrounded us all. He was the Alpha of the Craven Sea, a position claimed by a rogue dragon hundreds of years ago and regularly snatched up and stolen away. Not all betas were satisfied with their lot under the thumb of an alpha, and the Alpha of the Craven Sea was an opportunity for freedom, if you could defeat the man who'd come before you. My father had said it was a crown for the weak, for those who couldn't take the local title of alpha for themselves, but Seamus DeRoche had taken the mantle when my father was a young man and had held it ever since. His grip seemed unshakeable.

Seamus may not have had fields and farms and neighborhoods to command, but not one of us could set sail without his permission, and he held our trade routes in his fist. I respected the dragon, even if I found his cheerful humor tiresome. It was a mask that covered the steely beast beneath, I suspected.

"You're being patient for an alpha with an omega waiting on him," Seamus noted. "You're waiting for the others to leave?"

This was why he'd held his position for so long. He was more observant than his careless persona led some to believe. I respected Seamus DeRoche. Did I trust him?

"As you said, the betas of my isle are becoming...ambitious," I said, deciding that having him as an ally was worth the risk of hinting at what he likely already knew.

"It's about time you noticed, Cadogan," he murmured. "You'd better wait till Worthington leaves."

My eyebrows rose and I searched the crowd for Damian Worthington. He stood close to Torion, a pointed mark of support, but when I watched long enough I noticed an exchange between him and Francis Keane, a staunch beta supporter of the former Alpha of Grave Hills.

"I flew with Damian to face his father," I hissed.

Seamus shrugged. "You served your purpose. Bleake Isle doesn't offer anything to Skybern, and now Worthington must make nice with the old guard. He's a snake. Tries to cheat my fleet."

I glanced at Niall, who was making a thorough study of the crowd, his head buzzing, planning, untangling this new information for us both.

"Do you see his shadow?" Seamus asked me.

It took me a moment to sift through my own thoughts and the faces around us before I realized who Seamus meant. Damian resembled his father, classically handsome, not very large for a line of alphas, more a long-honed blade. And behind Damian was an echo of that resemblance—a taller, broader man, but one with the same fine features and dark hair. Unlike Damian, this man did not smile, did not charm those around him, did not wheedle alliances and agreements. If Damian was a snake, this man was solely fangs.

"Bennet Reeves, although they say he is Campbell Worthington's bastard," Seamus said. "I can't make out if Damian doesn't realize what a threat he has at his back, or if he thinks he's smarter than that man. Personally, I'd have him killed."

If Damian was cheating Seamus, the alpha had a perfectly good motive to steer my own alliances away from Worthington and to the bastard brother. After all, that was why we alphas came together. Torion's place in Grave Hills was recently secured, but certainly a man like Keane was already considering whether or not he might find a better ally. Torion was replacing a man like my father, and Grave Hills had an especially bad record of treatment to its omegas, so much so that the ratio of betas to omegas was ten to one. Some betas hoped Torion would improve the conditions, and thus the ratio; others preferred the cutthroat competition for women. If Keane was looking to replace Torion, then the new Alpha of Grave Hills and I were in a similar situation.

I wasn't sure if that made him the most powerful ally I could find—he might end up busy with his own problems before long—but unlike Damian Worthington, apparently, I planned to keep my word to another alpha.

"Come, it's time for the flight," Seamus said.

I nodded, following Seamus to where the other alphas were gathering around Torion, the betas in the crowd backing respectfully away until they were well clear of us. Torion's hands were clenched at his side, the only hint of tension he revealed. His brown chest was entirely bared today, forgoing the green woven sash he usually wore as a sign of his father's line. He was darker than the other men of Grave Hills. His mother had come from somewhere in the sunbelt region of the sea and caught his father's eye before the local selection. Lachlan was the first of the Feargus line to claim the alpha throne in Grave Hills, and without a serious family reputation and no inclination to follow in his father's footsteps in terms of *how* he ruled, Torion's reign was going to be a difficult one.

His chin was held high, but I thought I caught an easing around his eyes as he found me in the stretched ring of alphas who surrounded him. I offered him a nod of acknowledgement, then remained still.

"I am Torion Feargus," the newly risen alpha shouted, turning in a slow circle, his dark green wings stretching and flexing.

"Aye!" we answered back in unison, our wings beating once at our backs.

"I have defeated Lachlan Feargus!"

"Aye!" Air churned around us.

"I am the alpha!" Torion's feet planted in the ground, his scales shimmering back and forth across his bared, light brown chest.

"Aye!"

"I rule these hills!" Torion bellowed.

We roared back together, and our roars grew louder as wind swirled and magic changed our shapes. I'd always thought the transformation was somehow both an unbearable pain, like an explosion of my form, and also a release of tension, as if I'd been too tightly bound in my man's shape.

The threat of other alpha dragons around me left me restless and temperamental, and I stomped taloned feet against the ground, wings thumping and nearly striking against Seamus's. He leapt, catching air, and I followed, Torion's own horned nose and gleaming fangs pointed high to his destination, as if he might take his first flight as alpha all the way to the sun.

"TODAY MADE me question whether claiming my place was worth the trouble," Torion said, grimacing and then taking a long gulp from his glass. "Fang's fire, Roach, this is good."

DeRoche was on better terms with Torion than I'd realized before, and it was the four us, Niall included, left lingering in Torion's tent. My eyes kept drifting to the horizon, the setting sun, aware that I was in for a long flight home and another day was passing without me having my way with Mairwen. Would she be wondering where I was? Was she impatient? Or was she enjoying her freedom in the castle without me? Perhaps when I returned, she'd have an entire house up around the bed, bricked together with her collection of books.

The thought made me smile.

"It's time we put this poor bastard out of his misery and let him get back to his omega," Seamus said, slapping my shoulder hard.

Torion's eyebrows rose. "Omega? You claimed one?"

I dipped my head. "I did."

"What on earth are you doing here, then?" Torion laughed.

"Proving my respect for you," I grumbled.

Torion's head fell back, inky black curls rioting around his head with his roar of laughter. Wings the color of a forest in deep winter shook, his bared chest and shoulders revealing his scales with a shimmer of bronze. Whatever the local betas wanted to think, Torion had his father Lachlan's huge build and thick curls, even with all of his mother's warmer coloring.

"You're honest to a fault, Cadogan," Torion said, and Seamus snorted. "I never doubted your support. Go home. You smell like a rut, and now that I've ascended to alpha, my own won't be far off. Don't need you rushing me."

Niall and I glanced at one another, and my brother's eyebrows bounced. Seamus smirked at me.

Torion wasn't blind. "Oh, I see. Not just your gesture of respect."

I sighed, sinking deeper into the seat I'd been offered as I took another sip of Seamus's admittedly extremely fine liquor.

"I uncovered a plot for my assassination," I said.

"*Damn*," Seamus hissed, leaning forward. "I thought you were just hearing their snark behind your back at last."

I shook my head. "They planned to use the selection to plant an omega in my bed who would give them access to attack me after the rut."

"No wonder you're here—"

"No, no. I found out before the ceremony. I surprised

them all by picking another." *An infinitely better choice it was too*, I mused. "But it won't be long before they have a new plan."

"If you're going into rut, it might not be long until you have an heir," Seamus said, shrugging and frowning. "You know what everyone says about the strength of two dragons. Even if it's a load of nonsense, superstitions make people nervous."

But Mairwen would be the new target. My family line on the alpha seat was so long, Gamesby and any other beta who wanted me dead would never see my son as anything but a threat to their own rule.

"Do you trust your new omega?" Torion asked.

"I do," I said immediately.

Seamus looked to Niall. "Well? You're the real brains of Cadogan's rule."

I huffed a laugh, and Niall smiled smoothly. "Mairwen's an unconventional omega, but yes, she's trustworthy. Ronson made the right choice...in the end."

"An unconventional omega?" Seamus scoffed. "I look forward to meeting her. And since it's obvious you look forward to *returning* to her, I'll say this quickly. You have my fire, Lord Cadogan, Alpha of Bleake Isle."

A rush of breath left my chest, and Niall and I shared the briefest surprised glance. I'd come to Grave Hills for Torion's vow, and probably Damian's. I'd never have imagined even asking a man such as DeRoche to be an ally, but he was a promising one indeed.

Torion smiled at me. "I should make some terrible bargain with you, since I'm more than likely facing a mutiny of my own in the near future, but you're far too honest to let me down. You have my fire, Ronson."

"Thank you," I said, leaning forward and reaching a hand

for them to shake one at a time. "You have my fire, the both of you."

I should've stayed, finished my drink, continued making good bargains with these men. Instead, I accepted their laughter as I rose immediately from my seat and turned to Niall.

"Yes, yes, I know. Back to the isle," Niall said, nodding. "I'm right behind you."

I ARRIVED BACK at the castle late, the sky dark and the halls quiet. Niall had, thankfully, urged me on when we stopped to rest our wings on the tiny island between Grave Hills and Bleake Isle, and I'd briefly entertained the idea that this time it might be Mairwen waiting for me on a balcony instead of one of my siblings.

But no, it was far too late and chilly out. She would be safely tucked into the nest. Waiting for me.

I grinned against the crisp air of the night as I swooped down from the sky to my personal tower, boots landing heavily against the stone balcony. The room inside was dark, but I would light candles. Would Mairwen be asleep in a pile of books? Or would she be undressed and under the covers, dreaming and waiting for my touch?

As it turned out, the answer was *neither*.

I scowled, shoving the new heavy curtains of the beauti-fully built nest aside, digging through the pillows, as if Mairwen had somehow gotten lost in the finery of blankets and cushions and silk sheets. I didn't know where she'd found it all. This was the lushest, largest, most decadent nest I'd ever had for my rut, and I suspected she raided every linen cupboard on the isle to build it. But where was *she*?

"Mairwen?" I called, my voice sharper than I'd intended.

Not that it mattered. There was no answer. I hunted through the dark, opening cabinets and trunks as if the woman might be playing some sort of absurd *game* before rushing for the door, throwing it open and glaring into the hall.

I took a deep breath and snarled, my hands clenching at my sides, never more frustrated by Mairwen's elusive scent than I was now. There was no trail of perfume for me to follow, because I hadn't been here to keep her scent fresh.

"Mairwen!" Her name was harsh in my throat, tinged with something too close to anger.

Worry? Yes. A ferocious, frightened, desperate worry.

Had Gamesby grown impatient, or was he furious with me for foiling his plans? Had he taken Mairwen...or worse?

I tore through the halls of the castle, bellowing my omega's name, heaving breaths for any hint of her scent.

Chapter Fourteen

MAIRWEN

❧

"**M**airwen!"

The sound of my name, tearing and clawing into my dreams, startled me upright, and I slipped from the edge of the couch I'd been curled up on and down to the hard floor with an *oof!* of breath.

For a moment I remained frozen, groggy and lost, squinting up at the vast shelves of books and the enormous fireplace I could've stepped right inside, and the huge, luxurious furniture that could've served as a bed, forgetting where I was and how I'd gotten here.

"*Mairwen?!*"

Ronson's voice, booming and echoing, shredded with a growl.

"Here!" I squeaked out, shaking my head and grimacing at the crick of discomfort in my neck. I twisted, glaring at the couch I'd fallen asleep on and the book I'd used as a pillow. Heavy steps thundered closer, and I braced myself for the alpha's anger, trying to scramble up from the floor but finding myself trapped by the twist of my skirts.

"Mairwen!" My name gusted out with a great heave of breath as the doors to the library banged open and the alpha froze in their broad frame.

He was shockingly beautiful, hair rumpled from a flight, but he looked haggard and wild as he stood there staring at me, his skin pale. His eyes shut and his throat bobbed, and he scuffed a shaking hand over his face.

"Library. I should've known," he muttered.

"Where were you—Oh!"

I'd barely gotten my question started before Ronson was storming closer, the doors slamming and shuddering shut behind him. I reared back, gaping up at the rushing dragon as he approached, the brief slack openness of his expression tightened now to a familiar predatory intent.

And then he was lunging down, arms snapping around my waist as he threw himself to the floor. His hand caught the back of my head before it could hit carpet and stone, and his chest pressed roughly to mine, his face burrowing into my throat.

"Ronson?"

He laughed, a dark and slightly ragged sound. "The damned *library*," he said. "I thought... *Mairwen*," he breathed, body sinking into mine, pinning me beneath him.

There was a clock on the fireplace mantle, and it was deep in the night, nearing morning. I'd fallen asleep in the library, disappointed by Ronson's disappearance before I woke and his persisting absence throughout the day. A day I'd spent laboring over his nest, waiting for his return. Even Beatrice hadn't known where he'd gone, although she hadn't seemed very surprised or concerned.

Ronson groaned and rocked on top of me, and my breath caught in my chest, my hands hovering in the air near his wings.

"You-you were gone," I sputtered awkwardly. *I waited for*

you. And in a tiny private place in myself I admitted, *I missed you*. A dangerous confession. I couldn't afford to miss a man who would want to replace me in a decade.

"A new alpha ascended to Grave Hills," Ronson said, his lips nuzzling over my pulse, tongue flicking out. "Niall made me go."

I laughed at that, and Ronson lifted himself from on top of me, his own grin gleaming in the firelight.

"I didn't want to wake you," Ronson murmured, his hands sliding down my back to my hips, inching my dress up a little bit at a time.

"I...I couldn't have come?" I asked, wincing at my own question.

"Mmm, next time. The rut is too close, and I would've spent the day snarling at every alpha that looked at you," Ronson said easily, as if it were perfectly reasonable that other alphas would bother looking at me. He kissed across my collar, tongue teasing and lips suckling at my skin. "Mair-wen, why are you in a damned corset again?"

"My dresses don't fit without them."

"Then we need to get you new dresses," Ronson said calmly, lifting my ass and rucking my skirt up.

I flushed, squeezing my thighs together, pinching my chemise in place before he could expose me. "I can't—I can't just go around the island without a corset."

"You won't go around the island at all," Ronson growled. I stiffened, and he cleared his throat, lifting his face from my collar with what I thought might be a blush staining his cheeks. "For a little while, I mean. I'm sorry, I-I couldn't find you when I returned, and I'm going a bit..." He grimaced, and I couldn't help but settle my hands against his cheeks, smoothing my fingers over the short bristles of his beard. "Mairwen," he sighed out, eyes sliding shut. "Tell me it's my turn to explore."

My breath hitched as Ronson's fingers massaged and kneaded and circled their way up the back of my thighs. I'd suffered a heavy pit in my chest upon waking and finding Ronson gone from the castle, and I'd lost my train of thought too many times to count, sinking into the memories of his touch and imagining what would happen when he returned. But imagining was easy and careless in comparison to surrendering to reality.

Ronson was vast and handsome and terrifying and so, so tempting. His stare made me squirm with nerves, and his touch left me boneless and weak.

"I know it's late," he continued, dropping a wet kiss to the rise of my breast against the collar of my dress. "I know I've left you here at odd ends for days." Another kiss, a lick of his tongue into the tight crush of my cleavage. "Believe me, it's not what I'd hoped for. I planned to spend the days leading up to the rut...well, however you wished. But as much of them in bed with you as you'd grant me."

My eyes squeezed shut, a strange dip and soar rattling inside me at his words, like we were in flight. His hands were sliding up under my bottom, fingertips inching closer to the soft insides, the warm, damp place that was aching and pounding at my core.

"The-the nest," I said, as if I could pretend this dragon, the *alpha*, wasn't telling me he *wanted me*. "D-did you see—?"

"It's *perfect*, Mairwen," Ronson murmured.

I whimpered at the words, heat blooming in my chest, at the base of my throat, in my cheeks, and the place where Ronson's fingers were delving. He groaned on top of me, heavy and grinding and pushing up to press his open mouth against my pulse. There was a soft haze and an unfamiliar sweetness in my throat. My hands on his cheeks slid into his hair and around his shoulders, gripping his jacket in my fists.

Ronson groaned against my throat, huffing, body rocking

on top of mine. He pulled away and I let out a wordless cry of objection, trying to clutch him close once more, before he wedged one of his knees between mine and then another. I glanced down between us and found the picture of my ample bare thighs bracketing his own tight trousers and muscled frame.

I moaned and released him, covering my face with my hands. Ronson tutted above me, sinking down once more, circling his arms around my back.

"Don't hide, omega," he whispered.

I shivered at the way he said the word. *Omega*. I'd been one my entire life, but I'd never been *enough* of one, and there was something frightening and wonderful in the way he kept using it. His lips kissed against the back of my hand, and his fingers worked quickly at the laces of my dress.

"Let me look at you, Mairwen," he coaxed, all rasp and whisper. "Let me touch you."

I licked my lips and peeked out between my fingers. Ronson's smiles were rare, but there was a crinkle at the corner of his eyes that gentled the clench of his jaw.

"All right."

Ronson's head tipped to the side, watching me closely, and I reached for the crumpled skirt of my dress, lifting it up to my waist. He hummed and helped me as I arched and twisted, not rising up completely but enough for me to pull the dress over my head.

"Mairwen, you know I am the alpha of the isle, yes?" Ronson said, frowning down at me.

I blinked, my brow furrowing. "Of course."

"And that my word is authority."

I swallowed hard, scrambling back, searching for the point where I had made some error or done something wrong. "Y-yes?"

"Good," Ronson said, his expression cracking, laughter

twitching at the corners of his mouth. "Then please listen when I say it is a *crime* for you to bind your breasts so tightly."

I snorted and rolled my eyes, and Ronson's grin brightened the room. "Then I suppose you'd better help me out of this," I said, trying to be coy but knowing my face was entirely red.

He rumbled out a purr, hands sliding up my waist, barely tangible through the rigid structure of the corset. I started to roll over, and he tightened his grip. "No, don't move. Just—" The bite of boning dug into my breasts, and then a rending pop and tear cried out from underneath, the structure going slack. He'd torn my corset open!

I burst out in sudden laughter, shocked and delighted. I had another corset, but I supposed this was a lesson. He was serious about keeping me out of this one. I giggled as he finished tearing through the laces, unbinding my waist and tugging the contraption out from under me with a victorious grunt. The seams had popped and shredded, and one length of boning stuck out from its previous binding.

"What if this poked through? It could *stab* you," Ronson growled. He rose up onto his knees, wadding up the fabric and laces as much as he was able, and I let out another sharp bark of laughter as he sent the whole thing into the blazing fireplace.

"That was very wasteful, my lord," I said.

I liked this version of our alpha, wicked and playful. He terrified me a little too, mostly because this was so...new and unexpected. Being teased, flirted with, gazed down at like I was a bowl of ripe fruit drizzled with honey and he was a man who hadn't eaten in weeks, was such a foreign experience I sometimes wanted to search for a mirror to see if I was still... me. My hands rose to shield my barely concealed body from his stare, but he caught my wrists in his grip and then slid and fastened our fingers together.

"Delicious," he rasped, gaze stroking from my head down to my spread knees. "Do you remember what I promised you that first night?"

I'm going to go up in flames. I can't keep feeling warmer if I'm not about to combust, surely. But I nodded.

"May I?" Ronson leaned forward, still holding my hands, pushing them back to the floor as he stretched on top of me. But he held my stare and waited for my answer.

"May you..." I couldn't say it. I could barely even think it.

"May I suck and kiss and lick and squeeze your breasts until you can't stand another second, until the pressure in you is too great to bear and you *burst*, Mairwen?" Ronson rumbled.

Oh, that.

My tongue darted out, and my lips were numb and hot, and Ronson growled, diving down, catching my lips with his teeth, meeting my tongue with his own. Our hands separated only so our arms could twine around one another, his grip claiming my back and my waist and my thigh, drawing it up to hook around his hips, to grind our bodies together. I whimpered into his mouth, clutching the base of his wings, scrambling my hands up his side and then back down, realizing he had the right of it. Grabbing onto the firm flesh of his ass was *lovely* and gave me better leverage to lift my own hips, to rub myself against his trousers.

"Fang's fire, Mairwen, *please*."

"Yes, yes, I want—Ah!"

Ronson wasted no time, tearing from my lips and diving down. I mourned the loss of his mouth, but only until he was nuzzling and nipping and sucking on my breasts through the thin veil of my chemise. His purr vibrated into my chest and he found my nipple through the cotton, laving his tongue back and forth, creating a strange friction of slick fabric and hot pressure. His hips had drawn away from mine, but my legs could twist around his waist and back to hold him close, my fingers sliding through soft, dark curls to clutch him to me.

He was completely dressed, and I was wearing a chemise shoved up to my waist that barely disguised the soft texture of his tongue and the pattern of his teeth as he sucked a mark on the underside of my breast. We were in the *library*, for goodness' sake, and while it was incredibly late, there was no reason why we might not be discovered. Except Ronson's wings were lifting, stretching, shadowing us, and all anyone would see of me if they walked in was my bare legs tightening like a vice around the Alpha of Bleake Isle.

"R-Ronson, I—Please, t-touch me," I gasped, squirming and trying to press my bare sex to his body. There were too many layers, and he was mapping the heft and height of my breasts with kisses, and I'd been thinking of him making me reach some beautiful pinnacle and crash for days now.

But it wasn't my sex he reached to touch. With a yank of one hand, the collar of my chemise was down, the fabric now a useless, tangled circle around my waist, sleeves keeping my arms trapped to my sides.

Ronson's head lifted, eyes staring down at my chest, fingertips swirling over my right nipple, taking it and tweaking it gently to an throbbing point. He spoke between panting breaths. "You have the most divine form, omega. The sweetest, softest skin. Look at how perfectly pink you are. I would make a meal of your breasts, but once would never be enough. And these nipples—"

"Ronson," I moaned, flames of warmth licking over my skin, my body trying to stretch away from the praise.

"You're sweeter right here. Right at the tip," Ronson

whispered, the tip of his tongue circling first one tight, aching peak, and then the other. "Mmm, such a pretty color too."

I gasped, slamming my eyes shut and bowing my back, trying to silence his words by drawing his attention back to his feast.

"Those corsets leave marks on your skin, Mairwen," Ronson rumbled, stroking his thumb over a red line the boning had left. "And I am jealous. The only marks you bear should be the ones I make." He snarled, and then his mouth was fastened firmly to my breast, and I yelped, tangling my fingers back into his hair, digging my heels into his ass and thrusting my hips against his stomach.

He huffed a laugh around my nipple, but before I could blush or apologize or do anything but writhe and beg for more, he was suckling, a taut strand of pressure pulling my sanity up from between my legs and right out of my shouting throat. He worked my other breast in his hand, rolling and squeezing, pinching and tugging until I whimpered with the violent pulse of need.

"That's cheating, Mairwen," Ronson growled, and his free hand pinned my hips down to the floor before he switched breasts, feasting on the one sore from his hand, torturing the other with his fingers.

This was not the soft warmth of pleasure I'd built with shy pets and strokes between my legs and over my breasts. This was the wind of a storm and the tight hook of lightning in my blood and a rolling thunder calling over the sea, warning me of its arrival before it shook the whole house.

Back and forth Ronson went, soothing and sucking and coiling the rope in me tighter on one breast, bruising and plucking and gripping the other until it grew to be too much. I bucked against the hand holding me down, unconcerned with the dig of his fingers in my soft belly or the shameless snarl that slipped from my lips when he wouldn't let me budge.

"You're going to be fun during the rut," he rasped. "What a gift you are, omega."

Omega.

Not Mouse.

Not Mairwen.

A wonderful, precious creature who was just right. Who built perfect nests and had breasts to covet, in lovely shades of pink. Who tasted sweet and—

"Do you know how badly I want to feel your pussy, Mairwen? To stroke and pet you? To feel you fluttering on my fingers, slicking my palm? But I won't. Not till you come. I said I would make you gush like this, and I'm not in the habit of breaking my vows."

"Ronson, I—"

I was close, and I was somewhere entirely new, some wild, savage place, some greater height than I'd climbed on my own.

I have no wings, I wanted to cry, but Ronson's tongue circled my nipple, and I lost words to a simple shout of praise.

"Beautiful. You're so beautiful."

My face was hot and my body was quaking, and there were salty tears slipping from the corner of my eyes, but Ronson was laving and kissing at my breast, pulling sweetly in a steady rhythm on the other, and he must've been speaking about some other part of me, some part I'd never seen before.

"The taste of you—please, omega, I need to touch—" His mouth enclosed my tender tip and I screamed, arching into his mouth, my body clenching and clasping on nothing, begging for more even as I dove into pleasure.

Ronson growled and wrapped his arm around my back, holding me tight. He could fly for us both as I fell. I was safe.

I clung to him, one wave after another cresting, subsiding, taking all my strength and the rest of the world away, leaving me to float gently back into my own skin.

Feather-light kisses brushed over my chest, pausing to rest over my thrumming heartbeat. Ronson's short beard scraped between my breasts as he trailed his nose over my skin. My hands were lazy and limp on his back, soaking up the sound of his purr through my palms.

"Your jacket..." I murmured, blinking up at the high stone arches of the library ceiling, plucking at the collar of his coat.

"If I take a single stitch off, I'm not sure I can keep myself from... I'm only exploring," Ronson said, low and dark, as if to remind himself. His tongue mapped my belly button, and I squeaked and pushed at his head, not thinking about the *where* of directing him, only away from such a strange and silly place—

And then his breath ghosted and brushed between my legs. I froze, gasping, too afraid to glance down, afraid to move. He would be offended that I shoved him, would correct my error, or—

Calloused thumbs stroked down either side of my sex, and bristle-soft cheeks nuzzled against one thigh and then the other.

"Ronson—" I started, barely strangling his name out.

"Mairwen, the first thing you did was take my sac in hand," he said dryly. "I think I'm owed a little peek."

My mouth opened and closed, but his thumbs were sliding through embarrassing wetness, parting the folds of a place I was only just familiar with, and his face was *right there*.

"Fuck. Fuck, Mairwen, you're so *pretty*."

I made a small sound, fairly sure my heart was about to burst right out of my chest, that I might expire from some unfortunate blend of shock and horror and joy. No one had ever really called me pretty before. Certainly not beautiful.

And perfect was such a ludicrous thought that I assumed I'd imagined the word in some sort of lusty fever.

But then again...no one had ever taken so close a look at these particular parts of me. I softened and let my alpha look his fill.

Chapter Fifteen

RONSON

I was hard as stone. Harder. I was probably carving into the carpet and brick floor by sheer force of my outrageous arousal. My mouth was salivating to the point of nearly drowning me, and I thought the seams of my clothing might be just at the edge of tearing for how *imperative* it was to my mind and body that I get out of them and *into Mairwen*.

The air was thick to the point of heaviness, Mairwen's ambrosia of an omega perfume coating her skin and pooling on her in this perfect, shadowy, delicate, precious place. I hauled in a breath, and my purr roared in my chest. I nuzzled closer, ignoring the sharp pain of my stiff-enough-to-hammer-nails cock against the floor, my eyes rolling back as her slick arousal glossed against the tip of my nose.

"Ronson, what-what are you—"

"You know," I snarled back. "You liked my taste, didn't you, omega?"

She stiffened, her lush bottom flexing in my hands. I answered the gesture with a hearty squeeze and her breath gusted out.

"Oh."

Oh, indeed.

Oh, I had claimed an omega with a body made for touch, with breasts that tasted like spun sugar and honey and beeswax, whose perfume was a secret only *I* knew, and who quaked and shuddered and cried my name as she came from me feasting on her breasts alone.

Oh, I had not even been inside her yet, and I was certain I would never be satisfied with another woman.

Oh, my rut was hours away, and I would spend every minute making Mairwen feel pleasure, just to know all the ways she might reach her peak.

I opened my eyes for one last dark and sacred look at her, all wet and rosy, dark curls soft and tight, and then I set upon her with an open, starving mouth and a long groan in my chest.

Her taste was insanity and salvation—sweet and tangy, as rich and heady as DeRoche's fine liquor. One lick, and I was both sated and insatiable. Mairwen's whimper was a siren call in my ear. She was too quiet. I liked her voice and I wanted it loud and often, calling my name, pleading and praising.

I burrowed my tongue inside of her and got a sharp curse instead, one that drew a laugh from me. Her hips bucked, and I held them tightly, stroking my tongue up between her folds, searching for—

"Oh! Ronson! I-I—"

I resisted my grin. Victory. I teased my tongue around her clit, cleaning and claiming her flavor. Every little inch of her was so subtly different. Mine to memorize.

Mine.

I snarled and sucked on the spot until Mairwen was thrashing in my grip and then took mercy on her. Her breath sobbed, and I lifted my head to find her with an arm thrown over her face.

"You're not watching," I said.

"I *can't*," she moaned. I frowned, but she continued before I could object, "It's too much. Too much to feel. I can't look too. Not yet."

She's inexperienced. This is new. My head cleared a little, and I rested my cheek against her stomach, purring as she stroked a trembling hand through my hair.

"Do you want me to stop?" *Please say no.*

Mairwen's breath hitched, and her tongue slipped out, wetting her lips. It wasn't fair that I couldn't have my mouth on every part of her all at once. My dragon would devour her if given the chance. I would have to try and keep my head on during the rut, or I might end up...I didn't know. I suffered some unnameable craving to sink my teeth into this woman and never release her.

Mairwen's hips lifted and nudged against my chin. "Don't stop," she whispered.

I grinned, and set to my work. I memorized her with kisses, acquainting her with my mouth, learning all her flavors, until she was soft and sighing, occasionally wiggling for more. I slid one hand around her thigh and dipped my finger inside of her. Tight and giving at the same time, squeezing my touch in eager greeting. So fucking *hot* and *wet*.

Mairwen moaned as I took her clit in a long, sloppy kiss, easing my finger inside of her slowly, patient when she tensed, stroking till she was sucking me in deeper.

"Did you ever put your fingers inside yourself, omega?" I called.

"N-no."

"Do you like mine in you?" I asked, plunging it in and out gently.

"*Yes*," she moaned, following the rhythm with a soft hitch of her hips.

"Do you want another? Want me to stretch you?" *Please say yes. For both our sakes.*

"Will-will you make me come?" she asked, voice trembling.

She was already starting to clench around my finger, and when I nipped a kiss on her clit she made a sweet sound, close to the edge.

"Always," I answered, lifting my head, delighted to find she was propped up on her elbows, watching me, eyes dark with arousal, cheeks and breasts flushed.

"Yes. I want more of you," she whispered.

I groaned and pressed my face between her legs, panting at the plea. I could tear open my trousers, thrust inside of her and give her everything. Take her mouth in a kiss and fuck her here on the old carpet until we were both limp and satisfied.

No. Not yet. Just another finger. To ready her. So she wouldn't be too surprised by how it felt when I was inside of her... when we finally—

"Ronson?"

I clasped my lips around her clit before she could say anything else to drive me out of my mind, turned her gasp into a shout, and slowly worked in my second finger, pumping her steadily, stretching her with a little spreading gesture.

"Ronson! Oh! I—*Alpha!*"

My wings drummed in the air and I snarled, lashing my tongue across Mairwen's clit, moaning as her thighs clamped around my hands and face, a soft, muffling press around my ears that muted everything but her taste on my tongue and the clamp of her core on my fingers and the slightly faded sound of her calling my name, calling me *alpha*, crying out her release.

I kept at her, licking up every sweet drop of her, curling my fingers inside of her core, knowing the power I had over her, the same she had over me. *Another*, my dragon roared, and this time we'd have our way. Mairwen would come again. I would make her weak, destroy her with these touches, and I would cherish her in the wreckage.

I APPRECIATED Mairwen's work on the nest more the second time I saw it, with her bundled in my arms, dressed in a rumpled chemise and my great coat. She was sleeping, or at least pretending, her thighs chafed from my beard, breasts still rosy and tender, lips swollen from hungry kisses.

"It really is perfect, omega," I whispered.

Her cheeks turned pink as I laid her on the mattress. She was awake after all. An insatiable maw in my chest roared back to life as I pulled my coat away, revealing her gentle shape on the bed beneath me. The sun was rising over the isle, a hazy sugared violet staining the sky around the coral-pink bud of morning, but I had no intention of greeting the day.

No more petty beta disputes. No more alpha politics.

I pulled the curtains of the nest shut and turned back to the lovely shadows beneath me.

"Lift your hips," I said, drawing Mairwen's chemise up her thighs.

She blinked drowsily up at me but obeyed. "We're not sleeping?"

"Not yet."

Mairwen sighed and remained limp as I carefully undressed her. "You're still fully dressed. Is it still your turn? You don't...you don't mean to have your turn *all* day, do you?"

"What a wonderful thought," I said, grinning.

"Because I only had a few hours that night. It wouldn't be fair. In fact, I think we're even and—"

I shrugged out of my shirt, tossing it to the other side of the nest, and then dove down, muting Mairwen's speech with a firm kiss. She squirmed beneath me, not for escape but for closeness, tugging her legs out from under me to wrap around my waist, arching into my chest and nuzzling closer, parting her lips. I pulled my mouth from hers, digging my fingers into soft, cool sheets when she whined in complaint.

"No more turns, Mairwen. The rut is close. Tomorrow, I think." I grazed my mouth over her cheekbones, and she sighed. "All I want is for you and I to—"

Knock, knock, knock.

Mairwen barked out a sudden bright trill of laughter at the interruption—such a delightful, genuine sound that it managed to distract me from the immediate rage that tried to storm through me. She covered her giggle with her hand as I sat up, and I groaned at the sight of her breasts bouncing.

"Ronson—"

"Fucking *no*, Niall," I snarled in answer.

"There's a fire spreading from one of the estates toward the village," Niall called through the door.

Mairwen's laugh died abruptly and she scrambled up. I caught her in my arms, cursing myself as I found a bundle of deliciously lush curves pressed up against me.

Pin her down. Fuck her. Breed her.

It took so much effort to fight the order from my dragon that my body shook, resisting the urge to bury my face in Mairwen's neck and my cock in her soft, welcoming core.

"What estate?" Mairwen called, her own voice clear and sharp.

"Don't wiggle," I growled.

"Ronson, we have to go—"

I reared back, eyes wide. "You're not going anywhere!"

"The Quincy land."

Mairwen and I both stilled, and my eyes fell shut. *Fuck.*

"Ronson, that's right near *my* home," Mairwen breathed.

Your home is here, I wanted to snap, the fiery temper of the dragon too close at hand. I forced myself to shift away, cupping Mairwen's head with one hand and brushing a gentle kiss to her temple.

"I'm coming," I called to Niall, scrubbing a hand over my face as I pulled away from my omega, turning for the nest entrance.

"Where's my chemise? Oh! My dress and corset are downstairs and—Oh damnit, Ronson, you *tore* my corset."

I shoved aside the curtains of the nest and looked back to find a beautifully bare Mairwen scrambling after me. My hand lashed out without thinking, lightly shoving her back into the pillows.

"What do you think you're doing?"

Mairwen gaped up at me, her hair tangled and drooping around her face, body splayed in a deceptive invitation that took a painful determination to resist. "I'm coming with you!"

"Mairwen—"

The door creaked. "Ronson—"

"Don't you dare come through that door, Niall!" I roared. My voice shook in the air, and my mouth was hot and dry, a little dragon fire at the back of my throat.

The door clicked shut again and I gathered a breath, releasing it slowly, preparing to apologize to Mairwen for my temper, to urge her to stay here and keep me from losing my mind completely.

Instead, I found her standing, entirely naked, boldly glaring up at me, chin high and shoulders back like a queen. I salivated, and a growling purr rumbled in my chest.

"You can't *stop* me from leaving the castle," she said cooly.

Oh, I absolutely can, I thought, smirking.

Mairwen's eyes narrowed and then widened. "Are you considering *tying me up?*"

My knees buckled when her perfume floated around me, secretly teasing the idea she might not *object* to such a proposition under other circumstances.

"I am now," I muttered, forcing my steps away from the temptation that was my omega. "I need to go, to haul water. I'll be at my wit's end with you there in danger, exposed. Mairwen, I *need* you to stay in the nest."

"I'll be at my wit's end *here*, Ronson," she whispered, drawing up a sheet and wrapping it around herself. I wanted to rip it out of her hands, and I had to cover my face, shield my gaze, to try and hold onto any sense.

"I am coming. I will figure out a way to help," she said, a hard strength in her voice, one that I doubted many people realized she possessed. "That's my *home*, Ronson. My family."

A throat cleared from the other side of the door, and I debated the consequences of setting my brother on fire.

"It would be good for the isle to see you together," Niall suggested carefully. *They don't value her the way they should.* "Dress her practically. She can help me, or—Oh, quit growling, Ronson. She can help me, or she can fly with you. Better than charging there on her own and neither of us realizing."

I pulled my hands from my face at the sound of fabric rustling and was greeted by the sight of Mairwen's bottom bouncing as she tried to squeeze herself into a pair of my own breeches. It was working too, the wool offering just enough give for her ample curves, molding to her shape like a second skin.

"Fuck," I croaked, my teeth aching in my jaw. Breeches had never looked *less* practical.

Mairwen huffed as she buttoned them shut, spinning to face me. "I need a shirt."

She most certainly did. Because the sight of her standing

in skin-tight pants, bare-chested, skin marked from my mouth and nipples pert from the cool morning air, was going to make me *feral*.

"Come here."

Mairwen squinted at me and shook her head. "No. You've got a look on your face."

My teeth were sharp in my smile as I asked, "A look?"

"A look like either you're going to spank me or kiss me, and we don't have time for either."

"She's right, Ronson," Niall called, his voice raising my hackles once more.

"Damn. Damn this isle, damn my brother, and damn the fire—"

Mairwen waved her hands in the air and strode away. "Yes, yes. Aha! Stays. Come lace me up, and if you get handsy, I will tell Niall to come in."

"I'll break his fingers if he sees so much as an inch of you," I said, stomping after her, cursing her perfect, delectable, clever mind.

Chapter Sixteen
MAIRWEN

My shoulders ached, my hands burned, and most of my front lower half was cold and wet from spilled water, but I heaved another bucketful into my arms, stubbornly marching after Niall toward the shrinking blaze. I'd had to borrow his boots—slippers wouldn't do for such an occasion—and they were too big for my feet, sliding and chafing with each step.

Niall waited at the edge of the fire for me to catch up, and together we tossed the water, scorching steam making me wince and brace as the water crashed into the flames. Niall's hand wrapped around my arm, and he pulled me along with him back to the line of men repeating the same work. There were wagons pumping water not far from here, but every bucket counted.

The woods of the Quincy estate had grown dry in the hot summer, and a stray campfire—likely from a poacher—had caught a small area on fire, leaving it to blaze overnight before anyone realized what was happening. We'd managed to stop the fire from reaching the village, but there wouldn't be much left of the estate, although with what I knew from my wanderings, it was mainly made of brambles and weeds and pine trees.

"You're tired," Niall said, pulling me aside.

I huffed and glared at him. "So are you. So is everyone."

Even Ronson's enormous dark dragon had looked weary on the last trip back from the sea, bearing his huge burden of carted water.

Niall nodded his head toward the small cluster of women who watched us work. "Rest a moment with your mother. If you drop into a pile of ash from exhaustion, Ronson will roast me for dinner. You'll be safe there. I'll keep an eye out."

And checking on me sitting in the cluster of other drag-onkin women would be easier work for Niall than slowing his steps to match mine as he worked on dousing the fire. I sighed and nodded. "Fine. I'll save you a sandwich."

Niall's lips twitched as we parted ways, and I tilted my chin down to avoid the stares of the humans and beta dragons who were still working around the well. There'd been a fair amount of blustering when I'd arrived on Ronson's back and everyone had realized who I was. And then our alpha had roared and the objections had died down to whispered gossip as I hurried with Niall and set to work.

A whoosh of wings and stirring breeze swayed above me, and I paused to look up, shielding my eyes from the sun to watch Ronson's flight from the sea back to the fire, a great leather hammock gripped in his four massive, taloned feet. It was difficult to tell through the wavering heat of fire, steam, and smoke-sullied air, but I felt sure the alpha was watching me. I lifted a hand in a weak wave, and Ronson dropped two corners of the leather, a heaping flood of sea water crashing down onto the burning field.

He was flying the water to the center of the fire as the rest of us worked our way around the edges. The sun was high, and we'd been at work for hours already, but the first real signs of progress had only just begun. I was sticky and itchy with sweat, covered in soot, and only the refusal to rest had kept me upright with momentum thus far.

I paused, glancing at the huddle of women. I hadn't caught their notice yet. Most people weren't paying attention to me until they remembered I was here at all. It was such an outrageous notion for the alpha's omega to be dressed in men's clothing and helping in a crisis, most people managed to cheerfully forget my presence. Which wasn't so unusual for me, really. And in this moment especially, I didn't mind.

My mother stood with her friends, their heads bowed together, no doubt joined in some conversation that had nothing at all to do with the fire and more to do with what pairings had come of the selection, which omegas were likely to get with child, and who would make it through the births.

Behind me, a shout broke out in the distance, another group of beta men rushing back from a sudden blaze, the fire eating away at new territory, catching and spreading on a line toward town. I bit my lip and glanced at where Niall was steadily plowing on with the others, and then up at the shadow of Ronson as he turned back toward the sea.

Then I turned and ran for the spreading fire. Or hobbled as quickly as I could. Running was somewhat out of the question in Niall's borrowed boots.

None of the women noticed me passing, and I wasn't sure how likely it was that Niall would check on me right away. I *should* have been telling him where I was going, but I hated the idea of him tucking me back in with the omega matrons.

Perhaps I am less averse to real adventure than I thought.

I slowed as I neared the other group, my brow furrowing. They weren't moving. They weren't bustling and lining up as we had done, and though there was a well nearby and they all held buckets, they seemed to be...watching the fire. I swallowed and paused, eyeing the small patches of the fire to my left and the figures of the men ahead of me.

The Dunne brothers were there, a perfect mirror image of one another standing side by side. And Mr. Palmer too. I recognized his brilliant sapphire coat from the Huberts' the other day. The whole group had their backs to me, and I edged warily closer, holding my breath and waiting for them to act.

"How long do we keep this up?" Thomas Dunne asked, his voice raised just enough to speak over the fire, reaching my ears as I paused yards away from them, hiding behind one of the few beech trees to offer shelter. "At some point, the rut will take."

The rut?

"I don't know. It's only the Posy girl. Cadogan was desperate to grab her, but she can't be much incentive to take to his nest."

I stiffened, my face growing hot. Another day, if I'd heard the beta men speaking of me in such a way—not that they ever thought of me—I would've run from the scene. But this was more than just gossip and insults.

"We still don't know why he *did* take her," another beta said. "Unless he's mad. If he's not in rut, shouldn't we be trying to get him to change his mind? Dangle Adelaide back under his nose."

"Gamesby has new plans for the chit. He's locked up with her, hoping to sire before Cadogan."

My eyes widened as bile burnt in my throat. I'd never thought *much* of the betas of the island, but the polite society of garden parties and dinner tables had never revealed so much of their character to me. They were the grossest villains of the cheapest stories of my collection. Francesca wasn't silly at all—she was smart to run from them.

"What good will that do if the alpha gets his own heir on the Mouse?" the other Dunne brother asked.

"What do you think we're out here for, idiot?" Thomas hissed, and there was the sound of a thump and a scuffle of bodies.

"Enough," Palmer snapped. "We're delaying the inevitable, it's true. His dragon will demand he have her eventually. But the less opportunity, the more stress and distraction, the harder we make it for him. And she's practically an old maid as it is. He's not likely to get another rut out of her. Not one that bears fruit."

My fingernails dug into the bark of the tree at my back. I needed to get away from here. Get back to Ronson. These men made me want to leave the isle to *burn*, to take the alpha back to the nest just to prove them wrong. *But what if they are right?* a wicked voice in my head teased, sounding too close to their own mocking tones.

Did I want them to be wrong? Male dragon births, only achievable after a rut, were exceptionally dangerous, and rarely did both mother and child survive. I'd dreaded the prospect with Gryffyd Evans for a myriad of reasons, mentally dropping a period at the end of the sentence of my life when I'd considered my fate after the selection.

But I'd been chosen by the alpha. And there'd been a bit of dread mingling in with all of the confusion and shock, a sense of responsibility I hadn't prepared for, a massive turn in the path I'd thought I'd been resigned to. Somewhere between drugging kisses and wry, dark smiles, I'd wandered into a silly fantasy where I was favored by the outrageously handsome, breathtaking, and mind-numbing alpha.

Who had picked *me*.

To bear his heir and continue his line of alphas—a line that had gone unbroken for over a millenium.

The smoke in the air offered an excuse for the sudden

blur of tears in my eyes. I wanted to prove to the betas and omegas of the island that I was the *right* choice. I wanted Ronson's smiles and the weight of his body on top of mine and a thousand of his kisses—preferably in a *variety* of places. I wanted to be the perfect omega in the perfect nest, and I wanted to bear the heir, the next Alpha of Bleake Isle.

I also wanted to *survive*.

"Get busy. That halfling is headed our way," Palmer snapped under his breath.

I spun and found Niall storming toward my hiding spot. He would give me away and then the betas would realize what I'd heard. I flapped my hands uselessly for a moment, a breeze carrying smoke through the air and clearing the view of Niall's glare, and then I lifted one finger to my lips, nodding in the direction of the men I hid from.

He continued face unreadable aside from frustration, and then his eyebrows lifted and his steps slowed. He jerked his head, a sort of up and backward motion I didn't understand until the massive shadow of Ronson's dragon sailed overhead and then swooped, curving toward a landing in the field.

"You lot look like you could use extra wings," Niall called, redirecting slightly to pass by me without stopping. "How did this spread?"

His wings were stretched wide, hopefully enough to obstruct the view of me running back the way I'd come, back to the field where the omegas mingled and gossiped and fussed their way toward the alpha. Ronson's long and lethal tail swung and thumped against the ground, and the women's voices tittered with nerves, a few even skirting back. His long neck craned and searched the crowd, a brief puff of fire bursting from his nostrils, gaining a few cries of dismay from the men still working to put all other fires *out*.

"Ronson!"

The dragon's gaze, hot as coals, snapped to me as I burst

from the treeline and onto the field, a few stares turning in my direction but most remaining cautiously on the enormous and temperamental dragon. His talons dug grooves into the grasses and dirt, kicking clumps back as he took two steps toward the skittish crowd, and then the air simmered and stirred and Ronson shrank back to his gentleman's form.

His dragon scales had been dulled by the smoke, but transformation left all that behind, and compared to everyone out in the field, he looked so pristine it made me stumble. My belly swooped at the familiar intent sharpening his expression, my own muscles tightening in anticipation.

"Mairwen," he growled in greeting, and if I hadn't known better—known the way he spoke my name when he was crawling up my body to claim my lips in a kiss—I would've panicked at the thought of displeasing the alpha.

But the alpha was *Ronson*, and I knew the look on his face as he begged for me to touch him.

I ran toward him, accidentally knocking a pretty omega who was scarcely older than me out of the way—one of the omegas he hadn't chosen a decade ago. Ronson's snarling purr thundered in the field, and his knees bent as I leapt, his arms snapping around my waist, one hand clapping possessively over my bottom.

I wrapped my own arms around his shoulders, bowing my head to whisper in his ear. "The betas started the fire themselves. They're trying to keep you from your rut so you can't gain an heir before they have a new plan in place."

Ronson stiffened, although his chest was rumbling with a purr, and his hands absently squeezed my body as if reacquainting themselves with my shape. *Perfect*, as he'd called it.

Whatever the betas thought of me, of Ronson's choice, I'd believed that word as it was rasped into my skin. I believed the awe and hunger in Ronson's gaze as he'd watched me meet my pleasure with wide eyes.

I leaned back, my face hot, too many stares pointed in our direction. Ronson's eyes were black with hunger, just a hint of deep brown surrounding his wide pupils. I stroked his cheek and left a sooty mark.

"Take me back to the castle, alpha."

Chapter Seventeen
RONSON

I flew in my dragon form, Mairwen seated carefully between my shoulder blades, her arms wrapped around the back of my neck, hands holding to spikes to keep her seat. It was easier to think straight like this, to not tackle her down into the grass and rut her in front of the entire isle. I puffed a breath laced with fire, and the grip of Mairwen's thighs tightened.

Publicly claiming Mairwen was a tempting thought. An effective curse to the betas who plotted against me.

See me with my omega. See me breed her and create another future alpha to keep you in your place.

Except there was one tiny, decidedly human thought pricking the bubble of lust. What happened if Mairwen did become pregnant with my heir?

My dragon heir. The likely future alpha.

Mairwen might die. *Mairwen.*

My father had lost five omegas to early and still-births before my mother had survived my own. Those were especially bad odds for dragonkin—usually it was a little less than half of births that failed—but my father had said his own birth was one in seven. He'd acted as though it was a point of pride. I'd accepted it as the danger of how strong we were, larger and more powerful than the other family lines on the island.

But now that danger was on Mairwen's shoulders.

The crass mutterings I'd heard about women and their bodies battled against my own feelings for the curious omega. She had good hips for breeding. She was larger than a lot of the omegas. She might withstand the birth. But what did that make her odds of survival against my family line? Even if she was *more* likely to survive, there was still risk. Risk against her life, a risk I might lose this omega I'd only just found.

Her perfume was the secret I'd drawn out, savored and craved in equal measure. Her wide eyes and flushed cheeks as she raced across the field to me to whisper the betas' plot in my ear, so unabashedly loyal when the rest of dragonkin schemed and watched me from afar. The still, quiet peace of her body curled against mine in the morning. Could I risk losing all of her for the chance of an heir?

If Mairwen grew pregnant during the rut, there was a sickening, painful possibility she might be gone before the end of the year. Gone for good.

And it would be my fault.

My wings drummed through the air in protest, and Mairwen's breath caught, barely audible on the wind, as the island edge cut away behind us, leaving only the restless sea below.

"I love flying!" she called out from behind me.

I'd been careful to hold steady and straight, to follow some of the turns of the air so I wouldn't jostle her, but at the sound of her voice, bright and delighted, I leaned forward and tipped cautiously to the side. Mairwen laughed and clung tighter, and I glanced behind me to see her hair whipping back in the wind, braid loose and wild. Maybe I would just keep flying, keep her safe on my back, close to me but not in danger.

We passed the castle and soared higher. Mairwen's thighs squeezed against the hard, scaled nape of my neck, and even through the dense hide of my dragon, her warmth soaked into me.

I couldn't resist the rut. I'd barely managed to leave the bed this morning, and it hadn't even started yet. I might seek another bed partner, but the thought of going back to the nest without Mairwen, of bringing someone else into it to spend the rut with me, made me feel sick and disgusted with myself. I wanted *her*. I wanted her scent and her sounds and her touches. I wanted her slick heat and her curiosity and her shy smiles.

I wasn't even entirely sure I could withstand *not* spending the rut with her, now that I craved the possibility. I'd never been sincerely interested in a woman before, let alone an omega, never been so obsessed with the proximity of any person.

I didn't want to lose Mairwen, and I didn't know how to keep her safe. Not when the threat to her safety was *me*. I'd be lust-addled and ferocious during the rut, mindlessly driven by the breeding instincts. There was no *avoiding* spilling myself inside of her. It would be like telling myself not to breathe.

Even thinking too much about the rut was creating a problem. If Mairwen weren't on my back, I would've dove into the sea.

Perhaps...

Perhaps I could *leave* for the rut, leave the isle. Lock myself away somewhere?

Perhaps Torion might have a dungeon in Grave Hills strong enough to hold me?

I puffed fire and turned for the castle. If I could just

manage to keep away from Mairwen long enough to speak to Niall...

He would remind me that I'd been determined to choose an omega this year precisely for the reason I was now so reluctant: to conceive an heir. To hold my family line. To hold my own power.

I released a growl and made a sudden sharp turn for the castle, Mairwen squawking in surprise and holding tightly to me. She laughed, and my heart burned with restrained fire, wings and body arrowing toward my bedroom balcony.

I transformed midair, landing on the stone and catching Mairwen in my arms, hauling her against my chest before I could think of what I was doing, my mouth slanting over hers. I needed her close, needed her safe, needed her in the nest—

Under me.

Surrounding me.

Clutching me closer as she—

Mairwen gasped as I yanked myself away, holding her back by her shoulders, staring at her and guzzling in her scent by the lungful. Her cheeks were red and marked with soot, hair tangled from the wind and frizzy and wild from the fire. She was a mess, dressed in my clothing, eyes red and lips chapped. The impulse to soothe her marked skin was so strong, my mouth watered and my body shook.

"I need—" I rasped.

Mairwen smiled, holding out a hand to me. "Yes, I know."

Fuck. Fucking Belfry's ballocks. Because she was right, of course. I did need to take her hand, follow her into the nest, lose days in her taste and her skin and her welcoming body.

I shook my head, swallowing hard around the painful burn and ache in my jaw and throat. "No, I need to-to speak to—" *Who? Niall wasn't here!* "Beatrice," I blurted out, because there was no one else who made any sense.

Not that seeing my elderly sister before my rut made any sense, either—a fact Mairwen seemed to realize by the blank stare she answered me with.

"Oh. Of...of course." She stepped back, and I was an impulsive, indecisive idiot, because I lurched forward, catching her wrist, drawing it up to my mouth and nose to suck in a quick, smoke-sullied scent of her.

"Wait in the nest," I bit out. *Although I don't know if I can stand to come to you.*

I don't know if I can stand to stay away, either.

Mairwen's lips pursed and her brow furrowed. It seemed as though she might snap at me, demand I answer for my strange behavior, show some of that perfectly determined spine she'd had this morning. If she did, I wouldn't be able to resist tackling her into the nest and kissing every stubborn, strong word from her lips.

A shadow passed over her face, and she turned away, shoulders dropping with a heavy sigh. "Very well. I'll be here."

My fingers tightened around her wrist for a moment, but I forced myself to release her, to step back toward the balcony.

"Stay inside," I called to her retreating back.

She waved a dismissive hand, and I bit my tongue to keep from calling her name, then nearly swallowed it at the sight of her hips swaying, lovingly sheathed in my trousers. With a garbled choke, I spun and leapt to the edge of the balcony, wings spreading to catch the air, flying around the corner of the castle toward my office. I would wait there for Niall to return, even if I had to tie myself to my desk to keep from crawling back to the nest. Which, given the tightness growing between my shoulder blades, was growing increasingly likely.

"NOT THAT I object to the impromptu percussion taking place above my rooms, but aren't you meant to be... elsewhere?"

My feet froze, and I swayed in place, staring at my sister, who stared back with the particular pinched and canny expression that never failed to make me feel as though I'd been caught misbehaving.

"Cook is sending provisions up to the nest," Beatrice continued. "The omega—"

"Mairwen."

"—is waiting there, from what I understand."

I choked on the growl rising up my throat, grunted, and braced a clawed hand against my desk and the rough punch of desire from my dragon. My face was hot and flushed, and I turned my chair away from Beatrice's clear stare.

"Ah. I was concerned you were avoiding her from disinclination," Beatrice said.

"I don't want to discuss this," I bit out between clenched teeth.

"If you attempt to hold your dragon at bay, you will set upon that young woman like a beast when he breaks free," Beatrice said, stepping inside and shutting the door behind her.

Beatrice had always been too brave, too outspoken, too direct. After my mother had died, I'd looked up to her as some cross between parent and knight protector. She'd withstood the tempers of my father like a stone pillar in a raging storm, letting it wash around and off her without blinking.

"Is she afraid of you?" Beatrice asked.

My shoulders tightened, and I shook my head. "Beatrice—"

"I can speak with her—"

"Mairwen is *not* the problem!"

The chair I'd been seated on rocked and thundered

against the floorboards, threatening to tip over, and splinters dug into my fingertips where my claws pierced the surface of my desk. Beatrice arched an eyebrow, cool as ever as I huffed and puffed and leaned over the desk, groaning at myself.

"I'm...concerned."

"Concerned?" Beatrice echoed.

"For Mairwen."

Beatrice snorted. "Omegas have suffered the attentions of dragons for centuries, Ronson. She's a hearty enough creature. I'm sure she'll—"

"Survive childbirth?" I asked, falling back into my seat, blinking up at my sister. "The heir of the alpha? The *Cadogan* heir?"

I couldn't remember the last time I'd seen my older sister surprised. Beatrice swayed forward and braced her hand on the back of a chair before helping herself to the seat.

"Oh, Ronson," she sighed out. "The danger only just occurred to you?"

I scoffed. "Of course not. I've understood, even regretted, what we dragons ask of our women. But it's different when..."

"When you really like the woman?" Beatrice asked.

I sighed, sinking back against the spine of the chair, letting my wings droop and raising my hands to scrub over my face. "Mairwen overheard the betas. They've been trying to keep me too busy and stressed to go into rut."

Beatrice snorted. "Men. They make up the most absurd plots. As if they could prevent your rut."

My lips twitched. "It forced the consequences of the rut into my mind. I've been focusing on..." I wrinkled my nose and shook my head rather than admit my thought out loud to Beatrice. *I've been focused on the pleasure of fucking Mairwen.*

"You chose an omega specifically to gain an heir."

I frowned. "I know."

"You wanted the strength, the power of two dragons."

"Yes, Beatrice, I *know*."

"And that has changed?"

I swallowed hard. "Not precisely, but I don't want Mairwen's life to be the cost for my victory."

"I imagine she understands it's the potential hazard to her duty as your omega," Beatrice said coolly.

I gaped at my sister. "How can you... You have no idea—" Beatrice's eyes narrowed, and I wet my lips, starting over. "It doesn't feel right."

"Have you spoken to her?" Beatrice asked.

"I can barely look at her without—" I cleared the growl out of my throat. "The rut is *very* close."

"What is it you want, exactly? To refuse her your rut and heir?"

"I want to—I don't know! It's as if my options are to force this danger on her or deny her completely and-and—"

Beatrice straightened, leaning forward slightly, stare too keen. "If she had a choice, would you offer it to her?"

"Of course!" Although I might do my best to persuade her to choose the safer option, if one were possible.

Beatrice stared at me for a long moment and then glanced down at her lap. "You know I never had any children, in spite of the wishes of both Father and the dragon he passed me off to."

"Beatrice, I—"

She held up her hand. "My failure was a great blow. To *them*. For me it was a...a relief. And a success." She held my gaze, and a wry smile tugged at the corners of her mouth. "Sebastian didn't want a daughter, of course, so he only made an effort with me during his ruts. But I didn't want to risk his attention. So I drank a particular tea at the start of every month for the entire thirty years it took for me to outlive him and then Father."

My brow furrowed. "A tea?"

Beatrice smoothed the folds of her skirt. "It is illegal for dragonkin women to take any measures to prevent pregnancy. Our great-great-grandfather created that particular law. But before his rule, it was not uncommon practice for omegas to brew a tea with a collection of now outlawed flowers and herbs that would allow them to attend their dragon during a rut, without the consequence of a dangerous pregnancy."

"*What?*" My jaw was hanging open, but the rest of me felt quite numb, and I shook myself, as if I might make sense of these words. "Why...why have I never heard of this before now?"

"Because it is easier to prevent something from happening if you are able to erase even the suggestion it might be possible," Beatrice said with a shrug. "Which our forefathers did their very best to do. The birth rates of male dragons were dropping quite quickly for several centuries at that time. I don't know if our relative made the law to protect the isle's dragonkin population, or if he simply wanted to ensure his own heir."

"Beatrice, are you telling me... If the flowers were outlawed, how did you obtain them?" Was there time to get the tea for Mairwen too?

"Men take little interest in flowers," Beatrice said with a wave of her hand. "Especially our father. The library here at the castle has many texts that have been banned across the rest of the isle, including the records I needed. And Father gave me fair warning of his plan to use me as a political tool. I was able to track down the seeds I needed. I planted them in the greenhouse here, drank the tea on my monthly visits. I thought Father and Sebastian would grow suspicious, discover my deception eventually, but I don't think either of them knew enough about the real history of our island to realize what I was doing was possible. Erudite gentlemen, they were not."

My chest ached, and as Beatrice fell silent, I realized I'd been holding my breath. "And the flowers?"

Beatrice smiled, earnest and wrinkled, and she reached across the desk to cover my tense hand with her own soft and aged one. "I could brew Mairwen the tea today, if she wants it. But it must be her choice, Ronson. I gave the choice to your mother, but she *wanted* a child. And she loved you. I'm glad you don't want to take Mairwen's choice away, but I won't, either."

"Brew the tea, Beatrice," I said, the leaden weight in my chest easing, the prospect of the rut stirring interest and heat in my belly once more. "I'll speak to Mairwen."

Chapter Eighteen

MAIRWEN

My stomping footsteps echoed through the halls of the castle, and I realized as I made my way to Ronson's office that this enormous and intimidating structure was becoming slightly less of a maze. I would've been pleased by the fact, but I was too busy being itchy and irritable and annoyed.

The castle servants had arrived at the nest with a huge copper tub and a dozen pails of steaming water, and the prospect of a bath had been the perfect balm to the disappointment of Ronson rushing off *once again*, and this time for no apparent reason. And then one of the human women had stepped forward to speak.

"Lord Cadogan wishes to speak to you, Omega Cadogan."

I'd stared blankly at the human servant before the words registered.

"Then he can come back to the nest," I'd answered, a little too sharply. The busy servants stilled and I shook myself. "I'm sorry. Of course, I'll go speak to him."

"Your bath will be ready when you return, milady," the

young maid said, curtsying as I passed her, her nose pointed to the floor in a way that left me feeling like a bully.

I forced myself to draw in a deep breath as I approached Ronson's door. The last thing I needed was to lose my temper with the alpha too, no matter what kind of rapport was growing between us. Especially since I'd somehow managed to displease him on the flight home. Or was he angry because I'd wandered off on my own to spy on the betas?

I paused outside of his office, shuffling in bare feet, wishing I'd made him wait for me to bathe before going to speak to him, partly for my own comfort and partly just to annoy him. I could turn back. The servants would be gone by now, leaving that lovely and large steaming bath all to myself. If Ronson could storm off from the nest, surely I could storm—

"Mairwen."

I gasped and jumped in place as Ronson swung the door open.

"Why are you standing in the hall?"

"I was debating returning upstairs for my bath." My face twisted in frustration, annoyed by my habit of always blurting out the truth to this man.

Ronson purred, and his eyes darkened. "We'll bathe together. After we talk."

"You couldn't have come up to the nest to speak with me?" I asked, crossing my arms over my chest.

"Mairwen, if I went up to the nest, I wouldn't have spoken. I would've tossed you onto the bed and—" He grimaced and cleared his throat, backing away from the door. "This is...important."

Some of my ire softened. The *real* truth, the one I wouldn't even speak to Ronson, was that I'd worked myself into a bit of a lather after he'd left me upstairs, convinced he was changing his mind about keeping me as his omega for the rut, that he'd flown back to the betas to bargain for a better one.

I stepped forward, and Ronson backed away. Not as though he was trying to stay out of my reach, but more like...

Like he was keeping from reaching for *me*.

I crossed the threshold and stepped farther from him, pressing my lips together as he stumbled in my direction, keeping a precise amount of space between us.

"What is this about?"

"Sit, please," Ronson said, holding out his arm to guide me toward the chairs at his desk.

I sighed, tightening my fingers around my elbows, and obeyed.

———

"Oh," I murmured after Ronson had finished explaining his busy thoughts during the flight to the castle and his conversation with Beatrice. They hadn't been so different than my own this afternoon, and it gave me a soft, bitter ache in my chest to know he'd been worrying for me.

"I thought the only option was to avoid you during the rut, but I...didn't really want to do that. I don't even know that I would be capable of staying away," Ronson said, scowling, as if that wasn't one of the best compliments anyone had ever offered me.

"But it's not as if we are just—Ronson, you are the *alpha*. If anyone found out that I made certain not to conceive your heir... Well, like Beatrice said, it's criminal."

Ronson leaned forward in his seat, reaching across to take my hand in a firm grip—his first touch to me since he'd left me upstairs. I resented how that simple grasp seemed to ground me, settling some of the anxious thrumming in my chest. "Only you, Beatrice, and I would know.

Mairwen, I don't even need to know. This is *entirely* your decision."

I pursed my lips and stared back at him. "Is it? Really? Do you...not want an heir?" *Do you not want* me *to give you one?*

He sighed and leaned back, and his hand slipped from mine. "I don't want the matter of an heir to be an either-or question," he said.

Either the heir, or me.

"That's what we're discussing though, if I do drink the tea," I reasoned. "And the strength of two—"

Ronson waved his hands. "As far as we really know, that's just a proverb. My father's strength didn't double when I was born, and I certainly wasn't any use to him for the first couple decades. I was only a child."

I fidgeted with my skirt. Ronson could offer me this choice, wait another ten years, declare me useless, and take a new omega. Or he could even simply wait for me to die naturally, if he was really patient and men like Gamesby didn't come up with a successful plot before I was out of the picture.

"Everyone will think I failed," I said, speaking the words softly to my lap. *And they won't be surprised*, I added privately.

Ronson's chair creaked and his boots thumped, and I drew myself up, trying to force myself into a calm, unaffected expression. But when the alpha sank before me, gathering my hands and holding them gently in his own, those dark eyes shining up at me, I found my vision blurring and my throat tight.

"I don't want to refuse you the right to have a child, if that's what you want, Mairwen. But I don't want you to take this risk for anyone but yourself. You're worth more than a potential heir."

I sputtered, a garbled laugh slipping from my lips. "Ronson, that's...absurd—"

"I'm not going anywhere," Ronson said, shrugging. "And I've managed this long without one, haven't I?"

"You *know* it's not that simple. You are...you're the *alpha*. Even if you don't mind..." Did he need an heir? Society would say yes. And up until today, until *this moment*, Ronson and I both knew his intention had been to gain one.

Until he realized it might mean...losing me? Or just the guilt of my death? The answer shouldn't have mattered, but I was *so* close to asking.

The door behind me squeaked on its hinges, and I jumped, half expecting my family and Gamesby and all of dragonkin to burst inside this room, pointing their fingers and accusing me of-of—

I didn't know the word for it. Something disgraceful, embarrassing, and clumsy, no doubt.

But it was Beatrice walking into the office, carrying a well-loved porcelain tea set with faded painted flowers and slightly chipped cups. The steam rising from the pot was fragrant and a bit pungent, and my stomach turned queasily, eyes bouncing between Ronson and his sister.

"Mairwen, look at me."

I held my breath and met Ronson's gaze, and for a moment, there was no panic, no shame. Just the soft urge to lean forward and fall into him, seal my mouth to his and forget all the other little troubles that seemed to stack up around us. I flushed, and he caught my face in his hands before I could turn away again.

"Forget the rest," he said, voice low and heavy, like thunder on the horizon, his words echoing my own thoughts. "Make *your* choice. No one else's."

My eyes fluttered shut as he leaned in, grazing a kiss over my mouth and then pressing one firmly to my brow. Porcelain and silver rattled gently as Beatrice set the tray down at the edge of the desk. Ronson released me, standing up at my side so I was framed between the siblings. I swayed, untethered, as yellow and pink flowers gleamed out of the corner of my eye.

"You'll need to drink at least three cups, but given how close the rut is, I'd suggest finishing the whole pot," Beatrice said smoothly. "It's bitter, but you get used to it, and there's no physical discomfort."

"I'll wait upstairs in the nest," Ronson said. "Take as long as you need. Beatrice?"

"In a moment, Ronson."

I was trying to catch my breath, but each effort came in short, weak gasps, as if the air in the room was too thin. An heir would be my chance to prove dragonkin wrong about how they thought of me. I would not be the omega the alpha had chosen as a last resort, but the omega who'd helped continue the Cadogan line. The *right* choice instead of the wrong one.

Would dragonkin's opinions matter if I didn't survive?

Beatrice cleared her throat and I stirred, glancing around the room. Ronson was gone. It was only us. "It was always important to me that Ronson not grow up to become an alpha like our father. One who put his own interests and desires before all others, before the good of the isle. And he has. I knew that decades ago," Beatrice said, waving her hand. "What I failed to expect, because I've never truly seen an example of it in my entire life, was that he would also see us —see omegas—as more than the use of a broodmare. He means it when he frees you to make your own choice, Mairwen."

I licked my lips, blinking up at Beatrice, who waited for a moment before nodding and heading for the door.

"But is it right, then, if I have no gift to give in return?"

My voice was small, but Beatrice's quiet steps paused. I

didn't turn to look at her, wasn't really sure if she'd answer me.

"Are you sure there's nothing? Nothing but a potential child to follow in a line? What does it really matter if the Cadogans reign as alpha on this isle? Alphas rise and they fall. I'm not sure our bloodline matters to Ronson, and our father isn't here to care."

And perhaps even if there was a male dragon child, he might fail to grow into an alpha, take the position from Ronson. Dragonkin would be as unsurprised by that as they would my failure to produce one at all.

I groaned and leaned forward, dropping my face into my hands. My choice. *My* choice. What *was* my choice?

"Drink the tea, or dump it. No one need know your decision but you."

The door shut behind Beatrice, and I was left with the hundreds of bickering arguments in my head.

THE SUN WAS SETTING, and the room was cast in gold and copper rays of light when I finally made it back to the nest. I paused in the doorway, struck dumb by the sight of Ronson in all his blazing warmth, wings seeming to soak up the sunset and reflect it darkly. He was frozen too, halfway across the room, staring back at me, and he let out a long, heavy breath.

"I've been using my dragon fire to keep the water warm for you," he rasped out in greeting. It was on the tip of my tongue to tell him what I'd done, the decision I'd made, but Ronson held his hand out to me, waiting for me to reach his side.

And it was *my* decision. If he wanted to know, he could ask me.

I stepped inside and shut the door behind me, the click of the latch loud and final. "Did you already bathe?"

"I washed off a little, but no, we're bathing together. Are you ready, Mairwen?"

I turned to face him. He wasn't asking if I was ready to wash. This was more than that. We'd managed a great deal of *exploration* in the last two nights, but two nights would never be enough preparation for a dragon's rut. Especially not the alpha's.

"Is it true you shift into a dragon during...?"

Ronson grinned, his teeth sharper than they had been a week ago. "Not exactly. I grow larger, and more dragon features appear throughout, but I couldn't truly shift completely, not for the act itself. Not even an omega as perfect as you could take my dragon. Is that something people think?"

"It's just a rumor. It sounded false," I said, ducking my head.

Shadows churned out of the corner of my eye, and then Ronson was there, in front of me. Had he flown, or could he muffle his thunder and step silently when he wanted? Either way, he was surrounding me, the door solid at my back and him even more so in front of me.

His brow furrowed. "You're frightened."

"Nervous," I corrected, trying to avoid looking at him. But it was impossible. He was huge, and he was taking up every inch of my view. "Tired."

"We can—"

"Excited," I continued, glancing up, his gaze as black and difficult to decipher as ever. "Confused. It was a big day, Ronson."

"Just a bath, then," he said, gathering me gently and peeling me away from the door, cocooning me in strong arms and heavy wings.

"Not just a bath," I said, and his steps faltered. "I'm afraid if we wait another day, the betas will find a way to sink the isle into the sea and make it your job to float us back out again. But maybe... Can we move slowly?"

Ronson's arms circled my waist, drawing me back into his warm chest. He always smelled a little smoky to me, but it was a much fresher and more intense scent than the sweat and fire clinging to my own skin, and I turned my face to breathe him in.

"I especially enjoy moving slowly with you, omega," he purred in my ear, taking advantage of my twisted neck to press kisses inside the open collar of his shirt I was still wearing.

Will you be disappointed when you learn my decision? I wondered, but I didn't want the answer. It had taken a long time to dig through voices that didn't belong to me in order to discover my own, but by that point, it was a relief to discover it at all.

"In fact, before we even entertain the bath, I think I ought to start by very *slowly* undressing you," he continued, one hand sliding up to tug the uppermost button of my collar. His claws were sharp and glossy black, and they clicked against the delicate brass buttons.

"You're teasing me," I said, rubbing my cheek on his clean sleeve and feeling a petty pleasure when I realized I'd marked it with soot.

"I'm seducing you. Although that sometimes comes in harmony with teasing," he said. "Mairwen, would you be disgusted with me if I hired someone specifically to make you better undergarments? Ones that didn't aim to press you flat?"

"You are obsessed," I gasped out with a laugh, glancing down at the now gaping shirt that revealed my most comfort-able—although apparently still objectionable—set of stays.

"I am," Ronson answered, and then one claw sliced through the front band of material.

I growled, and Ronson growled back, bucking his hips against my ass. "I have to say yes now, or I won't have any undergarments at all."

"That's another very clever idea."

"Ronson!"

He gripped my shoulders and spun me to face him, the crinkles at the corners of his eyes the only clear sign of humor. I reached up and touched the firm line of his mouth, wondering what it might take to earn one of those startling and rare smiles, and his expression slackened as he stared down at me. My throat tightened, and for a moment there was no air—time had stopped.

He would ask what I'd done in the office, if I drank the tea, and I would tell him the truth, and then I'd know how he really felt about giving me such power.

His gaze darkened, and he stepped forward, guiding me backward, the moment vanishing and returning to this warm intent and anticipation.

"I don't think anyone really recognized me today," I said.

"I don't think this island really knows you, Mairwen," Ronson said, tipping his head.

My breath snagged in my chest. "And you do?"

"No. But I will." He pushed gently, and I found myself sitting on a wide cushioned bench. He stared down at me, imperious and impenetrable and handsome. "I have started my study in the most rudimentary way."

"Oh? What way is that?"

"Looking," he said, voice velvety. His thumb caught the collar of the shirt, drawing it aside to expose a long V of skin down my chest to my stomach.

"You've done more than look," I said, words dry.

Ronson's purr rattled with a laugh and he drew away,

circling the bench. I tried to look over my shoulder, but a hand caught me by my hair, holding me in place. One muscled leg looped over the bench, pressing to my left side, and then a moment later, he was wrapped around me, thighs bracing my hips, arms curling around me. His claws dug into my thigh, spreading my legs apart.

"That's true. I've learned the sounds you make, the way you taste, how your skin feels under my hand, against my own."

I shivered, and Ronson draped an arm over my chest, sliding his hand down to cup and roll my breast in his grip. I straightened, pushing into that touch, tipping my head in invitation.

"Superficial observations, I'll admit, and not nearly thorough enough to satisfy my curiosity," he whispered in my ear, licking the lobe and then ducking his head to mouth against my throat. "But there's more, Mairwen. I know there is. And I intend to learn it all."

"You might be disappointed."

"You plan on withholding what I want to learn?" Ronson asked.

That's not what I meant, I thought, but decided not to say. I twisted, reaching a hand back to draw his mouth to mine.

"Not quite so slowly now, alpha, if you please," I murmured against his lips.

Chapter Nineteen

MAIRWEN

The nest *was* perfect after all. It had taken me a fair amount of study, sweat, and tears to get it ready, but now that the work was done and the curtains were closed, I was able to enjoy the luxury I'd created. Walls layered in linen and velvet to keep our private world quiet and unpolluted. Down pillows and mattress pads piled high until I was fairly certain I'd recreated the sensation of lying in a cloud. A sensation that was even more luscious while gently crushed beneath the weight of a growling and purring man intent on kissing every inch of skin he could find.

"Ronson," I called, squirming in the outrageous cushion, reaching a hand out. He was too far away, down at my feet, his thumb digging into my arch and making me—

I gasped, a weak cry slipping from my lips as something that was *almost* an orgasm raced up from my foot into my core and higher until it reached my heart.

He rumbled, lifting my foot, a ticklish kiss pressed to my instep, the bristles of his beard making me shudder.

"I've never taken a lover before."

I wondered why those words had come from his voice and not mine, and then sat up to blink at him. "You don't mean—"

The nest was lit with just a few small hanging lamps, but it was enough to reveal the slight flush that bled over Ronson's cheeks.

"No," he choked out, a flash of a grin that only made me crave more. "I've been with other women...during other ruts. But human women can't last the entire rut, and I wasn't in a state to get to know them," Ronson said, sitting back on his heels.

I still had the urge to drag a sheet over my body and cover myself, but we were both entirely nude after the long soak in the bath, and there was a more tempting maneuver that would allow me to hide myself from view. I sat up, and Ronson's smile hitched as I helped myself to his lap, draping my arms over his shoulders and nestling my breasts to his chest. His hands took an eager grip of my ass, squeezing and clutching me closer, rigid cock wedged between our bellies.

"At least we are both new to one thing," I said, finding his shoulder conveniently in front of my lips and leaving a kiss there. "You're very warm. Are the betas warmer too?"

Ronson growled, and my hands tightened on his shoulder as he tipped me back into the soft mattress, the heavy weight of him dizzying and wonderful on top of me.

"Don't think about the betas, Mairwen," he said, hands caressing up my side, one gathering my hair in his fist to tug gently and tip my chin up. He kissed me, sharp teeth grazing over my lip, tongue stroking in as I gasped, stroking against my own. His body slid over mine, up and down, cock fitting nestling against my core and coating itself in my arousal.

"What if they do something else to draw you—"

Ronson paused, lifting up just enough to stare down at

me, a glow of candlelight reflected in his pupils, blazing in his darkness. "If they burn the whole island down or set a plague upon us or...I don't know, sink it like you suggested, then that will be the final note in the history of Bleake Isle. We should be fine, though. This is a very high tower, and it will take a long time for any danger to reach us."

I stifled my laugh and ground my hips up against Ronson. "Niall seems very capable, so everything should be fine."

Ronson rumbled with another growl, his eyes falling shut and his jaw ticking. "Mairwen," he warned.

"And I suppose not *all* the betas are scheming fiends. Some might be up for some heroism."

Ronson snarled and then squeezed me, rolling us over so that I was spilled atop him. "You're playing with literal fire, omega."

I grinned and I sat up. "I'll stop now, I promise. Roll us back over."

Ronson's gaze was hooded, studying me from head to toe, taking a more leisurely route along some of the stops I already knew were his favorite. I'd cursed my heavy breasts for so many years for being out of fashion, cumbersome, *hot* and sweaty. They were still all of those things, but it was a nice reprieve to know someone else could enjoy them so much.

"I don't think I will," Ronson said, gripping my hips and working me over his hard length. He was steely and soft and dense between my legs, rubbing sweetly against the shockingly sensitive spot of my clit. Ronson groaned and his head fell back, throat flexing with a hard swallow and body bucking beneath mine. "Fuck, you feel good on top of me, Mairwen. Lean down. I want you closer."

My breath was short as I set my hands on either side of his shoulders, just above his spread wings, a small whimper escaping at the ticklish brush of his chest hair against my breasts.

"Ronson, I..." I bit my lip and tried to shift on top of him, knowing what I wanted, even knowing the mechanics, but not sure how *exactly* to get there.

"You can ride me like this. I bet your sweet little clit likes grinding against my knot," Ronson purred.

I clenched a strangled moan behind sealed lips and buried my face in Ronson's chest before he could see it flame red with my blush. "Ronson, please, I need..." *You. Inside of me.*

"Tell me, omega."

I shuddered and shook my head. "You know."

"You need me to lay you down and lick you clean? To curl up behind you and wrap my arms and around you and stuff you with my fingers as you sleep?"

I gasped and looked up at the offer. It was *closer* to what I wanted, at least. But Ronson was smirking. He knew exactly what he was doing, hips churning to rub his length against me, his hands guiding my hips, occasionally traveling back to squeeze and knead at my ass.

I took a breath, wetting my lips, and Ronson's eyes latched to the spot. "I feel..." The words choked off, and I squeezed my eyes shut.

Ronson stopped his teasing movements, and one hand reached up to stroke my hair back. "Tell me, Mairwen," he said softly.

I swallowed and opened my eyes once more, meeting those impossibly dark and endlessly black eyes. "Hollow," I whispered.

Ronson groaned, and he sat up, drawing me with him, bending his knees behind me and making me a cradle. His wings spread and curved toward me, and once again Ronson was my whole world, everything quiet and terrifying and perfect.

"Rise up, Mairwen," he said.

I pressed my knees into the mattress and lifted up, glancing down and flushing at the sight of his slick, glossy cock and the wet sheen we'd made against his belly.

"Are you ready for me, omega?" he asked, and I couldn't tear my stare away as he reached between us, two fingers sliding and spreading over my swollen sex and then delving slowly inside. I moaned as they filled me, thick and stiff and somehow not enough. "Oh yes, you're all lovely and wet. And...oh, Mairwen, feel how soft you are." He pressed at my inner walls, and my body gave easily, a weak cry escaping me as the pressure and ache burst gently.

"I've never been inside an omega, Mairwen," Ronson said. "You're so plush. You're so tight around my fingers, but with just a gentle press you make room for me. Do you know why?"

I didn't know a single damned thing at this moment except that I needed *more*. My head shook, and Ronson leaned forward, dropping a damp kiss on the swell of one breast and then the other.

"You're built for my knot. *Mine*. No beta can give you what you really need. But I can."

I twisted and rocked my hips, trying to get his fingers inside of me to fill me deeper, touch more of me. The idea of there being any competition between Ronson and any beta on the island was laughable, knot or otherwise.

"Please," I whimpered, biting at my lip, and a sharp gasp flew from my lungs as Ronson hooked his fingers inside of me, coaxing my hips forward. The pressure was one fine point of perfection, echoing sweetly like a promise in my core, but it wasn't—

"*More*." The word was torn from me in a foreign voice, low and hungry, and Ronson answered the order with a growl.

He didn't obey, and I made a soft sobbing sound as his

fingers slipped free of me, both of his hands clutching my sides and shifting me backwards. "Sink down a touch, omega," Ronson rasped, urging me with a tug of his hands.

My eyes widened at the first scorching kiss against my throbbing flesh, and I stared down at Ronson, whose gaze was fixed between my legs, one hand shifting away from me to grip his cock and hold it against me. His thumb brushed against my clit once, and the tip of a finger slipped inside of me. Ronson's eyes lifted to meet mine, my chest still and frozen as he searched my expression.

"Take me inside of you, Mairwen," Ronson whispered.

I held my breath as my body found a natural answer to the invitation, knees spreading wider as I seated myself slowly on Ronson's length. I couldn't hold his stare, too startled by the invasion, by the shock of possession, full and heavy and sweet, so reminiscent of the man beneath me. I shivered and a mangled cry escaped me, a heave of breath caught in my lungs. My nails dug into Ronson's chest and he grunted, hunching forward and catching my breast with a nip of teeth and a lick of his tongue around my nipple that seemed to create a matching warm stir inside of me.

He was enormous, claiming my body as his with the simple act of my slick flesh enveloping him. *It ought to be the other way around*, I thought, struck by the sensation of being consumed.

And then Ronson groaned, resting his cheek against my chest, his breath gusting over my skin and leaving me trembling. His arm circled my waist, and his hand that held his cock in place slid up to caress between my legs, the ripple of need inside of me now clearer as it fluttered over him.

"Fuck, Mairwen," Ronson ground out through clenched teeth, then he tugged and there was *more*—the more I'd begged for and was now helpless to receive.

Our bodies were a tangle, my breasts brushing against the hair on his chest, his tongue laving over my pulse, one cramped hand between us touching and touching and touching, and all I could do was cling to him, my face turned up in awe at the peaked ceiling of the nest I'd built.

His lips brushed the lobe of my ear. "Are you all right?"

Another shiver raced through me, one arm slithering around his shoulder, now determined that we might simply... fuse together if we kept moving closer.

Ronson's nose nudged my cheek. "Omega," he called gently.

"I-I—Y-yes," I managed, and then I sobbed against his shoulder as my body seemed to shudder from the inside out, as if this previously untouched part of me knew how to claim kisses from the alpha.

Ronson purred, swirling a finger over my clit and drawing out another heady tremble. "Can you move?"

Move? So soon? I might have been shocked and overwhelmed, but I didn't want this to *end*. Not yet!

He nuzzled my cheek, and I shifted, blinking and leaning back just to catch his eyes. They were smiling, his lips still firm and serious, and we met in a smooth clasp of lips and tongue. And *oh*, it could get better. Ronson's mouth was gentle against mine, but it created a taut cord that ran through me like a dense pulse. And suddenly, I understood what he meant by his question, because I *was* moving and it was wonderful. I rocked on Ronson's lap, and his cock caressed me, those fluttering, drumming sensations building.

Ronson's teeth nipped at my bottom lip as I gasped and continued to squirm, a little clumsy and uneven, trying to find new territory inside of myself for him to touch.

"That's it." Ronson kissed my cheek as I hiccuped for air. "Does that feel good, omega?"

"Yes, yes, yes," I chanted in answer, grateful to put a word to the broken cries in my throat. My hands mapped Ronson's shoulders and back, sliding over to grip his wings and use the leverage to strengthen my uncertain motions.

Ronson's hand squeezed my ass, slowing my frantic jerks, turning them into a steady, slow rise and fall that cut the edge of pleasured panic and settled me back in our embrace.

"There," he whispered, grazing his mouth over mine, groaning as a burst of warm, slippery heat rushed between us. "You're close now."

"Yes," I answered, nodding and feathering kisses over his jaw. His hand was steady between us, gentle and stirring.

I was close. And yet...

I shivered and pressed my chest closer to Ronson, my head tilting back to find his gaze. I wet my lips, and his eyes traced the movement.

"I want your weight," I said.

Ronson's lips curved, and he rewarded me with a kiss, turning us slowly while keeping our bodies joined. His wings swept back, a cool breeze rushing in, and then I was landing gently on the bed with Ronson surging above me. My thighs wrapped around his hips and the first drive of him inside of me, plunging deeply, so thick and commanding, made my eyes fall shut on a shout. He made my efforts at moving seem graceless by comparison, the elegant tide of him on top of me driving all thought from my head but *need.*

"Oh, *alpha!*"

Ronson rumbled on top of me, his shadow looming as I opened my eyes, his brow furrowing and glittering faintly with sweat. "I like when you tell me what you want, omega."

Then I had only one option.

"I want your mouth on mine," I whined.

Ronson growled and stole my breath, his body landing heavily on top of me, tongue stroking against mine as we moaned together. His hand pulled away from my clit, arms wrapping around my back, but it didn't matter—our bodies were grinding together.

"I want-I want to come with you inside of me," I said into the kiss.

"*Yes*," Ronson snarled. "Come, my sweet omega. Coat me in your gloss. Come, and I will give you my knot."

I didn't care about his knot. I didn't even really care all that much about my orgasm at that moment. Ronson was covering me, and the island was gone, and the worries were gone, and I was *perfect* in this moment. One hungry kiss melted into sweeter nuzzles, then built into starving bites and laving tongues. The warm pressure began to fizzle and spark, and I shouted into Ronson's mouth.

"I can feel you sucking me in. So greedy," Ronson hissed, glaring down at me, so ferocious it made me tremble. Or maybe that was the steady build tightening in my core, shaking me in its grip, rattling like a thief with an upturned purse, waiting for its prize to appear.

"Ronson!"

"Come, Mairwen," he growled, lifting up slightly, digging harder inside of me.

My hands scrambled over his shoulders, feet searching for purchase in the bed as I bucked against him, short snaps of sound cracking on my tongue with every thrust inside of me, little whines of refusal with the retreat.

"Fang's fire, look at you," Ronson breathed, his glare turning tender. "You're stunning."

I flushed, heat crackling through me like a whip snap, and a shimmering, startling warmth followed. I came with my eyes wide open, with a fractured shout, and with Ronson staring down at me in wonder. He didn't stop moving and his hand reached between us, petting me softly, drawing out the quaking pleasure, encouraging it in easing waves until I was limp and breathless, a careless giggle gusting out of me.

"Who needs a knot?" I mumbled, a dazed smile on my lips.

Ronson's eyes narrowed and he settled closer, the knot in question rubbing against me, reminding me of its immediate presence. "I'm flattered, but I think you may retract those words, omega." His nose rubbed against mine, and I slanted my mouth over his, taking what I wanted from the kiss—long licks and brief nibbles.

Ronson's form was crushing, securing me to the mattress, pressing me down in its thick comfort. I stretched beneath him and grinned as his lips parted and he groaned. "You're teasing me," he said, brow tangling.

Was I? I was! What a thought. I ought to have apologized, except I felt quite...relaxed. A little drunk, and altogether the best I'd felt in...ever?

"A little," I admitted, wrapping my arms around his back, stroking the tense muscles. "It's your fault for putting me in such a good mood. I wonder if I can do the same."

I bit my lip and focused on where we were joined, trying to match the same circular motion he'd created with his hips. Ronson released a low moan, and his hips jolted forward, his knot threatening me with the first sharp edge of pressure. It might have hurt, except my body was set firmly on feeling wonderful, so instead the bite just made me clench around his cock.

"Fuck! Mairwen, I—"

Ronson's voice was ragged, fraying slightly into panic, and all at once, I recalled the power I'd felt that first night of having this man's pleasure in my hands. I wanted to claim that once more. I circled my limbs around Ronson and did my best to move beneath his weight, a slower and slightly less fluid motion, but one that did the trick in making him join me.

And oh, it was too delicious to have him inside of me, stroking neglected places that were now thoroughly awakened to what I'd been missing. I reveled in Ronson's groans, in his hands clutching my ass to hold me closer, but mostly I reveled in his scent, in the intoxicating taste of his kisses, in the heat of his skin pressing everywhere against my own.

He is mine, I marveled, and then amended, *For now, he is mine.*

If I had been given the choice, I would not have been brave enough to choose this man, this alpha.

He chose me.

A tear slid out from the corner of my eye, and I kissed my way to his jaw to keep Ronson from seeing any evidence. Not that he would notice, probably. His claws were starting to dig harshly into my ass, one hand sliding around to grasp and mold my breast against his palm.

"Mairwen, fuck. *Mairwen.*"

I tightened the grip of my thighs around his hips, squeezing my eyes shut to keep more tears at bay. Ronson's hips were jerking hard, his knot digging at my entrance, begging for my body to make room, to grant him closer.

"I wanted—I wanted tonight to be...just for us," Ronson panted against my throat, tongue circling over my pulse and teeth biting briefly. "The rut—"

"Let it come," I whispered, eager for the delirium, to see what else the alpha had in store for me, to lose myself in this whirlwind of physical discovery.

Ronson stilled, and for a moment there was only the cut of rough breaths from us both. Slowly and quietly, thunder grew, Ronson's purr, and I whined as he lifted himself away by a few inches. If he saw the sheen of tears on my face, he ignored it, ducking his head and settling his mouth gently over mine—a perfect, careful contrast to the rough press of his knot, now demanding instead of begging. I didn't know how to grant him access and the promise of pain stole my breath.

"Relax, omega," Ronson said, the words a sweet command.

I went limp in his grip, our kiss paused for our eyes to meet as he claimed me again, profoundly, undeniably.

There was no warning this time, and as ecstasy exploded from my core, storming through me, I realized that the brief, hollow echo I'd felt when he'd hooked his fingers inside of me had been a warning of what was to come.

You're built for my knot.

I was. I was made for this moment, this crescendo, this *unlocking*. Ronson held a key to a part of myself I hadn't known existed, and the flood that burst forth erased the woman I thought I'd known. I was caught in a tempest, this one turning the world around me, transforming me, and at first I was lost in the winds and the crackling lightning, alone and frightened by the force.

And then the thunder came, rattling my bones, purring in my ear, shaking the foundation of the nest. Hot skin and sharp claws touched me everywhere, and Ronson's quaking was as severe as my own. He was calling my name, pleading it, and I shook in his grip, found his dark, shocked gaze, and held onto it as my lifeline.

There was no escape now, the tug of his knot lodged inside of me and refusing any retreat, so we moved as one. Every nudge of him closer drew out new shudders of my release and every pleasured clasp of my body around his knot forced a groan from his lips and a soft splash of heat inside of me. We rocked in the nest, hands clinging to each other, mouths weak but still starving, and Ronson grew heavier with each passing second, more urgent, his gaze a little less focused.

The rut had arrived, and there was no question of holding onto my sanity as Ronson succumbed. Not when every slight movement, every kiss and scratch and grind, demanded I join him. Not when it was all so wonderful to lose myself with him.

Chapter Twenty

RONSON

I licked my lips and found my omega's nectar there. A growl scratched up my throat and I rooted forward, searching for more, snarling when her flavor was replaced with a cool, clean gulp of water. I jerked away, but a smooth hand caught my jaw, stilling me in place.

"Drink, Ronson."

I gaped at the vision before me. Perfect creamy skin, now marked with pink and purple, bruises from my kisses and bites, a map of touch that made my mouth water and long to repeat the claimings. Dark circles drooped under amber eyes, and my omega's lips were so red and swollen, they looked as though they might be just one more nibble away from breaking.

"Drink, *alpha*," she coaxed, a soft croak in her voice.

Oh, Mairwen, I thought, my chest aching, but I tipped my head back and accepted the draught of water she offered. The more I drank, the greedier I became, but also restless. I was erasing the taste of her. Unacceptable. My hands gathered silken bare flesh in their grip, and Mairwen's breath hitched.

"Claws, alpha."

I froze, jolting as I realized Mairwen's breathlessness was pain, not pleasure, and then spread my palms flat. I tried to clear my throat, but all that came out was a snarl. "I need—"

"You need to drink and eat first," Mairwen said, and her own fingers slid into my beard.

"How long?" I asked, blinking and trying to bring the nest into focus, but the only part that really mattered was the woman in front of me.

Her laugh was rough, and her touch moved into my hair, combing through tangles. "I lost track. Days, less than a week. Something like that."

Not even halfway through the rut. My head had probably only cleared because Mairwen was right and I needed the water and food.

"Will you hold the cup instead of me?" Mairwen asked, those ripe fruit lips curving up.

"*No,*" I rasped, my hands clenching briefly until I could rein my dragon once more.

She sighed and lifted the cup to my lips, waiting for me to drink it dry before twisting away to reach for a plate, the gentle flex of her body making my own tense with want. Scales glimmered over my arms, no longer hiding beneath my soft skin, and I glanced down to see them on my thighs too. Mairwen's body was stretched over mine, and it took me a moment to tear my stare from her glossy, reddened sex and to notice the chafed pink insides of her thighs.

"Are you in pain?" I asked, reaching between us to graze the scale-smooth backs of my fingers over the abraded skin.

"No, alpha," Mairwen said, catching my chin under her fingers and lifting it up, popping a cube of cured meat between my lips before I could press her for the truth. She sucked a berry between her lips, distracting me from my concern, and spoke around it. "You've been very attentive to my...comfort." She chose the last word with a blush on her cheeks, and I purred, leaning forward to nuzzle into her shoulder.

"You have to tell me the truth, omega," I said, letting a little alpha growl lace the words so she would listen. "What's tender?"

Mairwen squirmed against me slightly, and I shuddered as her slick sex stroked against my aching cock. "My breasts," she whispered, and then snorted. "Not that I'm surprised you've been focused there."

A bark of laughter escaped me, and Mairwen took the opportunity to feed me another bite of meat. It was salty and savory, but it was not what my mouth watered for most in this moment. I lifted Mairwen in my arms, ignoring her squawk of protest, savoring the feel of her body wrapped around mine, her plush weight cradled against my chest.

"Ronson—"

I lay her back in the sheets. "I need your taste on my tongue, omega. I'll be gentle."

"Ronson, you need—"

"After," I growled, drawing Mairwen's legs up over my shoulders. She opened her mouth to object, and I ducked down, running my tongue over the irritated marks on her inner thighs. Her words of protest died with a moan.

"WHAT'S—OHHHH..."

I rolled my hips forward, grinning into the terrible nest of Mairwen's tangled hair, and hissed as she fluttered and clutched against my cock and knot. I hummed in her ear, my hands sliding up and down her waist, one traveling slowly up to clutch her breast, massaging and waiting for her to whimper. She sighed and sagged against me. Good. She was healing quickly.

"What's that smell?"

I paused in my caresses and blinked into the dark shadows. It was night. Our candle lanterns had burned away the day before, and it made it easier to track the progress of the rut. Mairwen was smaller in my arms. No, I was larger now, my body more easily able to curl around her. I leaned up to stare down at her, and my jaw ached at the sight of her shoulder and the slope of her neck. I shut my eyes and held my breath, waiting for the strange urges to pass before clearing my throat.

"Smell?"

"It's...sweet. Like...like something melting?" she murmured.

My vision had sharpened as my dragon flexed and grew during the rut, and I studied the motion of her lashes with a kind of dumbstruck reverence as she blinked, a dark kiss of feathery softness against the tired circles growing deeper under her eyes. I couldn't clearly recall much of my previous ruts, but I was sure I'd never been so insatiable. I'd fucked to relieve the pulse and pain and demand of the rut, but it hadn't been so...celebratory and imperative.

"Omega...that's you—your perfume."

Mairwen's brow furrowed, and she turned her shoulders to glance at me, stare skidding quickly away. "I don't have a perfume."

"Ohhh, but you do," I purred, leaning down, swallowing the saliva that gathered as I pressed my lips across her bare shoulder. "A perfect, rich, drugging perfume. One I want to drown in, that makes me mad to touch you." I flexed my hips, and Mairwen gasped, a new flood of perfume bursting in the air and against my grazing mouth.

"But I-I never—"

"I'm learning all the ways to draw it out, omega," I rumbled in her ear, grinning at her answering shiver. "I covet every note of your scent. I want it coating me, and I want to keep it a secret, never let any beta or another alpha get a whiff."

"Ronson," she breathed, eyes falling shut and body rocking back against me, slick core sucking at my knot and stiffening my cock.

"On your knees, Mairwen," I rasped, but I didn't give her a chance to obey, already gripping her hips, rolling her onto her belly and pulling her up. My wings brushed against the walls of the nest, not as wide as my dragon's but twice as broad as usual. Mairwen was fastened firmly to me, my knot lodged deep, and she cried out into the pillows as I thrust forward, digging and rubbing my knot inside of her.

"You smell sweetest as you come for your alpha, omega," I snarled, the haze rising again, the rut claiming my voice and mind. "I want my prize. I want to slake myself on your scent."

Mairwen's perfume bloomed, brighter and thicker than ever, her legs and hands sliding in the sheets of the nest, her voice high and pleading. Pleading for relief, release. For me. Her alpha.

———

"WHAT DAY IS IT?"

"It's been... No, I lost track ages ago."

"I need—"

"Yes. Yes, yes, *yes*."

"Closer, *more*."

———

"ALPHA!"

I shuddered, my teeth clamped around my omega's shoulder, something like venom burning on my tongue.

Bite. Claim. Mine.

Mairwen whimpered, thrashing slightly in my grip.

"Hurts," she whispered.

Unclenching my jaw stung, as if my teeth had been bound closed with barbed wire I had to tear through in order to release the skin I'd tried to make a meal of.

Fang's fire, what is wrong with me?

I blinked, horrified and hungry in equal measure, staring at the imprint of my bite in Mairwen's smooth shoulder. I hadn't broken the skin, but it was a near thing, and already dark blue and purple blood vessels were bursting under her flesh.

A lie of a mark.

I shook myself and tried to pull away, realizing too late I was knotted in Mairwen. Her head tossed back and she shouted, and now her frantic movements were made of need, not nerves.

"So...so hot." Her hands slid over my chest, pushing me down into the mattress, and she rode me with that sweetly unpracticed urgency that made me buck in answer.

I reached for her cheek, drawing her gaze to mine and finding her stare glassy and absent. Her skin was burning under my touch, feverish, and I tried to sit up but was shoved firmly back in place. Her mouth hung open, breaths panting and whining.

"I need—I need—"

The truth reached me slowly, my head foggy from lack of sleep and food and anything but Mairwen's touch.

I'd put my omega in heat.

Pride pushed aside any lingering guilt at her bruised skin and anxious movements. I growled and rocked up, and Mairwen trembled above me as pleasure seized her. *A heat.*

An alpha's rut came every decade, an echo of the first mating urge we'd feel not long after taking our place as lead dragon, but omega heats were rare blessings, an equally matched biological *demand* for breeding. My father had called in quack doctors and supposed wise men, searching for some kind of recipe, a set of instructions, to put his omegas into heat. The truth was, no one knew what it took other than an alpha's pheromones, and most of the time even that didn't work.

"You need my knot," I said to Mairwen, licking my lips and ignoring another insane urge to bite her as her breasts bounced with her movements.

"Yes!"

"My cock."

"More, I need—Oh, alpha!"

I gripped her hips, rolling her into the bed and bracing myself above her, giving into the ruthless thrusts I'd been craving. Mairwen's eyes widened, her hands and feet scrambling in the sheets as she arched to meet my body.

"Yes, yes, yes! More!"

A triumphant laugh broke through my snarl. If only the island could see us now, beastly needs and bruised, weak bodies, still striving for more. Mairwen was a perfect omega, lusty and lush and so, so sweet, and they'd all failed to see.

I dove down, suckling on her breasts, and her hands dove into my hair, clinging to hold me closer.

"More, alpha," she whined, locking her legs around my hips. "I need *more*."

I woke to the sound of knocking and snarled at the interruption, drawing Mairwen's body tight to my chest.

"Ronson, are you *alive?*" Niall's voice called through the wood.

"Leave," I called back, my voice rough and crackling.

His voice muttered something inaudible, but his steps retreated with a final parting shot of, "It's been *three* weeks."

I ought to have been startled by the news. Even my first rut hadn't lasted a full two weeks. But I was too tired to be anything at all. Anything but...

I skimmed my hand over Mairwen's side, sighing as I found her skin warm but not scorching. Her heat had broken. My rut had settled. We were free from the breeding urges at last.

After *three* weeks.

My lips curved, and the tired skin burned as they stretched. Mairwen wasn't the only one sporting the wear and tear of the rut now. Her heat had drained me of my last reserves. I'd fucked her until my cock refused to last, suckled at her clit until my jaw locked up, and then given her my fingers until my body could rouse once more.

Insatiable omega.

Mairwen was entirely limp in my hold, not stirring at Niall's call or my touch, and it took me a few minutes of her stillness for panic to creep into my head.

It wasn't *unheard* of for a delicate omega to not survive an alpha's appetites in a rut, but—

I groaned as I sat up, every inch of my body protesting, and my breath froze in my chest at the picture of the woman on the bed. The wreckage of a woman. Mairwen was covered in love bites, some much closer to a *bite* than a kiss. I scowled at the marks, baffled and shamed at the recollection of how badly I'd wanted to really *mark* her, tear through her flesh. Her hair was a terrible mess, a little greasy but mostly snarled into impossible tangles. I picked up one slightly matted lock, ignoring the tired burn of my eyes, and set to work on repairing the mess I'd made of my omega.

If only I could quit smiling and feeling so damned *pleased* with myself at the same time.

Chapter Twenty-One
MAIRWEN

I screeched, jerking awake in a sudden shock of frigid water, splashing and flailing.

"Steady, steady. There you are."

My body shuddered and sagged reflexively at the purred words, settling back against a warm chest, thick arms banded around my waist, holding me upright in the churning sea.

"I was getting worried," Ronson said, leaning down and nuzzling against my cheek.

I twisted in his arms and gasped, the gently abrasive friction of touch shocking tired nerves over every inch of my body. I wet my lips and found them sore and swollen. Ronson's hold loosened, but he buoyed me in the cold water, and the icy lick over my breasts was a startling relief, even as I shivered.

"The rut?" It was as much of a question as I could get out through slightly chattering teeth.

"Try and relax," Ronson said, smiling. "You'll adjust quickly, I promise. The rut passed. And your heat broke yesterday, early morning. Or maybe before, but that's when I woke. You've slept since."

"M-my heat?" I murmured, but my hand tightened over Ronson's shoulder as I recalled the hazy, panicked, boiling heat within the nest.

"I'm so hot. I'm—Alpha, please, *I need... Cock. Knot."*

I blushed and slid down into the sea—Ronson was right, I was adjusting to the cold—ducking my head as if I could keep my memories from Ronson's view. As if he hadn't been *there* himself.

"Lean back."

A warm hand clasped the back of my neck, and I obeyed without thinking, my eyes sliding shut on a sigh as Ronson helped me dunk my head in the cold water. A small moan escaped my lips, and the hand on my hips tightened. An ache in my scalp I hadn't even realized was there melted away.

A tight fist gathering up my hair as I whined, scratching at the sheets, strong hips plowing against my ass, a soft, snarling purr sounding behind me.

My eyes opened, and I found Ronson's gaze taking an unhurried path over my chest, down to where my legs were wrapped around his hips. He looked hungry, although not in the same blazing, devouring way he had in the nest, abyss eyes roving over every inch of me. They were lighter now, in the morning, almost the color of dark chocolate, and he smiled gently as I caught him staring.

The sea swirled around our waists, and I studied the scene, looking up at the high cliffs and the spires of the castle. Black rocks dressed in seaweed and barnacles rose up around us, where Ronson had settled on a smooth landing.

"I perfumed."

He drew me up, and water sluiced down my back, heavy, long strands of my hair slapping against my bare skin. I shivered, and Ronson gathered me up to snuggle against his warm chest. If I didn't think *precisely* about the events of the rut, if I managed not to examine them too closely, there was still a kind of ease between us now. The hair of his chest was familiar against my body, the huge frame of him a memorized shape between my thighs.

"You did. Exceptionally," Ronson purred in my ear. He lifted my wet hair from the sides of my neck with gentle claws, grazing over sensitive skin, and then pressed his face to my throat, breathing there for a moment. "It wasn't the first time, Mairwen. You've been perfuming for me since the start."

I stiffened, and his hand on my hip slid to my ass, squeezing. "I have?"

Ronson nodded, stroking his beard over my shoulder. "Only barely at first. More and more every day since. I won't take the nest down now."

"But the rut is—"

"Over. And I'll wash the sheets myself. We'll use the velvet curtains for our blankets. But that nest is ours now, Mairwen."

It was too easy to fall into this alpha's dark stare, into his low rumbling words and the steady drone of his purring. Had he stopped purring yet since I woke? I didn't think so. *He wants me in the nest? Ours?*

"You're going to wash the sheets yourself?" I asked instead.

"I threw open the windows before I flew you down. It needs to air out," he said, flashing a grin. "But I don't want any other scents inside that room...for now. I'll wash the sheets after I've bathed you and fed you. You can rest more."

My eyes widened. "Ronson, you don't have to—"

He growled, cutting my objection off, and I caught my breath as his head ducked down, but his mouth landed so lightly over mine, just enough to steal the words from my tongue, to soothe my bruised lips and tease them with a feathering touch.

"Indulge your alpha, Mairwen," Ronson purred, his voice vibrating against my tender skin. "You have no idea... You were *a miracle* during the rut."

His words and the low rattle of his voice brought a dozen moments of the past weeks to mind, a shivering heat racing through my skin, *almost* tempting me to beg for more. His mouth on my breasts? No, they still felt bruised and aching. His fingers on my sex? No, I still throbbed numbly. A kiss? I licked my lips and ruled that out too—they were too raw and chapped. What I wanted would have to wait. My body needed more rest.

"A bath does sound nice," I said, circling my arms closer around Ronson's shoulders.

He rewarded me with a nuzzle against my temple, and his wings lifted from the sea, shaking water droplets off. I laughed as I was sprayed, and he nipped at my jaw. Even that spot was sensitive too! I wanted a look in the mirror.

Ronson's arms squeezed me against his chest, and I withheld my whimper as his body pressed to tired bruises. The water seemed to pull in refusal as his wings beat, dragging against my hips, my legs, my toes, but we broke free with a splash, and I held my breath as Ronson raced up the cliffside and to the tower, trying not to think about the fact that we were both bare and flying up past the windows of the castle. We would only have been a flash of skin. No one was likely to be looking, surely.

My face was hot as we landed on the windowsill, but any embarrassment quickly evaporated under the sudden shock of stepping inside the room. Ronson had thrown the windows open, allowing a delicate breeze to circle the space, but it only seemed to carry the scent with it.

And the *scent*.

I gaped for a moment, dizzy in the churning air, the rich sweetness and subtle smoke, like the incense inside one of the old temples for the great dragons. Ronson's purr thickened, and his hands on my hips began to stroke.

"Good, isn't it?" he rumbled.

It was...intoxicating.

My eyes watered and I tried to cling to Ronson's shoulder as he peeled me away. The enormous tub was filled with fresh, steaming water, waiting for me. Ronson's head ducked, and his brow furrowed as he found a tear sliding down my cheek.

"I did this?" I asked, breathing in.

His expression softened and he tugged me closer. I nuzzled my face into his chest and recalled burrowing there during the rut, catching my breath and kissing the skin. I pressed my lips tentatively over his heart, and the gesture was easy and comforting.

"You did, omega," Ronson said, bending slightly to press his lips to the crown of my head.

I sighed and let him direct me into the tub, down into the water. The alpha's omega was meant to serve him, not the other way around. But I didn't protest as Ronson ran a sponge carefully over my skin, kissing the red marks and purple bruises he'd made during the rut. I closed my eyes and let the sudsy water wash from my hair, his fingers traveling gently through the strands. I parted my lips for the bites of food he fed me as the water eased my tired muscles.

And when he led me back to the nest, only gauzy cotton curtains still standing, bed dressed in fresh sheets but no less potently coated in our scents, I slid into the pillows and blankets and accepted his kiss on my brow before falling back to sleep.

AFTER TWO DAYS of quiet rest, recovering from the exhausting weeks of the rut and my heat, Niall put his foot down.

"The betas have started to ask questions." Niall's voice echoed from a distance. Ronson hadn't let him—or anyone else—approach the door. He'd been making any trips for food and water himself.

"Tell them the truth, then," Ronson grumped, but he was sliding his arm out from under my shoulders. "Their alpha was rutting his omega like a mad beast—"

"Ronson," I hissed, lifting the book I'd been reading aloud up to cover my flaming cheeks.

"—for weeks on end and had no real intention of stopping," Ronson finished, grinning at me and winking one dark eye. "At least not after some well-earned rest."

I squeaked and dragged the blanket up over me. We'd been fairly chaste—kissing and gentle touches aside—since I'd woken from the heat. I'd talked Ronson into letting me wash him, and while he didn't sport as many love bites and bruises as I did, there'd been no disguising the irritated redness of his cock. But I was curious about what it might be like once we were healed, without the urgent craze of the breeding instincts.

"Believe it or not, I did tell them that."

"Niall!" I cried, throwing the blanket off.

Ronson laughed, drawing his trousers up his hips.

"I'm just not sure they...believed me," Niall said.

I swallowed and turned my face away. Of course the island didn't believe Ronson would be *enjoying* his rut with me. I'm sure if Niall passed along the information I'd gone into heat, it would've been a society-wide joke to share. The awkward, scentless, improbable omega in heat? Laughably outrageous.

But it did *happen*, I reminded myself. Whether or not society believed it, Ronson was pleased with me.

"Give me five minutes," Ronson called to his brother.

I turned back and tried to make my face blank, but Ronson was watching me as usual, prowling back to the bed with his pants half-buttoned and his chest bare. He was too beautiful, too powerful. Dark scales gleamed under tan skin for a moment as he crossed through a stream of sunlight, and I recalled the way those scales had come forward during the rut, his cheekbones sharpening to dragon spikes, his shoulders armored between my thighs as he licked me clean.

"You can't dawdle," I said.

"I can if I want to," Ronson said, bucking up his chin. My eyebrows rose, and his gaze glittered with hidden mischief. He was still young by dragon standards, but he hid that boyish mischief well, buried under stern command. Not from me, though.

"I think you like riling Niall up. You know he wants what's best for you," I said, leaning back as Ronson crawled onto the bed. I fell back into the pillows, and Ronson braced himself above me.

My body still throbbed slightly with aches and bruises, but there was a quivering interest in this moment with him above me, the slight urge to spread myself in invitation.

"He does. More importantly, he wants what's best for the isle. I'll leave in a moment. But first..." Ronson lowered himself on top of me, and I caught my breath, eyes widening.

"First?"

"I want my omega to kiss me goodbye."

I laughed, but I lifted my chin. Ronson had been treating my lips and inner thighs with a light salve that tingled but seemed to do a world of good, and it didn't hurt at all to open my lips to him. The bedsheet covered me up to my breasts, a thin barrier as Ronson settled his weight against me, not grinding, simply pressing, and I couldn't help but squirm beneath him. His tongue traced my lips, and I parted them eagerly. We hadn't kissed like this since the heat, and I found myself suddenly starving for his taste.

He purred into my mouth, tongue delving, and I sighed, suckling and answering him with a lick of my own. Every spare second he'd bought from Niall was given to the kiss, and I wasn't nervous or shy at all. The foggy hours of the rut and heat had changed me. I knew this man, knew the hitch of his breath and the weight of his body and the taste of his hunger. I moaned as he stroked inside of my mouth, whined as his knees trapped my legs shut.

And slowly, the air between us filled with a thick, heavy sweetness. Ronson groaned as he pulled away, dropping fully onto me, burying his face in my throat.

My perfume. He'd wanted my perfume. He was dressing himself in it before leaving the nest. For his own comfort? Or for the betas?

I tucked my face into his silky hair, kissing aimlessly, and stroked the back of his neck with my hands.

"The dressmaker is coming today," Ronson rasped, not moving from on top of me.

"When did you have time to manage that?" I asked. It was difficult to catch my breath with him using me as a mattress, but I didn't mind.

"Put Beatrice onto it before you woke."

"It'll still be weeks before they have anything ready for me. And in the meantime, I have next to nothing to wear since you destroyed—"

"Rightfully. I have no regrets."

"—my undergarments."

"Good riddance."

The rogue didn't deserve my laughter but I couldn't resist, and Ronson purred, nuzzling against the thrum of my pulse.

"You're running out of time," I murmured.

He grunted but peeled himself away from me, stopping to

sit up at the edge of the bed, scuffing his bearded jaw with his hand. "I think I'll shave for dinner."

I tried not to pout. I liked Ronson's beard. It scraped a little, yes, but—

"And for dessert," he said, eyeing my lap with dark hunger.

My breath hitched, my perfume bloomed, and Ronson left the nest grinning.

"WELL, I certainly see the necessity for a change in shape," Miss Priscilla Pettyfer said as her measuring tape pinched around my waist.

I flushed but held my chin high to keep from seeing the picture of us in the mirror. Miss Pettyfer, in her perfectly pristine flocked muslin and polished leather boots, was a delicate and miniscule woman who walked and snapped her dreaded measuring tape with authority, but spoke in the gentle and demure tones of a human amongst dragonkin.

And there I was, in a shabby and well-worn chemise, my skin marked and reddened, dark circles still shadowing beneath my eyes, and my usually drearily straight hair attempting to escape out of the braid I'd hastily arranged. Something about being so close to the sea seemed to coax my hair into an unruly halo of waves. I was precisely this human's opposite, and I wobbled in place on the cushioned stool where I was perched.

"Your waist is quite small. It would be a shame to drape it under swathes of fabric," Miss Pettyfer remarked, almost to herself. It took me a moment to hear the words for what they were—a compliment.

"Small?" I echoed, glancing into the mirror and seeing the

point where the strip of brown leather hatched with black lines tightened around my waist.

"An hourglass figure was all the rage only a century ago," the seamstress continued, drawing the leather strap away and then holding one end to my waist and letting the other hit the floor.

Hourglass. Not plump. Not...all the other disparaging words I'd heard murmured from my mother's lips, or from someone like Adelaide.

"It's not...not really small," I said, reaching my own hands tentatively to my stomach. The soft swell of flesh hadn't vanished in the rut.

"It draws in," Miss Pettyfer said matter-of-factly, catching my wrists and then moving my hands to either side, settling them in the crook of my waist before it spread out to generous hips. "Dresses now are cut to create long, straight figures of women, but I've always believed the best dress will admire the woman within it, not reshape her. Your waistlines need lowered, for starters. But I think we must start beneath the dress." She stepped back and eyed me head to toe twice before lifting her keen gaze to mine. "Forgive my impertinence, Omega Cadogan, but would you lift your breasts for me?"

I ignored my blush and raised my hands to my chest, lifting the heft of my breasts and trying not to imagine what Ronson would say about this situation.

"Yes. I see. We need support, not constraint." Miss Pettyfer flicked her measuring tape and squared her shoulders. "Hold that position, please. We have a few more measurements to take."

Chapter Twenty-Two

RONSON

❦❦❦

"There are barely enough viable omegas to go around as it is—"

"If a man might provide for more—"

"There'd be more if the alpha wasn't letting them dash off the island to ancients know where."

"—and you want to claim new ones and keep the old too?"

"Discarding a woman who served me well with a son just because she is no longer likely to provide a second is hardly the *gallant* gesture, now, is it? And my estate—"

"I think we've had enough," Niall whispered to me under his breath.

I stirred in my seat, glaring at the gentlemen gathered around Lord Cambeth's table, and caught the tail end of the ridiculous conversation I'd been doing my best to ignore. Which had been surprisingly easy, considering the much more pleasant recollections readily available in my head.

"Cambeth, *sit*," I snapped, with the full weight of my alpha strength.

The conversation died abruptly, a screech of wooden legs

on stone tearing against my ears as Lord Cambeth obeyed, against his will or otherwise.

"My lord," he tried.

"Lady Cambeth granted you a son, as you said. A nice, healthy heir, if he is the one I saw racing past the window on your excellent horseflesh earlier."

Lord Cambeth's chest puffed. "He's a fearsome rider. Very strong lad."

"And you have a daughter too, I believe," I said.

Lord Cambeth nodded, smirking slightly. "A great beauty."

Lord Cambeth had partnered an omega once before that I could recall, but there'd been no heir or issue, and she'd taken ill one winter a couple decades ago and passed away. The circumstances were only the slightest bit mysterious, and the investigator I'd put to the case had come away with nothing to incriminate the lord.

"You've been blessed," I continued, nodding to the man, feeding his pride. "You're correct that it would be quite ungentlemanly of you to cast your omega aside just because she is now past the age of fruitfulness."

Lord Cambeth's eyes gleamed with victory. The fool thought his absurd argument had won.

"Just as outrageous as it would be displace her in the home she has built you, in the bed she has made for you; to hand the keys over to a new woman, while she remains trapped to watch her position usurped," I continued, clasping my hands together on the surface of the table. "You ask too much, your boon is refused. You have the riches of your family. Be grateful for what your omega has granted you."

Silence rang around the room, and I knew from Niall's raised eyebrows and downturned glance that I had perhaps spoken too harshly against the older beta. But his request was absurd. To claim a second omega and hold two in his home together? A new one to bed and breed, while the elder, the *mother* of his dragonkin children, was set aside?

"Then I request—"

"Do *not* request to me you be granted the right to break contract with Lady Cambeth," I snapped, rising from my seat. "You have your heir. Your estate is secure. Be *grateful*," I snarled softly.

Too harsh, Niall's voice cautioned in my head. But it was too late. And I wondered if maybe it wasn't time for me to start showing my teeth to these betas. Had I been too timid with them, trying to prove I was not my father, approaching their queries with reason and bargaining? I was the alpha. I didn't need to *cajole* these men, not when I could command them.

I narrowed my gaze and looked around the room. "The selection ceremony has confused you gentlemen. You think your omegas are a *right*. They are our *privilege*."

Betas shifted irritably around the table, some slack-jawed with shock, others eyeing one another as if to say *See, he's against us*. In truth, I *was* against those men. I'd been treading gently, trying to grease palms and make friends out of enemies. It meant I'd had to compromise where compromises were not deserving.

"They are *your* right, alpha, are they not?" Gideon Millward called out from the far end of the table.

Damn. I wet my lips and avoided Niall's eye, meeting only Gideon's gaze. "By the law of the selection, yes, an omega is my right. But as you gentlemen may remember, it was a right I refrained from for a great many years." Half-hearted chuckles answered my raised eyebrows. "Until Omega Cadogan."

And I dare one of you to tell me you really wanted her, I snarled in my thoughts, answering myself with, *Mairwen would be wasted on them*.

I leaned back in my chair, shoulders rolling and wings flexing restlessly. Thinking of Mairwen only reminded me how badly I wanted to be back in our nest. Preferably with her pinned beneath me, begging and gasping.

"My lord, be reasonable. You have denied us at every turn today," Redmond Palmer said, forcing a tense attempt at a jovial grin on his face. "You are our alpha. You are meant to serve the interests of the island. The interests we present—"

I raised my hand, and the man's words died on his tongue, the corners of his eyes flinching at my interruption. "The interest of the *island*. Which are not *solely* the interests of the beta gentlemen who seek to make a profit or claim young women to their bedchambers."

"Lord Cadogan!"

"Mr. Buchanan, your mine has thrice now claimed lives. It has been sucked clean of profit, sir. I would be a fool to grant you the loan to reopen, to send more human workers—"

"They desire work!"

"—to their graves in the hopes of another thin vein of tin," I said. "I agree that men out of work is *not* what we wish for the island, but families without fathers will serve no better. We must divert the efforts elsewhere. Alpha DeRoche has opened his seas another fifty miles to us."

"You want me to become a *fishmonger*," Mr. Buchanan spat. Lionel Buchanan was young and the only son of a once-prosperous mining empire, the only inheritance left to him and one that had been drained of its fortune long before his birth. He was very handsome but at the brink of being entirely penniless, and had persuaded no omega to his side yet.

I gathered in a deep breath, fire swirling in my lungs, my claws digging into the arms of the chair, and Buchanan paled slightly.

"Should you change your mind, a suitable account will be arranged for you to start a small fleet of fishing boats."

"And the new mine?" Redmond Palmer asked, eyes gleaming brightly, almost as if he were *eager* for my refusal.

"There is no evidence to suggest it would be successful and certainly not safe. You need certifiable studies, Palmer. It will serve none of us if the isle crumbles into water pits you all insisted upon digging."

Palmer's lips pursed, but he sat back.

"There's no cause to evict paying tenants from their homes," I continued, waving to another beta who'd wanted to unhouse a number of human farmers to add hunting land to his estate. "And as you already have an omega, Lord Cambeth, no, you may not take another. If you gentlemen wish to gain my permission, I suggest you bring me better causes."

Grumbles circled the table, a few betas brave enough to mutter choice words. I collected my courage and turned to glance at Niall. He was already staring at me, face *nearly* blank. Except I'd known him all my life and there was a sliver of humor in his eyes, the faintest twitch at the corner of his mouth. Good. If Niall were truly angry with my decision, if he thought I'd done wrong, there'd be no hint of a laugh. We pushed back our chairs in unison, and I immediately debated the merits of flying to the village before returning to the castle. I could stop at a bookseller, see if I could find anything for Mairwen that wasn't already in the library. Then again... there were likely plenty of books in the library she hadn't read *yet*, and she was there, waiting—

"Alpha Cadogan, a word as you leave, if you have a moment."

I paused, and my head cleared of russet locks and pink skin. Gideon Millward stood at the edge of the room, his eyes on the milling and exiting gentlemen as if he hadn't spoken a word. Interesting. I glanced at Niall who nodded, waiting.

"Speak to Lord Posy. Issue an invitation to the castle for him and his wife in..." Mairwen was only seeing the seamstress today, and for some reason I didn't want the rest of dragonkin to see her in her old dresses again, even her parents. Not now that she was mine. "In ten days' time."

Niall split away from me, weaving through the betas to catch Mairwen's father, and I dipped my head to Millward, continuing on my path toward the exit.

"I'll warn you now, I'm no more likely to say yes in private to something absurd than I am around that table." We would have to walk together, and it would slow my progress back to the castle. To Mairwen. At least it wasn't late.

"And certainly not to a beta with as little to offer you in influence as I do," Gideon answered.

I shot him a glance over my shoulder as we stepped outside of Lord Cambeth's manor, but he seemed easy, unbothered by the truth of his statement. I grunted in answer, and his lips quirked.

"For what it's worth, I don't think this request is absurd, but you're welcome to correct me," he added. "I never did congratulate you properly."

My steps slowed. Some betas were stepping into carriages already. Many remained milling in Cambeth's drawing room, no doubt to speak my name in foul tones.

"On selecting your omega," Gideon said, matching my pace to walk beside me as we headed for the gates of the Cambeth estate.

"Ah. Few did," I muttered, but a smile curved at my lips. "But given my fortune in Mairwen, I'm inclined not to be offended."

Millward stared at me, full of questions. Did he think I was as mad for choosing Mairwen as the others did?

"That's her perfume, I take it," he said, obvious curiosity lacing his voice.

I stopped still, turning to stare down my nose at the man in warning. "I am willing to hear you out, Millward, but I suggest you take a different track."

"I don't mean to offend, but there was never any sign—"

"You're being very bold."

Gideon laughed. "I'm being honest with you, alpha. You seem the type to appreciate that sort of thing."

"Any dragon lucky enough to have an omega will have her perfume on his skin, yes?"

"If your aim was to prove to dragonkin that we are wrong to doubt your choice, presenting Omega Cadogan would do more. Now they'll just think you wear false perfume," Gideon said, shrugging his shoulders and turning to pace forward.

I gaped briefly at his back. The *nerve* of this beta. He reminded me of...Niall. Damnit. That meant I *liked* him. "*This* is what you wanted to speak to me about?"

Gideon paused, and I marched to catch up with him. "It's all that any of dragonkin wants to speak about, my lord. But you're right—it isn't why I asked for your time. I know a man, a farm laborer at the moment, who grew up north of Skybern. His father worked for a pearl farmer, and he learned the process himself when he was young. He uses it still, although on a small scale."

I kept silent, my eyes on the high tower of the castle, where I hoped to find Mairwen waiting for me when all this was done. The longer I was quiet, the more Gideon Millward fidgeted in our walk, turning to me, waiting, then turning away again.

He huffed. "You think I should've brought this proposal to the table."

"That is how these things work." I was curious, though,

not that I wanted to let him know as much after he'd been so impertinent about Mairwen's perfume.

"It is also how someone like Gamesby or Palmer would've purchased this man's expertise out from under me before I had time to persuade you to loan me the capital. It's not a quick return on investment, my lord."

"I imagine not. How long?"

"If I want to do it right, at least a year and a half before the first harvest. Preferably longer. But after that point, profit is easy."

I nodded. I knew enough of the market to know Damian Worthington owned portions of several pearl farms. That investment had made him rich, and with his wealth, he'd secured influence over his betas.

"How much are you offering me?" I asked, not tearing my stare from the castle.

"Five percent," Gideon answered.

I laughed. "Five percent is very low."

"Five percent, and you can choose me a partner. Another beta gentleman. One who would be..."

I stopped. Gideon and I were safely away from anyone else. His own home was in the opposite direction, but he was following me toward the castle. I turned to face him and waited for him to finish.

"Grateful," he said at last, shrugging. "One whose gratitude might sway his ear away from other influences."

I recalled the faces around the table today. Gideon Millward was smart to offer me this. I didn't *need* more than the five percent share. I needed allies who'd want me alive to keep their pearl farm invested until it bore fruit.

"Can you stand to work with Buchanan?" I asked. Niall had seen Gideon going to Buchanan's house after I'd denied him Francesca, but I'd never seen the men interact in person.

There was something *private* between them, and I wondered how it would affect Gideon's decision.

He paled slightly, staring warily at me, but I'd never been very good at expressing myself, and it suited me in moments like this to be impenetrably obscure.

"He's not the worst of them, really, just desperate," Gideon said, holding my gaze. "Give him a fortune, and you'll have his loyalty back. It won't take us much to start. Just a few men."

"Bring the numbers to the castle. Not today," I said, catching the sharp gleam of triumph in his expression. It was after luncheon, an early time to declare myself done with business, but...

Gideon only bowed. "Yes, Alpha Cadogan. Thank you."

I spread my wings and leapt to the air without another word.

Chapter Twenty-Three

MAIRWEN

Sex was rather wonderful.

I rolled my hips, shivering as cool air trickled through the parted curtains, teasing against the sweat that beaded on my back and between my breasts. Beneath me, the Alpha of Bleake Isle groaned and twisted, body bucking up, pleading with me.

I grinned, and Ronson huffed.

"You love to torture me," he rasped, propping himself up on one elbow and reaching for a breast with his free hand. I stiffened, but he was gentle, brushing his thumb across my nipple till it pebbled for his touch.

"I don't think you know the meaning of that word, my lord," I said, leaning forward and grazing my breast against his mouth. His tongue flicked out as dark eyes stared up at me, and my breath hitched in my throat.

"I don't think you've fully considered what I will put you through in exchange." Ronson's smile was sharp, but his hands stroked softly up my back as he drew me closer. Our eyes slid shut as his lips enveloped my nipple. I whimpered and rode his length, that perfect fit inside of me, and for a few minutes we were wrapped around one another, harmony in motion, a matching rhythm of heartbeats.

I cried out, partly in delight and partly in mourning, as heat burst within and Ronson growled, sitting up and holding me close, kisses coating my throat and shoulders. His knot pushed against me and I gasped, halfway crashed from the height I'd reached, ready to fly again. Ronson's voice was buried into my skin as I thrust my hips down and accepted his knot. The grip of his teeth on my shoulder was the harsh edge against the hazy ecstasy that billowed through me at the union, and my fingers flew into his hair, tightening roughly, holding his bite at bay.

"Ronson!"

He snarled into my shoulder, fingers digging into my back, and for a moment—and the recollection of a dozen moments in the rut and heat where I'd held him back—I thought he would fight the restraint, take what he craved. I would let him. I hadn't told him so; we hadn't really discussed some of the events of the rut—neither of us were entirely lucid at the same time—but there was a strange thrill racing through me when he bit me, a kind of impossible joy.

Slowly, as pleasure simmered inside of me with the slow pulse of his knot and our release, Ronson's jaw loosened. His tongue swiped around the edges of his teeth, a glittery warmth like the shimmer of sunlight on the waves of the sea racing through me. My fingers stroked through the strands of his hair, and Ronson and I both sighed.

"Forgive me," he whispered, kissing the bruises that still healed from his bites. "Fuck, Mairwen, I—"

"It's all right," I soothed, rocking on his lap. His hands gripped my hips, stilling me, and his head shook, falling back into the cradle of my palms.

He's mine, a little voice whispered.

"I don't know what's wrong with me. I'm going—I feel as though some kind of madness is taking hold," he murmured.

It was difficult to tell—his eyes were too dark—but there was a kind of haze in his gaze that reminded me of the rut. I combed my hand through his hair, and his eyes blinked slowly.

"You really want to bite me?" I asked. He'd come so near so many times already, but that had been the rut and it had passed now, hadn't it?

Except that when he'd returned from his meeting with the betas, he'd snarled and tackled me into the nest, nearly tearing my robe in his haste to be inside of me. I hadn't been *much* less urgent, clawing at his trousers, rucking my hips up to draw him into me before either of us were fully undressed.

It was late now, dark outside. We hadn't left the nest.

"I don't want to hurt you," Ronson said, slowly easing back, turning us to face one another on our sides. He was still firmly fastened inside of me, but without much movement it was just a pleasant glowing feeling, a warm union.

"But..." I prompted.

He sighed, and one hand left my hip to cover his eyes. "It's... Mairwen, I know..."

"Ronson, I'm hardly in a position to run screaming from the room at the moment, just—"

"*Yes.* I want to *bite* you. I-I-I've never... I have no idea what comes over me, but—"

I stretched, pushing Ronson's hand away, covering his mouth with my own, breathing with him as much as kissing him until he settled.

"It is strange," I admitted, and he flinched. "No stranger than the impulse I have to *let* you bite me."

He stiffened and then his arms were wrapping around me, chest purring against my own, body leaning closer. I laughed and pressed my palm to his chest.

"Ronson, stop. You're *not* going to bite me."

"Just a little nibble," he teased, rocking closer, distracting me with a sudden wave of pleasure.

I snorted and wrestled against him, which did very little to persuade either of us to stop moving. "Hasn't it occurred to you there might be *consequences,* you mad beast?"

He blinked, pushing me onto my back, settling comfortably between my thighs. "Consequences?" he repeated, brow furrowing.

I stroked his shoulders. "It's not a...a reasoned impulse, is it? The urge to bite me?"

He stared at the mark on my shoulder, freshened by his latest attempt, half in hunger and half in worry. "No, it isn't. It feels like... I don't usually feel separate from my dragon, but this is his impulse. You think there might be more to it than just a monstrous desire to devour you in every manner possible?" His lips quirked and his head ducked, kissing my lips, chin, and the tip of my nose in succession.

"I think it merits some research."

"Ahhh, I see. This is an excuse for you to get back in my library," Ronson purred.

"You did catch me before I could visit today. And it's been weeks, you know," I said, fighting my grin.

This was lovely. This teasing. This man who *liked* me and kissed me and apparently desired me so much, he wanted to *bite* me. Perhaps that shouldn't have been so flattering. Perhaps Ronson was as wrong an alpha as I was an omega.

For now, I didn't mind.

"How on earth did she manage to get these done so quickly? It's only been a few days!"

"You're the alpha's omega. I'm sure she's eager to please,"

Ronson said, rising from the bath we'd been enjoying together, twisting a towel around his hips and pacing closer. "Go on, let's see."

My hand hovered over the delicate tissue paper, scattered with dried lavender and tied shut with a sprig of rosemary. I lifted my face and narrowed my gaze at my alpha. "Whatever she made for me, you musn't tear, slice, rip—"

Ronson barked out a laugh, and for a moment I forgot the small delivery of clothes—only a partial deposit on the order Miss Pettyfer had arranged for me—or indeed anything but Ronson's smile.

"If she's done her work adequately, I agree, but if we find another narrow-boned corset designed to torture your—"

"You are absurd," I said, huffing and pushing the tissue aside. My lips pursed at what I found.

"That looks like boning to me," Ronson muttered.

I sighed and pulled the contraption up from the box, my head tipping to the side. It was similar to a corset. "You may have to resign yourself to my need for structure to acquire a pleasing shape." Ronson growled, and I rolled my eyes, grateful he was at my back.

This wasn't a typical corset—at least that much was true. I pinched what I assumed was boning in my fingers and found that instead of a rigid pole inside, it was something flexible but thick enough to offer support. Instead of being slightly curved but primarily cylindrical in shape, the corset also included what could only be referred to as...cups. Rather obscenely sized ones. Made partly of lace. For my breasts.

"I suppose I'd better try it on," I murmured, standing up, finding my face unexpectedly warm. It was one thing to have Ronson tearing my clothes off, but it seemed an entirely more intimate thing to have him watching me put on my undergarments. "I'll call a maid."

A tan hand plucked the linen and lace from my fingers. "Nonsense. I think I can manage to offer assistance."

"My lord, that isn't—"

"Don't be prim, omega, or I will be forced to use these laces to tie you up and remind you that there is no one better acquainted with how pleasing your form really is than myself."

My mouth dried, and I glared up at Ronson through my lashes.

"Disrobe," he coaxed, his eyes crinkling at the corners.

I was only wearing a robe in the first place, having risen from the bath when the maid knocked on the door to deliver the parcel. It'd been almost a week since the rut, but Ronson was still steadfast in not allowing anyone else into the room, although he now allowed the castle staff to approach the door.

I sighed and untied the robe, sliding it from my shoulders. Ronson's shadow was cast in three directions across the floor, lit up from behind by the candlelight in sconces. A rough purr thrummed across my shoulders as the silk robe hit the floor, and I found myself fighting a smile. Whether it was his intention or not, Ronson never left me in any doubt of his interest.

"Don't get distracted, alpha," I teased, surprised by the slightly husky rasp in my voice.

Ronson grunted and cleared his throat. "Lift your arms, omega."

I shivered but obeyed, and Ronson stepped closer with a rustle of fabric as he examined the new corset and then stretched it around my form.

"I disagree, by the way," he murmured as I adjusted the shape of the contraption against my chest, swallowing hard as I realized the lace of the cups extended down over my nipples, the shelf-like cups lifting my breasts high.

"Disagree?" I asked absently. The lace felt scandalous

against my sensitive tips, and I was already anticipating a reaction from Ronson when he realized.

"Your shape needs no structure for enhancement. I like you in that robe best of all," he said, soft and rough, amending a moment later, "Aside from bare, of course."

The corset fastened around me, and he hummed, one hand cupping my waist. The curve of the corset was more of a deep V, settling comfortably at the narrowest part of my stomach. It was not the slim slope of fashion, but it was comfortable, and it did prove Miss Pettyfer's point about my waist.

"Laces," I prompted, glancing over my shoulder, only to find Ronson giving my behind a heated stare.

"You don't need to be strapped in, Mairwen," he grumped.

"This corset has no straps and needs to stay up, my lord. Please, I want to see how it's meant to look."

He harrumphed but began the laborious process of tying in the laces.

"Tighter," I said.

"No."

"Ronson," I huffed, rolling my eyes and reaching my hands back to do it myself. "It's not pinching me, and if it's too loose it will chafe."

He batted my hands away. "Fine, fine. I don't see the point of this. If your dresses fit properly, what need do you have for this?" But with gentle tugs the corset grew comfortably snug. It was strange to wear it against my skin like this; I should've put my chemise on first, but I wasn't planning on keeping it on for long. Only now I realized I was wearing this corset and *only* this corset, my sex still exposed to the warmth of the room, the towel wrapped around Ronson's hips occasionally grazing against my bottom.

"That's good," I said, twisting a little and finding that

whatever magic Miss Pettyfer had worked into her new boning allowed me a comfortable range of movement. I glanced down and blushed at the high heave of my breasts below my nose. "I think I ought to put a dress on to see—"

"Oh no, you don't!" Ronson laughed, catching me by my shoulder. "I put in a good effort on those laces, I deserve a—"

His hands on my shoulders had turned me to face him, and his words died on his tongue. I was staring steadfastly at his chest, but I didn't miss the telltale movement tucked beneath the towel around his hips, and it gave me the bravery to glance up to meet his eyes.

Ronson's mouth hung slightly open, still frozen mid-sentence, and slowly his hand guided me to step back, to offer more of myself to his view, his black eyes caressing slowly over me, always pausing to linger at my breasts. His purr started, loud and approving, and I blushed as my own perfume answered automatically.

"A mirror," I murmured, trying to twist out of his grip.

"I changed my mind," Ronson rumbled.

"About what?" I whispered, unable to meet his eyes again.

"This is a lovely piece of invention." Ronson's hand slid from my left shoulder, tracing the delicate edge of lace that covered one breast down into the narrow V between, the slight callus of his finger scraping against my skin.

"I think it might be a bit..." I waved my hands in front of my chest, and my eyes rose up to the ceiling.

"Oh, it is absolutely..." But Ronson's gesture was to pinch my nipple through the lace, my breath hitching roughly as his claw pressed into my flesh.

"You can't—You promised—" He hadn't. "Ronson, *don't* tear this off of me," I said, meaning it as a stern warning but finding it came out as a breathless plea.

His sharp smile and the dark, hungry pierce of his stare against my skin did nothing to reassure me, even when paired with him rumbling, "Oh, omega, I don't intend to take it off you at all."

I squeaked as Ronson bent just enough to scoop me off my feet, his hands helping themselves to my ass. "Alpha?"

"I think I might be jealous of your seamstress, Mairwen," Ronson growled, hefting me against his chest, marching us toward the nest.

"Miss Pettyfer?" I laughed, my legs wrapping around his waist.

"I thought I alone understood your body so well," Ronson said, his head ducking down to bury itself between my breasts. "I underestimated her."

I snorted. "I think you likely have her beat in other areas, Ronson."

He arched a brow, and I found myself riveted to the sight of his lips parting, his tongue grazing over thin lace, dragging closer to my right breast, teeth glinting briefly in a grin. "I should hope she doesn't know your taste as well as I do."

Such a claim was so patently outrageous it deserved a hearty bout of laughter, not the breathless catch in my throat as Ronson latched his mouth to my nipple and began to suckle me through lace.

"It did not come up at the fitting, no," I murmured as the shadows of the nest enveloped us and I was laid down on my back.

"Just to be sure," Ronson purred, nipping my breasts before shoving me farther up the mattress and delving between my thighs.

Chapter Twenty-Four

RONSON

❧❧❧

"**B**rother! Halt!"

I paused, my chin raised high, the tantalizing promise of Mairwen's perfume just a thin thread on the air, a trail for me to follow toward—

"Ronson, for the love of flight!" Niall huffed, catching me by the shoulder and shaking me slightly. I glared back at my half-brother. "Don't you *dare* go into that library," he snapped.

"What on earth—" I tried to shake him off, but he tightened his grip on my shoulder sternly.

"You can lie to yourself if you like, but not to me," Niall said, an exasperated flush spreading over his face. "Dalton is on his way here *now*."

I glanced at the open door of the library, my mouth watering and teeth aching. "He's not expected for another half hour—"

"If you go chasing after Mairwen right now, the pair of you will be in the nest before ten minutes is up, unless you plan on knotting her in the library."

My body swelled and my eyes narrowed, a growl bouncing off the stone bricks surrounding us. "Niall, I am warning—"

He raised his hand and rolled his eyes. "I'm not trying to be an ass, Ronson. I'm happy for you, but Tylane's tail, you have no *focus* lately. One whiff of—"

"Ronson?"

I straightened and spun toward the door at the soft call from inside the library.

"Is that you?"

"Damnit," Niall hissed.

Only the fact that my intolerable half-brother was *right* kept me from charging through the open door. I had been... easily distracted as of late. *More like obsessed with your omega*, I thought to myself, a smile bursting onto my lips as Mairwen appeared in the frame of the doorway. I took a step toward her, guided by an immediate, imperative to touch the purple mark just peeking out of the collar of her new dress. The mark of my teeth, the bruise she let me refresh each night as we gasped and held onto one another with the endless urge to touch and taste and sate our mutual craving.

"Omega," I purred, wrapping an arm around Mairwen's waist and tugging her to press against me.

"Mairwen—*Omega Cadogan*," Niall corrected at my snarl. "I'm begging you. Lock yourself inside that library until dinner and do *not* let Ronson in."

Mairwen laughed as I growled, but she sobered as she realized Niall was serious. I had been late to two meetings Niall had arranged this week so far, it was true, but Mairwen hardly needed to *sequester* herself.

Except that my head was ducking, cheek nuzzling into her throat, tongue dipping out, and I tried to nudge her back inside the library where we could be alone.

She grinned, pushing at my chest. "I see. I *am* trying to do my own work here." Her hands caught my face and tipped it up until my vision was full of Mairwen's flushed cheeks and bright smile, her amber eyes glittering with humor and an answering need. "Quit making Niall's job harder than it already is, alpha. I will see you at dinner."

"In our rooms," I rasped as she lifted her face up for a kiss. I would've missed the slight flinch if I hadn't been so close to her already, but it vanished and Mairwen slipped free of my grasp too quickly, her delicately-shaped waist so perfectly showcased in her pretty new dress, making her hard to catch.

"Very well. Our rooms for dinner," she murmured.

I frowned in confusion as she ducked back into the library, shutting the doors quickly behind her. My shoulders hunched as a lock turned, snapping loudly into place, as if baiting me to break it open just to prove I could.

Niall cleared his throat, and I shot him a glare. *He* was the reason I wasn't currently kissing my omega.

"She's quite taken Cook in hand, you know. Our dinners have seen great improvement," he said, quietly and wisely moving out of reach. "You should consider attending one."

I snarled, but Niall only laughed, marching swiftly toward my office and leaving me to follow sulkily after him.

"I DON'T BELIEVE Alpha Feargus plans to bring his new omega, but there is some...expectation of seeing Omega Cadogan," Ewan said, chin propped on his fist, seated across from me at my desk.

"Torion took an omega straight away?" Niall asked from behind me at the same moment I blurted, "*Expectation* of Mairwen?"

Ewan glanced between us, and I restrained my growl as he addressed Niall first. "Weeks before any selection ceremony could be arranged, he claimed his right to another dragon's omega. The circumstances... Well, it depends on who you speak to. I believe he may have done the woman a favor. She'll remain at his keep, preparing for the impending rut."

I sat back in my chair, stunned. Was Torion trying to beat me at ill-advised actions? I was incurring the ire of my betas left and right lately, refusing to compromise. But I had *never* even so much as flattered a local beta's omega. Even my father hadn't gone that far, although there were rumors of extended affairs.

Ewan shifted in his seat and met my gaze next. "Gamesby and Palmer have been spreading information to the other isles, my lord."

"Rumors," I spat out.

Ewan hummed and shrugged. "Not...rumors so much as, well, the general opinion of local dragonkin on your choice of omega." I bristled in my seat, but Niall set his hand on my shoulder.

"Mairwen's made no real public appearance since you claimed her," Niall said.

"There hasn't been *time*," I muttered. And I had firmly banished Mairwen's old clothes, making it next to impossible for her to leave the castle. Not that I really wanted Mairwen leaving the castle. I barely tolerated these extended periods of tackling business and politics without her.

"Palmer and Gamesby have exaggerated her unsuitability, I suspect," Ewan said, waving a careless hand.

I stiffened, glaring across my desk at the Skybern spy who had served me well for many decades. He blinked, hands stilling on the arms of his provided chair as the air around me shimmered with restrained fire.

"No doubt," Niall said, calm where I could not be.

The next person who made any remark regarding Mairwen's suitability as my omega was going to meet my dragon's claws.

"Bring my omega here," I said, voice low and stony.

"I'm sure that isn't—"

"Ronson, honestly," Niall sighed.

I twisted toward my brother. "Go to the library and bring her here to meet Mr. Dalton."

Niall's eyes just barely resisted rolling, but he left immediately, Ewan Dalton shifting uncomfortably in his seat.

"My lord, I meant no offense."

"I am aware of the general misconception surrounding my omega, Dalton. I only wish for you to make your own opinion. Meet her, and then share whatever gossip you like."

Ewan Dalton shrank in his seat and nodded. "Of course, my lord."

Niall must've flown down the halls, because it took him very little time to return. Perhaps he understood the risk to Dalton's neck if left alone with me for too long. The door to my office creaked, and Niall stepped aside, holding it open to make room for Mairwen's entrance.

"Omega," I purred, rising from my seat, Ewan hurrying to do the same.

Mairwen could not have responded better if she'd been trained for this moment. The call of her rich, hypnotizing perfume slowly filled my office as she approached. Her cheeks and chest were flushed, and she'd undone the long braid of her hair so that silken strands swayed against her back as she walked. She'd chosen one of the less rigid stays to wear under her dress, but had foregone the lacy fichu, leaving the swell and curve and shadow of her breasts exposed above her collar.

I held out my hand to her, only sparing a glance for Ewan Dalton when Mairwen rounded my desk, her thick lashes batting shyly against her blush.

The beta looked stunned, his nostrils flaring, one hand braced against the back of his chair. I didn't know what nonsense he'd heard filtered down from Gamesby and Palmer, but I was sure it bore no resemblance to my omega.

I'd been an idiot not to see the jewel Mairwen was right from the start, but I would admit privately that the subtle changes she'd undergone since I'd claimed her would make a significant impression on those in her acquaintance. The presence of her perfume alone would likely set Gamesby back on his heels.

"Mairwen, this is Mr. Ewan Dalton of Skybern," I said, wrapping one arm around my omega, stroking my other hand from the tip of her chin down her throat, the flush increasing at my touch, more perfume blooming eagerly. Mairwen blinked at me, her pupils growing wider, and it took her a moment to tear her stare from mine to notice the stranger.

She leaned back in my arms for a moment, shrinking. Then, as if catching herself, her shoulders and spine straightened, and she offered the dazed man a steady smile.

"How do you do, Mr. Dalton," she greeted, a pristinely creamy and delicate hand raising in offering.

I met Niall's gaze as Ewan stumbled closer, accepting Mairwen's hand and bowing low over her knuckles. Niall's lips twitched, and he nodded to me—a concession.

"Omega Cadogan, an honor," Ewan rasped.

I cleared my throat in warning, and the man jumped back, his legs hitting the seat of his chair. Mairwen looked back up to me, eyebrows slightly raised. I brushed my thumb down the line of her spine, wanting to dismiss Ewan immediately and reward her for...for being her, really.

"Mr. Dalton arrived with news of an impending Flight of Alphas," I explained. Mairwen's eyes widened, and she glanced between us, her breath catching and pressing her breasts to strain against the squared collar of her dress. "I think Mairwen ought to join me at the Flight, don't you, Dalton?"

The man huffed out a laugh, still gazing in shock at my omega. I twisted my arm tighter around her, tugging her chest to lean against me. He'd stared quite enough for my taste.

"I absolutely agree, Lord Cadogan," Ewan said, ducking in respect to me. I swallowed my growl as his gaze darted to Mairwen's round hips.

"I'M GOING to say something I think you won't like to hear."

My steps scuffed over the stone floor, and I shot an exasperated glare at Niall. We were on our way to dinner, which I had sent word to Mairwen *would* be in the dining hall, doing my best to ignore my brother's goading look.

"Have you considered not saying it?" I answered dryly.

Niall grinned. "Almost since the beginning."

I sighed and scuffed a hand over my face, wondering if I was about to come to blows with my brother. We'd done it plenty as young men growing up together. My father had even tried to set us against one another, although that had generally failed, for we were never enemies of one another more than we were enemies of *him*.

"I worry your regard for Mairwen will make her a target," Niall said, hands clasped behind his back, hidden under his tucked wings.

I blinked and continued walking. "Ah."

"I *am* happy for you, Ronson. And as you know, I said from the start that she was—"

I shoved at Niall's shoulder, and he laughed as he bounced off the wall of the hallway.

"You think I shouldn't have introduced her to Dalton," I said.

"Not exactly. I trust Ewan's interest is in our favor. And I do think it's about time to correct misconceptions about Mairwen's suitability as your omega. But it isn't just tales of her remarkable perfume he's left here with. He'd be a fool to have failed to notice *your* response to her."

"He seemed awfully busy with his own response," I grumbled.

Niall shrugged. "Perhaps. But if it'd been Gamesby in the room today—"

"I would've made Mairwen a target. Yes, I know," I rasped. We were nearing the stairs down to the dining hall and I slowed, shaking my head. "I wasn't expecting..." It was unfair to admit what I'd thought of Mairwen in the beginning. "She is..."

Niall reached for my shoulders, gripping me by the arms. "What she is to you, brother, is plain to see. All I'm saying is that perhaps you should attempt to make it *slightly* less so when around men we don't trust."

I frowned. Mairwen deserved to have me making a fool of myself over her in front of all of dragonkin, not just the isle. But Niall was right. I wanted her safe at my side for many years to come, not in the arrow sights of one of Gamesby's plots.

What if there is an heir? What if she didn't drink the tea? What if...

We reached the bottom of the stairs, and I stopped still. Mairwen was smiling, her arm wrapped around Beatrice's, the pair of them laughing softly. She twisted, glancing over her shoulder at me, eyes bright and welcoming, and my entire body lurched in her direction at the rough tug from within my chest.

She is mine.

I would do what I must to keep her that way.

Chapter Twenty-Five

MAIRWEN

❦

"**M**y lady."

"I have been wondering if perhaps the cream sauce *and* the souffle won't make the meal too rich after all," I said, chewing on my lip as I hovered over Cook Guinney's great tome. The pages open revealed a shocking collection of scribbles from my edits.

"Omega Cadogan," the older woman snapped.

I flinched and glanced up, and Cook sighed, gently prying her book from my clammy grip.

"There will be no more changes made to tonight's dinner, Omega Cadogan," she said with rare patience.

"I just want—"

"It to be perfect. So you've said." If I wasn't mistaken, there was a hint of a smile on her lips. "And I will do my best for you, Mairwen. But you must *leave my kitchen*. Please," she added with a roll of her eyes.

I fidgeted, and her eyes narrowed. My lips parted, and the human woman made a not un-dragon-like growl.

"Yes, Cook Guinney," I relented with a sigh.

"Find your alpha, girl," the woman muttered, marching

away, and I wasn't sure if she really meant me to hear the words. "Surely he can keep you out of my hair for a few more hours."

My lips twitched, and I twisted and wove through the busy staff of the castle. Her suggestion was not a bad one. Ronson had wrestled me back into bed when I'd tried to rise before the sun, and while Niall had caught him for a quick question earlier, I knew Ronson's aim today had been to soothe my nerves.

Which were rioting.

One would think I was preparing for the Flight of Alphas, not the simple dinner planned for my parents' visit. Except that I knew what to expect from my parents, and that was so much worse than the prospect of the unknown.

"There you are."

My breath caught and I gazed up the stairs to find Ronson at the top, his wings blocking the light from the windows behind them.

"More dresses from Miss Pettyfer arrived. I thought you might—"

"Would you take me flying?" I called up to him.

He was quiet for a moment, and I caught a glimpse of his handsome profile, so strong and sharp. "It's chilly today...but yes, a short one. You wouldn't rather see the dresses?"

I hurried up toward Ronson. I was more used to the excessive climbing and walking this castle took now, but the flights of stairs still left me breathless. He caught my waist before I'd reached the top of the flight, and I laughed as he lifted me the rest of the way, clutching me to his chest.

"There isn't much I'd rather be doing than flying with you, if I'm honest," I said, looping my arms around his neck.

Ronson took me for morning flights when Niall wasn't dragging him to business straight away. I'd grown addicted to the wind against my skin, the view from high above the isle and the water, the touch of morning rays on my cheeks.

"I think *you'd* rather see the dresses," I teased.

"It's not the dresses themselves so much as you putting them on and taking them off again," Ronson said, grinning.

My right hand reached automatically for his cheek, studying the swell of his smile against my palm. *I love when he smiles.* I brushed the thought away before it could carry on, growing into something uncomfortably large and achingly heavy. I'd had to do that more and more often since the rut had passed and Ronson and I had become...

Still hungry for one another, sometimes shockingly so. But more than that too. We'd become friends. And I'd never had a friend who laughed when I was dry and sarcastic, who read books with me, who offered compliments and praise.

Certainly not one who made me tear at my bedsheets as I cried out their name, I thought wryly.

"Mairwen, if you keep looking at me like that, our flight will be very short indeed," Ronson purred, gazing up at me with hooded eyes.

"Flight first," I murmured, kissing Ronson's lips. "Seduction after."

He continued to purr as he carried me to the nearest balcony.

"MY GOODNESS, Mairwen, you will drain the alpha's coffers, putting on dinners as extravagant as this one," my mother trilled, pushing her pork nervously around her plate. She batted her lashes at Ronson at the far end of the table. "You really mustn't let our little mouse run amuck with your pocketbook, my lord. She does know better."

"Please, Lady Posy. Don't discourage Mairwen. She's made a world of difference to all our tastebuds," Niall laughed.

My mother's answering sound was uncertain, a small squeak of nerves as she caught Ronson's glowering expression.

The dinner was not going well.

Ronson had been calm to start, calmer than I, despite his best efforts to exhaust me in bed after our flight. He'd laughed as I changed my dress thrice, and growled and distracted me when I tried to lace one of my new corsets too tightly.

He'd greeted my parents warmly, shaken my father's hand, kissed my mother's cheek, guided them on a tour of the castle, which my mother had never visited before.

And then it began.

"Dear Mouse, with all these stairs, I'm quite surprised to see you're still so plump. You mustn't just laze about, you know."

Ronson had stopped dead on the stairs, glaring down at my mother, and it had been up to Beatrice to lead us on. She'd chosen the library.

"Mairwen's favorite room, of course," Ronson had said, stroking a hand down my back and resting it at my waist.

"Too curious for her own good, as usual, I expect," my father had bantered, laughing. "But I doubt Lord Cadogan has many of those silly novels you waste your time on, does he, Mouse?"

My tongue tied in my mouth, and my head ducked to hide my flush, Ronson's hand sliding away as he'd stepped in front of me almost like a shield.

"Mairwen and I read together nightly."

"Don't let her bore you with that drivel, my lord. Mairwen knows a man's interest doesn't extend to those trivial stories," my mother had cooed, taking my arm and drawing me to her side. "Goodness, Mouse, what *are* you wearing?"

Niall and Beatrice had tried their best, making up for my awkward silences and Ronson's souring mood, managing to get us all around the table. But even Cook's divine efforts at dinner hadn't distracted my parents, and the flavors I'd been so excited to arrange were now ash on my tongue.

Ronson cleared his throat, and my mother's nervous laughter died away, the entire table turning towards his words, forced out through almost clenched teeth as they were. "In every respect, Mairwen has exceeded my expectations of what an omega might be to her alpha."

For a moment, all the little slights and subtle chastisements of the evening melted away. Ronson's eyes caught mine, and the vision of him blurred slightly through grateful tears. I sat up in my chair, wanting to soar over the long table and into his lap.

"Very generous of you, Cadogan. Very kind indeed," my father said.

My eyes blinked, and I swallowed the stone in my throat, finding the food on my plate nearly untouched.

"Sir—" Ronson growled.

"You have been very good to us," my father continued. "I considered myself quite lucky when Mr. Evans stepped in and could be persuaded to take on our little mouse. But it was an exceptional honor, and quite a surprise, I might add" —he chuckled here and my mother laughed delicately in agreement, their eyes flashing fondly in my direction— "when you claimed her for yourself! And very considerate of you to settle things between Gryffyd and me."

Ronson's knuckles were white around his silverware. I'd left my own abandoned on the table, my appetite ruined for the night.

"I wonder, my lord, if you would be open to discussing a proposal I brought you some years ago," my father continued.

"Darling," my mother cautioned lightly.

My eyes narrowed, stare bouncing between them, and Ronson shifted in his seat, brow furrowing.

"A proposal?" my alpha repeated.

Niall was frowning now too, staring at my father.

My father chuckled again, but the sound was reedy and tight, not earnest. "Not long after you took the helm of alpha from your father, in fact. When you declared indentured servitude unlawful."

"Father." I sat up sharply, but only Ronson spared me a glance, not that my voice had come out more than a whisper.

"I understand your position, of course, my lord," my father said, waving a hand. "But if you recall my proposal—an amendment, if you will—to better those humans' conditions, provide some token payment—"

"Father!" This time, there was no ignoring my voice. My mother called my name, but I ignored her, ignored the stares from everyone, even Ronson, as my father turned cooly in my direction. "Not only is this not the time nor place for you to propose business to Lord Cadogan, but on such a topic? I know it was your trade once—"

"Mairwen," my father began.

"—but it was an immoral and cruel practice. You said yourself the terms were never designed to benefit the humans. There is no civilized society now that still abides by servitude, so how precisely would you propose finding—"

"Mouse, you know *nothing*," my father snapped, a rare fire in his tone that set me back against the spine of my seat. "That trade you think so little of was what built the roof you resided under for nearly twenty-seven years!"

I wet my lips but couldn't find the words. Not before the alpha spoke.

"Omega Cadogan."

I blinked, looking at Ronson, but it was my father he was staring at with narrowed black eyes and fists clenched upon the table.

"My lord," my father murmured, ducking his head. "Forgive my daughter's temper. Our Mouse is softhearted and knows little of these matters."

"No," Ronson said, voice heavy and the word clipped. "Her name is Mairwen. Or Omega Cadogan. Not *Mouse*. And in fact, Lord Posy, your daughter—*my* omega—knows quite a lot. Not least of which is my position on indentured servitude. I am aware that the restrictions I placed on the flesh trade impacted your own investments, but no bond between us, no matter how precious," he said, eyes flicking to me and words rasping sweetly, before facing my father once more, "will influence my decision on that matter. I recommend, sir, that you listen to Mairwen's advice on this and drop the subject."

And with that declaration, coldly given and yet leaving me warm from head to toe, dinner resumed in silence.

MY MOTHER HUMMED as she sipped the second small glass of sherry I'd poured her and shot another hopeful look toward the parlor door. Beatrice had retired just a few minutes ago after carrying the lion's share of our after-dinner conversation, and I knew we were both only waiting for one thing at this point. For Niall, Ronson, and my father to join us, preferably only to say our goodbyes for the evening. My head was pounding and there was a tight ache at the back of my neck, and I must've been right that the dinner menu was too rich, because I'd only taken a few bites but my stomach had been turning ever since.

"I do worry for you, Mou-Mairwen," my mother stammered, carelessly tripping over my name.

I blinked at her, baffled that Ronson's sharp words at dinner had made enough of an impression for her to even try and correct the slip of the nickname.

"Worry?" I repeated.

Her eyes were watery, but they often were and the tears rarely spilled over. The implication of her sentiment was enough for my mother. "It's a terrible burden for a girl like you, Mouse, to be the alpha's omega. Everyone will be waiting for you to produce another alpha. And oh, my darling girl," she gasped out, leaning forward and clasping my hands in her feverish grip. Her voice trembled, and this time a tear, a beautiful one, did trickle down her cheek. "They are such *terrible* births. My mother lost a sister to the last alpha, you know. And so many other families lost girls too."

I swallowed hard, biting down the confession that itched at my throat. My loyalty was not to my mother now. It was to Ronson, my alpha. *My omega knows quite a lot.*

I straightened, squeezed my mother's fingers, and breathed slowly in and out, trying and failing to expel the ragged pain in my head. It didn't work, but it did make my voice steady when I spoke.

"Gryffyd Evans has lost a number of omegas in births as well, Mother. Many women are lost to dragonkin with every match." I searched my mother's lovely, smooth features as her brow furrowed. *Did you drink the tea, Mother? Is that why there was only ever me?*

"It's-It's true Mr. Evans was not what we might have wanted for you—"

I pulled my hands free from my mother's grip, giving her a simple pat. "Things will turn out as they will. Ronson—Lord Cadogan—he isn't careless with me."

"He's very severe," my mother murmured, shaking her

head and saying more to herself than me, "and you are such an unusual sort of omega."

I wanted to scream. I wanted to throw open the windows of this pretty parlor—one I met with Cook in to organize meals and took tea with Beatrice in, but still felt as though it belonged to someone else—and leap from the windows and take flight over the sea. Not forever, not like Francesca longed to leave the isle and seek adventure, but at least until my parents had loaded themselves into their carriage and returned home.

But I need Ronson to fly, and he was—

A rumble of male voices approached from the hall, and my composure gave way, sinking me back into the cushion of the chair I sat in and drawing a sting of relieved tears to my eyes.

Please let this night be over, I thought, even considered shouting, as the door opened.

Chapter Twenty-Six

RONSON

Where is my omega? I thought, entering the parlor, staring at the wilted creature in the armchair by the fire. Mairwen's eyes glittered in the light, but their amber glow had dulled. I swallowed hard around yet another snarl and then cleared my throat.

"The Posy carriage is called," I managed, refraining from the rest of what I would've liked to say. *It's time to say goodbye to your damned parents. Unless you'd rather I simply toss them out without another word. Let's not invite them back.*

I claimed a greedy gulp of air, stepping inside the parlor. Mairwen's perfume lingered here, remnants from another day, but it had withered to nothing since her parents' arrival. Still, any taste of her was a relief.

Mairwen rose from her seat, smoothing her skirt and wearing a placid smile as her mother babbled wishes of staying longer, her worry for her daughter.

"Please, M-Mairwen, you must—"

No! "Omega," I called, cutting the woman off. Mairwen's glazed expression drifted in my direction. I extended my hand, and Mairwen sagged with a released breath, crossing toward me.

All night, the Posys had seemed to grasp and pluck at Mairwen's luster, like pulling feathers from a beautiful bird. And I had made the terrible mistake of keeping silent, of letting Mairwen take their subtle jabs and sweetly-delivered doubts. At first, I'd been more concerned with showing the Posys that I wasn't a tyrant of an alpha like my father, that I was taking good care of Mairwen, that she was happy here with me. Mairwen's quiet seemed out of character, and I'd thought it was only nerves, that she would want her parents to be pleased by the castle or by me, by her situation.

The truth arrived too late. The Posys had as little faith in their daughter as men like Gamesby, a fact they were not shy to express.

Mairwen reached my side, and I spared no time in wrapping my arm around her shoulders and tugging her against me. She was listless, leaning into me, her perfume vanished and replaced by a slightly bitter note. Here was the woman they called *Mouse*. Her shoulders had drawn up during dinner, closing around her as I might use my wings to shield me. Her eyes had dropped, rarely lifting, and the only flare of life I'd seen since the start of dinner was when I'd rebuked her father, color and life rising to her cheeks. Embarrassment, yes, and shock, but at least she'd been *Mairwen* in that moment. I should've gone on chewing her parents' ears, correcting every rotten word they'd said, praising every moment I'd spent with their daughter, but I'd been tied up in knots of anger, fairly certain that if I spoke another word, it would come with dragon's fire.

Better to get them out of the castle and coax Mairwen back to herself. I had a better idea of how to draw her perfume out now, but it wasn't her perfume I missed. Or not most of all.

"You look tired," I whispered to Mairwen as her mother bustled closer.

"I have such a headache," she admitted, her voice even softer than my own.

Mairwen's father watched us, something like understanding taking over his expression, his gaze on my hands where they spread over the base of her spine. *Yes, you fool, I have the sense to be grateful for your daughter. To see her value. To to—*

I stiffened, blinking down at Mairwen's head. It was tilting on her neck toward my chest, but not helping itself to its place there.

Albert Posy was still watching me as I lifted my stare, his eyes narrowed slightly and a bemused smile on his lips. He'd tried to press his case again over brandy, but he'd been docile and almost resigned at my stern refusal.

"I could not have dreamt of such a superior match for you, my dear," Lord Posy said to Mairwen.

You should have! I wanted to scream. *You should've demanded it for her.*

"Thank you, Papa," Mairwen said, but she didn't pull free of my embrace, only extended her hand to her father for a brief and gentle shake of hands.

"I hope you will both excuse us. Niall will see you to your carriage, but I should like to take my omega up to our nest," I said with the merest hint of a bow to the older couple.

Mairwen's mother's eyes widened. "Nest? Your—*your* nest?"

My hard smile came easily, my hands stroking up and down Mairwen's back as I puffed with pride. "I refuse to dismantle it. Mairwen did such a superb job." My omega pressed closer, her face lifting, eyes growing bright. I raised one hand to cup her jaw, to refuse her parents her gaze as I continued, "I could not have chosen a finer omega. Not if I had scoured every isle and all of dragonkin."

Mairwen's mother gaped, but I wouldn't let my omega look away from me, not until Niall had led the Posy's out of the parlor and down the hall. Mairwen's eyes welled, glossy tears clinging against her lower lashes, and her cheek pinched in where she chewed at it from the inside.

"I'm sorry," she gasped out.

I battled the urge to go tearing down the hall, roaring and snarling and scorching the backs of the Posys. They should've been Mairwen's respite from the judgment of the dragonkin. Instead, they appeared to have been one of the worst sources.

"You have nothing to be sorry for," I said, my voice too rough and harsh.

Mairwen stiffened in my arms, braced herself, and opened her lips to say more. I dove down and stifled the words with a kiss. She didn't relax, just accepted the firm press of my lips to hers. The bitter edge of her scent eased, and she let out a whimper.

"Don't say another word on the topic, omega," I said, and this time I was able to purr through the growl. Mairwen's eyes fluttered shut, her shoulders softening with a sigh, and she wrapped her arms around me automatically as I bent and lifted her from the floor.

Mairwen was silent as I carried her up to our tower, her head resting on my shoulder. The longer she was quiet, the longer *I* said nothing, the more tense she grew in my arms. I needed to get her into our nest, to kiss every inch of her, to pay her every compliment, before she managed to vanish in front of me completely.

"I meant what I said to them, Mairwen."

Her breath caught, and I glanced down, my heart dropping several stories at the sheen of tears on her cheeks. She didn't answer me, but her fingers dug fiercely into my shoulder, crumpling my dinner jacket in her fists.

"I've never considered myself a lucky person, but I can

only grant the moment I saw you wandering through the woods as Gamesby and Adelaide plotted my murder as divine intervention—the old dragons showing me the better path."

Mairwen's brow furrowed, and she lifted her chin. "You wouldn't have chosen Adelaide after hearing all that. I didn't need to be there."

"Discovering the plot was not the part where I got lucky, omega," I purred.

And there! I praised every star in the sky for the little puff of Mairwen's perfume.

"Then again, the first time Niall saw you, he told me you were the most interesting omega of the lot," I continued. "So perhaps I would've taken his advice while on stage."

Mairwen was silent all the way until we reached the door of our room.

"If the first words you had ever said to me were 'You'll do,' I would certainly have vomited on your boots," she said.

I laughed, and another whisper of her scent reached me. "I should've chosen those words more carefully. I should've said..." *You're mine*, I thought, but couldn't quite say.

"'Hello, have you considered foregoing your corsets?'" Mairwen suggested, the bright note of her voice that I'd ached for all evening finally reappearing.

I laughed again and hurried us into the nest, depositing Mairwen in the cushions and turning back to yank our curtains shut. The fire in the grate illuminated the room, and the curtains were sheer, so there was just enough light to see the tiny smile on Mairwen's lips and the tired droop of her eyelids as she fell backwards into the pillows, rolling onto her side. She had a headache, and she was bruised, my perfect, succulent little omega.

I climbed over her, and Mairwen's face buried itself into the pillow as I untied the laces of her dress. Her seamstress had altered many of Mairwen's garments—formal and intimate alike—in ways I wholeheartedly approved of, including the silk shifts Mairwen wore against her skin. They had delicate little barely-there straps and were trimmed with lace, the back and collar plunging low so that when I opened her dress, there was lovely bare skin in view.

I leaned forward, kissing the nape of Mairwen's neck, brushing my thumb over the goose bumps that rose. "I should've said, 'Hello, I know we haven't spoken'" —another kiss, this one below the first— "'but I think,'" I continued, purring and whispering, gently pushing the sleeves of Mairwen's gown down until they reached her elbows and she drew her arms free, "'you are *exactly* what I need.'"

The words might not have been true at the time. I had fewer doubts about Mairwen than the rest of dragonkin, but not none. Still, they were the words I wished I could've given her.

Mairwen sniffled into the pillow and I paused, hovering above her, wrestling with the urge to strip her bare, plunge myself inside of her, and bring her so much pleasure, all thoughts of her parents or the rest of society were washed away.

There was another impulse. A gentler one. Mairwen knew our bodies hungered for one another, but there'd been little time to share much else with her.

I undressed her slowly, purring all the while, stroking her back and her hips when she shuddered with tears, rubbing her legs as I unrolled her stockings, until she was left only in the beautifully-shaped silk slip, one so perfectly crafted that it wrapped around her like a breeze or the sea water we sometimes went swimming in together. If Mairwen had to wear anything at all, it should only have been those slips.

I kept that thought to myself, pulling a sheet up to cover her from any chill before undressing myself with more haste. I kept my purr rumbling. If I wasn't going to give her my knot, purring was my next best alpha gift on offer. I kept an eye on her body, the little trembles that came and went, the incredible rise and fall and rise again of her silhouetted figure.

When I was bare, I slid under the sheet, the thrum in my chest roaring as Mairwen's hand reached back for me, catching my own and drawing my arm around her. It wasn't enough. I bundled her up, tangling her legs between mine, circling her in my arms, pressing myself to her back so closely that she too rattled, as if producing her own purr.

Little by little, her quavering sighs melted to steady breaths and her perfume laced around us, even as she sank into a weary sleep. I remained awake, remained purring, telling myself it would assure that even her dreams were safe for her that night.

IT WAS UNSETTLING to wake the next morning and find that Mairwen had slipped away before I woke. It was even more aggravating that it was not her I found in the hall, but my brother.

"Where's Mairwen?"

"In the library," he said, as if he'd known precisely what question would be first out of my mouth.

I'd only dressed in a loose linen shirt and worn trousers, and I paused in the hall, narrowing my eyes at Niall. "Why do you know that?"

He smirked. "Because I spoke to her there."

"Whatever business you have for me will have to wait a little," I said, scuffing my hand over my hair and eyeing the stairs, wanting my omega to appear. "I need to speak with Mairwen about the Flight of Alphas."

"Mm, that's what she's working on. Researching all the families," Niall said, nodding and turning to follow me.

I froze, blinking back at Niall. "Is she?"

Niall stopped too, reading me too easily. His voice lowered, and he leaned in, glaring. "Ronson...*what* about the Flight of Alphas were you hoping to discuss with her?"

I sighed, stretching my wings back to touch their spines to the cool stone wall. "I am wondering if it wouldn't be better if Mairwen remained here instead of joining me."

Niall's expression flattened, and he drew himself up. I sometimes forgot that my brother was nearly my own height. "Do you? Ronson, I..." He shook his head, rolling his eyes skyward. "Do you realize what a monumental mistake that would be? I know your motivations. I know what you feel for that young woman—"

"You were there last night," I hissed. "You saw what the Posys put her through."

Niall stepped forward, and I was too baffled by his raised fist to do anything but watch as it approached my face. If he'd been inclined, he could've landed quite the punch in that moment. Instead, he thumped firmly against my forehead, as if knocking on a locked door.

"You're an idiot," he said simply. "I *saw* Mairwen's parents express every possible doubt as to her competency as your omega."

"Fuck." The word grunted out of me as Niall's words sunk into my thick skull.

"And, yes, I saw how it belittled her confidence until she bore next to no resemblance to the woman I'd grown acquainted with here in the castle," Niall continued, leaving the obvious unspoken.

If I suggested to Mairwen that she might not be ready to join me at the Flight of Alphas, I would be confirming those doubts the Posys had tossed about last night. Which was unacceptable.

"I'll admit that I can't guess what the others will think of

Mairwen, but I will give even the worst of the lot the credit that they probably won't offer her insults to her face. Not like the ones she suffered last night," Niall muttered with a shake of his head, matching my pose against the wall opposite me. "If you show half the restraint you did with the Posys, we won't have a diplomatic issue on our hands either."

I laughed and let my head thunk against the stone behind me. "You would've made a good alpha," I said.

Niall was quiet, and I lifted my head to find him staring back at me, startled. "Thank you. But believe it or not, I do prefer my current position," he said.

"You deserve more respect."

Niall huffed and waved his hand, turning back to the end of the hall. "Much easier to get my work done when people only pay attention to me for the wrong reasons."

I followed, catching my brother by the shoulder, turning him to face me. "I mean it, Niall. *Thank* you."

He flushed, and his eyes darted every direction but mine for a moment, but he let out a breath and settled, nodding. "You would've been intolerably distracted if you'd hurt her feelings. I can barely keep you focused as it is. But come, no doubt by now Mairwen will be ready to teach *you* a thing or two about the history of dragonkin politics."

I clapped Niall's back and hauled him alongside me to my omega.

Chapter Twenty-Seven

MAIRWEN

'**O**ur *Alpha Falk, a goode reign of one hundred years or more, following the death of her mate—*'

I blinked at the page, my finger beneath the word *mate*, my other hand lifting a cup of tea to my lips. Slowly, I lowered the tea and set it aside, safely away from the ancient text.

'Following the death of her *mate...'*

Alpha Falk was a *woman?*

I'd found the word *mate* a number of times in regards to these historic alphas, and as near as I could tell, it referred to the omega an alpha had chosen to remain by his side for a lifetime. They usually produced male heirs at an irregular rate —more frequently than the ten-year cycle of a rut, to be sure —and were included in histories of flights, battles, and politics. But never had I heard of an omega mate rising to the rule of *alpha*. Had it been an honorary title offered during a time of peace?

No, I remembered this area in the records of battles, and there'd been at least three in the century she would've ruled.

I'd only assumed that she was the same Alpha Falk as her alp —*mate*.

I marked the page with a ribbon and then pushed back from my seat. Niall and Ronson were at the ports today, meeting with local merchants, which left me and Beatrice with the run of the castle. Her office was only two corridors away, and I hurried there, my hands fiddling in the deep pockets of one of my new dresses.

I'd told Ronson I would be researching the family lines of significant dragonkin today, and in a way, I was, but I'd long since worked through any information that might be relevant for the upcoming flight. No, for the past two days, I'd been searching for more mentions of mates. It seemed as though the further back I searched, the more I found, and I *knew* there must be some piece still missing, something that explained what made an omega mate different than an omega rut partner. It was possible that the word had simply fallen out of fashion, but every time I tried to push my curiosity aside, it continued to itch in my thoughts.

There had to be more.

I burst into Beatrice's study, and received her usual arched eyebrows in reply. But she smiled slightly too and set down her pen.

"What seems to be the matter, Mairwen?"

"Where...where do we keep the portraits of old alphas? The ones we no longer display?" I asked.

Beatrice hummed for a moment, head tilting. "There are a few attics that might serve as storage for that sort of thing," she said, rising and drawing a heavy ring of keys from her desk drawer, older and simpler-looking than the ones she carried at her hip day-to-day. "Some underground storerooms too, though I can't say what state anything would be in, if that were the case."

"I don't mind searching on my own, if you'd rather not," I

said, almost *wishing* Beatrice might hand me the ring and leave me to it.

Not that I didn't like the older woman—she was wonderful and we'd grown to be friends. And I suspected if anyone else in the castle would be thrilled to learn of a woman alpha in our history, it would be Beatrice. But it was *my* mystery for the moment.

Beatrice pursed her lips, and I sighed, relenting. "But I think...if I find what I'm looking for, you'd like to see it too," I admitted.

"Lead the way, Omega Cadogan," she said with a smile.

I blinked, turning toward the door, then paused and winced. "Well...actually, I don't know the way."

Beatrice laughed, and we set off together.

Two attics, one lower keep, and a very large closet later, I was giving up hope.

"Perhaps they didn't keep them after all," I murmured.

"Unlikely," Beatrice said, huffing and throwing a large sheet back over a collection of boxes that housed old dinnerware. "Dragons hoard, not discard."

I chewed on the inside of my lip briefly. "There is much of our history that it seems was...nearly erased."

"*Nearly*, yes," Beatrice said, leading us back out of the closet. "But you found it in the library, didn't you? Because whatever our alpha predecessors did not want the public to know, they couldn't bring themselves to destroy outright. If it exists, Mairwen, it will be here. Somewhere. Come, there's a long flight directly up to the attic just this way."

Truth be told, I was quite tired of running up and down *long flights* of stairs and starting to wonder whether I really needed to see a portrait of this woman alpha anyways, not when there was written proof, however brief, of her existence. But Beatrice was in motion, and I followed, partly embarrassed to admit I could barely keep up with her and partly afraid she might find the portrait before me.

My thighs burned, and I was making a galling amount of noise, huffing and puffing my way up the narrow spiraling stairs, always watching Beatrice's skirt disappear out of sight. When I thought I was near to fainting, near to falling backwards and toppling my way back to the hall, near to sitting down on this exact step to wait for Ronson to come and find me and fly me about—up or down, I didn't care—I finally heard a door creak above me.

"Aha!" Beatrice's voice curled its way to my ear. "This looks more like it."

And with that, I regained my last reserves of energy and hurried up after her.

The air was hazy with dust, light falling through two opposing stained glass windows with simple diamond patterns in a mismatch of colors, painting the large rectangular drapes of sheets. Beatrice hadn't touched a single one, and she stood at the center of the room, smiling and waiting for me.

"I assumed you'd like to do the honors," she said.

I *really* liked this woman.

"Thank you," I said, nodding. I was breathless and my legs were trembling, and my pretty new dress now clung damply to me in uncomfortable places, but I smoothed my skirts with clammy hands and stepped forward.

The first few portraits I uncovered were fairly typical—an alpha standing alone along a cliffside, or perhaps with an omega at his side, sometimes even a child. I grunted as I pushed aside a family portrait that Beatrice examined in the shifting light of the windows.

One after another, I uncovered a painting, frowning to

find another man, another pair of wings, another dragon on the skyline. She had reigned for one hundred years. Surely. *Surely* there'd been a portrait. Or had that been a line too far for the preservation of history? Had her portrait been destroyed? Was she only one of the women in the many I'd already uncovered?

"Mairwen, there is...something curious in these," Beatrice murmured behind me.

But I was busy lifting another sheet of linen, pausing halfway to see a solitary figure in an enormous brocade skirt filling the frame, gilded with beads and pearls and a belt made of lattice gold and huge rubies.

"Beatrice," I hissed, jumping up to throw back the curtain of linen, marveling at what I found.

The portrait was very old, the style of figure stiff and simplified, but the subject was undeniable. Beatrice gasped behind me, stumbling closer, and together we stared at the woman in the frame.

The woman...with *wings*.

"Alpha Falk," I murmured, finding the broach over her chest with the Falk family crest. She'd kept her own alpha mate's name and crest, instead of whatever family line she'd been born into.

"She is...she was... Mairwen, are those wings...symbolic?" Beatrice asked, her eyes wide and lips remaining parted.

I shook my head. "I don't know. But...how?"

An answer was impossible, so for a long stretch, Beatrice and I remained standing together in silence, staring up into the hard and mischievous eyes of the woman in the portrait. What had her first name been? Had she kept the name Falk because she was mated, whatever that meant, or because she loved the alpha who chose her, or simply for the sake of her rule as alpha?

Had she been able to fly?

I smiled as I studied her. She'd not been very pretty, I noticed. Not by today's standards. Her face was quite round and her shoulders very broad. There was no hint of a bosom in the image, and her waist was almost squared to her chest. But she looked clever. She looked like the kind of woman who could rule as alpha—a concept I hadn't ever considered before today.

Her wings were a warm shade of brown, and they took up most of the background of the portrait. It was obvious the intention was to show them, to show that she'd *had* them. They had the most detail of any piece of her, even of all the jewelry, the leathery texture so carefully transcribed in paint, the glow of a sunset bleeding through the wing on the right.

"Mairwen, look," Beatrice said gently, tiptoeing closer, raising a hand up to Alpha Falk's throat.

I frowned, inching up to join Beatrice, squinting at the slight discoloration of her skin, little pink and silver highlights at the curve where neck met shoulder.

"Is that...is that a bite?" I asked, almost whispering.

"I'm not sure," Beatrice admitted, taking my hand and drawing me back, turning me to face the other portraits. "But she isn't the only one with the mark."

It took me a moment—my head was still spinning at the discovery of Alpha Falk with *wings*—but finally I caught a glimmer on the throat of a young and pretty woman smiling cheerfully at the side of an absolutely terrifying alpha. I hurried closer, hunting their clothes until I found a family signet ring on the alpha's hand. Blue stone, rose marking. Alpha Grimshaw and his *mate*.

My hand rose up to press over my chest as I rushed to the next portrait, no mark on the woman's throat this time. Alpha Brand, who'd chosen a handful of omegas to rut with, without any mention of a mate.

And the next, marked, *bitten*. Alpha Unger. His mate was

recorded as having established the first schools for young women on the island, both human and dragonkin.

The bite marks. They were *mating* marks.

I couldn't recall every family crest—my head was spinning too fast—but I knew enough to confirm a few more of the portraits, until the sun started setting outside and the room we stood in grew dim. Ronson would return soon. He would take me back to the nest with him, all eager and hungry. He would...

My cheeks were warm as I turned and found Beatrice watching me, her gaze on my throat, at the curve of my shoulder, where curved dark bruises marked my skin. I resisted the urge to lift my hand and cover the marks, it wouldn't do any good now.

"We should...we should cover these back up," I rasped out.

Beatrice glanced at the portraits that surrounded us, lingering on Alpha Falk, glowing in the last rays of the day. "For now," she murmured.

Yes, I thought. *For now*.

Chapter Twenty-Eight
MAIRWEN

Ronson rumbled beneath me, his huge plated body pointing toward the high peak ahead of us. We were reaching our destination after a long, cold morning of flying. We'd stopped briefly in Grave Hills, in an open valley that Ronson said belonged to their new alpha, just long enough to eat the food Cook had sent us with—what I'd considered an insane amount but Ronson explained as necessary.

"Flying as a dragon works up a dragon's appetite," Ronson purred to me, his eyes stroking over my shape from my seat on the picnic blanket. Niall had cleared his throat to remind the alpha we were not alone.

I squinted my eyes through the foggy shield of my helmet, watching the mountain grow with a good bit of relief and a dash of mourning. Ronson had been right to warn me about flying long distances. It was bitterly cold through the air, even against the many layers I wore, but mostly it was exhausting. I braced and bent with Ronson's flight, using muscles I hadn't known I possessed, not to mention the incredible ache in my thighs, stretched around the wide nape of a dragon's long neck. I'd been given a seat and stirrups to lock my feet into, but even at our resting point, I'd barely been able to dismount, let alone do so with any grace. Now, after what Ronson claimed would've been another two hours of flight, I was fairly sure he would simply have to transform and leave me to drop to the ground.

"It looks like others are arriving now too," I said, although Ronson probably couldn't hear me, my voice echoing beneath the helmet. But dark shapes were swirling in the sky, shimmering through the warp and pebble of the glass that guarded me from the wind.

We'd passed castles and villages and more sheep than I'd known existed in the world, a patchwork quilt of landscapes and roads, but there was nothing quite like a mountain rushing closer to prove how fast and graceful Ronson's flight truly was.

I leaned forward, grunting against the fiery stretch in my inner thighs, and rested against the back of his neck. The plates of his leather hide reminded me of the rise and fall of the land below us, but up close even the sharpest points weren't painful to lean against. I wiggled my hands out from the long leather cuffs of my coat and stroked them over Ronson's hide, surprised by the pleased rumble that rattled through us both. He could feel my light touch, even in this form?

The air warmed as we descended, and I was relieved that Ronson seemed intent on landing rather than circling the mountain as some dragons appeared to be doing. I wanted a long draught of water and a good stretch, after perhaps a little time to enjoy being on the ground again.

Flying would be more fun if I could do it myself, I thought with an amused smile.

The alphas were conferring on a long, low plateau of ground cradled between the mountain and a smaller peak to the south, toward the foggy overhang of Skybern. Ronson aimed us at a large open patch of frosted grass in front of two green tents, wind rushing and whipping at my clothes as his wings beat in the air to slow our descent.

We landed with a slight thump, and I thought Ronson must be weary too, grateful to give his wings a rest.

A cluster of humans in simple uniforms ran closer, and Ronson squatted to the ground before I realized the humans were there to assist *me*.

You are an alpha's omega, I reminded myself, reaching out and stifling my groan as two men pulled me down from my seat. They held me steady between them, which was good because my legs were something between stiff boards of wood and boneless jelly. Another pair of men hurried forward, quickly unstrapping the seat I'd rode on and pulling it from Ronson's shoulders.

He transformed immediately, the humans stumbling back, beaten by the wave of warm heat and dragonkin magic.

And there was my alpha. If my legs hadn't been useless before, they were now. Tall, handsome, windswept, and regal, he'd barely returned to himself before he was turning and striding toward me, as if transforming from a dragon—let alone one who'd spent the last five hours flying—wasn't a burden.

"Give her to me," he said a little sharply, and I wobbled as I was abruptly pushed in Ronson's direction.

"Oof."

Ronson's arm caught me around my waist, tugging me snugly to his chest, and then he pulled the helmet from my head, the air sharper and his face clearer before me.

"Are you all right?"

"I'm fine—Oh! Ronson!" I laughed, scooped up from the ground in a tangle of buckled and strapped layers of wool and leather.

Ronson was peering up at the sky. "I think I see Niall in the distance. He'll meet us in our tent."

"I can walk," I murmured as Ronson marched us toward the larger of the two tents.

His lips quirked, dark eyes flashing down to me. "Can you?"

"Probably not," I admitted as Ronson grinned, and then words died on my tongue as we stepped inside.

Ornate lamps were lit in every corner of the square tent and hanging from the central post, gentling the transition from bright daylight to the shadowy interior. A lush and rich interior, as fine as our own rooms in the castle.

"They put carpets on the grass!"

"Skybern does like to show off," Ronson said, dropping the helmet I'd worn onto an ornate side table laden with platters of fruit and meat and crystalline jugs of wine and water. "Let me wrestle with your layers," Ronson said, chewing around a morsel of beef he'd popped into his mouth and lowering my legs to the floor.

I had to lean against Ronson's broad form, or at least I chose to, but his hands were quick on the many fastenings of my cloak, coat, and fleece tunic, until I was dressed in a long velvet gown with slits up to either hip and a pair of fitted leather leggings.

"I have to refix my hair and change before we go back out," I murmured.

"You're too sore to walk," Ronson said, frowning.

I shook my head and slipped my hand under his own coat to press it over the quilted tunic he wore. "I'm just stiff. I'll recover quickly."

Maybe not recover completely, but certainly enough to walk around the pasture outside of our tent and to stand and speak. Which I found myself strangely eager to do. Maybe not to speak; polite conversations and small talk weren't something I'd ever found myself very adept at, but I wanted to see the other alphas. I'd spent the better part of two weeks —the entire time I'd had to prepare for this event, when I wasn't worrying about that disastrous dinner with my parents —researching dragonkin and all of the many families that had given their bloodlines to the role of alphas.

Ronson's family boasted a long reign as alphas in Bleake Isle, but in Dire Peakes, north of the mountain range we gathered at today, it was common practice to ensure the next alpha did not come from the same family as the current one. The competition for the role of Alpha of Skybern was fierce and bloodthirsty and full of political deals that took place behind closed doors. And on the Craven Sea, an alpha rose from the waves with feats of strength and a good deal of canny trade.

The history of dragonkin was not a bad collection of tales for an avid reader like myself, in fact.

I reached up and cupped Ronson's face, distracting him from his own change of clothes. He tossed his tunic aside and stripped down to one of the loose linen shirts I sometimes stole to sleep in.

"Your name might be in a book someday," I said, and Ronson froze, blinking down at me. "A history book, about dragonkin. Do you think about that?"

His hands caught my waist, drawing me close. "I try not to," he said, cheeks flushing a little. "I might be marked down in a very small text about the isle as the worst alpha on record."

"I doubt that," I said, rising onto my toes. I meant to tease Ronson with a kiss on his chin, but he clutched me to his chest, dipping his head just enough for our lips to slide and fit together. Perhaps I'd known this would be the kiss instead, because I surrendered easily, humming and looping my arms over his shoulder, sinking into his chest.

A light slap of waxed canvas and a sharp breeze announced a guest.

"I told you," Niall said dryly.

Which was an odd kind of greeting, until I lowered back to my toes and twisted as much as Ronson would let me to find that an enormous man had followed Niall into the tent.

An enormous man with a roguish smile, exceptionally long and glossy dark hair, and an undeniably piratical swagger that swayed to and fro as if he hadn't quite regained his land legs.

"DeRoche, get out," Ronson growled, fingers tightening on my waist. "You too, Niall."

Both men ignored Ronson, and I scrambled out of his embrace, stumbling on awkward legs before managing a respectable curtsy.

"Alpha DeRoche."

Seamus DeRoche was precisely what I would've imagined the Alpha of the Craven Sea as, although perhaps in my more fanciful moments he had an eye patch too, rather than those vividly midnight-blue eyes that glittered with poorly restrained humor. His nose was large, his features pronounced and a little craggy, but there was a kind of handsomeness that belonged on a large man—masculinity and strength rather than beauty.

"Omega Cadogan," DeRoche greeted, his voice deep but more musical than I'd expected from such a rough and rugged person. "I will admit that I lacked faith in Cadogan's judgment up until this moment. What a pretty treat she is, my lord."

I wondered if I should've been embarrassed by the sudden bloom of my perfume or the blush on my cheeks, but Ronson only draped a heavy arm over my shoulder and purred, ducking his head in acknowledgement of the compliment to me.

"He's been insufferably pleased with himself ever since the selection ceremony," Niall said to DeRoche, who laughed without any reserve, a boisterous sound that must've carried over waves and through storms.

To me, Ronson had always been like thunder, heavy and quiet, comforting and threatening at the same time. This man *was* the sea, huge and dangerous and beautiful.

"It's a pleasure to meet you, my lord. Ronson speaks with great...animation about you," I said.

And as all three men laughed, I found myself strangely light, my body straightening easily, the flipping in my belly settling beneath the weight of something...unfamiliar to me. I glanced up to find Ronson staring hungrily down at me.

"I'm no lord, my lady. A *mister* will do. Or you may call me *darling*, if you'd rather," the alpha teased.

Ronson snapped a glare in his direction. "She certainly may not, you bastard. Get out and leave us to refresh ourselves."

"And here I thought we were gathered together for diplomacy," DeRoche laughed, winking at me and turning on his heel.

"Ronson's rudeness is a compliment, trust me," Niall said to the other alpha. He arched a brow at the pair of us. "Almost everyone else is mingling. *Don't* get distracted."

Ronson huffed and waved his brother out of the tent, but when he turned to me, there was no disguising the wicked tilt of his smile.

"Distracted, omega? What on earth could he have meant?"

I squeaked but could only laugh as Ronson swung me up into his arms and hurried us toward the richly-dressed bed at the far end of the tent.

AFTER MORE OR less behaving ourselves in the tent—Ronson had tortured me with a thorough massage of my hips and legs that did *not* end in my release but did leave me much more comfortable to walk around—and after I was freshly dressed with my hair braided and twisted and pinned up, we joined the rest of the company on the lawn.

"You didn't bring your new omega?" Ronson asked the Alpha of Grave Hills.

Torion Feargus suited the name of the region he ruled over, in my opinion, with inky dark curls and smooth bronze skin, his brighter gold scales shimmering over his throat and chest. He scowled as he stared out over the field, eyes narrowing on someone behind me.

"Brigid asked to remain at the castle," he said. He shook himself and then forced a stern smile to his lips. "She finds alphas oppressive to be around."

"Well, if she's been stuck with you, it's no wonder," Seamus said, eyes glinting with mischief.

Damian Worthington, the Alpha of Skybern who had wandered over with his own omega—a beautiful, petite woman named Helena, who I was trying very hard not to resent for her remarkable resemblance to Adelaide—barked out a laugh and elbowed at Torion's shoulder.

Torion's smile was stiff, and there was a flinch in his eyes. I wondered if he thought Seamus was perhaps correct, and I struggled, my eyes bouncing around the small party we stood with, trying to think of the right thing to say.

"Or perhaps she simply has a preference for only one alpha in particular," I said, urging a smile to my own lips as I looked up to Torion on my right.

The somber man glanced at me, and the tension around his eyes eased into warmth. He bowed his head toward me in thanks, and Ronson's arm around my waist squeezed gently.

"It's an adjustment," I murmured to the alpha.

"For us both," Torion answered, his tone equally quiet. Seamus covered our exchange, chastising himself for his rudeness and praising me flirtatiously.

"Enough. She is spoken for," Ronson growled at Seamus, clutching me closer.

"You make it too easy for him to tease you, alpha," I said, settling my hand over Ronson's chest. My alpha thrummed with a purr, gazing down at me, and my cheeks warmed.

"My, my, Ronson. I thought the latest rumors about you were an exaggeration, but it appears to be true."

The ease of our conversation stalled in the wake of Alpha Worthington's declaration. Ronson tensed at my side, wings stretching slightly, and I pressed my hand in place, holding him back.

"Rumors travel through so many lips. Whether or not they bear any resemblance to the truth is often a matter of chance, my lord," I said.

Damian Worthington blinked at me. He bore some resemblance to Ronson, with dark hair and handsome features, but he was a slightly smaller man and seemed to lack my alpha's *potent* quality. He reminded me of the dragonkin gentleman who'd laughed when Adelaide had teased me and who had ignored me at balls.

"If you've heard that I consider myself very lucky in my choice of omega, then for once the gossip has served true," Ronson purred, his hand stroking down my spine as he dipped his head in Worthington's direction.

"Of course," Worthington said stiffly, forcing a smooth smile onto his lips. "A great compliment to you, Omega Cadogan."

Ronson bristled, and behind me Niall huffed in annoyance, but we were saved from any further polite antagonizing by the blaring declaration of a horn at the center of the field.

"That's our cue," Seamus said with a sigh of relief and a

wink in my direction. He bowed. "Ladies, gentlemen, we alphas must take our leave for the flight."

Ronson tugged me backwards and then circled me, curling his wings around us to create a moment of privacy, his head ducking toward my mouth. I lifted my face, smiling slightly, ready for his kiss, but instead he nuzzled his nose to mine and whispered against my lips.

"Be careful. Some of the betas here are only waiting for the right moment to become the next alpha." Ronson sipped and grazed his mouth over mine, our eyes open and catching at one another. "Tell me what you think of them when I get back. I trust your judgment."

Now that I knew my own perfume better, I was more aware of its bloom, filling the little cocoon of wings around me. I laughed as Ronson growled and clutched me in earnest, slanting his mouth over mine for a brief but deep, licking kiss. He pulled away, eyes black and chest heaving. I pushed him back, smiling at his growl.

"They'll fly without you," I said.

"Then we could just go back to the tent and—"

"Seamus!" I called, laughing as a tanned and scarred hand caught Ronson by the back of his collar, tugging him away from me.

"Let the girl have a few hours of peace, you menace," Seamus said, dragging my alpha along.

Ronson shot me a sharp grin, his eyes glinting in warning, and then spun and strode away with Torion and Seamus on either side of him. Niall stepped up to my side, and I avoided his eyes for a moment, too aware of the heat of a blush on my cheeks and chest.

"He's showing off for the others, isn't he?" I murmured. *Showing me off. Playing up being smitten.* I wanted Niall to break the spell, to crack the bubble of happiness that was growing painfully large in my chest. Better to do it now before I really started to believe it, surely?

"Ronson isn't the calculating sort. That's my job. He can stifle his feelings when he needs to, wear the stern mask of an alpha when it's called for, but I've never seen him feign in the opposite direction," Niall said. That bubble in my chest grew and floated a little higher, nearly choking me. "You're doing very well today, Mairwen. He is *right* to be proud of you."

Niall wouldn't lie to me. I wasn't sure why I knew this as a certainty, perhaps because of how wholly Ronson trusted him, but I did. I nodded, raising my chin, and turned to watch as the alphas in the field spread out in a circle, leaving plenty of room between one another.

"I've never liked this part," Helena said, wandering to my side. "All that magic at once makes my hair stand on end."

Niall and I wandered closer to the circle until the air started to shimmer around the alphas. I gasped at the sudden sizzle that ran over my skin. Helena was right! The power of so many dragons transforming at once made the fine hairs on my skin prickle and rise. I'd seen a few betas flying as dragons in the past, although only from far away. My father had never transformed—he wasn't strong enough—so the only dragon I'd been up close to was Ronson.

Damian Worthington transformed first, the air around him crackling with blue lightning, a brief glow bursting and then revealing a large and elegant dragon. He was the color of dark oil spilled, gleaming with hints of violet and sapphire but also bronze and black. With a crack and a boom, the older alpha from Dire Peakes transformed next, dwarfing Worthington's dragon with a brutal and craggy beast, all stone gray and flecked with white.

One by one, the men in the circle vanished, replaced by the magnificent and deadly forms of their dragons.

"Brace yourself," Helena said, reaching up to her carefully coiffed curls.

I was busy marveling at the dragons. Ronson was one of the larger of the group—only Seamus DeRoche and the Alpha of Dire Peakes were larger—and his dark scales shone with heat under the sunlight. The glistening Alpha Worthington raised his head high, snapping his jaw, and as one, the alphas raised their wings, stroking them through the air in unison.

Wind gusted, and I laughed as it stirred against my skirts, rifling through my hair. Ronson's head turned, one black eye with a fiery pupil sighting me. He thumped his tail—they all did—and I laughed again as the ground shook, echoing up into my legs until my bones were numb with the ringing.

"Beastly," Helena muttered, shaking her head as the dragons all raised their voices to roar together.

Beautiful, I thought, my breath freezing in my chest as the dragons' wings slashed through the air, their enormous and powerful bodies pushing against the ground, thrusting them as one into flight.

Chapter Twenty-Nine
MAIRWEN

I glanced up at the sky, hoping for a hint of the alphas' return, but if the dragons were on their way back, the clouds lingering around the top of the mountains hid them from view.

"And of course, I've grown quite sick of all of last season's gowns, but Worthy doesn't hear a word I say on the matter," Helena continued, just as she had for well over an hour, her arm linked though mine as she led us in aimless circles around the field, always careful to avoid stepping too near any of the lingering beta gentlemen.

I searched them now for Niall, wondering how I might make my escape from this woman. He was in conversation with one of the dragons from Dire Peakes, a rugged and mildly terrifying-looking man who scowled at the halfling while nodding along.

"But you know, I quite fancy this new cut of yours. I had no notion that little *Bleake* Isle might offer anything in the way of innovation for fashion," Helena said.

The more time I spent in this omega's company, the less certain I was that she wasn't a great deal like Adelaide after all. She only seemed to wield her blade of superiority with more subtlety than my local nemesis.

"Not every dragonkin woman wants to spend hours speaking of fashion, Helena," a dry, dark voice announced from behind us, accompanied by a breeze that carried the scent of smoke and caramelized sugar.

I twisted toward the man, but Helena stiffened, her arm squeezing around mine as if prepared to drag us both away.

It was the beta from Skybern with a sly tilt to his gaze. I hadn't been introduced to him properly yet. He seemed to evaporate the moment one of the alphas turned in his direction, always lingering at the fringe of the small party. Bennett Reeves, suspected to be Damian Worthington's bastard half-brother.

He bowed to me, courtly and polite, and stepped forward. The air was heavier around him, almost as if he were on the verge of shifting into his dragon form. At my side, Helena's cheeks were splotched with bright streaks of red. Why? Because of his teasing words? They were rude but easy enough to shrug off.

"I heard you accompany Alpha Cadogan on dragonkin matters around the isle, Omega Cadogan," Reeves said, his too-keen stare piercing into me.

I opened my mouth to tell him he was mistaken, then recalled when Ronson had brought me to the Huberts', or when I'd joined him to help put out the fire on the island.

"Only occasionally," I said. I turned to Helena and smiled. "We were just discussing how often gossip amongst dragonkin seems to be made of exaggerations."

"Indeed. Excuse me, I must have a word with Omega Quigley," Helena rushed out, suddenly tearing her arm from mine as if I had her trapped at my side.

I watched her rush away toward the elderly omega, a little

relieved to be free of her and yet also wondering if I might not be better off to follow.

"I am the persistent stain in Helena's otherwise pristine lifestyle," Reeves muttered darkly, but when I turned, surprised by the bitter candor of the words, I found him smirking as if his goal had been to irritate the other omega. He blinked at me, and the smile smoothed into something that ought to have been charming but left me uneasy. "It's clear Alpha Cadogan sees you as more than an ornament to display at his side."

What did this beta—barely a beta; he walked with more weight and power than many of the alphas here, certainly more than his elder brother—want from me exactly? Or did he simply take enjoyment from unsettling omegas?

I paused for a moment, deciding between the wise choice of excusing myself from his company or the impertinent choice.

"I've never considered myself very ornamental. That, at least, is gossip the isle and I might agree on," I said.

Bennett Reeves's eyes glinted with humor, although his expression remained slightly superior. He wore a mask, not unlike Ronson had at the start, but I suspected there was a man in there somewhere.

"Yet, as you mentioned, gossip is often wrong. Certainly in this case," he said with a gentleman's nod.

"A very courtly reply," I said, rolling my eyes.

And he laughed, a rattling, rough sound as startling as his own wide eyes, surprised by my response and his own laughter.

"I've always liked Alpha Cadogan," he said, eyes crinkling and some of that smug, stony mask slipping away as my eyebrows rose. "His choice of omega is another point in his favor."

"I wasn't aware you were acquainted."

Reeves shrugged, glancing around the field. "No, not at all. But I've studied the policies of all the alphas here, and their predecessors. It's rare for an alpha to chart a course so at odds with those who came before him. It takes a combination of confidence and courage. Or ego."

"Most would say those are the markers of an alpha," I said, now as eager to study this man as he seemed to study everyone else around him.

He hummed. "Perhaps. Genetics certainly seem to create a pattern."

"In Dire Peakes—"

"In Dire Peakes, they follow a matriarchal lineage—makes it harder to track the families who ascend. If you do the work" — and with that, he shot me a sly look to say he *had* done the work — "there are three specific male lines who've taken the role as alpha regularly, and one who ascends most frequently and most quickly." And then Bennett Reeves tipped his head in the direction of the beta Niall was speaking to, without even having to look. I suspected if I'd blindfolded him at this moment and asked him the locations of every individual in the field, he would've known them, perhaps even of the alphas in the sky.

"Alpha Cadogan follows a genetic pattern, but in all else, he seems willing to take great risk to make great change. I admire him for that," Reeves said.

"I won't dissuade you," I answered, smiling on behalf of the compliment to Ronson.

"I imagine your guard has realized I'm occupying your time by now," Reeves said, and I glanced over to find Niall staring at us with his brow furrowed.

"You have eyes in the back of your head, sir," I laughed.

"Just a very good sense of timing. I'll take my leave of you." He bowed, and I resisted the impulse to curtsy.

It was a little easier to breathe as he walked away, the

weight of the air easing, and I turned to head in Niall's direction at the same moment he started to stride toward me. Either Damian Worthington couldn't sense what I did when in the company of Bennett Reeves, or he had good reason not to be threatened by his brother. The man was an alpha-in-waiting. And likely a formidable one.

"I'm very curious about the conversation you just had," Niall murmured under his breath as we reached each other.

"Oh, I'm sure you are, and you should be. But for now, I'd like you to introduce me to the man you were just speaking to. I have it on curious authority we should expect him to rise as an alpha in the near future."

"Ronson will end up replacing my help with yours if I'm not careful," Niall answered cheerfully. "Or at least allow me a day off."

RONSON HUMMED, fingertips grazing a torturous path up and down my spine, stirring new arousal, even as we caught our breath and sweat cooled on our skin.

"We'll fly to Torion's keep tomorrow, rest there for the night before we return home." Ronson's voice rumbled beneath my cheek where I relaxed against his chest, more vibration than sound. "DeRoche too. No doubt he's not done flirting shamelessly with you just to annoy me."

"You like him."

"He's a good ally." I snorted, and Ronson heaved a sigh. "Yes. I like him."

"Partly *because* he flirts with me," I teased.

"I deny this," Ronson growled.

I grinned and turned my face, burrowing into his chest as he sometimes did with me. His muscles were soft as we lay together, and they made a comfortable cushion to nuzzle against.

"What did you discuss during the flight?" I asked.

The dragons had returned just as the sun had started to set and the table for the feast had been laid. I thought Ronson and Torion looked a bit grim, but they eased at dinner, and by the time the bonfire was high and ale was liberal, my alpha was easy again.

Ronson turned us onto our sides. "Alpha Quigley wanted a universal sanction against omega migration—"

"Because of Francesca?" I gasped.

"No. Unlikely, at least. Torion just lifted the sanction in Grave Hills that his father imposed. His betas are angry because it means omegas will be free to leave. And Quigley is angry, because it means his omegas will have somewhere to go if they manage to escape."

"There's no sanction in Bleake Isle?"

"No," Ronson scoffed. "No, not since I ascended. But I do the best I can to make the isle safe for omegas so they don't need to escape. Quigley was outvoted. But Damian Worthington argued in favor. Skybern doesn't even have the sanction."

"What of Dire Peakes?"

"Dire Peakes is the only region that never had a sanction, actually. I've only seen a couple omegas from there in my life, but they looked almost as ferocious as the men."

"Good for them," I murmured, my eyes dragging down. "I'm glad the sanction didn't pass."

"As am I. I'm glad Torion ascended. But Quigley had to know there was no chance. I had to get permission for Millward's pearl farming too. Quigley and Damian used my vote imposing the sanction against me. DeRoche stepped in. The seas are his, after all."

"If Bennett Reeves decides to ascend, you'll have another strong ally," I said, blinking heavily.

There was a long pause of silence, and then I rolled onto my back, stirring from my near slumber to find Ronson hovering over me with wide eyes. "You spoke to Bennett Reeves?"

I grinned. "He approached me. Said he admires you."

Ronson looked thunderstruck. "We've never even spoken."

I hummed and stretched, and for once Ronson wasn't distracted by the display of my body on offer. "I think he avoids others so you don't all realize how strong he is. I wonder why it doesn't bother Worthington."

"What do you mean, 'how strong he is?'" Ronson asked, scowling.

"He has a lot of...presence."

Ronson's eyes narrowed. "Oh, does he?"

"Pft, you're so jealous. Don't be absurd. Just sneak up on him tomorrow and you'll see. There's power, a great deal of it. Almost oppressively so. But unless he was trying to use me, to convince me he'd be a better ally than his brother—which I suppose is possible, actually... Goodness, politics are so tangled, aren't they?" I frowned, now less certain that Reeves had been genuine with me at any point.

"I am jealous, you know."

"What?" I blinked up at Ronson.

He shifted, and my body knew every movement so well, my legs parted without a thought, inviting him to settle against me. We'd grabbed for one another in a rush when we'd finally returned to the tent, like we'd been separated for days rather than hours, trying to stifle our gasps and moans. I was tired, but I wanted my alpha's attention once more, now that the revelry outside was silent and the night was quiet.

"I am jealous of DeRoche when he flirts with you. Jealous

that Niall got to spend the day with you while I flew. Jealous that Bennett Reeves has impressed you with his *presence*." Ronson purred as he spoke, and I couldn't help but arch and rub myself against him.

"You know I don't—"

Ronson ducked, stealing my protest with a gentle kiss. "I am proud too, Mairwen. So proud," he whispered, and I couldn't respond because he'd found his way inside of me, slowly and sweetly, our bodies perfectly attuned to one another after the rut and the heat. "Proud you are mine. My omega."

I whimpered, and Ronson silenced the sound with another kiss, rocking into me, over me, surrounding me in his arms, tilting my hips just so, driving all thought from my mind.

Almost all thought. There were two almost constantly playing in my head every morning and night, every hour.

I reached between us, grasping his face, speaking the simpler, easier of the two confessions out loud. "I am proud too. Proud to be yours. Proud you are my—" Ronson snarled and bucked, and I gasped, almost shouted in pleasure. "My alpha."

"Touch my wings, Mairwen. Wrap your legs around me."

I obeyed, and Ronson rewarded me with a thrusting kiss and a patient, practiced pace inside of me.

Chapter Thirty

RONSON

E ven in my dragon form, the sound of Mairwen's happy laughter was music. I swooped and swerved around the squawking gulls we passed, playfully snapping at the tail feathers of a brave little creature that darted towards me.

"Don't snack on them, Ronson!" Mairwen cried.

I rumbled, a softer warmth than my fire easing through me. Small hands stroked down the back of my neck, like the faintest breeze, but I relished the touch of my omega.

We'd taken a slow journey home, resting a day in Grave Hills before setting out at first light. I was looking forward to a long soak with Mairwen in my arms and a good nap in the nest. Niall had even promised us no disruptions until tomorrow morning. I was looking forward to making Mairwen perfume as I told her again how proud of her I was. For charming the other alphas. For gaining insight on the betas who waited to rise to power. For spending days flying without complaint, even though I knew she must be sore and tired with skin chapped from the wind.

I was looking forward to massaging her and spoiling her

and praising her until she was a trembling mess of perfume and slick, and then wearing us both out in bed.

My eyes narrowed on the horizon, where the subtle spires of the castle pierced the bright blue sky. Seamus DeRoche was a dark inkblot above the castle, spinning in a circle, not landing, and as I flew nearer, Niall leapt from the dragon's back, a small speck in the sky hovering over the balcony.

A stony inkling settled heavily in my belly, a warning that my delicious plans might be interrupted after all. Was it too late to change course? Perhaps there was a small remote island somewhere nearby where I might rule as alpha with only Mairwen to please and impress and keep for my company.

DeRoche turned back in my direction, soaring closer, slowing in his approach. His ship was behind us, halfway between Bleake Isle and the southern coast of Grave Hills, waiting and ready for his return, but he didn't pass us, instead transforming in midair and aiming for my flight path. He swerved around my head like a slightly less appetizing, but significantly larger, seagull.

"What's wrong?" Mairwen called from my back, her legs tight in the saddle.

"You've got visitors. Niall seems to think you won't be pleased to see them," DeRoche warned.

I snarled, and a burst of flame nearly caught the edge of DeRoche's coat, but he only barked a laugh and darted away.

"Raise your fire if you need me," he called, flying overhead and transforming back into his dragon.

Mairwen's weight settled at the nape of my neck, her arms wrapping around my scales. I wanted to roar, to bolt forward and snap up the intruders and crunch them between my huge jaws. My little omega patted me lightly.

"Better dealt with than ignored," she called up to me.

I grumbled, but she was right, and I certainly wouldn't

remain the alpha of the isle if I snacked on my subjects. I leaned forward, and it was only another minute or so before the figures that waited for us on the balcony were close enough to make out.

Gideon Millward was there at least, with Buchanan, but also Gamesby and Adelaide and Redmond Palmer. A small lash of dragon's fire escaped from my nostrils, and Beatrice and Niall gestured the uninvited guests inside, making room for me to land.

At least Gryffyd Evans hadn't been invited. After getting the full story from Mairwen, I would not have been able to resist making a tough meal out of the older beta.

Mairwen slid from my neck and shoulder with a slight *oof* of her breath as her boots hit the stone, and I twisted my neck, watching her stiff movements as I crouched low and she removed the saddle from my back. She looked a little tired but mostly troubled and nervous, tiny teeth plucking at a full lip.

"Why'd they bring her?" she whispered, adding under her breath, "Of course I look like this."

The saddle dropped to the balcony, and I didn't waste a second before transforming, ignoring the blaze of heat and the whip of wind, reaching for Mairwen. Her cheeks were flushed from the magic, but she came willingly, her hands fussing with the squashed braid of her hair and the askew folds of fabric she wore.

"We'll manage them easily," I said, my voice low as I bent and grazed my lips over hers. "And you look delicious, as always."

The balcony doors creaked as they opened, and Gamesby strode towards us, barely sparing a moment to offer too-shallow bows. "Alpha and Omega Cadogan, forgive us our intrusion. We thought you would've returned last night."

"Forgiveness will have to wait, Gamesby," I said, enjoying

the beta's flinch and attempt at hiding the expression. "My siblings will see to your party's comfort as my omega and I take a moment to recover from the long journey. I'm sure you understand."

"If you might just—"

Mairwen gasped as I snatched her about the waist and leapt into the air, weary wings beating in a determined path upwards.

"Are you sure we should leave them to wait?" Mairwen whispered.

"I am the Alpha of Bleake Isle, and you are my omega. We do not wait on men like Hugh Gamesby. He waits on us," I said, not caring whether or not the words might fall on the subject's ears.

"Very well, alpha," Mairwen said, restraining a laugh and drawing out my purr as she nuzzled my jaw. "Have it your way."

"Tease me, and we'll make them wait even longer, Mairwen."

Chapter Thirty-One
MAIRWEN

"Oh, my. Why, these curtains, they're positively ancient, aren't they? Of course, I couldn't tell at first glance, as they're very well cared for. Naturally, the staff you now possess knows what they're about."

I rolled my eyes as Adelaide carried on.

"But quite, *quite* outdated. I suppose the rumors *must* be true," Adelaide said, gaze flicking slyly over her shoulder at me and then snorting. "In which case, you haven't had the time to address your role as mistress here."

The rumors, the ones Adelaide no doubt imagined impossible, being that Ronson kept me in the nest, insatiable for his omega.

My spine straightened, and I found a smile curving my lips. The rumors *were* true.

"My role as mistress of this castle is to respect, honor, and protect the legacy of our isle's longest line of alphas," I said, watching Adelaide's coy glance tighten around her eyes. "This room was arranged by the first omega of Lord Francis Cadogan, the first of the Cadogan alphas. That pattern of weave was specially commissioned. It is the Cadogan crest, in silk and Bleake Isle wool, stitched with sea pearls and gold beads."

Adelaide blanched and turned away from the curtains. Which was for the best, considering my entire speech had been a bunch of nonsense, aside from the bit about the crest pattern.

"I would certainly be failing my alpha if I allowed fleeting fashions to overthrow the prestigious history of his family home," I said, the rare sensation of triumph sliding warmly through my veins.

Spending the afternoon with Adelaide had been wearying as she scattered a constant breadcrumb trail of slights, insinuations, and the occasional outright insult delivered with a giggle and wave of her hand, as if it was all a joke. As if a joke couldn't sting.

I'd accidentally gotten us lost on the way to the portrait gallery, a room I'd only seen on my tour with Beatrice, and Adelaide had quipped that I'd never learn my way around the world if I kept my nose in a book as I walked. When I explained that we'd just attended the Flight of Alphas, she nodded sagely and declared that must be why I looked so wind-chafed and weary, and what an overwhelming and intimidating experience it must've been for me. When I tried to settle us in the library for tea, she'd moaned about the smell of mold and how it would "cling" to her if she spent too long there, as I must always do.

The words did sting, like little mosquito pricks of discomfort, delivering the lingering itch of irritation and urge to retaliate. But they didn't *hurt*.

For the first time in our lives, Adelaide had lost and I had won. We'd never been in a competition before, not really. As far as our society was concerned, Adelaide was too far above me. I suspected the real reason behind her targeted attack was not so much the loss of Ronson to me, but that it was driving her mad to not know *why* he had chosen me.

I was glad she didn't know. It would've been the only weapon she might've used to really hurt me. The truth. That if Ronson hadn't learned of her planned deception, he would've chosen Adelaide.

He was lucky to have discovered it—he told me so often enough, and of course it was true. And I was starting to believe that there was something between us that no one else, no other more perfect omega, might've had with him.

Still, if not for that brief moment in the woods, the whispered plot and my stumbling blindly into Ronson's arms, Ronson would not have seen the mistake he was about to make...and he would not have seen me at all.

That did hurt, softly and deeply—an open wound at the very heart of me that Ronson unknowingly staunched when we were alone. It was hard to imagine Ronson wanting anyone else when he spoke words of praise and perfect, explicit filth in my ear.

But he'd *almost* made a different choice.

"Speaking of family," Adelaide started, rallying and straightening her shoulders. Her hand lifted from her side, hovering over her belly, and a nervous sinking weight settled in my chest. But the fates were looking after me, and the door from the hall opened into the parlor.

I couldn't help myself. I released an audible sigh at the sight of my alpha in the doorway, my cheeks warming at the way his stare fixed to me without so much as a flick of acknowledgement in the other omega's direction.

"Our meeting is concluded," Ronson said.

"I spoke to Cook. Our guests will remain for dinner," I answered, smiling at Ronson's scowl. "Beatrice is seeing that rooms are prepared for their stay."

"Their stay?" Ronson repeated, an eyebrow arching.

"For the night," I said, nodding.

Ronson prowled into the room, and I noted the way Adelaide shrank away from him slightly. I didn't understand how—I could barely keep myself from swooning into his chest as he neared. Behind him, Niall and the four betas we'd found upon our arrival stepped inside.

"You're in luck, Palmer. My omega is far more gracious than I. You'll have time to continue haranguing me over dinner," Ronson said, but he didn't bother looking over his shoulder at the beta.

I did, and what I saw left me wondering if I hadn't made a mistake. Palmer and Gamesby shared a smug, satisfied expression. Which meant whatever they'd come for, I'd given them the opportunity to still pursue.

"Niall will show you the way," Ronson said as his arm fastened around my waist, holding me firmly to his side. Adelaide was staring at where he held me, a puzzled frown on her lips, but she followed when Gamesby called for her, a peevish bite of her name, and the party filed out of the room.

"They're up to something," I whispered when Ronson and I were alone.

"Of course they are," he said, spinning me to face him and then crowding me backward.

I knew that hint of heat in his black eyes, the spark of fire in the depth of his irises warning me of his hunger.

I laughed and planted my hands on his chest, trying to slow him as he backed me against the wall. "Ronson!"

He rumbled pleasantly, hunching and surrounding me. "They heard about Millward's scheme for a pearl farming endeavor, and they claim they want the right to do the same."

I frowned and shook my head. "That can't be all."

"It certainly can't," Ronson agreed, hands sliding around my waist and down to grip my bottom, tugging my hips to press to his. "I don't want you alone with any of them."

"I won't be—"

"Not even what's-her-face, Annabelle."

I pursed my lips and tipped my head. Did he really not remember her name, or did he know that would please me? *Does it matter?*

Ronson growled and ducked his head, teeth gently claiming my bottom lip. "You remain at mine or Niall's side tonight. Drink and eat nothing they hand you."

"You're worried they mean to harm me?" I asked, eyebrows raising.

"It's what I'd expect from a coward like Gamesby," Ronson muttered.

"I shouldn't have invited them to stay. We could change our minds?"

Ronson sighed, leaning into me, and his hands on my ass slid up to stroke my back. "No, you did precisely what an alpha's omega should. We'd be foolish to pretend they aren't a threat but just as foolish to show fear. And we have extra allies on hand tonight too. Millward and Buchanan aren't just here to defend their pearl farm. Come, we'll dress for dinner together." He stepped back, offering me his arm, a half-smile on his lips.

"More dresses from Miss Pettyfer arrived while we were gone."

Ronson purred. "Then I at least have something to look forward to tonight—unwrapping you."

DINNER WAS TENSE BUT HARMLESS. Palmer and Gamesby made a show of wheedling Ronson over the pearl farm plan, but anyone could see it was pointless. They had no one who knew the process, and they had no need to ask Ronson for the capital when it was obvious they could provide it on their own.

In between snide jabs about favoritism, Ronson's restrictive measures against mining, and appropriate pay for farmers, Gamesby made an entirely different case.

"Don't eat that, love," he said, scooping a plate of fish out from under Adelaide's nose. "You know it won't sit well with you."

"Not another glass, my darling. You really shouldn't, you know," he said, shooing a servant away from Adelaide's wine goblet.

And with rude, snapping fingers raised in the air, "You look flushed! The fire is too warm for you. Open a window."

I knew what Gamesby was almost shouting at in his hints, what Adelaide had started to tell me before we were interrupted. What was funny was that Ronson was absolutely oblivious to the performance in front of him. When he wasn't batting away Palmer's petty arguments, he was simply enjoying his dinner, speaking with Gideon Millward, watching me with a hooded and warm gaze—the one I'd mistaken for a dark glare at our first acquaintance.

Gamesby was growing impatient.

It was Adelaide who fascinated me. She was not the effervescent girl of cozy parlors and garden picnics now. She appeared dwarfed by our surroundings, washed out by dark stone and glittering candlelight. Had she changed since the selection ceremony, or was I seeing her through new eyes? Even *she* seemed irritated by Gamesby's charade, although she caught his hand after the finger-snapping incident and gave us all a reprieve, holding him in his seat with a gentle glare.

Ronson cleared his throat as the last of the plates was removed from the table, catching my glance with a glitter of mischief in his eyes. He was going to send everyone on their way to bed, early as it was in the evening.

I stood and opened my mouth without thinking, only

knowing that if I was called upon to play the role of the alpha's hostess, I wanted to do it properly, leaving no room for my hospitality to be called into question.

"The ladies and I will leave you to your drink and discussion," I said, but Ronson was already circling the table toward me. "You may find us in the blue parlor."

"Oh no, you don't," my alpha purred, grinning. "We'll join you there now."

"My lord," Palmer protested.

"You've had my answer since you arrived. No. Millward and Buchanan have the resources they need and my offer of capital. You have no resources and no need of capital." Ronson's arm slid around my middle, cupping my waist and leading me to the door, the rest of the room following suit. "Let that be the end of the discussion and the start of a more pleasant evening."

I tried to free myself from Ronson's grasp and take his arm, as would be polite, but his grip was too firm. At least it was only Beatrice behind us.

"What if it was not your capital being offered? They want a share of the profits, don't they?" I asked in a whisper.

Ronson glanced down at me, brow furrowing. "That would be a solution. I'll speak to Millward and Buchanan first. Thank you, Mairwen."

I blushed. "You were having too much fun thwarting them."

"I hope you've been doing the same," Ronson said, fingers squeezing my hip.

I hummed and shrugged, and Ronson let out a small, stifled growl.

"I should've sent Bea to—"

"No," I hissed, shaking my head. "No, I'm fine, Ronson. It's better if I am the one with your guests." If Beatrice had been the one to keep Adelaide company this afternoon, it would only have given the betas reason to think Ronson didn't have confidence in me.

"Very well, but I insist on having my omega's attention for the rest of the evening," Ronson said, not bothering to lower his voice by the end.

He dotes well, I thought, unable to hide my smile as Ronson settled me in a cozy armchair near a stack of books I'd left on a table the week before. I liked the blue parlor best in the evenings. It looked over the island rather than the sea, all the delicate lights of homes and the farther towns sparkling and fading over the course of hours.

Gamesby was doting too, or mimicking the concept as he hurried Adelaide onto a chaise, fetching her a blanket.

"You see, Lord Cadogan, I had hoped to share a toast with you, celebrating our good fortune," Gamesby said, too loud for it to escape anyone's notice, even as Niall and the other betas sat down to a card game.

Ronson sighed, his back to the room as he poured us drinks by the bar cabinet. "I don't see why we can't do so—"

"For our dragonkin community is shortly to celebrate another entry to society," Gamesby continued, rushing the words over Ronson's, his hand clamped on Adelaide's shoulder.

Whatever reception Gamesby expected, it probably wasn't for Ronson to turn, two short glasses of whiskey in one hand, and stride toward him with a calm expression on his face—not a smile, those were rare.

"Congratulations are indeed in order," Ronson said, passing Gamesby one of the glasses and then tapping his own lightly against the rim. He offered Adelaide a brief bow, and her eyes widened. "I wish your family the very best."

The pair were silent, Gamesby's fixed smile tightening and Adelaide's cheeks flushing slightly. Ronson returned to my side, offering me a small glass of sweet brandy, a syrupy heat on my tongue that we'd discovered I liked best. He leaned against the high back of my chair, one hand dangling down to toy with a braided loop at the nape of my neck.

"We are...very lucky to know so soon," Adelaide said, straightening. She found my eyes and held them. "And certainly, we will be delighted to raise our son in the same generation as the alpha's. When do you plan to announce, *Mouse*?"

Ronson's hand tensed, tugging briefly on my hair before stroking over the side of my throat in apology. It struck me, in the sudden inhale of breath that circled the room, that of course this had been their aim. Had Ronson succeeded? In spite of his choice of omega, in spite of their efforts to distract him, would the alpha produce an heir this year?

And I was the only person in the room who knew for certain if such a thing was even possible.

I glanced up at Ronson and found his gaze already hunting mine, an urgency there, a worry. I would've given anything to banish the others in the room and ask him what he was thinking, to dive into his head and know the absolute truth of his thoughts.

"I admire your curiosity, but you know as well as I do that any announcement is too precious to precede in a parlor. The island will know as one when the time comes," I said, doing my best to hold my calm as I turned back to Adelaide.

Her eyes narrowed, and I refused to flinch.

Chapter Thirty-Two

RONSON

My claws dug into my palms as I stared at Mairwen.

Perfect. She was so fucking *perfect*.

I wondered if she realized how Palmer's stare slid in her direction every so often, brow puzzling into a knot. How Gamesby couldn't bear to look at her, but his nostrils flared with hunger when she passed him.

Mairwen was gleaming, pale skin shining like a jewel, mouthwatering bosom lifted and presented like a feast, only the first course revealed by the heart-shaped neckline of the dress that stroked over her, velvet laced to a cinch around her waist, scooping below the silk of the gown. Her smooth, shining hair was twisted back, pinned in soft loops and thick braids, a few heavy locks left to hang in loose curls over her shoulder. Her eyes glowed in the firelight, ambers lit from within.

It was laughable to imagine that I or anyone else had ever considered Mairwen plain, insanity to think that a poorly-fitted corset could've disguised the truth. She was almost too beautiful to behold. The welcoming stretch of her full mouth as she smiled, lips peachy-pink and glistening from the brandy she sipped, pursed as she struggled to restrain a laugh at some dry remark of Beatrice's. It was all I could do to keep from dropping to my knees, crawling to my omega to beg for the gift of a kiss.

As if I'd be able to stop at one.

I was going mad.

Not because I found Mairwen beautiful—that was proof of some sanity left in me.

No, I was losing my mind because I was seriously considering letting out a roar, transforming into my dragon to chase our company out of the room, so I might be alone with my omega. So I could ask her the words burning on my tongue.

Mairwen rested her empty glass on the side table, and I licked my lips, watching her long, pale fingers cup and then clap together. Adelaide had started playing the pianoforte and singing some time ago, and it was a relief to have the room's attention turned away from Mairwen so that I might admire her in peace. I wanted the entire world to acknowledge how exquisite she was, and then I wanted them all to leave us *be*, so I could appreciate her privately.

"Oh, Mouse—"

I let out a growl, a reflex at that absurd nickname, but Mairwen's elbow launched off the arm of her chair and into the side of my thigh, cutting off the sound abruptly.

Adelaide swallowed but forced a smile to her lips, her narrowed stare on my omega. "Shouldn't it be your turn by now?"

Mairwen murmured an assent, her cheeks flushing, and she made to rise from the chair.

Across the room, Gamesby let out a bark of laughter. "Does the Mouse play music?" He was deep in his cups, too free with his tongue, and even Palmer shot him a quelling glance from the card table. "I've never heard such a thing."

"Nor have I, truth be told," Adelaide said, smirking slightly.

It was some kind of trap, an obvious attempt to belittle Mairwen. And come to think of it, I had also never heard Mairwen play, so perhaps she didn't, or maybe she was terrible, neither of which I cared the slightest about.

"No," I said, too sharply.

Mairwen was on her feet and she flinched, her eyes wide and the lovely blush over her cheeks turning spotty and red. Beatrice glared at me from her seat, and Niall refused to lift his eyes from the cards, but I knew straight away the error I'd made, all but confirming Adelaide and Gamesby's lack of faith.

"Unless...you want to, of course," I stumbled out, catching Mairwen's hand with mine. "I know you are...tired from our travels."

Mairwen's stare searched me, and I wanted to drag her into my arms, kiss away the worry on her brow, apologize for being an idiot, and tell her I'd be more than happy to listen to her sing bar songs and sea shanties and nursery rhymes if it suited her. It wouldn't matter if she were awful. I might not even be able to tell, too thoroughly besotted.

"I enjoy playing," she said softly, squeezing my fingers.

Oh. Well. If she *enjoyed* it, then I was incapable of arguing.

I took the seat she vacated, and Adelaide remained smug, flouncing her way back to Gamesby's side. If they laughed, if they so much as *blinked* in mockery during her performance, I would eat them alive. Niall would forgive me. Eventually.

Except as Mairwen sat calmly down on the velvet bench, the spotlight glow of the oil lamp enveloped her, casting her in gold, and my attention was hers entirely. She closed the sheet music Adelaide had been using and set it aside, not pulling anything out for herself. Her hands rested on the keys, and I was jealous of every place where her fingertips touched ivory instead of me.

It was obvious by the first bar of music that Adelaide and Gamesby really never had heard Mairwen play, or they wouldn't have dared issue the challenge. The melody was simple, but the music was liquid, notes not plucked and tapped but blending into one another. My lips curved, an unguarded smile taking over my face. It was obvious Mairwen did enjoy playing. She was calm and proud, back straight and eyes drifting, not needing to stare down at her hands.

But when she sang...

When she sang, I stopped breathing.

The card game came to a halt, and I only noticed because it meant there was no other sound in the room, no other voice but hers. Mairwen's voice was heavy and open, hollow and echoing, swinging low and floating high, and it carved through my chest like dragon talons. The words were there, a pretty and tragic story about betrayed love, words I wanted to steal from her lips because Mairwen should never even have to think about such a thing.

Why did it sound as though she knew heartbreak? Why did her voice cry with tears? Had she loved someone? Someone who'd left her behind?

I would tear them limb from limb, then thank them for leaving the road open for me to claim my omega.

Her breath shuddered on a sigh, and the room breathed with her before going still as her voice rose sweetly, a perfect contrast to the desolate woe of the heroine.

Mairwen was casting a spell, or perhaps she was pulling aside the enchantment, the one that had fooled this island into seeing a mouse, so easily overlooked. And what was behind the curtain was terrifying and divine, a woman capable of offering salvation or devastation to your heart. I wanted to slide off the chair and down to the floor, to crawl across the room and offer myself prostrate to Mairwen's whims, but I was frozen in place.

Her voice sank, down into the dark fathoms of water where the heroine was left to perish, and my heart in my chest cracked open to let the sea in to drown me too.

Mine. Mine, mine, mine, the dragon in me crowed in victorious chorus.

For a moment, as the last chord of the music hung in the air, we all remained trapped. *Don't leave us here*, I thought irrationally, as if Mairwen might suddenly vanish before us, the magic of her now at an end. But then her hands fell to her lap and her face turned toward us, toward me, eyes open and a little nervous.

And still I couldn't move.

Thank the ancestors for Niall and Beatrice, who started the applause, a jarring cacophony after Mairwen's offering of pure music, but it did the trick of rousing us from her spell.

Buchanan's chair squawked as he rose from his seat, clapping quite roughly, and Palmer joined in, although his eyes were wide on Mairwen, seeing her for the first time.

I didn't want him to see her. I didn't want *any* of them looking at her.

Mine, my dragon growled.

And so she was.

I rose from my chair, noting them all—even Gamesby and Adelaide were offering compliments, although in a daze, as if they'd forgotten why they coaxed her into playing—but not bothering to look anywhere but at Mairwen. Just as she never tore her gaze from mine, licking at her bottom lip and then tucking it between her teeth. I prowled to her, blocking her from their view. My omega. My... There wasn't a word for what Mairwen really was to me. I needed one. I needed *her*. Immediately.

"That's enough for the evening," I said, my voice rough, and Mairwen blushed and looked down into her lap.

No. Look at me. See me as I see you, I wanted to shout.

There was a brief bout of laughter, but cards were abandoned on the table, and soon footsteps were retreating.

"I'll see them out in the morning," Niall said, the last to leave.

I nodded without turning. "Good. Thank you."

"Ronson—" Mairwen started.

The door clicked shut, and I dropped to my knees before her, sighing in relief as I found her eyes again and watched them widen in surprise.

"You were *never* a mouse," I growled out, and Mairwen's lips parted. I grasped her hips in mine, trying not to let my talons prick the fabric. The dress was a rich shade of copper, earthy but regal. I hadn't noticed before, too fixated on the way it touched her. "A mouse could not have worked the magic you just did."

"Magic?" Mairwen echoed, reaching for me, fingers brushing against my jaw.

I leaned into her touch and tried not to let the desperate urge to consume her take me too soon. "You held the heart of every dragon in the room in your grip, Mairwen. You lured them into the water, deep into the ocean's belly, and then left them there to freeze. You are a *siren*, omega."

Mairwen's breath hitched and her eyes watered, but she blinked the sheen away. "What...what about *your* heart?"

I gaped up at her, marveling at the words, the tremor in her voice, the uncertain shyness of her eyes. I caught Mairwen's hand in mine as she started to pull away, dragging it back, flattening it over my heart.

"*Mairwen*. Is this not your fist in my chest? You clasped it around my heart, and you now demand every beat it issues." Her eyes were huge, liquidy, and luminous, and I saw the question on her lips, couldn't bear her doubt. "Mairwen," I pleaded, releasing her hand on my chest in order to grasp her face, to rise up and meet her and seal my mouth over hers, tongue stroking in to steal the wonder. Was there a way to kiss my omega so that she would know, *know* for certain, what I saw when I looked at her? I tried to find it, tried to pour in my gratitude and amazement, my hunger and affection.

"Mairwen," I sighed as her arms circled my shoulders, as she pulled me over her, our bodies bowed over the piano bench. "Mairwen, I can't lose you. Please...please tell me."

"I'm yours," Mairwen breathed, reaching for my face again, nipping at my lips.

I purred, my dragon pleased with her answer. But it wasn't what *I* needed to hear. I groaned as I sat up, then quickly gathered Mairwen in my arms, shifting until I sat on the bench with her cuddled against my chest, skirts pushed high so I could fit between her thighs. And as urgently as I needed her answer, my hands needed the feel of her in their grip, sliding beneath her skirt, trembling with satisfaction as I found the backs of her thighs, soft and ample and in my possession.

"Tell me you drank the tea, Mairwen," I said, and the words cut a wound on my tongue.

I'd waited decades for an heir. It had been my only goal since I'd defeated my father, the one tool I needed to acquire to secure my rule. But I'd pursued it half-heartedly, and now I knew why.

I need Mairwen *far* more.

"Tell me," I whispered, squeezing my eyes shut against the damp sting that grew there, biting at her jaw, her cheek, her earlobe. "Please, I need to... I need to know you are safe. That you're mine and I won't lose you. Tell me you drank the tea."

"Ronson?" She pushed gently at my chest, but I didn't

want to meet her eyes as she told me that it was her *duty* to give me an heir. "Ronson, my love—"

I gasped, bucking up against her, squeezing and pulling her closer. My *love*. Not my alpha or my lord. Had I imagined the words? Or were they meaningless sweetness?

Mairwen's hands clasped my face as she leaned back, and I helped myself to a generous gape at her bosom, flushed and full and mouth-wateringly perfect, before she forcefully dragged my gaze up. There was an indulgent smile on her lips, one I wanted to lick into, swallow whole with every other bit of her.

"Ronson," she said softly, thumbs stroking my cheeks. Her voice lowered to the most delicate whisper, body bowing forward to rest her brow against mine. "I drank the tea. It's all right. It's...fine, I'm safe, I—"

I groaned, swallowing her words, my hands—two was such an inadequate number when it came to touching Mairwen—fumbling eagerly at her hips, up to cup the nape of her neck and hold her close as I claimed her lips. Her breath caught on pretty sighs as she looped her arms and legs around me, and I debated the comfort of the piano bench compared to the floor or the time it might take to fly up her to the nest. A few broken fragments of thoughts clambered in my head, spiraling in the burst of relief still coursing through me before linking together.

"Just-just for the rut, or—" I asked, panting. There were still dangers, even when birthing a child without wings, and the thought of Mairwen at risk created a panic in my chest that it didn't seem capable of containing.

She shook her head, nuzzling against my cheek in the process, and I traced the tip of my tongue against her jaw.

"I wasn't... I was afraid you might..."

I knew that fragile note in Mairwen's voice, and it calmed me enough to meet her eyes just as they skittered away.

"Omega," I pressed, my tone darkening in a command I knew she softened for.

"I wondered if perhaps you might...prefer there was no child. So you could choose—"

I clapped a hand over her lips, my eyes wide, head shaking automatically. *No. No, Mairwen*, I wanted to cry. It hadn't occurred to me at the time, before the rut, that Mairwen might assume I wanted no issue between us for my *own* sake.

Her fingers caught at mine, pulling them from her face. "And I'm not quite ready yet," she added gently.

I puffed out a breath, and Mairwen offered me a crooked smile. I drew her back against my chest, breathing in her perfume to calm my racing heart, my tripping thoughts. Mairwen melted into me, and my eyes shut on the sting once more.

"I will *never* let you go, Mairwen," I murmured, pressing a kiss to the curve of her shoulder.

She sniffled against me, her hands finding my wings and grabbing their base.

"The only thing I want more than to have a child with you, is to ensure you remain at my side for as long as possible," I added with another kiss. Already, the disparity in our lifespans was digging a hole into my chest. Mairwen would age too soon, die too soon. I wondered if I told Gamesby that when Mairwen died, I would lose all strength to fight him, that perhaps he might leave us in peace until that time. *No*, that would only put Mairwen in the firing line.

"Do you believe me?" I asked, lifting us from the bench, wrapping an arm under Mairwen's ass to hold her wrapped around me. She was still for a moment before nodding against my shoulder. That wouldn't do. "Look at me, Mairwen. You have to say it. Do you believe me? Believe that I want *you* more than anything else in this world? More than an heir, or to be alpha. More than this castle or this isle. Fang's fire, omega, the number of times I've thought about carting you off to find somewhere just for the two of us to live in peace..."

Mairwen laughed at that and finally lifted her head. She was perfuming so strongly I could've drowned in it, but for once I could focus through the haze of hunger. Her eyes were damp but bright, her smile wide, her cheeks pink and full.

"Yes, Ronson, I believe you," she murmured, quietly and sweetly, but without hesitating or glancing away.

"Good," I said, which was an inadequate word for the enormous second sun that was growing in my chest, lighting me from the inside out.

"There's-there's something we should discuss. Something I found in the library," Mairwen said as I carried her to the tall windows.

"Later. I'm taking you up to our nest, my pretty siren." I squeezed at her hips, grinning up at her, panting in the gasps of perfume she was granting me.

Mairwen's gaze hooded, her smile languid and wicked. If there had been a beta in the room to see that smile, I would've had to kill them. I opened the window, stepping up onto the ledge, and Mairwen tightened her thighs around my hips, preparing for the flight up to our nest.

"Alpha, you must promise not to bite me until *after* I've shown you what I've found," Mairwen said, kissing along my jaw, nipping at my lobe.

The words should've struck me, but my omega was so close, so warm, and the scent of her made my mouth water and my cock stiffen.

"Don't tease me, omega, or I'll be inside you before we've reached the nest," I answered, groaning as she perfumed in answer.

Chapter Thirty-Three

MAIRWEN

S trong hands with calloused fingers stroked down my back, occasionally digging into muscle. I tried to fight my smile, my squirms of pleasure, but it was useless. Daylight crept into the nest. I was awake and Ronson knew it.

Ronson.

My siren. My omega. My perfect girl.

I buried my face into the pillow, clinging to all the impossible things he'd said the night before.

"Mairwen," Ronson purred, my name sweet and coaxing.

And I remembered that those wonderful words he'd spoken weren't impossible after all. I grinned and rolled over, and Ronson's always somber and serious face brightened in an answering smile.

"There you are. Fucking beautiful," he whispered, head ducking and lips soothing gently over mine.

I wrapped myself around my alpha, sighing at the weight of him against me. "Good morning, alpha."

Ronson rumbled and groaned, kissing up my jaw and

down my throat, and I arched for him, offering the spot I knew he was searching for.

He stopped there, breathing roughly against my shoulder, and then pressed a long, chaste kiss to the bruises. "Mairwen," he started slowly, lifting away to meet my gaze. "What did you mean when you said I couldn't bite you *until after* you'd explained what you found in the library?"

I stilled, and thought rose up in a flurry. I'd spoken in the heat of the moment, in the shelter of Ronson's warm stare and loving words, but what if he'd only been reassuring me? What if he'd been responding to my perfume and a moment of pride? What if the words he'd said—that I had his heart—were temporary? Because what I'd learned about mating was...*permanent*.

Ronson watched me, brow tensing, lips hardening, but he relaxed with a brief brush of my fingers over his jaw. "Whatever it is, you can trust me, Mairwen."

I can't lose you.

I took a deep breath and nodded. If Ronson didn't want to be mated to me, to tie my life to his, then he would know not to bite me. And if I didn't tell him, perhaps his control might break one day, even in another ten years during another rut...he might mate me without realizing the consequences, and it would be worse to know for many, many decades that he regretted doing so than it would be to accept that he would *choose* not to.

"Are our unwelcome guests gone?" I asked.

Ronson frowned again, nodding. "Beatrice saw they got a good meal before politely urging them on their way. It's nearly midday now. Niall is taking care of matters for me today."

Which meant there was nothing in the way of our spending the day together. It probably wouldn't take *very* much effort to distract Ronson from his question, keep him in bed with me...

And if he bites you in a moment of passion? I wondered.

"Come with me to the library," I said.

Ronson sat up with me, holding me close, even as he glowered. "This isn't news we can discuss in bed?"

"Perhaps, but I think you'd have questions. Better to show you everything I've found." It might take a trip up to the portraits too, come to think of it.

Ronson sighed and nodded, but he didn't release me as he left the bed, just carried me along with him as I laughed, arms tangled around his shoulders. "Very well. But we're not getting properly dressed. We've earned this day of rest, and I plan on ensuring we enjoy it."

"This could wait—" I started, unsure what would come of our conversation about the mating marks.

"Oh no, you don't," Ronson said, lips twitching, voice lowering. "You said I couldn't bite until *after*. Which means you've cause to think I *can* bite you. And Mairwen, my teeth *ache* every time I look at you. My jaw grinds to keep me from sinking my bite onto your lovely throat. I'm not sure how much longer I can avoid it."

I licked my lips, and Ronson set me on my toes by the wardrobe, pulling down the slip I'd draped over one door, helping me dress, his hands greedy to touch.

"Perhaps you should go and see a dentist," I murmured.

What if Ronson didn't want to bite me once he learned what it would mean, but he still physically craved the act? How long could he withstand the urge? How long could I keep myself from arching my throat and drawing his mouth to the spot, begging him to make me his?

Ronson groaned and dragged me to him. "You're *perfuming*, and I want to know why," he growled.

I shivered, his breath ghosting over the temporary marks he'd made, the ones he might make permanent.

"After," I breathed.

I HELD MY BREATH, standing at the opposite side of the table in the library, the one I'd covered the surface of with open texts. Every mention of an alpha and their mated omega. The very few descriptions of mating ceremonies I could find, in the oldest and most fragile of texts. The small pamphlet from centuries ago referring to the savage and base act of "biting," apparently propaganda opposing the mating marks. I'd done my best before we'd left for the Flight of Alphas to collect everything I could find that might relate to mates or bites.

Ronson stared at a page in one of the oldest texts. "This mentions the strength of two dragons."

I nodded, but Ronson hadn't looked up from the table. His eyes kept bouncing from one book to another, brow furrowed and back straight.

"Yes, I noticed that too." I wondered about Alpha Falk and her wings, wondered how literal those words might really be. I'd nearly brought her portrait down the day Beatrice and I had found it, but I was glad now I'd left it in the attic. It would've been a disaster if Gamesby had come across it while here.

"The dates," Ronson murmured next, looking at the life records of the isle's alphas and omegas, their children.

"Yes. The mated couples had male heirs outside any rut cycle I could track."

What was he *thinking*? I was desperate to know. I wanted to crawl over the table, into his lap, and force his eyes to mine. I remained in place, trying not to fidget.

"What? Oh...oh yes, they do, don't they? But the omegas...they live..."

Suddenly, I couldn't bear to keep still, my body pacing back and forth with quick steps, matching the length of the broad table. "As near as I can tell, the bite changes something within the omega. Their lifespans match their mates. The estrus cycle changes too, I assume. I'm not sure if there's more ruts or more-more—"

"Heats," Ronson finished, and I glanced over nervously, only to find him watching me. His eyes were dark, hot, hungry. I shivered and stumbled and then stood still at the corner of the table.

He'd put me into heat during the rut. He'd been resisting the urge to bite me. He'd nearly been in tears last night, begging me to tell him that I'd drunk the tea to prevent a pregnancy, that I'd chosen my life over my duty to him.

"And no mention of deaths during the delivery of a child," I breathed, trying to hold onto the facts, the information I'd found, and not fall into the tension between us that called me *closer, closer, closer* to my alpha.

"Mairwen—"

"It's irreversible. I don't know why...why..."

"Come here," Ronson purred.

"Why they would've put a stop to the marks, but the pamphlet originates in Skybern, so perhaps the answers are there. And even after the law forbidding bites, Alpha Brooks is still noted as having taken a...a..."

Ronson rumbled and I staggered back, swallowing.

"Mate," he said, and my belly clenched. It sounded less like he was finishing my sentence for me and more like he was calling to me. "Come here."

"Ronson," I protested, but it was useless—I was already rounding the edge of the table as Ronson pushed his seat back. He held his hand out when I paused, and I found myself sliding between him and the table, his hands cupping the backs of my thighs as he leaned in and stared up at me.

"You discovered all this on your own?" he asked.

"More or less by accident at first. I was only researching

family lines. The further back I went, the more I found mentions of mates."

Ronson purred, and I sighed, my eyes falling shut as he drew me a little closer, pressing his lips through the silk of my robe and slip to kiss my stomach.

"What a clever omega I have," he said against me. My hands found their way into his hair, sighing in relief, anchored in calm simply by being able to touch him. "I thought I was going mad, losing my mind to my dragon's or worse."

I combed my fingers through the thick, dark strands, soothing us both. "It was only instinct," I said softly.

Ronson nodded, turning his head to rest his cheek against me, his fingers tightening on my thighs. "A very good instinct."

I blinked, and my breath hitched.

"I should've bitten you the first time I had the urge, Mairwen."

My eyes widened and I stared down at him, but he was hidden against me, his words soft and warm, rumbling with his purr.

"My omega," he rasped, turning his face back into my belly, nuzzling there, hunching lower. I gasped as his mouth opened, teeth biting dully against me. "My *mate*. Ohhh, yes. That word tastes almost as good as you do, Mairwen."

"Ronson." I tightened my fingers in his hair, trying to make him lean back to look at me, but he only moaned at the tug, and he was much stronger than me, lifting me off my toes and settling me down on the edge of the table, the silk of my slip sliding up so easily at his urging. "Ronson, it's-it's—"

I whimpered as he burrowed his face between my thighs, purring against my sex, breathing roughly there.

"Permanent," he moaned, and he nodded, his nose just barely rubbing at my clit. "Yes, Mairwen. That's the best part."

A rough sob cracked out of my chest, my body crumpling, but Ronson was fast, standing up, arms circling my back and giving me a cradle to fall into. His face wasn't unreadable now. He was radiating warmth, pleasure, *pride*, just as he had last night.

"Shh, it's all right, omega." He drew me into his chest, tucked my head beneath his chin, and heave in air as I clawed and groped at his back. "I know. I know what they made you believe, what they let you think of yourself. But it isn't true. Not a bit of it. You are *everything* an alpha could want. I just happen to be the extremely lucky fool who had the chance to claim you."

I wasn't crying, not with tears, but I couldn't catch my breath, couldn't contain the voices in my head that contradicted every word Ronson spoke. I whined and tried to climb into Ronson as if he were shelter I might take. He lifted me from the table and sat back in his chair with me nestled against his chest.

"I want my mark on you. I want a *life* with you—my whole life, not part of it. I want you to have my strength, and I desperately need yours, Mairwen. I don't want an heir. I want a *child*. Your child. Ours. When and if you're ready." He stiffened and then tipped me backwards, frowning. "The tea? Will it still work?"

He was asking me a perfectly reasonable question, while I was busy falling apart because I was so relieved, so *happy*, so honored by him that for a moment, I could only squeak and stare up at him, hiccuping for breath.

"I love you," I gasped out.

Ronson's face went slack, and I was too stunned to even doubt the words, to doubt that he might want to hear them.

I reached up and grasped his face in my hands. "Ronson, I love you."

Sound roared from his chest, a shocking thunder of a purr.

The room swung around me, then my back was pressed awkwardly over a mismatched collection of open books— books far too old for this treatment—and the weight of my alpha was making the table groan, his mouth tenderly and sweetly and reverently pressed to mine.

"I forgot," he rasped, nodding and then kissing me again. "I forgot to say that last night, didn't I?"

I could fly, after all. That was the only explanation for the soaring sensation racing through me.

"Forgot what, alpha?"

Ronson groaned, nose digging into my cheek, chest heaving against mine as he gulped for air. "I love you. I love you. I love you, Mairwen."

And for some reason, I didn't doubt for a moment that he meant it.

"Nest, alpha," I murmured against his ear.

"Nest, *mate*," he corrected.

Chapter Thirty-Four

RONSON

ate, I marveled, laying Mairwen back inside of our nest, crawling in over her.

Mate, my dragon thundered in approval. *Mine.*

It had been a fact I hadn't known the word for, and now that I did, the truth rested perfectly in place, a brilliant jewel in a precise setting. Mairwen was my mate. My clever, beautiful, desperately sweet mate.

And she loves me. My breath caught in my chest, and I gazed down at Mairwen, at the soft glitter in her honey eyes as she stared back, the way she eyes traced over my features in equal wonder. Her fingers smoothed around my jaw, and then brushed the backs of her knuckles against my cheek. I turned my head and kissed there, nipping at her knuckles and earning a soft giggle.

My hand on her waist slid to the tie of her robe, but for once, I wasn't impatient. I wanted to unwrap my mate slowly, savor every bit of her. Mairwen wiggled beneath me and the robe parted, sliding over her smooth skin and off her shoulders, revealing more of the bruises on her left side that I'd been both proud and ashamed of. Now that I knew why they were there, why I'd been so obsessed with marking her, *biting* her, I admired the restraint of not actually breaking her skin.

Yet.

I leaned down, smiling as Mairwen released a soft, eager sound and arched in offering, lifting her bruised skin to my lips. I kissed softly over the patterns I'd made, faded watercolor circles of pink and purple and yellow.

"Do you want my mark, Mairwen?" I murmured, unable to resist the urge to suck softly over my most recent work. Mairwen gasped, hands tearing at the snaps of my shoulders, wrestling away my own clothing to rub her silk-clad skin to mine.

"*Yes*, alpha."

"It's permanent," I reminded her, settling myself on top of her, knowing well enough by now that she liked my weight. And sure enough, Mairwen moaned and sighed, sagging into the soft bedding of our nest. She blinked drowsily up at me as I shifted. "You thought that might be a concern for me. And so it might be for you," I said, catching her hair behind her neck, freeing it gently and draping it back over a pillow so it wouldn't tangle beneath us.

"I want to be yours. Your mate," she said, blushing but not looking away from me.

I purred, my eyes falling shut, enjoying the moment of Mairwen's lush form beneath mine, her full thighs cradling my hips, her hands ghosting over my back, her perfume full and rich, layers of the satisfaction I'd given her coating our nest. I'd never imagined such a sense of *rightness* with any omega I might choose, not this completion and ease, this *imperative* understanding that I could love Mairwen and no other.

"How long have you known about the bite?" I asked.

"Since the day before we left for the Flight of Alphas," she said.

I nodded. There hadn't been time before now to tell me, and there hadn't been much chance of me going so far as to bite her while we were traveling. She'd thought to warn me last night.

"I'd found mentions of mates, but nothing that connected to you wanting to..." She blushed again and squirmed.

I grinned down, moving just enough to coax the slip up over her hips. "Bite you," I prompted, glancing at those marks on her throat.

She nodded. "But then Beatrice and I found old portraits —Oh, I meant to show you!"

"Later, Mairwen," I rasped, too eager now that her warm skin was wrapping around me.

She laughed and lifted her hips, her chest, arms sliding back to allow me to strip her bare beneath me. I swallowed hard, forever dazzled by the vision of Mairwen beneath me, so much exquisiteness on offer.

"I thought at first that maybe this was just an urge between any alpha and omega," she said softly.

I shook my head, frowning. "Not possible. No man could resist wanting a woman as much as I want you," I said.

Mairwen gasped, and her eyes glittered with tears. "Ronson, you are so—"

"Devastatingly in love with you," I finished for her, ducking down to kiss the swell of one breast, then the other. "Yes, I know."

My father was certainly not a man of restraint. If he'd wanted to bite an omega, he would've. And this craving hadn't been there from the start with Mairwen, although I thought perhaps the start might've been sooner than the rut. The night I'd found her in the nest, surrounded by books, shockingly sweet and lovely.

"Wonderful," Mairwen sighed out as I trailed a damp line of licks and kisses down between her breasts to her belly. "Ronson, I need you."

As much as it thrilled the dragon in me to hear her call me *alpha*, it made me ache in an altogether more tender way when she used my name. We were alpha and omega, and the bite was an instinct I'd barely managed to resist up till now, but this was more than a base urge, more than my dragon's desire. I loved this *woman*, her appetite for knowledge and for story, the core of her that had persevered with humor and curiosity, in spite of being so constantly discouraged by those around her. I'd spent my many decades as alpha attempting to be fair, catering to men I didn't respect. But if I was going to be worthy of Mairwen, I need to be as good as her, as strong for *all* of the island as she seemed to think me capable.

I rose up only long enough to work my way out of the loose trousers I'd donned for our trip to the library, falling back into Mairwen before she could follow and chase my touch.

"Bite," she pleaded, arching her throat until the muscles were taut, offering me that divine stretch of skin I'd claimed.

No, I'd claimed all of her. I'd claimed her on the stage, in full view of dragonkin and the human locals. I'd claimed her on the floor of the library with my lips and hands, in our nest during my rut, in front of the other alphas at the Flight. Even in front of her parents.

The bite was not my claim. It was my means of survival. Because if I lost Mairwen, in childbirth or simply in her too-short lifespan, I was sure my dragon would wither and so would I.

I wrapped Mairwen's legs around me, stilled her eager wiggles and squirms by finding my way to her opening, just barely poised to enter, and then took her face in my hand.

"I love you, Mairwen," I said again, because the words were a relief and a joy.

She softened, *sparkled* up at me like the treasure she was. "I love you, Ronson."

I swallowed hard and then flexed my hips forward, watching her pupils grow, her lips part on a pant. "I love you, *mate*," I corrected, grinning.

Mairwen's voice cracked sweetly, a pleading note, and her hips tilted into mine, pink tongue flicking out to wet her bottom lip. "Mate," she rasped, begging.

I groaned, and my eyes fell shut, thoughts sinking help-lessly into Mairwen's heat and warmth and wonderfully soaked core, narrowing down to the simple and primitive ache and complete solace of being inside the only woman I'd ever *really* wanted.

Mairwen met me stroke for stroke, her hunger a match for an alpha's, a match for mine. I licked the skin of her throat, syrupy perfume filling my lungs, coating my tongue. My hands were full, one massaging her breast, the other cupping her ass to hold her close. I wanted to lick her arousal from the source, wanted to put her on her hands and knees and grip the back of her neck, and pound into her to make her scream, wanted to be everywhere on Mairwen all at once.

But I opened my eyes and found her face, her beautiful stare and lips begging to be kissed, and wanted nothing more than this—our chests pressed, arms wrapped tight, to be as near to her as I could until our heartbeats hammered together and our rocking thrusts dawdled, savoring every slide of slick flesh.

I smiled as Mairwen's gaze went unfocused, her eyelashes fluttering and a slow, deep moan rising from her lips. Oh, yes, she liked this. My lovely, greedy omega liked when I was patient and thorough, when I filled her as completely as I could, rubbing my knot against her clit. Her hands squeezed

KATHRYN MOON

low on my back, a high sigh released as her eyes squeezed shut when I pushed inside of her, a tremulous whimper as I pulled nearly out.

"Ronson, *yes,* please," she breathed, turning and arching for a kiss.

I licked into her mouth, gave her my groan as her wet sex squeezed my length, pressed a little harder against her, debated knotting her, biting her, making her mine *forever* right at that second. But she made such magnificent, tormented, pleading sounds as I eased back, and I could be patient, could make her unravel for me and then take her there again faster with my knot, drive us both to the brink of oblivion. And this time, I would let it take me.

I rolled Mairwen's nipple between my fingers, bit gently at her bottom lip as she cried out, hiked one leg up higher to her side. Not long now. I knew her so well, knew what pleased her, what drove her past reason. I knew she grew shy when I kissed her belly but also so wonderfully wet. Knew she shuddered and fluttered around my cock when I gripped her tightly, almost to bruising. She loved my possession as much as she bloomed for gentle brushes and kisses.

If I rose up on my knees, I could find the angle that would make her shout and twist and tremble on the bed, losing control completely, but it would leave her limp and embarrassed after, so I stayed close, grinding myself against her until she lost the ability to speak, to breathe, her nails digging into my ass. I released her breast and caught her chin.

"Look at me, my lovely siren," I hissed. "I want to watch you as you come for me."

Her eyes fell shut, but she opened them once more for me, and now I knew that the sounds she made as she fell apart, as she clutched and soaked my cock with a body that fit me perfectly, were a good match for the hauntingly beautiful way she sang.

I couldn't help myself. I gave her my knot without waiting, watched her eyes widen in shock and fresh ecstasy as it drove her back up to the height of her release before she'd finished falling. I allowed myself one long study of her as she whimpered and sighed and clamped down on my knot, her cheeks and throat and chest flushed, her hair tangling behind her head, her lips bitten rosy, and then I surrendered.

My mate. My omega. My love. *Mairwen.*

I groaned and bucked, drawing out the flutters and quakes of her tight core on my knot, the pulsing squeeze slowly shredding the thin thread of control I'd gripped so tightly. My wings beat at my back in a chorused agreement of movement and urgency. Mairwen chanted praise, my name woven with the words *love* and *mate* and *yes.*

My mouth watered and my teeth ached, and her pulse throbbed on my tongue, calling to me in steady waves of perfume—a plea or an invitation or both, I didn't know. I didn't care.

Mairwen was mine, and this would make her even more so. I purred and found her skin against my tongue, the muscles of her throat flexing with babbling words of encouragement. So gentle. So sweet. So tender as it gave beneath my hungry teeth. Her arms clutched and she froze beneath me, the first squeak of discomfort like a distant alarm in my foggy head. Then copper and honey syrup laced the inside of my mouth, and Mairwen melted, moaned. I bellowed as tension snapped, heat and lightning racing through me, velvet softness and electric crackling. I snarled into the throat of my mate and collapsed into the cradle of her body at last.

TWO CRESCENTS of little rubies fitted in slightly pink and swollen flesh. Mairwen's bruises had faded in the wake, but the mark of my bite was still fresh, blood occasionally welling as she stretched or turned her head, drawing my gazeback, as well as my lips and my tongue to soothe the spot.

"Does it hurt?" I rasped, ringing my tongue around the marks.

"Not when you do that," Mairwen murmured. I frowned and lifted my head, and she offered a smile. "It's a little sore, that's all. The books about the mating ceremony say it doesn't last long. And you're doing exactly what you ought to to help it heal."

I stiffened and then groaned, dropping my head down to Mairwen's bare chest. "*Damn*. I forgot you mentioned a ceremony. I should've—"

"Should've taken me out to the village square, stripped me bare, anointed me in oils, and then mounted me from behind as the isle feasted and watched you bite me?" Mairwen asked. I growled, and she laughed. "I prefer our rather more private method. The ceremonies fell out of fashion before mating did."

I sighed and started to settle back against my mate—she'd been stroking her hands through my hair like she might to a house cat, and I was not ashamed to admit I loved every second—when she sat up suddenly, nearly knocking our heads together.

"Oh, Ronson! Mating is *illegal*. We've done something illegal," she gasped, hands flying up over her mouth.

I grinned and rolled onto my wings. "Ahhh, I see I'm not the only one who was forgetting something important. *That* one I did remember."

She slapped me gently on the chest. "Why didn't you *say*—"

"I'm the alpha, Mairwen. I hereby declare mating legal again," I said, sweeping my arm out in a grand gesture.

"There, all settled. No one even knew that law existed anyway."

Mairwen's eyes narrowed, and she snorted. "I'm sure Niall won't have anything to say once we tell him." I blinked at that, and her lips twitched. "Ah-*ha*! You didn't think it through, did you? Bet you thought you could just keep it all a secret, as if no one would notice I wasn't aging—Ronson!" she squawked as I tackled her back into the pillows, wrestling my arms around her and glaring down at her flushed and magnificent face.

"Keep it a secret, *mate*?" I growled. Mairwen's lips pressed together as she realized what she'd said. "Keep *you* a secret? Not tell the island, the entire *world* how proud I am to be yours? To have you at my side for my *life*? To have my mark on you so they all know what you are to me, what you mean to me? Not likely, Mairwen."

She'd mellowed as I spoke, and she reached between us now, fingers traveling gently back into my hair. "Of course," she said, leaning up and kissing my jaw. "Of course not. Silly of me."

I purred and then curled up on top of my omega like the oversized feline she apparently knew I was, resting my cheek on her chest, sighing as we settled together once more.

"We do have to tell Niall, though. And it won't be so simple as just announcing to the island that I'm something most of them have never even heard of," Mairwen said. "If we're lucky—if we're going to get away with it—none of them will have heard of mating."

I sighed and nodded, but I refused to open my eyes. "Tomorrow," I bargained. "We'll tell Niall and Beatrice tomorrow." *Let me have you today, mate*, I begged privately.

Mairwen was quiet, the path of her fingers slow and steady, soothing me towards a nap. I felt calmer now. And while I was still quite tempted to cup and squeeze and roll

Mairwen's breast that sat just out of the corner of my eye, to draw it to my mouth and make a feast, there was less of the sense of lust *riding* and possessing me and my actions now. Mairwen was mine and I loved and craved every inch of her, but I loved this too—holding her, resting with her, having her scent and her touch around me in a moment of calm contentment.

"Tomorrow," she murmured as I pet a hand over her hip.

Chapter Thirty-Five

MAIRWEN

I held my breath, my hands clasped firmly in Ronson's where they rested on his lap. We sat side by side at Ronson's desk as Niall and Beatrice gaped at us across the table. Actually, Beatrice didn't look even half as surprised as Niall. She'd been there with me when I discovered the connection between the bite marks and the mention of mates. She'd seen the way Ronson had been soothing an impulse we didn't understand by gnawing on me anytime we were alone.

Niall, on the other hand, had *not* seen this coming.

He'd been studying Ronson through the whole conversation, aside from one quick confirming glance at the healing marks on my throat, his face slowly paling, eyes widening then narrowing, lips flattening. He stared at Ronson now in silence, and the *only* thing I could read on his face was shock.

Then he shook his head and looked at me. "I trusted you," he said.

I startled in my seat, looking at Ronson who scowled at his brother. "Niall," Ronson growled.

Niall held up a hand, head shaking, but he didn't look

away from me. "Him? No. From him, this...this...this thing I'd never even imagined makes a kind of sense. But Mairwen, you? You were my sensible one."

"Niall!" Ronson repeated his warning as I garbled out the start of an apology and then swallowed it down.

I wasn't sorry I'd mated Ronson. I wasn't even sorry we hadn't discussed it with Niall first because that moment was *ours*. Mine and Ronson's.

He loves me, a cheerful voice reminded me for the hundredth time since he'd said the words. I glanced up at Ronson at my side and found myself smiling. I caught his eye, and he relaxed back into his seat, answering me with the same as he squeezed my hand.

I turned back to Niall. "What makes you think our mating isn't sensible?" I asked instead.

Ronson huffed out a laugh, and Niall glared at him, but I thought the corner of his lips were twitching. "Persuade me to your case," Niall said.

"W-what?" I asked, rearing back.

"Mairwen is—" Ronson started, more prepared than I for Niall's prompting, but Niall cut him off with a raised hand. A shame, because I would've liked to hear Ronson's argument.

"Tell me what makes the bonding sensible," Niall said to me.

Ronson's chest swelled, his scent growing rough, and I thought he might start an argument with Niall he would later regret, so I spoke.

"There's several mentions of mating bonds creating the strength of two dragons, just as an heir would."

"In texts society has no access to," Niall pointed out.

"It would be easy enough to take them to a printer," I answered, sitting up. "There's more research to be done, of course. We still don't have a clear picture of why it vanished in history."

"You're talking about something that's going to take a great deal of time, and the pair of you *already* are mated."

"Yes, we are," I said, bucking my chin up. "And I also have the texts that talk about what it takes to resist a mating urge. A dragon is barely capable of focusing on anything but his mate until the bond is satisfied."

"I can attest to this," Ronson said, smirking at Niall, who rolled his eyes.

"As if this is going to stop you from chasing her skirts," Niall muttered.

Ronson grinned and shrugged. "Not likely."

I nudged my elbow into his side. "It should help, actually."

"We'll see," Ronson said, goading his brother.

I huffed and continued, "Bonding increases the chances of a male heir outside of rut, and it offers an omega the physical strength to manage the birth. There's *no* record of a mated omega dying in childbirth anywhere in our histories."

Niall looked between us, losing his sardonic expression. "Is that... Are you...?"

"No," I admitted, blushing.

Ronson released my hands only to drape an arm over my shoulder. "We're in no rush now. And I wouldn't have wanted to risk Mairwen's safety. But we would like to have children when we're ready."

I would keep drinking the tea, since as far as we knew, it prevented conception regardless of any bonding. If we were going to remove the sanction against bonding, I wondered if we might make the contraceptive legal again too. That was likely a step too far, at least for the betas of dragonkin. But it was better not to consider those men at all in this case. Ronson and Niall didn't respect most of them. I didn't. Ronson had given Francesca a choice, given me one. Perhaps together, we could give all the omegas of the isle their choice as well.

"I know that the island doesn't have confidence in me," I said, pressing my hand to Ronson's knee before he could interrupt me. "I didn't try to change their minds before, and I started to believe that some of what they said was right. But I know better now. And as impressed as I am with what you both have accomplished since Ronson became alpha, it isn't enough. Not for omegas."

Niall's head tipped, but he didn't argue with me, just raised an eyebrow and waited.

"An omega was considered equal to her mate, and I would like that to be the case again. The omegas of Bleake Isle might consider me an unlikely ally, but I hope to be able to speak up for them. I hope you'll listen," I added, turning to Ronson.

"You know I will," he murmured, lifting my hand from his lap to his lips, whispering the word *siren* against my skin as he kissed there.

I sighed and nodded, looking back to Niall. "Someone will find that bonding was outlawed, you're right. There will be controversy. Just as there is controversy now for almost anything Ronson does. But he will have me at his side for it, and I believe we can weather the storm."

Niall was quiet for a moment, and then he said something entirely unexpected. "The bond makes you stronger."

My brow furrowed. "Me? I haven't read—"

"She was always strong," Ronson said, smiling. "The bond assures her she's not alone. Her strength is backed by mine, and mine by hers."

"The strength of two dragons," Beatrice said softly, eyeing me.

"The truth is, brother, I don't want to rule as alpha if I don't have my mate at my side," Ronson said, his hand squeezing gently around my shoulder. "And I'm no longer sure that compromises are worth making."

Niall wilted into the chair he sat in, his head falling back to blink up at the ceiling. "It's not a very good case, Mairwen."

Ronson rumbled a snarl, but it stuttered and choked away as I leaned into his side, smiling at Niall's weary tone.

"Then you'll have to help us make a more convincing one," I said.

Niall nodded. "Yes, I suppose I shall. Can you bear to have her mark covered for a little while?" he asked Ronson.

Ronson frowned but nodded. "I suppose."

"Good. I have reading to do. Take Mairwen with you today to the Lords' Council," Niall said. My eyes widened, but before I could protest, Niall narrowed his eyes at mine. "Remember what you just said to me when they talk down to you, Mairwen. You are Ronson's equal—"

"Better," Ronson said.

"—and they owe you as much respect."

I sucked in a breath. Silly me, to make such a speech thinking I might apply my leadership to some indefinite future. No, Niall must throw me in straight away.

"There are the omegas to consider too. A fair few of the island have influence, although they wield it more subtly than the betas," Beatrice said, scooting forward. "We should arrange a meeting amongst them. A tea, perhaps, for the sake of appearances."

I wondered if my nerves showed on my face as I turned to Ronson, who did his best to hide his humor, although it glittered brightly in his gaze.

"It is time for the island to properly meet *my* omega," Ronson purred.

MY CLAMMY HAND lifted from my lap, reaching for my chest, where fire seemed to burn inside, anxiety a hot tempest in my heart. I forced my fingers to the teacup waiting in its saucer instead, listening to the cheerful murmurs of the women around the table, waiting for my opportunity to speak.

The Lords' Council had been bad enough. Once the men had gotten over their utter shock at my arrival and their near refusal to discuss anything of importance in front of me, they'd carried on their business as if I weren't there at all. Or at least they'd tried. But I knew more of their business than they'd expected, and when they wouldn't listen to me, they were forced to acknowledge Ronson. By the end of the afternoon, I'd received a scant few respectful words from two of the lords in attendance and I was in a rare hot temper. Which Ronson had promptly fucked out of me in our nest before dinner.

But Ronson wasn't here with me now for this tea. Even Beatrice, who had helped me plan everything from topics to tarts, had left me on my own.

And the truth was I was more intimidated by these omegas than by their beta counterparts. These women had helped shape my identity as 'Mouse.' Not as directly as Adelaide and her rotten nickname, but in smaller and equally cutting ways.

Lady Hudson had once suggested to my mother and myself that if I was to have a new dress for her ball, it might be best if it matched the colors of her walls to better allow me to blend in for the night. When Mrs. Finch had caught my mother bemoaning my increasing inches at the dressmaker's when I was fourteen, she'd recommended that if a reducing diet was not working, I might consider fasting when not at a public event. I'd once overheard Lady Keegesby tell her daughter to be sure to stand near me so as to appear slim by comparison.

These matrons had belittled me as easily as breathing. They were not meant to be insults but friendly advice. I hadn't existed to them, not as a girl with feelings, and that was somehow worse.

I swallowed down the heat of bile in my throat and straightened in my chair. If Ronson had known any of that, he'd be at my side. Just the thought made me more aware of the healed bite hiding beneath my gauzy fichu, and I found myself smiling, catching the eye of Lady Keegesby as she leaned forward to inspect the spread of food I'd ordered for this "informal meeting of friends."

"Lady Keegesby, I'm very glad you could attend. I wish you would share my heartfelt congratulations with Jane on the birth of her latest daughter," I said.

"Thank you, M—Omega Cadogan," the older woman said, blinking back at me.

"It is a pity, though, that she should've gotten with child so soon before the rut," Lady Hudson cut in, glancing between us. "Another daughter for Mr. Sampson, and another cycle without an heir."

Lady Keegesby flushed and pursed her lips to bite off a retort. I resisted the restless stir in my chest that wanted to tell these women that they were all speaking to one another and playing these games by the rules of horrible men who discarded and wasted their lives so carelessly. Instead, I took a breath and smiled at Lady Hudson.

"Ahh, but Mr. Sampson eagerly dotes on those daughters. And besides, we omegas are still outnumbered. Another daughter might do our island good," I said.

The easy conversation between the other women had settled as I'd spoken up, and now they were all ears, eyes keen and eager. They wanted to watch verbal cuts and jabs. Perhaps some of them even wanted to see me win against Lady Hudson, who had a rapier for a tongue. But I didn't want a tea of catty conversation and delicately-phrased arguments. I wanted to *unite* these women. I had to tread carefully and not let this new and eager temper of mine have its way.

"And so she might, if any of the betas had the sense to listen to women," a sharp voice croaked out. It was Agnes Hubbard, an elderly omega who'd survived not one, but two beta partners—the second had claimed her supposedly for the double fortune she'd amassed before the age of thirty-five—and whose only sharp words to me growing up had been, *"Well, speak up, if you're going to speak at all."*

A woman trilled with a nervous laugh. "Oh, quite! My John never does attend a word I say."

"The betas may not all be our ally, but Alpha Cadogan would be," I said, lifting my teacup once more to my lips, letting my softly spoken words rest in the stirring sounds of muslin and lace shifting in seats.

"And what good does it do the isle to let a barely grown omega go tearing off on a ship to seek a silly fortune elsewhere, eh, girl?" Agnes grouched, snatching one of the tarts from the tray. She sniffed it, but at least *that* she gave an approving glance.

I laughed, thinking of Francesca. "I see your point. But what harm does it do?"

The women in the room blustered and shot wary looks at one another.

"He gave me the chance to leave too, and I stayed," I said, shrugging. "Not all of us want to run. It's not *so* dire, I think. Still, you must admit there's room for improvement."

"This is...is...heresy. Or-or treason," Mrs. Finch hissed to the woman at her side.

Agnes Hubbard snorted and rolled her eyes, plumping herself more comfortably into the cozy chair she'd claimed upon entering. "Of course it isn't either, you goose. You're sitting in front of the alpha's omega. If she's here, it's not to start a coup against her alpha."

"I like him rather a lot, actually, so no," I said brightly, finding my footing, if only by knocking all the other women out of of their usual stride. And hearing that I *liked* Ronson? Well, that threw a lot of women back into their chairs in a stunned silence.

Not Agnes, though. She huffed, but it was a sound of humor. She was tall, like me, healthy and full-bodied too. She'd birthed two sons—one to her second beta, quite late in life by dragonkin standards—and while her family and her sons' families had no grand titles and no marriages to high-born lines, Agnes Hubbard herself owned a number of successful businesses in part or whole on the island. She had deep pockets, and deep pockets always held influence, even if women like Lady Hudson would've rather not acknowledged as much.

One omega, Lady Evelyn Grant, cleared her throat to catch my eye. "If you really do have your alpha's ear, then perhaps you can persuade him to my Reginald's—"

"I'm not here for your betas," I said firmly, cutting her off and refusing to shy from her shocked gasp. "I am here for you. For your daughters. For *their* daughters."

And still, the room was quiet, the women eyeing one another, waiting for someone else to speak. I wanted to rise from my seat and shake them all. These matrons had survived, it was true, but it was equally unlikely they had not lost someone too. A sister or a daughter. As omegas, our deaths were almost commonplace when it came time to bear children. Being chosen in the ceremony was like tossing a coin to see if you were going to the gallows.

We all *knew* what was wrong on the isle, with dragonkin. Why wouldn't anyone say it out loud?

"My granddaughter is expecting," Lady Hudson said,

smoothing her skirts and turning her cup in its saucer. "From the rut. Already she is bedridden. Lord Quincy has informed the doctor to cut the babe from her if there is any chance of her not being able to deliver."

I nodded and met Lady Hudson's gaze as the other women looked away.

"Doctors on the isle prioritize a birth at great risk to the mother," I said.

"He's lost two omegas already," Agnes Hubbard muttered, and Lady Hudson winced.

I drew in a breath and considered the problem, the question Lady Hudson hadn't asked. "I am, as some of you might've noticed, a voracious reader. There are old birthing practices traditional to the isle that have fallen out of fashion, but they offer considerable benefits to the mothers."

"Wing breaking," one woman whispered.

Wing breaking was a practice of causing the break of an unborn male's wings to allow for an easier birth, but it didn't always have the best record of those wings being reset properly.

"Perhaps. I was thinking of a text I'd read regarding the regular habit of swimming," I said, receiving a few scoffs. "It sounds trivial, I agree, but the physics make sense. We float in water. It takes the pressure off the mother's body, as well as building muscle without excessive strain."

"Isn't there a chance of-of drowning the child in the womb?" Mrs. Finch gasped.

"Don't be a ninny," Agnes Hubbard groaned.

"Of course, we must first find a way of dissuading doctors of some of their more brutal methods," I continued.

I had their attention now, and for once, it didn't make me feel small and foolish and embarrassed. Ronson wasn't here to purr and compliment me. This strength was, at last, my own.

Chapter Thirty-Six

RONSON

I was getting used to the sensation of smiling.

I turned, my arm tight around Mairwen's waist, her hand warm in mine, and my cheeks felt full and a little sore as I watched a loose strand of her hair fluttering as we spun. The ballroom's plentiful candles and lamps glittered around us, warming Mairwen's skin to gold. Her hand on my shoulder tightened, and her breasts caught my eye, just the faintest glimpse of the dark valley that made my mouth water, almost hidden by the lace collar worn to disguise her bite. Mairwen's eyes slid shut and she stumbled slightly, carried along to the music by my leading.

"Are you all right?" I asked, slowing a touch, but not enough to cause a hiccup in the dancers around us.

"Just a dizzy spell," Mairwen laughed, and she swayed closer, like she was about to lean against me, before recalling that we were in public.

I found a gap in the dancers and ushered us through it, guiding Mairwen off the floor for the moment, ignoring the polite rules of society to pull her close against my chest. If dragonkin was inclined to be scandalized by the sight of me holding my omega, then so be it.

It'd been a long time since I'd attended a ball. I might've declined this invitation too, if it hadn't been for Mairwen saying, "Oh, I always hated attending the assemblies. Standing to the side for hours in a crowded room, while others got to dance? What a bore."

My omega hadn't danced? That wouldn't do.

"You were dizzy this morning on our flight too," I said, bending my head so only she would overhear.

Mairwen hummed and shrugged, but she didn't pull away from my support. I slid my hand at her waist up to the back of her neck. She was hot to the touch, but the room was crowded and we'd just danced two rowdy dances in a row together. Even I was sweating.

"Are you tired?" I asked.

Mairwen shook her head, smiling and watching the isle swirling around the floor. "Although I suppose we won't get to dance together again," she murmured, brow furrowing briefly.

"Why shouldn't we?" I asked.

She twisted to stare up at me, lips parted to answer the obvious—we'd had our three socially polite dances already, and it was time to share our attention with the rest of dragonkin—but then her mouth hooked a wicked curve at the corners. "You're right. I don't mind being a scandal with you."

In that case, I thought, grinning and ducking my head for what I hoped would be a kiss worth all the gossip the isle could muster.

"Time to share her, Ronson."

My growl rumbled, and I didn't straighten, glaring out of the corner of my eye at my brother, who possessed all the inconvenient timing in the world. But if Mairwen had never had chances to dance at any of dragonkin's balls, she certainly hadn't been escorted about by a collection of partners. I'd kept her to myself thus far. Niall would be a good second partner.

"Go on, then," I said with a sigh, diverting my kiss to Mairwen's temple, her lips stretched in a broad smile. "Don't accept a next partner we wouldn't—"

"I know," Mairwen and Niall choroused together, and then she slipped free of my hold and accepted my brother's arm.

I watched them take the floor together, Mairwen talking quickly as Niall studied the crowds around them. I had to clasp my hands behind my back to keep from rushing after, stealing my mate back for myself. With Niall escorting and Mairwen at a distance, the expressions of the surrounding dragonkin became clearer, and I eyed the company critically.

Betas stared at Mairwen with a mix of confusion and curiosity, and some with outright admiration. I couldn't decide if I was more offended by those who seemed baffled by my omega or those who looked a little too eager to renew their acquaintance. In the corners of the room, clusters of omegas whispered to another behind the cover of their fans, their gazes dissecting Mairwen, and I wanted to believe I saw approval in some of their eyes. The omegas of dragonkin had been out of my reach during my rule as alpha. If Mairwen succeeded in gaining their trust, the influence they might wield over their betas in the privacy of homes could be a great boon for any cause we wished to champion.

The slow advance of light brown wings pulled me from my study, and I stiffened at the sight of Mairwen's father approaching me. I hadn't forgiven Mairwen's parents for the horrible evening we'd spent with them, although I wondered now if my omega was more equipped to manage time with them. I wouldn't test the theory. We'd deal with the Posys if and when Mairwen asked to see them.

I considered turning away, snubbing Albert Posy, but he

reached me before I made up my mind, murmuring my name with a deferential bow. I ground my jaw, glanced briefly at the dancers to make sure Mairwen was still smiling, and then answered him with a nod of my head.

He straightened and moved to stand at my side, watching the same scene, the same subject, that I couldn't help but be drawn to.

"I underestimated my daughter," he said softly, so none of the nearby eavesdroppers might hear.

"You did," I said, an easy enough answer to make.

"I am grateful, for her sake, that you proved us wrong."

"Mairwen is responsible for her own achievements, Lord Posy."

"You'll allow, at least, that you saw the potential we did not," he murmured.

I sighed and shrugged, already searching the room for a reason to escape this conversation. My gaze drifted, skipping back to Niall and Mairwen before returning to the edges, and I'd made nearly a full circuit of observation when I landed on a lone figure in a shadowy corner of the hall. A girl, nearly too young to be in attendance, I thought, stood at the fringe of the company.

"We do love our girl, Lord Cadogan," Albert Posy said. "Gwen and I are a love match, and it is more than we hoped for to see Mairwen in one as well."

The girl in the corner was short and plump, and her pale hair was scraped cruelly back from a plain face. She was staring at Mairwen with a kind of wonder shining in liquidy eyes, one I could relate to. I wouldn't have noticed her while I was dancing with Mairwen, but I suspected she hadn't been asked to the floor yet. Even the youngest betas seemed to give the girl a wide berth, their eyes turned away from her to avoid being caught and required to play the part of the gentlemen they were meant to be.

"I know it is of general society interest whether you might have an heir. But I do wish to say, as a potential grandfather, that we look forward to any grandchild with a great deal of familial joy," the beta continued.

"No doubt," I said, then turned to face him before he could continue and press for information. His motivation might've been as Mairwen's father, or simply as one of the many of society who'd wanted the same answer. Had I been successful? Had I claimed an omega and achieved an heir at last? "Any announcement we might make, privately or publicly, will take some consideration between Mairwen and myself."

"Of-of course, my boy—"

I cleared my throat, and Albert Posy's voice died. "If you might excuse me," I said when his silence settled. He flushed but ducked his head and set me free.

I crossed the room. I'd vowed earlier not to dance with anyone but Mairwen or Beatrice, but since I'd only sworn that to myself, it was an easy enough one to break. The girl was too focused on the room to notice my approach. When it became obvious, with me only a yard or two away, she balked visibly, stumbling back toward the wall, searching side to side in the hopes she might find some other reason for my nearness.

Do you always walk like you're on your way to claim your right as alpha? Mairwen's voice rang in my head, along with her bright laughter, and I reminded myself to slow, to put on a smile I usually reserved for one woman and one woman only. I stopped when I was close enough to be heard but not so close as to drive the poor girl to climbing the wall to escape me, then offered a short bow.

"Forgive my interruption," I said, and the girl's eyes widened. "I hope you'll forgive me for not seeking an introduction from another source."

She gaped at me, pale and startled and no doubt confused. "Lord Cadogan," I offered, to prompt her.

Her eyes searched our surroundings, her face turning almost green when she realized the nearby dragonkin were staring. Perhaps I should've waited for Mairwen to return from dancing. She would've instructed me on how to soften my approach. But the girl rallied, curtsying low. "M-Miss Rebecca Underhill, my lord."

I sighed, relieved to be done with that part, at least. "Miss Underhill, I wonder if you might do me the honor of joining me for the next dance?"

She froze and so did the men and women around us, but her cheeks regained color and she straightened and smoothed her skirts. "It would be my pleasure, Lord Cadogan."

It occurred to me as we stood side by side watching the dancers, that I should've asked for the remainder of *this* dance, because making conversation with the terrified girl was awkward at best and the gawking of the room were stifling. But none of it mattered because my eyes were fixed on another pair, honey and warm and shining, Mairwen's smile reaching me from across the room.

My mate accepted Gideon Millward's hand for the next dance, and I led Miss Rebecca Underhill to join them—conveniently, a dance where partners would be exchanged. And the girl brightened as she exchanged hands with first one gentleman and then another, all who paid her courteous attention and a polite compliment. And all the while, Mairwen beamed at me, holding my gaze.

Gideon secured Miss Underhill for the next dance, and I would offer him some sign of my gratitude later, because Mairwen's hand was in mine and she was leading me from the floor, through the throng of watchers at the edges of the room, out a pair of double doors and into the cool night on a large open stone terrace.

"Mairwen?"

"I love you," she gasped, dragging me out of sight of the windows full of shadowed figures and candlelight, her hand pulling free of mine, grasping my sides instead, tearing open the buttons of my coat so she could press herself closer to the softer cotton of my shirt. "I love you, I love you."

I groaned and sank against her, nuzzling my face to hers as she dressed my jaw and throat and cheeks in kisses.

"It was only a dance," I murmured, wishing I could go back in time, wondering if I would've had the sense to pick Mairwen out from the shadows too, to ask her to dance.

"She will never forget it. *I* will never forget it," Mairwen whispered, arms wrapping under my coat. "I'm dizzy again, Ronson."

I frowned and lifted my head, reaching to cup her face, but her gaze was clear and bright when I found it.

"Take me to the nest, mate."

I bent and Mairwen was ready, slipping her arms up to loop around my shoulders as I scooped her up beneath her knees.

"We'll go to every ball from now on," I said, my wings stretching and starting to beat, stirring the air around us.

Mairwen laughed. "Only if you promise to ask a young omega looking out of place to dance at each one."

"To make you happy? I'd ask a thousand," I said.

"Mmm, not a thousand. I'll want to dance with you myself, my love."

I growled and leapt to the air, flying us home.

I PULLED the curtain of the nest back, and Mairwen winced and rolled away from the sunlight, burrowing under blankets and pillows. My stomach twisted nervously.

"I should call a doctor."

"It's only a little heartburn, Ronson," Mairwen said, voice muffled from beneath the pillows.

"And dizzy spells. And that nausea last night."

The blankets rose and fell. "I think perhaps Cook is right, and I do like foods that are too rich."

I frowned, debating undressing and crawling back into the bed with Mairwen. Not that I could do anything other than stare at her and fuss. But she'd had little symptoms like this ever since the ball a week prior, and while she didn't seem to be getting any worse, she wasn't getting better either.

And part of me kept wondering... *What if?*

What if Mairwen was sick? I would tear the island, the entire world apart until I found a doctor who could cure her.

But what if she was pregnant? What if the tea *didn't* work for mated dragons?

"Ronson," Mairwen grumbled. "I can feel you staring."

"I'm worried."

"I'm *fine*."

"Mairwen—"

"Ronson—"

"Mate."

A pause. A huff. A twitch of my lips as the blankets were flung back and the pillows tossed in the air as Mairwen sat up, beautifully rumpled and obviously irate.

"I love you," I said. Whether it was a reflexive response to seeing her, or an attempt at deflecting her irritation, I wasn't sure.

She smiled while glaring, and I decided that Mairwen, annoyed and affectionate at the same time, was almost as arousing as when she was soft and amazed and desirous.

She rose to her knees and sighed. "I feel better already," she said, scooting closer to the edge of the bed, pressing her hands to my chest before I could wrap her up in my embrace and take us both back down to the mattress. "And I love you too. I'm resting today, I promise. And telling Cook to make lighter fare for a little bit. She'll get to tell me she was right. She'll like that. You don't need to worry."

"Don't take this as an excuse to spend the day researching in the library," I said, bending for a kiss and nipping at the scowl on her lips. "Read for *fun*."

Mairwen's eyes brightened, and then I brushed my mouth over hers and she hummed, lashes falling and draping over full cheeks. "If you insist," she sighed as I pulled away.

"If there are any changes—"

Mairwen's hands stroked up my head, and she skimmed another kiss over my lips. "I'll call a doctor and I'll send someone to bring you back. But honestly, Ronson, I'm all right."

She did look fine. More than fine. Her cheeks had color but not too much, her eyes were clear, and her smile was earnest. Her skin felt warmer than usual, almost feverish, but she didn't seem to notice the change the way I did. I sighed and nodded, stepping back at last, turning for the door, not quite able to tear my stare off of her.

"Don't let the betas get away with whatever it is they're scheming about now," Mairwen called, falling back into the bed with a lazy wave.

I grinned and relaxed at last, marching away. "Never."

———

I BRACED myself against the wind, keeping my eye on the familiar outcroppings of rock, the old and abandoned outposts of now retired mines. The Dunne mines were located at the southern end of the isle, away from the villages and estates and farmland, almost at the cliff's edge. They had closed after the death of Edgar Dunne, his widow unwilling to sell the mines away but also unable to manage them on her own, and had been kept in reserve for the twin brothers until they were old enough to manage.

I had my doubts about whether the mines were safe or had any ore left to offer, but since they'd still been producing at a trickling amount when they closed, I owed the Dunne twins a meeting and, most likely, my approval to reopen.

Niall and I touched down on the ground a few meters away from the modest stone building. Some windows had cracked glass panes, but it was still the warm season, and the rest of the building looked to be in decent shape.

"This won't take long, at least," Niall said, glancing at me as I grunted. "What's wrong? You haven't been this surly and silent since before you claimed Mairwen."

I rolled my shoulders and shook my head. I hadn't realized I was tensing up, but the farther we'd flown from the castle—from Mairwen—the more uncomfortable I'd grown. Was this because of the mating bond, or because I was worried for her? I opened my mouth, not quite sure what my answer would be, when we turned the corner and saw the small crowd of beta gentlemen waiting for us.

The Dunne twins, Lord Cambeth, Gryffyd Evans, and of course, Hugh Gamesby. Niall's stride halted just after mine, and he stiffened, twisting in my direction.

"A challenge?" he whispered.

"No doubt," I answered, frowning.

"I should—"

"Go to Torion. DeRoche if you see him on the water too," I said.

Niall glanced back to the betas, who stood still and solemn, waiting for my approach. "This should be done publicly."

I nodded. "It would require a vote. This way, he can make me accept in private. Go. I'll manage."

Niall moved, wings spreading, and then paused once more. "Should I tell Mairwen?"

I licked my lips, only a little embarrassed to realize I wanted her here with me, supporting me. I flexed my wings, glaring at Gamesby. "No. I'll tell her myself when this is over."

Niall nodded, legs bending and wings drumming, taking roughly into the air. Gamesby's eyes widened at his departure, grim features snaking into a smile, and a flicker of doubt rushed through me. Whatever his plan was, it suited him for me to be alone.

My hands fisted at my sides, and I stepped forward with sinking acceptance. Whatever he had planned for me, I would meet it as I was—the Alpha of Bleake Isle.

Chapter Thirty-Seven

MAIRWEN

"**O**mega Cadogan? Lord Posy is here and has asked to see you," the maid announced from the doorway of the library. I blinked at her, and she offered a nervous smile, her hands twisting in front of her apron. "Should I tell him you're unavailable?"

Yes, please, I thought, then grimaced and shook my head. "No. No, I'll see him."

"I should bring him here?" the girl asked.

I glanced around me, then sat up, dragging my legs off the couch. Every flat surface in the library was covered with open texts about mating or birthing practices.

"No, I think the blue parlor would be best," I said, rising and breathing a sigh of relief when the room remained steady and no dizziness struck me.

I'd promised Ronson I was fine, and for the most part, I believed I was telling the truth. If anything, I felt *stronger* than usual. Even the many flights of stairs between the nest and the kitchens hadn't made me breathless and wobbly earlier. But there was something *different*, and I couldn't decide between the urge to ignore it entirely, afraid of what I might find, and my usual curious impulse to study it and make sense of the symptoms.

I smoothed my sleeves and skirts as the maid hurried to escort my father. I could take my time, do my best to soothe my nerves, if possible. My hair was down, braided, and for anyone else I might try and twist it up, but it was only my father visiting. I tucked loose strands of hair behind my ears and picked up my shawl from the arm of the couch, draping it over my shoulders to hide the bite mark on my throat.

Good enough for Father, I thought, a bittersweet ache in my chest as I headed for the hall.

I'd always been grateful to my father. He'd seemed to accept me as I was—a great relief in contrast to my mother, who had plucked and pushed and ordered my corset laces tighter at every opportunity, wanting me to be more like the other omegas. Since Ronson had claimed me, I realized that my father's acceptance was slightly tainted. He accepted the daughter the rest of dragonkin saw me as, flawed and disappointing and not worth as much as the other omegas. It was something more like resignation, really, not love. I was what he'd had to work with, and so he'd made the best of me. He'd sold me to Gryffyd Evans.

I couldn't imagine the life I might've had, if not for that chance moment with Ronson. I was too far removed from that woman by now, even in the few months it had been. I would've been miserable. No, much more than that.

I shuddered as the door to the parlor opened, the maid departing, and caught sight of my father standing at the center of the room, his back to me.

He earned his way contracting humans' labor and lives. Why not sell his daughter too? I thought bitterly, wishing now that I'd sent him away, waited for Ronson's return.

My rough sigh was too loud, and my father turned to face me before I could devise an escape.

"Mairwen! There you are." His smile was bright, and his arms stretched wide, open for a hug. A year ago, I would've been overjoyed if he'd looked so happy to see me. Now there was only a brief, cool relief that he'd used my real name.

"Hello, Father," I said, forcing a smile to my lips and entering the room. "Forgive my informal dress. I wasn't expecting anyone."

"No matter, no matter. What is the use of formality between father and daughter?" he asked, bracing his hands on my shoulders as I reached him. He stepped back, still smiling, although up close, there was less joy in the expression than I'd realized. His gaze studied me slowly, searching more thoroughly than ever before, and I crossed my arms over my stomach and stepped away.

I twisted to seat myself in an armchair and gasped at the sight of a second man in the room. Redmond Palmer stood on the other side of the door where it hung open, out of my view as I'd entered the room, and he smirked as I startled, offering me a low bow.

"Apologies for intruding on the visit, Omega Cadogan. Your father and I were out on business together when he asked to stop and see you," Lord Palmer said, tugging his scarlet waistcoat back into place as he straightened.

I fought my frown, but the maid had already vanished. I would have to find her later and speak to her about announcing *all* my guests to me, rather than some.

"Please, sit," I offered, watching them carefully. Palmer sat near the door in another armchair that faced me, and my father at my side. "Lord Cadogan is away at the moment, and I have my own work to attend to shortly, but it is nice to see you," I said to my father. I glanced at Lord Palmer and tried not to let my suspicion show on my face. "What business do you have together?"

Lord Palmer's lips twitched in amusement, but my father

blustered, smoothing his palms over his knees and forcing out a chuckle. "Mouse, what need do you have to know men's business?"

"The isle's interests are my interests, just as they are my ma—Lord Cadogan's." I corrected my near slip with a huff, wetting my lips and hoping neither man noticed. Would they even realize I had almost called Ronson my mate?

My father glanced at Palmer, plucking at the fabric of his trousers, a nervous fidget that made me want to shift restlessly or rise and run from the room.

"Surely, Omega Cadogan, your most important role is to bear and nurture the alpha's heir," Palmer said with sickly sweetness.

Rat, a dark voice snarled in my head, but it came with a sense of comfort, of not being alone in the moment.

This was no heartburn blazing in my chest. I lifted my chin and tried to swallow against the scorching sensation in my throat that begged to be let loose.

"Surely, Lord Palmer, Lady Palmer will see to the rearing of your two boys, the managing of your household, the bookkeeping of your accounts, and any interests of her own. We women are raised to widely share our talents and attention," I said cooly, even as the fire built inside of me. I tipped my head and glared at Redmond Palmer, my fingers digging into the arms of my seat like claws. "Why did you bring my father here?"

"M-Mairwen," my father murmured. "Perhaps, sir, it would be better if—"

Palmer raised his hand and nodded. "Say no more. I'll give you both a moment."

"Remain in the hall, if you don't mind, my lord," I said, voice sharp and teeth snapping shut. The last thing I needed right now was Palmer snooping about. I watched him rise and leave, the door almost completely shut. And then I turned back to my father, sighing. "Father, why would you bring that man—"

"Mairwen, hush a moment and listen to me," Father said, leaning forward earnestly and grabbing my hands. "Are you pregnant with the alpha's heir?"

"Father!" I reared back, but my father's hands were tight around mine, his eyes wide.

"This is important, daughter. Palmer knows of a doctor who can safely rid you of the alpha's offspring, but it must be soon," my father whispered.

I gaped at the man before me, familiar and a stranger all at once. It wasn't the concept I rejected but the source—that men like my father or Palmer might know of such a possibility and reserve it for their own whim.

"I think it very obvious why Lord Palmer might offer such assistance to me, Father. How can you not see his motivations are to thwart our alpha?" I asked, barely lowering my voice. My skin felt too tight, hot and aching, and my nausea had returned.

My father blew out a breath and shook his head. "His motivations are meaningless when he is offering you the security of surviving, Mouse."

"I am not a mouse," I spat, yanking my hands from my father's, fisting them into my lap.

"Mairwen," my father pleaded.

"This is a *scheme*, Father. A bad one. A treasonous one," I said. Ronson had given me the choice, and in a cruel, backwards way, my father was doing the same. I wanted to march into the streets and scream at top of my lungs what omegas were being denied, these secrets that our dragonkin had kept from us.

"Mairwen, listen!" my father snapped, and I flinched and then wanted to roar at him and myself for the reaction.

"With the alpha gone, there will be no one to protect you. Even if you survived the child—"

I stood, a loud, sharp ringing in my ears, a dark vibration in my chest. When the warning note settled, the sound of my own snarl was all that remained in the quiet.

"What did you just say?" I asked, and my voice was lower, thicker, a growl in the words.

My father sat back in his chair, eyes darting to the door.

With the alpha gone...

"Mou-Mairwen, wait!" my father cried out.

But I was already racing for the door, tearing it open and ignoring the resulting *bang!* as it crashed against the wall. Palmer startled outside, just across the hall, and his lips flattened with one glance at me.

"Where is he?" I growled.

"What did you say?" Palmer asked, looking over my shoulder to my father.

I'd had enough of men speaking around me for one day, enough of being overlooked for a lifetime. There were sharp points pricking into my palms, and my hands stretched for Palmer, grabbing him by his gaudy coat and yanking him into the room. Ivory claws tore holes in the wool.

"Where is my alpha?!"

Palmer paled now, surprised by my strength, perhaps, or by a woman's anger in earnest. Or perhaps it was the sight of the blue flames that licked out between my lips, reaching for his face.

"Precisely where he told you he would be, Omega Cadogan," Palmer answered, taking a breath, trying to straighten in my grip, to regain his footing. "If he's not dead by now."

I shook him hard, staring down at him, watching him grow smaller in my grip, my knuckles sharpening, the room too hot and tiny and crowded with *men.*

"Fang's fire, what's happening?!" my father shouted.

Palmer's eyes were wide enough to see white around his irises now, and there, in their terrified reflection, was a ferocious creature with sharp horns and bright eyes. I was dizzy, breathless, but I couldn't faint in front of Palmer. I didn't dare.

"Posy, get back!" Palmer shouted, and I was buffeted by waves of sharp, crackling energy, like lightning. He was going to transform into a dragon, here in this small, pretty blue parlor.

He would tear the castle open.

Eat him, the new voice in me purred. *He will stick between our teeth, but it will silence his tongue.*

I roared at him instead, delighted by the sound, by the release of pressure in my chest, and dragged him over to the windows.

"No, wait!" Palmer scrambled, pulling a chair onto its back as he grabbed it in a panic to stop our progress.

I threw us into the glass, shattering it against hard scales.

"Mairwen!" my father screamed.

The air outside was warm and fast, caressing against me, and falling was not so different than flying with Ronson as he teased me and dove toward the waves.

Ronson.

My mate. Our *mate.*

I roared, lifting my head to scorch the air with excess fire, and with a scalding, tearing sensation, I spread my wings to take flight. Caught in my claws was a smallish dragon, gray-brown with flecks of blush red, and he snarled and twisted, biting at my scaled grip, but his fangs were weak and his body was light.

It took my wings a few tries, my rhythm unsteady, but soon, we were rising. I barked a sound, a cry of joy. This was *my* flight. *My* body.

My dragon.

The dragon in my hold snapped its jaws hard around my front left leg, finally catching a tender spot of my hide, and I roared and loosed my claws, dropping him free. He screeched and turned midair, wings beating frantically to escape me.

Not so fast, little rat, my dragon purred, and together we swooped down to catch the beast in the clamp of our jaws, dragging him out toward the sea.

Squash this pest first, then rescue my mate, I thought, and I soared through the air, chest full of pride and fire.

Chapter Thirty-Eight

RONSON

I grunted and snarled, twisting toward the dragon that had just jutted its horns into my right flank, snapping forward to bite. Claws swiped at my left wing and I roared and flailed briefly, irritated and tired, swarmed by too many enemies at once.

I shouldn't have told Niall to go.

Gamesby hadn't been issuing a challenge. He'd come for a cold-blooded mutiny. And I sent away my only chance of a witness.

But I wasn't dead yet. Gryffyd Evans was crumpled on the ground, leg broken and unconcious. Tybalt Dunne had a broken tail, and in spite of catching my wing, his own on the right was nearly done for. One more good hit, and I would ground him.

Unfortunately, that still left me—

A large, heavy body threw itself into my side, and my flight faltered, sagging in surprise, giving Gamesby time to gouge his claws into my belly. But no matter what he wanted to believe, he wasn't as strong as me. He hadn't fought my father for the role of alpha—he wouldn't have survived that challenge. And I didn't intend to let him survive this mutiny.

I belted fire and charged forward, rolling us midair, letting his claws dig in to hold him against me and turn him onto his back. He released me then, twisting and diving, trying to stay out of the reach of my claws, but they caught his spine, tearing down his dense hide—not serious damage, but enough to make him scream in protest. Jaws gripped my tail, but I ignored them, finishing my swipe at Gamesby before turning to address Cambeth's bite.

I would survive.

I would win, and then I would have a *very* good reason for taking these men, these thorns in my side, and stripping them of their titles and their lands, locking them up, and putting them through a humiliating court of justice. If they had omegas and children, I would put all their properties and assets in the women's hands.

I kicked Cambeth away, bit through Tybalt's wing, wrestled Julian into a retreating somersault, and turned back to Gamesby. If I could finish him off, the others would likely back down. I just needed to—

A roar sounded at a short distance, rolling through the air to reach us, and a shiver raced down my back. Gamesby and I grappled at one another, and I allowed him to spin me around, just so I could see the dragon approaching.

My heart sank.

The beast was *enormous*. And it wasn't Seamus or Torion, which meant it was likely someone here to assist Gamesby. I might be able to beat these four—no, three now; Tybalt was grounded—dragons, but not if this fearsome creature came to help them.

I had never seen such a dragon before. Could it have been from a different isle? Even Gamesby had lost focus, and for a moment we all caught our breath, hovering above the ground.

Their golden scales shone brilliantly under sunlight, and the large body was adorned with sharp horns, their color dipped in the blue-green of the surrounding sea. The bones of their wings were thick, the sweeping motion long and a little uneven, but the talons on the tips were deadly looking.

And then the dragon tipped its head and roared again, an eye like gleaming honey and amber blinking.

Mate, she cried in that thunderous voice.

Mairwen.

I answered the desperate call, a great echo of triumph, shock rippling through me in equal measure with joy and wonder.

That dragon was *my mate*.

My mate was rushing closer, headed to join me in a fight against three other dragons.

Suddenly, it didn't matter that I'd known a moment ago that she could outclass me. If a single one of the betas around me so much as scratched one of those perfect golden scales, I would tear them to pieces. My wings drummed, and I charged at Gamesby, grabbed his neck in my jaw, and shook him hard, hearing his fangs rattle together.

Behind me came a crash of claws and scales, and a roar that vibrated through my bones announcing my mate's arrival to the fight. I twisted, swinging Gamesby by my grasp on his throat, just enough to watch Mairwen land on Cambeth's dragon, to hear his rough yelp of pain as her body bore him down to the ground. Julian swirled around her head, the fool, and she butted roughly into his belly, her deadly crown scratching at the sensitive scales there.

Fools! her dragon snarled, jaws snapping. *Dead fools.*

Gamesby scratched a claw up my ankle, and I tore my focus away from Mairwen. Well...most of it. But she was magnificent! I could've left her all three of them, and she would've held her own. Now I simply wanted to make her proud. I tossed Gamesby from my jaws and then rose high, catching him once more by the shoulders before he could plan another attack. He screamed, thrashing in the grip of my claws, but he couldn't fly with the roots of his wings held tightly.

On the ground, Tybalt Dunne had transformed back to a man, his wings folded in close and hands lifting up to his mouth. "Come down, Julian! We're better off running now. Gamesby hasn't a chance."

Rivals as the brothers often were, Julian listened, rising up out of Mairwen's dangerous reach and then diving down to his brother. Cambeth surrendered too, slack in Mairwen's grip, his lack of resistance and her strength carrying them down to the ground. Which left me with Gamesby.

I should kill him, I thought, shaking him in my grasp. On the ground below, Mairwen's dragon watched us, glowing eyes narrowed in anger.

My father would've killed a man like Gamesby for challenging him, for planning a *mutiny* outside of any legal and honorable channels. Which cleared some of the fog in my mind. I was not my father. And Gamesby hadn't chosen a *challenge*. He'd chosen a murder attempt. With men on the ground that could testify as much and be charged as well. I grinned toothily at Mairwen as I looked down to see her spiked tail curved around the Dunne twins, preventing their escape.

I raised my own tail, striking it roughly against the side of Gamesby's tough face, hearing his scream as one daggered tip scratched his eye. A distant roar heralded the arrival of more dragons, and the dark inky-blue wingspan was that of an ally.

Gamesby groaned and shuddered, and I dropped him to the ground as he transformed. I followed him down, noting the bloodstains on his shoulders and side, the eye I had scratched, and then pinned him carefully under one clawed paw. Mairwen huffed a breath of fire in his direction, singeing some of the honey-blond strands and drawing a whimper from the man. Her jaw lifted, and I ducked my head down to hers, nuzzling her chin, avoiding her dangerous spikes and puffing my breath, catching some of that warm scent of hers, now candied and darkened with dragon's fire.

"I yield," Gamesby wheezed beneath me.

I spat near his head, and it sizzled in the grass. Yielding was for legal fights.

"Ronson! Fang's fire, who is that?!" Niall shouted from above.

I looked up to see my brother on DeRoche's back, Torion's dragon not far behind. They were headed straight for us, and DeRoche's fangs were exposed as he snarled at Mairwen's dragon.

I transformed quickly, kicking Gamesby hard in his wounded side to keep him down, nodding at Mairwen when she put her own claws on his back.

"You're too late for a fight," I called back, then pointed at the deep blue dragon barreling closer. "Don't you dare let your fire loose, DeRoche, or I'll skin you for hurting my *mate*!"

DeRoche floundered for a moment mid-flight and then slowed to cruise, Niall leaping from his back to finish his journey down to the ground.

"Mairwen?!" he gasped, jogging closer, wings occasionally lifting him for a few beats.

He gaped at Mairwen's dragon, who blinked slyly back at him, a burst of sea blue beneath her golden gaze. From my perspective on the ground, as a man again, she was even more remarkable than before. The red of the other dragons' blood that had spattered her form glowed against her scales, each one painted in shades of fire and treasure. Her horns were like sapphires in precious metals, the faintest iridescence at their ends.

"What happened?" Niall asked me.

I stared at Mairwen and shook my head. "I haven't the faintest idea. She just arrived and made quick work of the fight. Gamesby said he *yields*. Didn't you, my lord?"

"Get it off me," Gamesby snarled weakly, and I thought Mairwen might've been using more of her weight than was strictly necessary. Cambeth transformed back and crawled out from under her, but he fell slack to the ground, bleeding and pale.

Seamus and Torion approached from behind, staring up at Mairwen.

"It can't really be..." Torion murmured, dropping a sack to the ground with a heavy thump and the rattle of metal. Black steel, I suspected, to cuff the men before us, keep them from transforming back into dragons.

"It's her," I said.

Seamus's lips just twitched, and his arms crossed over his chest. He spoke to Mairwen directly. "We found a dragon barely alive in the sea near the castle. Was that your work?"

Mairwen huffed in confirmation and her wings stretched and flexed, Gamesby groaning beneath her foot. My brow furrowed, and I hurried to her. "A dragon? Who was it? What happened?!"

She rumbled and shifted, head tossing, and I realized the woman was trapped in the beast, unable to answer me when our forms didn't match.

"Grab them," I said, pointing to the betas. Torion dragged the bag of chains over, and Mairwen released her prey one by one, sighing as I stroked a hand over her side. "Mairwen, darling, can you shift back?"

Mairwen's feet stepped restlessly over the ground, wings rising and lowering in a shrug. This was new for her, and if she'd been fighting, if she'd transformed because of a *threat*, her dragon had likely taken over for her. I spread my arms, and her head lowered, breath hot on my belly as she huffed and let me embrace her snout. Around us, the men watched, the betas and even Torion, with disbelief in their eyes.

"It's all right now. You're safe," I murmured. Mairwen grunted and nudged me gently, nearly knocking me off my feet. I laughed and rubbed firmly between two horns. "Fine. *I'm* safe now. See? They're all secured in steels. Give me back my pretty mate," I said in a low whisper, just for her.

Mairwen grumbled and then shuddered. I'd never been so close to a dragon when they transformed before, and I winced, bracing myself at the pound of magic sweetened with Mairwen's scent. Wind struck me hard in the back, air filling the place where Mairwen's dragon had been, and I ran forward, catching the woman in my arms as she reappeared.

Catching her...and finding a slight impediment.

Wings.

Mairwen's wings were a slightly more burnished shade of gold than her scales, and they flailed briefly, lifting her off her toes before snapping shut and dropping her back down again.

"Oh my," she gasped, steadying herself with a grip on my shoulder.

I couldn't restrain my grin. "You're stunning. You're so beautiful. Mairwen—"

She blushed and ducked her head, raising one hand to cover my lips. "Alpha, *please,*" she hissed, glancing around us. I turned and took in the thunderstruck expressions. The only person not absolutely flabbergasted to see an omega with her own wings was DeRoche. Which meant...somehow, somewhere, he'd seen them before. Interesting.

But not as important to me as the woman in my arms.

"Who was it, darling?" I asked again.

"Palmer," she rasped. "He said...he said you might be dead, and I—"

I squeezed Mairwen against my chest, knuckles brushing the inside of her wings and finding her leather soft. "What did you do with him?" I asked DeRoche. "The dragon you found in the sea."

"Fished him out, left him with my crew. He's no threat at the moment, if he's even still alive, and I'll get word to have him brought here. What will you do with the others?" DeRoche asked, nodding his head at the remaining five traitors, most too beaten to move and all now in chains.

"They'll be jailed for now. Torion, can you take some? We don't usually have large-scale mutiny to deal with," I said.

"Of course," Torion answered. "The keep has an uncomfortable abundance of strong cells."

"You'll have a trial?" Niall asked me, raising an eyebrow.

I was within my rights to have them executed on my orders. Gamesby glared at me, knowing as much.

"It may be the same outcome in the end," I said, partly to warn the betas. "But yes, I want their crimes to be known to the island. And their defeat."

"And what of *her*?" Gamesby spat. "Will you want the island to know of that abomination?"

Mutiny, I might tolerate temporarily. But slights against my mate?

I released Mairwen with a gentle kiss on her brow, then turned and marched for Gamesby. He was goading me now, begging for a swift end. But he deserved to be publicly humiliated, starting with—

My arm swung, and DeRoche held the beta steady by the wing roots, giving him no way of dodging the punch. Gamesby shouted a garbled yell as his face was snapped roughly to the side by the force of my fist.

"You'll be busy rotting in prison, Gamesby, but yes, I plan on *celebrating* my mate with all of the isle's dragonkin," I said.

"Ronson," Mairwen called, and I turned to find her with a weary and unimpressed expression on her face.

"Apologies, but that was overdue, my love," I said, returning to her side. "Niall, I'll trust you and the alphas to escort these gentlemen to prison."

"Of course," Niall said with a low nod. "You're all right, Omega Cadogan?"

Mairwen was swaying slightly, her eyes glassy and pupils huge, and she blinked away whatever thoughts were busying her mind to glance at my brother. "Fine," she said, her voice too high and tight. Her wings rustled and then squeezed to her back again, as if she surprised herself each time she remembered they were there.

"Are you injured?" I whispered, ignoring the movements of the others around us.

She shook her head and then frowned, glancing down at herself. Mairwen leaned in, and I wrapped my arms around her waist. "I feel as though I don't quite fit in my own skin," she whispered, looking up at me.

I nodded. "It will settle. I felt the same the first time I transformed." Granted, I'd only been thirteen at the time, and I'd known it was coming. "I'm going to fly us back home. Can you keep your wings against your back?"

Mairwen stiffened, clenching her whole body, and I fought my answering chuckle. She would grow used to her wings soon enough, but for now, it was cute to see the struggle.

"You don't seem surprised," Mairwen said as I scooped her up. Her wings were a slight impediment to carrying her and flying with her in my arms, and a new added weight, but not a serious struggle.

"Oh, I am *shocked*," I said, bending my knees and leaping

as my wings thrust us upwards off the ground. "My dragon is not surprised, however, which makes the adjustment easier. Did you suspect?"

"I was starting to. The symptoms—the dizziness felt like the urge to...to fly, almost," Mairwen murmured, her hand rubbing over the back of my shoulders. I restrained my hiss as she stroked a wound, but she gasped and pulled her hand up, her wings flexing open in surprise and adding resistance to our flight. "You're hurt!"

"Just a scratch. Tuck your wings in, darling," I reminded her, laughing as they snapped shut again and Mairwen went rigid in my arms. "You'll get used to it, I promise."

"C-could I try flying?" Mairwen asked, cheeks flushed and eyes lowered.

Was my omega *shy*?

I squeezed one arm around her waist, pausing my flight to hover us and turn her carefully in my arms, adjusting my hold on her so her back was to my front, my body tucked between her wings. Her hands clutched over my arm around her waist, but her wings stretched slowly open.

"Stroke them through the air," I said.

Mairwen's wings flailed and flapped, and it took me a moment to balance us, to make up with my own flight for her awkward movements.

"Match their beats to your heart," I suggested.

"But my heart is racing!" Mairwen laughed.

I wrapped my arms around her more firmly and tipped us forward, Mairwen's wings snapping wide, braced against the air.

"Can you feel my heartbeat?" I asked. There was a pause as she considered. I was coasting us, letting us sink gradually, heading towards the edge of the isle. Mairwen nodded after a moment. "Then try and match that."

It took her a moment, and I probably impeded some

movement, pressed so close to her back, but with a little trial and error she found the steady one-two rhythm to fly to, my own wings pausing to then match hers. We rose in the air, and Mairwen let out a bright giggle of excitement, faltering for a moment.

"Don't worry. It doesn't always take so much concentration. This is just new for you," I promised.

I'd learned to fly not long after learning to walk, if Beatrice could be believed. Most betas didn't really remember the *learning* part—it was part of our nature. I tried not to think about how lucky it was that Mairwen had even made it to me safely. Her dragon had seen her through.

Gradually, I eased my grip around her until I was only gently holding the sides of her waist. Mairwen was *flying*.

Chapter Thirty-Nine

MAIRWEN

The wind dried the few tears that slipped from my eyes, and I tried to remember to *breathe*, but the ground was racing beneath us and my wings—*my wings*—were rushing through the air, every stroke caressing against new flesh. *This* was what I'd wanted all those hours of flying with Ronson, of watching the alphas transform. I'd wanted to *fly*.

Not to be flown or carried, or to ride on the back of a magnificent dragon. I'd wanted to be the magnificent dragon myself. And I was. I was *soaring*. I had dragon fire burning in my chest and claws that had fought enemy dragons back from my mate. My mate, who'd looked so...*small* to me when I'd been transformed.

A laugh broke out of my lungs and my flight wobbled, and I realized Ronson wasn't holding me now. I was on my own and—

I yelped, wings slapping backwards, arms and legs flailing as if to make up the work.

A shadow rushed over me and then Ronson was there,

catching me around my waist, making up for my imbalance with strong beats of his own wings.

"Tuck in," he said, grinning. My wings squeezed close to my back. "We'll practice together. But right now, I don't want you fighting for your life on the way back to the nest. Is that all right?"

My arms looped carefully over his shoulders, mindful of the wound I'd found earlier, and I tucked my head beneath his chin. I might've been a bigger dragon than him, but like this, Ronson was still reassuringly strong and *much* better at flying than me. And he always gave me a choice.

"Yes, that's all right," I murmured, breathing in his scent.

His arms tightened around me, a gentle crush. "Tell me how on earth this is possible. You're too clever not to have some idea."

I explained the portraits Beatrice and I had found, how some of the mated omegas were painted with wings, and even about Alpha Falk.

"All my symptoms hit at once when I realized you were under attack. I was fairly sure I knew what was coming, but it didn't occur to me that the wings would be a permanent addition after the transformation," I admitted.

Ronson growled and shook his head. "I would've rather you'd destroyed half the castle as a dragon than jump out of a window before you were *completely* certain of what was happening," he muttered, glaring down at me, but the anger cleared quickly. I was safe. He was safe. "Why do you think some of the omegas had dragons and others didn't?"

"Some betas can't transform," I mused. "But I wonder... I found in some of the documents that some mates were referred to as 'chosen,' and others not. I wasn't sure if it was just a turn of phrase, or..."

"Or if some alphas mated for the sake of an alliance rather than by instinct," Ronson murmured, nodding against the top of my head. "That would make sense. And you were certainly *chosen*. Chosen, claimed, always meant to be *mine*."

I smiled against his throat, kissed a mark to his pulse.

"You were glorious, Mairwen," he murmured.

I tipped my head back and found those dark eyes glowing warmly down at me. "I was, wasn't I?"

Ronson grinned and ducked his head, and I stretched to meet him. Kissing my mate felt a lot like flying.

"Poor Miss Pettyfer," I murmured, twisting and contorting in front of the mirror, stretching my wings this way and that to see the ruination of the back of my dress. My new stays at least had managed to survive, all straps and edges safely away from the roots of my wings. Which were *tired* and a little sore. Flying took so much work.

Ronson shut the door to our room behind him. "Beatrice has already sent word we'll need alterations. She thought of it before I did. And she said your father returned home after an hour of fretting. Mairwen...I..."

"You'll have to question him," I said, carefully shimmying out of my dress. Perhaps Miss Pettyfer might only have to replace the backs of my gowns rather than the entire garments. "I understand. Will you...will he..."

"He won't be put in prison yet," Ronson said, crossing to me and pulling me into his chest. He was right that any of his injuries were only surface marks, and I'd patched them up straight away when we'd arrived back at the nest. "If his inclination was to go home and not run for the docks, it's doubtful he has much to hide. Palmer probably only made use of him in the moment."

I sighed and nodded, rubbing my cheek over the soiled linen of Ronson's shirt. I hoped, for my parents' sake, that was true, but I wouldn't stand in the way of any decision Ronson had to make regarding my father. My loyalties were to my mate, and upon reflection, my family hadn't made that a strenuous choice.

"I love you," I whispered, my hands clutching against Ronson's lower back, wings tensing as if prepared for flight or another battle to protect him. "I was so afraid I would be too late."

Ronson soothed his hand over the back of my head. "Nonsense. I would never stop fighting, mate. Not while I have you to return to." His hand slipped under my chin, lifting it for me to meet his stare, soft crinkles in the corners of his eyes. "But I will never forget the sight of you soaring to rescue me. You are the most beautiful dragon I've ever set eyes on."

I warmed from the inside out. "Am I...am I a pretty dragon, then? I haven't seen."

"You were terrifying," Ronson said, and he laughed as I gasped in offense. "And yes, very pretty. You looked like very dangerous treasure."

Yes, we are treasure, her heavy voice purred in my head, approving of Ronson's description.

"We'll have to have a very large mirror crafted so you can see," he said.

I huffed. "Excuse you. 'Very *large?*'"

Ronson's belly laugh made my own lips twitch. "You're a dragon now, darling. Very large is *ideal*. Do you know, I think if you challenged me, you'd win. You could be alpha of the isle."

"I'll keep that in mind," I quipped, nudging him in the stomach, eyeing the nest around his shoulder.

Ronson took the hint with an answering purr, his hands on my arms guiding me along as he walked backward to our bed. "Niall would back you in the fight, no doubt. DeRoche too, the charming bastard."

I rolled my eyes and Ronson growled, tugging me hard against him and ducking down to slant his mouth over mine. I surrendered to the kiss. Strong as my dragon might be, I had no complaints with my alpha, certainly not enough for a challenge. Ronson's purr thickened as I opened to him, his fingers working quickly at my back, untying laces and groping sweetly at bare skin.

"Do you remember," he began with a pant and leaned back, feathering kisses over my cheeks, "our first night together?"

I blushed and nodded, recalling my unguarded curiosity, the strange power and triumph of having Ronson at my mercy. We'd barely known each other, really, but he'd let me touch and explore him, so eager and responsive. I'd never felt desire before, never been desired, and it was like opening the floodgates.

"The very first thing you asked to do was—"

"Touch your wings," I said, smiling and reaching out to do so.

Ronson's purr thrummed steadily between us, and his gaze hooded. "It's my turn now, omega."

I opened my mouth but Ronson was quick, lifting me up by my waist and tossing me onto the mattress. My wings spread and flapped aimlessly, more like flailing arms still, and I let out an *oof* of breath as I landed in the pile of pillows and soft blankets.

"I'm not a sack of potatoes, Ronson," I scoffed, trying to hide my smile as I settled myself more comfortably.

"You most certainly are not," he agreed, climbing onto the bed, his knees on either side of my legs as he scooted up. His hand paused to squeeze appreciatively at my ass. "Spread your wings."

It took me a moment, slightly distracted by his hands kneading at my bottom and up my back. My wings stretched, and I sighed as they came to rest against my back and the bed. Ronson's hands worked their way up my spine, and I buried a groan of relief into my pillow.

"The muscles for our wings are thin but very strong. Yours will likely be sore after flights for a while, but that will ease quickly too. I'll take good care of you, my treasure," Ronson said, voice softening at the end.

I rested my cheek on my folded arms. "You always do."

"Your talons are exceptional," Ronson said, shifting over my back, one of my wings lifting briefly as he examined the talons at the ends of my wing bones. "I've never seen longer and sharper. And the blue tips remind me of the sea."

I wondered if I'd ever grow used to the profuse compliments Ronson was able to offer me. I hoped not.

A touch landed on the upper edge of my wing, and I startled in place, Ronson chuckling. "Sensitive?" he asked, his hand gently cupped around the thick ridge of bone and muscle and leather.

"Y-yes, and it's so...new. Your touch is suddenly reminding my body or-or my brain that it's there at all," I said, trying to twist to watch his gentle caress. I had wings, new limbs, and they had never been touched before this moment.

"Mmm. They're still soft," Ronson mused. "You still have the velvet on your hide. Wait here."

He slipped from the bed, and I lifted just enough to finish undoing my loose corset and then to shimmy out of my torn slip, kicking it down into the sheets. Ronson returned, purring with approval. I squeaked as it was his lips and not his hands that found the lower curve of my bottom, slow, wet kisses passed back and forth over my cheeks and up to the base of my spine. His tongue circled there for a moment and then vanished.

"Good girl, getting yourself ready for me. Now relax while I have my revenge," he said.

I shivered at the first brush of his fingertips over the flesh of my wing, the sensation still slightly foreign but no less arousing, and then moaned as he pushed my wings into a spread. I'd spent a long time studying his wings, and now that I knew just a small fraction of what it must've felt like, I was beginning to understand the true nature of his revenge.

"This will help keep the velvet soft and the leather from growing tight or dry," Ronson said, ignoring my buried whimpers as he rubbed the fragrant substance into my new skin. "Now we can tend to each other."

"Gamesby wasn't entirely wrong," I whispered, trying to distract myself from the deep thrills rushing up my wings, into my back, and down into my core.

"Mairwen," Ronson warned with a growl.

"Some of the island will be too shocked to accept an omega dragon," I said.

"They haven't a choice," he said firmly, but he settled his weight on the backs of my thighs and then sighed. "Some will balk, yes. But you are my omega, and I am their alpha. What's done is done. I wouldn't change a thing. You don't think any omegas might be envious of you?"

I blinked and propped my chin up. I hadn't thought of that. I wondered if perhaps there were other women on the island who would be pleased to see that an omega could have her own wings too. Francesca would've run riot with wings. Katharine would appreciate the dignity...

Adelaide. Adelaide *would* be jealous. Spitefully, marvelously, viciously green with envy. And humiliated once Gamesby's betrayal was revealed.

And pregnant. And alone.

My petty victory cooled quickly.

I sighed and stretched beneath Ronson. "We have to make changes, Ronson."

"We do. We will. Lift your wings for me, mate."

I did so and Ronson shifted, pausing at my side, his gaze traveling slowly over me, lips faintly curved. When his eyes met mine at last, his smile stretched.

"What are you thinking?" I asked, grinning and expecting wickedness in answer.

"That you are the most beautiful dragon, woman, omega, everything that I have ever had the incredible fortune to stumble across in my life," Ronson said, the answer soft and simple.

I blushed, but I didn't hide from him, just spread my wings a little more, shifting slightly to my side to offer him more to admire.

"If I recall correctly, I was the one who stumbled into *you*," I said.

Ronson laughed and bent, his arm circling my waist, lifting me up and over his lap. Our wings curled around us, meeting at the edges, the hooked talons at the top of the joints linking together like hands clasped.

"Right as usual, mate," he murmured, hiking me up slightly, our soft moans lost in a kiss as our bodies centered and joined in a smooth stroke. "Perfect as always. *Mine.*"

"Yours," I whispered, gasping as our wings moved, dragon skin and velvet brushing together, a perfect private shelter created between them, light just barely stretching through the skin to make us a rosy cave to hide in. "As you are mine."

"Oh, yes," Ronson said, grunting as his hips hitched, grinding against me and making my own breath catch. "Yes, I've been yours ever since I caught you in my arms. Seduced by an ill-fitting corset."

It was patently absurd, so I hushed him with a kiss and held him deep inside me, rocking us softly to our pleasure.

Chapter Forty

MAIRWEN

I paced in front of Ronson's office, pausing every so often to let the rustle of my skirts and wings settle, hoping I might make out some of the softly-spoken words from the other side of the door.

This was silly. Ronson had *offered* to let me sit in on the conversation with my father. Except I was afraid of what I might hear, that I might try to influence Ronson in the wrong direction. I did love my parents and I understood that they loved me, but there were pieces of our relationship that were broken, and if my father had schemed with Gamesby and Palmer against Ronson, I didn't want to excuse those actions.

My mother's voice trembled from inside the office, and my hands twisted in front of me. I hadn't wanted to see them yet, not until after Ronson had made his decision. Father had likely seen me transform, and according to Niall, there were already *several rumors* floating around the island regarding the golden dragon who'd flown in a lather across the sky yesterday. Rumors about the incarceration of the betas who'd attacked Ronson too. Already dragonkin and humans were gathering in the festival field, waiting for our arrival, for the answers to their many growing questions.

The door cracked, and I startled, stepping back out of the way. It was Niall who exited the office rather than Ronson, and I breathed a sigh of relief as he offered me a reassuring smile.

"Coming in?" he asked softly, tipping his head back into the room.

A small part of me, the part society called Mouse, wanted to scurry back up to my rooms or into the library. I shook my head and rolled my sore shoulders, my wings flexing as I stepped forward. Ronson had taken me flying in the dark the night before, getting in enough practice for me to be steady on my own. He wanted me to fly with him for the announcement this afternoon, for the island to see me as a dragon in my own right. Beatrice and I had even done a little clumsy work to one of my dresses to make it acceptable in the meantime, splitting open the shoulder seams and two slits down the back before relacing it around my wings.

Better not to delay, I reminded myself, then walked into the office.

My mother gasped, falling down into the chair behind her, but my father remained standing, eyes wide.

"It's true," he murmured, stepping forward and then freezing. "I could barely believe what I'd seen, but..."

"Wings... I read a-a silly story once where an omega had wings," my mother murmured, her stare glazed as it traveled across one of my wings and then the other.

My eyebrows rose in surprise. "I wondered if some traces must've remained, in literature or art." I shrugged and my wings moved with me, and both of my parents stifled another gasp, as if they still weren't quite sure if they could believe their own eyes.

"I-I owe you...many apologies, Mairwen," my father said

as he took two more tremulous steps forward, almost as if he were afraid of me. I suppose I had been fairly fearsome when I'd transformed in front of him. "Most pressingly for allowing Palmer's influence to coerce me here yesterday."

I glanced at Ronson behind his desk, and he offered a subtle nod. He believed my father. That was a relief.

"If you hadn't come, I might not have realized Ronson was under attack," I said. I shifted toward my father, wondering if he would flinch back, but he only heaved out a breath and lurched, meeting me halfway, circling his arms around me in a tight hug.

"I thought you'd leapt to your death," he whispered, a fragile tear in the words.

"Mairwen's arrival certainly settled the matter amongst the betas. *We* are the strength of two dragons," Ronson said firmly, smiling at me.

It had been literal after all. A mated alpha had another dragon at his side, fighting with him, making him stronger. And according to Ronson, I made a formidable addition to his strength, which was a compliment I hadn't expected to enjoy so much. It was nice to be considered ferocious instead of forgettable.

I was a dragon. The alpha's mate. Ronson's siren. My spine straightened, and the tension in my chest faded away.

"Could we have a moment alone?" I asked Ronson.

"Of course." Ronson rounded his desk, reaching me without a moment of hesitation as he drew me closer, lips grazing over my brow. "I'll be in the hall with Niall."

I lifted my face to kiss his jaw before he slipped out of the room, leaving me alone with my parents. It was quiet in the room, the sun cutting through the window panes, stretching across Ronson's desk to reach the three of us.

"May I...may I touch?" My mother's hand was

outstretched, hovering next to my right wing, and I fought the urge to tuck them close.

This was a small sample of how the isle might respond—the disbelief, the curiosity, the wariness. There would be outrage too, I was sure. Omegas were meant to be dainty and delicate and talented at pouring tea and stitching. We weren't meant to be *dragons*.

But we were *dragonkin*, so perhaps it was time for society to catch back up.

"You may," I said, flexing my wing open, letting it butt into my mother's fingers. She gasped, her hand retreating and then returning.

"My goodness. My word. Oh, Agnes Hubbard will be *quite* envious," my mother said, finishing with a trilling laugh. "She always did think wings were a waste on gentlemen. They never have so many things to do as an omega."

My father's eyes were fixed to my face rather than my wings, searching me, studying. "Can you forgive me, Mairwen?"

My mother startled, retreating to his side, glancing between us, delivering that watery, pleading stare to me, urging me to say yes.

"I will forgive you for coming here with Palmer, for letting his words twist your judgment," I said.

My mother sighed, a tremulous smile offered to my father, but he was still watching me.

"But?" he prompted.

I wet my lips, wondering if might be better to bid them goodbye for now, to push no further. I didn't *need* their support. I couldn't, *wouldn't* go back in time to change anything, but only because I had what I needed and wanted most now. Still...

"But...I wish that it hadn't taken someone else—a stranger to me, to you—to see that I was not wrong, or inappropriate, or less than the other omegas," I said softly, drawing a deep breath and continuing before they might interject. "I wish not that I had been enough for you both, because I was *always* enough. I wish that when all others had found fault in me, you had loved me as your daughter, exactly as I was, so that I might've loved myself too."

My mother's breath caught, her eyes wide, tears slipping free. "Mairwen," she murmured, and I wasn't sure if it was a plea, or an objection, or a refusal of what I spoke.

I shook my head. "I am not the wrong size, and I'm not strange. I am beautiful, I have a perfume, I have a nice singing voice, and I *do* know my place. It is here, with the alpha. With my mate."

"We see that, Mairwen," my father said, dipping his head. "We see that *now*."

I nodded, smoothing my hands over my skirts. "I can't say I won't forgive you for how long it took. I think I am the forgiving sort, and I do love you both...but I haven't yet. That will take more time."

My mother was flushed, avoiding my gaze, but my father would soothe her shame in private. He reached for me and I accepted, squeezing his hand in mine. I didn't know exactly when I would be ready to see them again, to risk another dinner, but I did know that I would not shrink or fall silent or fail to defend myself again. Ronson would take up arms for me, if I asked it, but I was strong enough on my own too, and now I knew as much.

THE CROWD WAS FAR LARGER than I'd expected, fuller even than the day of the selection, although Niall had said those crowds had thinned out over the decades, since Ronson never elected to take an omega for himself before me. But this must've been every soul on the isle. Perhaps even some travelers from the nearby port. All here to see me.

To gawk at the omega with wings.

"Mating is natural to dragonkin, an honored practice we lost over time and one I am wholly grateful to discover with my own omega," Ronson continued, his voice loud but unable to cut through the murmurs and mutterings of our audience.

His expression grew darker by the moment, and I resisted the urge to fidget at his side. Niall had arranged for the pamphlets we'd had printed to be passed around, but it was clear that most people were discarding them or tucking them away.

They didn't care about Ronson biting me, or that I was his mate. They cared that they were looking at a woman with wings. The more he spoke, the more restless they grew.

When Ronson took a steadying breath, a rough voice rose up from the crowd, accent strange and thick.

"Wings look damned fake to me!"

My eyebrows rose, and I turned to Ronson, whose eyes were full of irate fire. His body tensed, as if prepared to launch himself into the crowd and fight whoever had spoken.

"Show us yer dragon, then!"

I squinted and found movement in the crowd, a figure in a strangely heavy cloak shifting from one spot to another. Their head lifted briefly, revealing a pronounced nose and a roguish smile.

Seamus DeRoche...egging on the crowd?

No...

Encouraging me.

Let them see me, my dragon purred, shifting restlessly, hot in my chest. *Show them my beauty and my claws.*

I squeezed Ronson's hand, his teeth bared in a snarl, and he calmed again with one smile from me. The crowd quieted into sudden silence as I stepped forward.

"Very well," I said, and a collective breath was stolen, a great shift in the air, anticipation electric.

I hadn't transformed since Ronson coaxed my dragon back after yesterday's fight, but she was there in my chest, ready and eager, equally amused with Seamus's scheming.

Ronson tugged at our hands to catch my attention, searching my face for a moment before relaxing, satisfied that I was comfortable. "I'll give you room," he said, stepping back and then surging forward for a firm kiss that made our audience titter.

My eyes slid shut as I opened to him, but he was gone too quickly and the entire island was looking at me now. I took a deep breath, steeling myself against the inevitable censure and alarm of their stares, then reopened my eyes.

They're small. Just snacks, my dragon soothed me easily.

And through her eyes, the crowd on the ground, the notable dragonkin in the winged risers that surrounded the field, were only strange human faces, ones she couldn't even tell apart.

I released my breath slowly, and heat circled me, crackling in my ear and raising the fine hairs on my skin. I'd wondered if transforming was painful for Ronson, and while there was a discomfort in the expansion, the truth was simpler. My dragon reached out to part the curtain of one small, fragile form and to reveal the strength within. I moaned, and the sound was low and rattling. My wings spread back, huge and majestic, and my face rose high to the sky, stretching up, up, up, until the sun glinted off my horns.

The stage beneath me groaned at my weight, and I huffed a chuckle as the audience—their faces so tiny now, their eyes so wide, their collective scent far too potent—swirled and gasped and fluttered like a little flock of agitated birds upon a field of seed.

"Beautiful."

I turned my head, cocking it to catch the sight of my mate approaching my side, smiling up at me, his voice clear above the rest. His hand stroked the tough hide and scales of my leg, and the touch was as light as a feather, almost ticklish, but it was *his* hand on me, so I hummed with pleasure.

"Fly," he said.

Yes, let them see how strong we are. How lovely. Let them watch our flight.

I needed no further encouragement. My legs bent and my wings beat, and the stage heaved out a wheeze of relief as the audience shrieked in excitement and I took to the air.

At last. At last. At last.

The sun on my scales was as warm as my alpha's stare, the air under my wings as rich and silken as the sea. I spiraled higher, Ronson's voice growing smaller below.

"Mating is our true dragonkin gift. It is the true strength of our blood. It gives our omegas their own power, their own flight, and the safety to bear our sons and daughters without the great risk to their lives."

I twirled in the air, flying easier and more instinctive in this form, and a soft sound of appreciation circled the voices below me.

"It is a permanent bond, a lifetime, *my* lifetime devoted to my perfect match."

Pretty words, I thought, in tandem with my dragon now. *Let's hear some more.*

I circled back down, a little sorry to land and give up my transformation so soon, but my dragon relented easily, patient to wait for more time in the air. I shifted once over the stage, the crowd large below me, my back and wings tired, my skirts floating out around me.

I slapped my hand over my skirts to settle them back down and struggled to catch my descent for a moment. I would need to start wearing clothes more similar to those I'd worn on the way to the Flight of Alphas if I was going to be flying around the island. Ronson was reaching for me as I lowered down to the ground. His hand caught my hips, and my wings tucked in, grateful for the support at the last moment. My feet touched the stage, and Ronson's arm circled my waist tightly, his forehead dropping to mine.

The isle was quiet now. They would have questions—I certainly still did—but they couldn't refute that I was a dragon. I reached up and stroked my hands over his cheeks and jaw.

"We knew this wouldn't be easy," I whispered.

Ronson nodded, planting a kiss on the bridge of my nose. "I'm not afraid of the work," he answered. "I have you."

I fought my smile to kiss him softly and then pushed at his chest. "Go on, then."

Ronson sighed, keeping me in his grasp for a moment longer before finally releasing me and turning to the island. Someday, probably not so long from now, I would raise my voice with his, be as much a part of the role of alpha as he was. For today, I took a step back, finding Niall at my back.

"Did you suggest that to Seamus?" I whispered.

Niall huffed, shifting a step up to my side. "Perhaps."

Ronson cleared his throat, wings spreading at his side, shoulders back and chest broad. He stood with such natural authority, just as he had in a little drawing room for an afternoon gathering a few months ago. The Alpha of Bleake Isle.

My mate.

The man who shared his secrets and laughter with me, who loved me playfully and with starving hunger and incredible, patient kindness.

"There will be no future selection ceremony," Ronson said, voice full and firm, continuing before the shock of the statement could raise new voices. "I have my mate and no need of another omega. From now on, ladies, any gentleman who seeks your company ought to work quite hard to earn your favor. Any choices made will be yours, and you may seek my authority, or my mate's," he added, twisting to smile briefly back at me, "if that right is challenged. May all of the isle dragonkin find such happiness and completion as I have."

I blushed but tried to remain serene in my spot.

"He's getting better at speeches," Niall noted as Ronson continued. "And it only took half a century."

THE DOOR to the bedroom closed, and I stirred from my book at the rough sigh that announced my mate's arrival. I glanced at the candle at my side and realized it'd been hours since I'd come up to wait for him while he dealt with more panic from the betas.

"They gave up?" I asked, setting my book aside, open and face down.

Ronson groaned, sagging against the door. "Hardly. I banished them for the night. Have I told you today what a brilliant, magnificent blessing you are?"

"You have," I said, grinning, folding my knees up against my chest and wrapping my arms around them. I was in my favorite armchair in our bedroom, but now I had to sit in it sideways to let my wings drape over one arm. "First was this morning, because...well, you know..."

Ronson's gaze grew hot. "Ah, yes. I remember. A very thoughtful way to wake a man up."

"And then, of course, before the announcement to the isle. After too," I said, now counting on my fingers.

Ronson nodded. "Naturally. You did so well."

"And then once more before I came up to bed. What was it that earned me the praise again now?"

"Agnes Hubbard," Ronson said, finally pushing away from the door, hurrying to pull at the shoulders of his shirt.

"Ah," I said, nodding.

"I only had to do half the talking. Give that woman an inch of authority, and she uses it with the most shocking precision and efficiency I've ever seen in my life," Ronson said. "And she knows so many of the betas' mothers. Her threats were elaborate, artistic even."

I rested my cheek on my knee, watching Ronson undress, carelessly tossing his clothes in one direction and another. I had suggested that before agreeing to meet with any betas— who would undoubtedly argue every single change we had just announced—we ought to put some omegas on the Lord's Council and make it an Isle Council. Agnes Hubbard was the obvious first choice.

"Half of them have folded under her force...for now," Ronson said, kicking his linen undergarments aside and falling backward into the nest with a heaving sigh. He lay there for a moment, and I wondered if he'd fall asleep like that, exhausted by the day. But his head popped up, brow furrowed and lips just nearly suggesting a pout. "Why are you over there? Come here. I need to taste you," he said, patting his chest.

My body warmed in agreement, but I rose slowly, leaving my shawl on the chair and joining him in the bed, although not in quite the way he'd suggested. Instead, I circled to the other side, crawling up to hover my face over his so he was looking at me upside down.

"We will wear them down," I said, brushing my fingers through Ronson's hair. His eyes slid shut, and his purr thrummed in his chest.

"And we will build the omegas up. Until dragonkin learns to stand on even footing."

My heart ached, and I ducked my head, brushing kisses

over every inch of Ronson's face.

"There is no better man than you. No better alpha," I murmured.

"No better lover," Ronson prompted.

"Presumably. I wouldn't know," I teased, squawking a laugh as Ronson growled and sat up, twisting and quickly wrestling me down beneath him, his grin sharp and his hair ruffled in all directions from my fingers. "What a pretty speech you gave. How nice for the omegas to have their choice," I continued, squirming with breathless gasps as Ronson snarled and groped, snapping kisses against my cheeks and jaws, until I found myself spread beneath him, my slip torn up to my waist.

Ronson paused there, hips pressed to mine, just a few inches from being inside of me, gaze blazing and smile wide. "Do you think I won't work hard every day to deserve you, mate?"

I sighed, and he released my hands so I could touch his face, draw it down to mine, our lips parting and tongues meeting familiarly with grateful moans to taste one another again.

"You do deserve me," I breathed, rocking my hips up to his, trying to draw him into me. "As I deserve you."

Ronson's eyes lit up. "Ohh, my sweet little omega knows how to please her mate. And I will prove I know how to please you," he said, rewarding my little words of confidence with the slow drive inside of me, my gasp of relief mingling with the slick sound of our bodies joining. "Every day, Mairwen. Every day of our lives."

"Closer, alpha. Come closer to me," I pleaded, circling my arms around his shoulders and my legs around his hips.

And when we were as close as we could be, wings held and hips snug and lips open to one another, I knew I was precisely where I was meant to be.

Epilogue
RONSON

ONE HUNDRED & FIFTY YEARS LATER

The moon was perfectly framed by the window, just a sliver of silver sea visible at the bottom edge. Mairwen stirred in my arms, and my lips curved up, strangely pleased that we were both still awake. Every moment, even the still and silent ones, were precious to me, but especially tonight, our last night in the nest Mairwen had built me so long ago.

"Are you nervous about tomorrow?" she whispered.

I laughed, combing my fingers through her hair, sorting through the tangles I'd created just a bit ago. "What do *I* have to be nervous about?"

Mairwen puffed a sound of annoyance. "It doesn't matter to you who wins the challenge?"

I sighed and considered. "It does, but...I'm confident the right person will. *A* right person. We have a lot to choose from."

"As long as it isn't Bernard Davies," Mairwen muttered.

I scoffed. "He doesn't stand a chance."

Mairwen shifted, rolling half onto my chest and propping her chin up on the backs of her hands. "I know Blair thinks it should be him because he's the oldest," she breathed so softly, as if our son were in the room and might hear her otherwise, "but I do think one of the others stands a good chance."

I hummed in agreement. All of our children would make a good alpha for the isle. Which was why I was less concerned with *which* one and more eager to simply enjoy my retirement. At last. I wanted my remaining years—and plentiful I hoped they would be—spent traveling the world with my mate. Or just lazing about in bed with her as she read me books. Either option was promising.

Our tiny island, with a home just for the two of us an easy flying distance away from the isle—not so close as to threaten the new alpha—was ready and waiting for our arrival. Mairwen hadn't seen the house yet, and I was looking forward to her reaction. Perversely, I hoped it was not quite up to scratch. I wanted my omega to boss me about on improvements. Mairwen was magnificent when she was determined to have her way. I'd admired her management of the isle and our brood of little dragons for a century and a half, and now I was looking forward to her managing me, and me alone.

I'd always been greedy where Mairwen was concerned.

Her finger prodded my chest, drawing my attention back to the present. "Go on. You must have a favorite."

I laughed, reaching down to squeeze Mairwen's full bottom—fuller now than when I'd met her. Deliciously so.

"I will tell them you asked that," I said, hissing as she pinched my nipple in retaliation. "I don't have a favorite. Not of *ours*. And I do hope it stays in the family..."

"Because you don't want them to come moaning to you if they don't win," Mairwen said.

I nodded. "Precisely. But I will say that even if the Millward boy does win, at least the isle will still be in good hands."

Mairwen hummed, softening against me, settling in for sleep at last. "Arran will struggle with the feats of strength, but I think he might still come out ahead when it comes to the rest of the challenge."

We were quiet for a moment, my fingers still carding slowly through her long hair. "Mairwen?"

"Mm?"

"Have you noticed that Iona has been...cagey lately?"

Mairwen's breath hitched, and she nodded slowly.

"Do you think *she'll* enter?" I asked, now whispering too.

"Would you mind if she did?" Mairwen asked in that delicate way that meant she already knew the answer to my question.

It didn't take me long to decide. I shook my head. "She would make a good alpha. It would change things. Again," I added with a chuckle.

"A lot has already changed," Mairwen said with a sleepy sigh.

"Mm...that's time passing, I suppose. A great deal more change to come, I'm sure."

Mairwen's hand lifted, reaching back to catch mine, tangling our fingers together and resting our hands over my chest. "But not this, my love."

I smiled, stretching my head up for a moment to kiss the top of her head. "No, my darling mate. Never this."

The End

Afterword

I really hope you enjoyed Mairwen and Ronson's story. I've been dreaming of these characters since the start of 2022, but so much changed over that time and their world grew and developed well beyond my initial itch for some dragon loving. And as is probably clear, there's lots of change left to come in this world!

Torian's book is the second in my plans for sure, and of course Seamus and others need their own stories. As is pretty typical for me, I already know that the moods and themes and nature of the characters won't always be the same across every book, but I hope you'll find more of what you enjoyed in the next one. I'll even keep my fingers crossed that I might even make you love each book a little more than the one before.

There are many ways to keep updated on my progress but the best places where are in my Facebook group and on my Patreon!

Also by Kathryn Moon

COMPLETE READS

The Librarian's Coven Series

Written

Warriors

Scrivens

Ancients

Standalones

Good Deeds

Command The Moon

Say Your Prayers - co-write with Crystal Ash

Secrets of Summerland

The Sweetverse

Baby + the Late Night Howlers

Lola & the Millionaires - Part One

Lola & the Millionaires - Part Two

Bad Alpha

Faith and the Dead End Devils

Sol & Lune

Book 1

Book 2

Inheritance of Hunger Trilogy

The Queen's Line

The Princess's Chosen

The Kingdom's Crown

Tempting Monsters

A Lady of Rooksgrave Manor

The Basilisk of Star Manor (novella)

The Company of Fiends

Sanctuary with Kings

SERIES IN PROGRESS

Sweet Pea Mysteries

The Baker's Guide To Risky Rituals

The Knitter's Guide to Banishing Boyfriends

The Florist's Guide to Summoning Saints (coming 2024)

Monster Smash Agency

Games with the Orc

Howl for the Gargoyle

Lessons with the Mothman (coming 2024)

Dragonkin Series

The Alpha of Bleake Isle

The Alpha of Grave Hills (coming 2025)

About the Author

Kathryn Moon is a country mouse who started dictating stories to her mother at an early age. The fascination with building new worlds and discovering the lives of the characters who grew in her head never faltered, and she graduated college with a fiction writing degree. She loves writing women who are strong in their vulnerability, romances that are as affectionate as they are challenging, and worlds that a reader sinks into and never wants to leave. When her hands aren't busy typing they're probably knitting sweaters or crimping pie crust in Ohio. She definitely believes in magic.

You can reach her on Facebook and at ohkathrynmoon@gmail.com or you can sign up for her newsletter!

Milton Keynes UK
Ingram Content Group UK Ltd.
UKHW010845280324
440101UK00001B/15

9 781959 571285